Almost Wrecked

THE SONG WRECKERS BOOK 1

CRYSTAL FIRSDON

SOUL MATE PUBLISHING
New York

ALMOST WRECKED

Copyright©2014

CRYSTAL FIRSDON

Cover Design by Christy Caughie

This book is a work of fiction. The names, characters, places, and incidents are the products of the author's imagination or are used fictitiously. Any resemblance to actual events, business establishments, locales, or persons, living or dead, is entirely coincidental.

All rights reserved. No part of this publication may be reproduced, stored in a retrieval system, or transmitted in any form or by any means (electronic, mechanical, photocopying, recording, or otherwise) without the prior written permission of both the copyright owner and the publisher. The only exception is brief quotations in printed reviews.

The scanning, uploading, and distribution of this book via the Internet or via any other means without the permission of the publisher is illegal and punishable by law. Please purchase only authorized electronic editions, and do not participate in or encourage electronic piracy of copyrighted materials.

Your support of the author's rights is appreciated.

Published in the United States of America by
Soul Mate Publishing
P.O. Box 24
Macedon, New York, 14502

ISBN: 978-1-61935-807-2

ebook ISBN: 978-1-61935-501-9

www.SoulMatePublishing.com

The publisher does not have any control over and does not assume any responsibility for author or third-party websites or their content.

Acknowledgements

I would like to acknowledge those who helped me along the way—I wouldn't have kept going without you! To friends who were willing to read my story and give me feedback: Thank You!! I needed all the positive comments as well as the constructive criticism. I would especially like to thank my mom whose faith in my ability to get published never seemed to waver, and also Nancy, whose excitement kept fueling me to keep going. Last, but certainly not least, I would like to thank my husband for more than twenty years of love and commitment. I could never write about love or romance without being wrapped in it for so long.

Chapter 1

I unplugged my guitar and set it in its case, then grabbed the towel I always brought and wiped the sweat off my face and neck. Some guy yelled out a semi-lewd yet oddly flattering comment about my ass as I stood up, so I cracked a smile and half-waved. If I wasn't already so hot I'm sure they would've seen my face turn red. The air conditioning in Brett's Bar was fighting a losing battle thanks to August's high heat and humidity and the couple hundred customers, many of whom had been dancing.

Since turning the big three-oh a couple weeks earlier, vocal appreciation of my backside didn't bother me like it did ten years ago, but it still made me blush. It was nice to know that all the hours I'd put into running, yoga, lifting weights, and dancing wasn't wasted.

But man, good thing whoever yelled that couldn't smell me.

"Whooo!"

"The Song Wreckers, baby, yeah!"

I smiled bigger. Song Wreckers fans were the best. They had to have been roasting hot, and we were done playing our three sets, but they still cheered for us as if it were starting—rather than quitting—time.

"Good Lord," Katie, my best friend and lead singer said, "It's hotter 'n hell in here."

Fanning my face with my hand, I asked the rest of the band, "You guys wanna sit outside for a few before packing up?"

I needed fresh air and a cool breeze, but wasn't going to stand in the back alley by myself while everyone else did all the work.

Courtney set down her violin case. "I could use a few minutes outside." She looked at her husband, Josh. "You coming?"

"Yeah. I'll grab some waters." Josh set his drum sticks across his snare and headed toward the bar, while Katie yanked the curtain aside that ran along the back of the stage so we could hop down.

Once off the stage we took the few steps to open the door that led into the back alley where we all parked. Our footsteps crunched on the gravel as we each found a spot against the wall to lean, away from the Dumpster and our cars. The humidity was high, but the breeze was strong enough to feel somewhat refreshing, even with the smell of garbage twenty feet away. I lifted my ponytail to let the air cool my neck.

None of us four girls talked. After being in a loud bar for the past few hours, the quiet was a welcome change.

Josh walked out and handed each of us a cold bottled water. I rubbed mine on the front and back of my neck before opening it and guzzling half the bottle.

He walked toward his wife, and because he was wearing heavy boots, the crunch of gravel practically echoed.

"God, that's a creepy sound," I said. "Especially late at night with no one else around."

Our bass player Heather hummed the "Doo-doot, doo-doot" of the *Jaws* theme song, then said, "Seriously, Molly. We've been parking in this alley for years. Nothing scary has ever happened back here."

The Song Wreckers had been playing at Brett's for almost a decade, but six months ago we struck a deal with Brett to play at his bar exclusively the first Friday and Saturday of every month, known as Wreckers Weekends. We were tired of traipsing our asses all over metro Detroit to play. A once a month set schedule, Brett's makes a killing during Wreckers Weekends, total win-win.

"Hey, Mol. Speaking of scary," Katie twanged. Her southern accent was always more pronounced when she was tired. "Can you believe this is the last Wreckers Weekend before the school year starts?"

We were both high school teachers and had to report back to work at the end of the month. "I just hope it cools down by then. Being in a room with thirty sweaty teenagers . . ." I took another drink. "Yuck."

The back door opened and all our heads turned to see Brett poke his head out. "Good show, guys. As always. You need any help getting your stuff off the stage?"

He knew we never wanted help because it was faster and easier to set up and break down the equipment ourselves, but he was a good guy with a huge crush on Katie so I resisted rolling my eyes. "No thanks, we're good. Just needed some fresh air. We'll be back in soon."

"Okay then. Uh, Katie, can I speak to you for a minute?" Brett asked.

I whipped my head toward Heather and Courtney. The lighting in the alley was crap, but it was just enough to see them smile. We all knew Katie had as big a crush on him as he did on her. Heather's lips parted to speak, but she was close, so I put my hand over her mouth.

"Leave them alone," I whispered to Heather. Katie stood up straighter and followed Brett inside. I tapped her arm for support as she passed me. "Do not ruin this for them."

Heather pushed away my hand. "Dude. How long have we been waiting for him to make his move? I gotta say *something*."

I glanced at the ground behind me to make sure there was nothing nasty, then sat in the gravel, legs out in front.

"Better watch out, you may be a Wrecker, but that man is your boss."

Heather was both Brett's right hand girl at the bar and our bass player. She chuckled. "Dude, I can't help it. Watching those two get all flustered with each other is funny."

It was funny. If they started dating, I would miss it.

We spent another couple of minutes cooling off, then went inside to pack up our equipment. The crowd had finally settled down some, and the area around the bar wasn't so clustered. Brett was nowhere to be seen, so he and Katie were probably in his office. God, I hoped he was finally going to ask her out.

I wound a cable from elbow to hand. Kyle hopped up and sat on the edge of the stage.

"Hey, what's up?" I asked. "I'm surprised Midnight isn't playing tonight." Kyle plays bass for Crawling Home After Midnight, a damn good grunge band. He'd also played for The Song Wreckers between our original bass player and Heather.

He shrugged. "We play tomorrow night. Sorry about Adam earlier."

I rolled my eyes. Ah, Adam. The kind of man who gave all men a bad name. He had a hard time taking "No!" for an answer, and carried himself as if he were God's gift to everything. Adam was a great drummer, and I liked the rest of his band, but I preferred to steer clear of him.

Adam heckled us a bit tonight, but Katie put him in his place by dedicating our song "You Suck, Let Me Tell You Why" to him. He seemed to take it in good fun.

"Don't sweat it. So where you guys playing tomorrow night?"

Kyle and I chatted about Midnight's upcoming gigs, then Heather, Josh, Courtney, and I set our equipment off the back of the stage in the hall by the back door, ready to be loaded into Josh and Courtney's van.

Katie and Brett walked out of his office, Katie trying to suppress her excitement. We've been best friends since the first day of ninth grade, so I knew she was trying to play it cool but was really bursting inside.

I watched Brett walk back behind the bar. Heather shoved the door open and we each grabbed a piece of equipment and brought it outside.

I shot Heather a *don't you dare* look. "So?" I asked Katie with a huge smile.

She stopped walking toward the van and turned to me with an exited look. "He's taking—" Her excitement turned to confusion. "Molly, what is that on your car?"

"I believe it's called a large trash receptacle, known by its more socially accepted name, Dumpster. What happened with Brett? Come on, spill."

"He's taking me out to lunch tomorrow. Not *by* your car, *on* your car, idiot. *That.*" She pointed to the hood of my Jeep.

I spotted the . . . whatever is was the crap lighting couldn't let me make out on my hood, and jogged over to it.

"Mol, stop! You don't know what it is," Katie yelled. "Let Josh get it."

Josh hopped out of the van when he heard her. "What should you let me get?"

Katie pointed to it. "That thing on her hood." The rest of the band walked over to my Jeep.

The lump was actually a big, brown teddy bear holding a heart with its hands. Cute, I guess. The heart was shiny red with an opening at the top where a mix of multi-colored roses stuck out. Crammed in with the flowers was a piece of paper with something written on it.

"It's a teddy bear," I announced. "Just another Wreckers fan with a crush." Crushes were usually aimed toward Katie, though, and didn't involve gifts left on anyone's vehicle. More like business cards slid in our back pockets, or names with phone numbers scribbled on cocktail napkins and left on the stage.

Courtney took a step closer and craned her neck forward. "Is that a note in the heart? What does it say?"

I picked up the bear to read the note and noticed a stick, maybe six or eight inches long, protruding from its back. Someone had taken the time to rip a hole in the seam of its back to shove the stick into it. What the fuck? Not cute. I took out the note and had to turn to get in the beam of the alley's one light to be able to make out what it said.

Bitch.

It also had a hand drawn smiley face.

"Good Lord," Katie said next to me. "How did we not see that? We were just out here."

I handed the bear to Courtney and she examined it, turning it all the way around. "Do any of you know anything about this?" she asked the others. Of course everyone said no.

"Dude. That is disturbing. Especially the smiley face," Heather said. "Who the hell did this?"

No one with a crush, that's for sure. "I don't know." I took the bear from Courtney and threw it in the Dumpster.

"Mol, you shouldn't have done that. You should've taken it to the police station or something," Katie insisted.

"For what?" I asked. "Listen, don't make a big deal out of this. It's someone trying to be funny. Let's go."

The Song Wreckers were a country band, but our fans were all types. Including creepy, disturbing freaks who liked to scare guitar players apparently.

Heather was right, a creepy ass bear left on my Jeep was disturbing, and I drove home feeling uneasy. I don't know if the stick in the back or being called a bitch bothered me more. The stick in the back was mildly threatening, sure, but I am not a bitch and I don't like being called one. Maybe the bear from Hell was meant for Katie or Heather. Not that I wanted it to be meant for them, but they're more likely a target for a creep. They're the ones who go out in the crowd and party it up during our breaks, not me. I usually hang out in Brett's office and read or stretch or rest my eyes. Most likely Katie or Heather flirted with a guy who became infatuated with one of them. And he obviously didn't know whose vehicle was whose.

The whole thing was stupid. And somewhat upsetting and definitely annoying. This was probably orchestrated by some jerk trying to get a rise out of me or one of the other girls. After all, my name wasn't on the thing.

I chose to ignore the creepy bear because most likely this was the end of it.

Right, and monkeys will fly out my ass.

Chapter 2

The next night, Saturday, I shoved the back door open and carried two mic stands out into the alley. Instead of taking them to the van, I went to my Jeep, which I had parked closer to the alley's only light.

Rose petals covered my hood. Tons of them, all different colors.

I slammed the mic stands down. "Shit." The rest of the band walked over to me. I leaned forward to get a better look. Most of the petals were stuck to my hood by red goo. Ketchup? No way in hell I'd put my nose close enough to take a whiff and find out.

On the plus side, there were no bears, no notes, and no makeshift knives. Only rose petals. "Shit," I repeated. That would not be fun to get clean.

The five of us just stood there in the alley, staring at my Jeep, checking out the flower and red goo display.

Katie broke the silence first. "Whoever did this is crazy as a shithouse rat. Brett agrees with me that you should've called the police last night. You need to call them now."

She set down the two guitar cases she was holding and took a step closer to my Jeep, but I wanted to stop looking at the gory mess. I picked up the mic stands and loaded them into the van.

"You finally go out with Brett and you talk about me? That's pathetic."

Katie started walking again, slowly, still looking at the mess. "Cut the crap, Mol. Don't downplay this. Two nights in a row someone leaves you disgusting stuff on your car."

I sat on the van's bumper and crossed my arms over my chest. "But . . . and . . ." Damn it, I had nothing. I threw my head back in frustration. "Ouch." That's right, the van.

Courtney and Josh chimed in while I rubbed my new sore spot.

"Katie's right, you should go."

"This is nuts, you need to report this."

Heather had my back, though. "Dude."

Well, sort of.

Two things I really hated: crying and people thinking they had to worry about me. I put my hands up in surrender. "Okay, I'll go to the police," I said, "just not tonight. I'm tired and want to go home."

Katie put her hands on her hips and raised her eyebrows. "That's code for 'I will say what you want so you leave me alone but I have no intention of doing it'."

Damn it again. Having someone who knew me so well was totally inconvenient.

Heather shrugged. "It's Molly's decision. If she wants to be a dumbass then let her."

Katie retrieved her guitars. Walking back into the bar, she yelled over her shoulder, "I'm gonna go tell Brett on you."

My shoulders slumped. Great. He's going to get all protective on me and of course he would take Katie's side.

Heather, Josh, Courtney, and I loaded almost everything in the van before Brett stormed out of the back door with Katie on his heels. "God damn it! Molly, you are going to the police station tomorrow to get it on record. If you don't go I'll call them myself."

Katie stood there with a smug look on her face, while Brett and I stared each other down in the crappy light of the alley. Put up a fight, or give in and agree to go to the police?

With a sigh I gave up. "Fine. I'll go tomorrow, I promise." This was a fight I was going to lose anyway. If I refused to go then I would never hear the end of it from Katie. That woman would nag the living hell out of me and then I would give in to shut her up. I'd learned that from her, and it's a tactic I love to use myself. And what's an extra hour out of my day when reporting the creepy bear and gooey rose petals to the police would give the closest thing I had to a sister—or any sibling—peace of mind? The only thing I'd planned on Sunday was to go for a run and visit my mom. Do the laundry.

Oh, and wash the heck out of my car.

Who knows? Maybe a talk with the police would give me peace of mind, too. I was freaked out more than I wanted to admit. Why would anybody do this to me? Since both incidents were on my vehicle, it had to be meant for me specifically. Was it a stupid joke? And if not, what next?

I went to the police station on Sunday as promised and spoke to Officer Anita Layne. She took a report on what happened and told me she'd get someone to look into it. She also commented that there wasn't much to go on, especially since the Dumpster I threw the bear into had been emptied this morning. I agreed.

"Well, I'll let you know if we come up with anything," Officer Layne said. "Call us if anything else happens. Hopefully it won't."

"I would like nothing more than to have no more contact with you regarding this, no offense. Thank you officer, I appreciate it."

I walked out of the police station feeling no better about anything, except that I kept my promise to Katie.

I started the engine, but didn't put it in gear. I was due at my mom's for lunch at noon. It was eleven, so even with the forty-five minute drive I could spare some time.

I used my phone to get a list of all the flower shops within a five-mile radius.

Seventeen? People buy that many flowers?

There were five between the police station and the freeway entrance, I had some extra time, why not check some out? Surely someone buying that many roses would be remembered.

Except when it's still wedding season. Damn it. I gave up after visiting the third flower shop because *yes, lots of men came in buying roses. It is wedding and anniversary season after all. No, we don't have the time to look up the information you need. Do you know how many baby showers we're doing this afternoon?* And my favorite: *Honey, I'm sorry if your man bought another woman roses but that's not my problem.*

Well, great. I was still completely clueless as to who left those things on my Jeep and why.

I walked out of the last shop and sat on the bench right outside the door. Despite the cloud cover, it was uncomfortably hot. I just needed to think for a minute and it smelled really good so close to the entrance, so I let myself sweat while I tried to figure something—anything—out. My thoughts went in circles, only reviewing the little I knew. Was there anything worse than feeling as if you had no control? Someone out there was having a good laugh, knowing they'd pulled one over on me.

My skin was wet wherever it touched the bench so I stood to air myself out. I checked the time on my cell. Shoot, there was no way I'd make it to my mom's on time.

I dialed her number. "Hey," I said when she answered. "I'm going to be late. Is that a problem?"

"Molly?" she asked.

Really, Mom? "Yeah, it's me and I'm running late." I unlocked and got in my Jeep. Thank God I'd kept the windows cracked.

"Oh honey, I didn't know you wanted to come down today. I'm about to leave."

I clenched my teeth to keep from reminding her that we agreed to have lunch today after she canceled on me last weekend. I slumped back in my seat and cranked the engine, turning the air conditioning on full blast. I needed cooled off, in more ways than one.

Whatever. It was time for me to forget everything out of my control, like creepy jerks and emotionally distant mothers.

I wished her a good day and headed to Katie's. I had other things to focus my energy on—songwriting, for one. Katie and I write all the songs for The Song Wreckers, and our fans expected new stuff every once in a while. Channeling the negative feelings I had into songs—usually revolving around getting even, partying, too much drinking and too little ass shaking—was a form of therapy for me. The anger and negativity in a new song I was almost done writing called "See You In Hell" was perfect for my frame of mind, so yeah, I'll feel much better in a few hours.

Chapter 3

The months flew by and before I knew it the heat and humidity of August became the nearly frigid chill of the end of the year.

The asshole who messed with my Jeep was always in the back of my mind, but rarely made it to the front anymore. I've been busy at work since they gave me AP Government to teach—yikes!—on top of the regular Government and Economics classes I already taught. Katie was the choir director at her school, and I helped her organize her annual fall musical. And honestly, when something's bothering me I work out like crazy. I was a serious dancer all through my youth, and after I quit I started running and lifting weights. And swimming and playing softball, volleyball, tennis, and anything else I could. I learned early on that beating myself down physically and staying busy kept my mind off of unpleasant bullshit. So by the time winter vacation rolled around, I was ready to get the last of The Creep—that's the nick name he'd earned—out of my head once and for all.

I pulled into Katie's driveway and popped my hatch for her to load her suitcases in with mine. Cold December air mingled with the heat blowing from the vents. Her luggage and ski boots were a tight fit, but we'd been going to Traverse City to snowboard and ski over our schools' winter vacations for five years now, so we knew how to cram as much as possible into my Jeep.

She plopped into the passenger seat and immediately adjusted the vents to blow directly on her.

I handed her a small, wrapped present. "Happy birthday."

She grabbed and shook it. I padded the box so nothing rattled. Usually I got her a new calendar for the next year that had pictures of cute, fuzzy kittens—she loves those—and a bag or some other accessory. This year, the box was too small for either of those.

She tore the paper off and lifted the lid. "No way!"

"Way," I said, as she admired the custom guitar picks done in a multi-colored glitter look, with *The Song Wreckers* printed on one side, and *Katie* on the other.

She had been looking at these online a while back, but never ordered them. She lost guitar picks like crazy, so I ordered her a box of one hundred. Hopefully that would last her for a year.

She thanked and hugged me. I backed down her driveway and headed north to TC, where we would meet up with some other teacher friends and hit the slopes.

After stopping for breakfast, she admired her new picks again. "Did you order some for yourself too? These are really cool."

"I did," I said as I merged onto I-75 north. "But mine are black and I didn't put my name on them."

She nodded. "Maybe that's a good call considering your new creepy admirer. He might find something with your name on it and want to keep it."

Thankfully Wreckers Weekends yielded no more creeptastic presents and I could finally stop cringing every time I walked out the back door after a show. "It's been almost five months since anything was left on my Jeep. And really, it was only that one weekend in August."

Katie reclined her seat and put her feet on the dashboard. "You probably just blew off some guy and wounded his ego."

"Well, if I hurt someone's ego, it was unintentional." I merged into the slow lane, and turned on the radio. "So, how bad are you going to miss Brett?"

She sighed loudly. "A lot. We've gone a few days without seeing each other, but never because one of us was out of town. I am seriously in love with this man. This is going to be tough."

I glanced at her sad face with my smiling one. "Well I'm glad one of us isn't an emotional retard." Yeah, I have issues.

The roads were snowier the further north we drove. Great snowboarding weather, but scary to drive in. Six hours after I'd left, we met up with our small group and settled into hotel rooms. I immediately hit the slopes, and stayed there for nearly three days, only coming in to eat and sleep. Katie thought I was crazy, but she knew I cleared my mind by physically working myself to exhaustion.

I snowboarded my heart out until an old dance injury to my knee was aggravated when I took a hard fall, so I came in for good the day before we were scheduled to leave.

The other women I came with were done as well, so we did what all mature adults do on the last night of vacation: got rip-roaring drunk.

Somehow, Katie finagled us an invite to a party. I would've rather stayed in one of our rooms with just us girls. I was out-voted and forced to party with strangers, but better than sitting alone in my room. To cover my discomfort, I drank. And drank. A lot.

I didn't know exactly how much I drank, because when I woke the next morning—with the worst hangover of my life—my memory only held the first hour or two of the party.

I spent a good hour ridding my body of the leftover toxins, and cringing when Katie pieced my night together for me. She had stopped drinking when she saw how drunk I was getting.

I lay sprawled out on the bed, face down and buried in a pillow. I lifted my head. "Oh my God, Katie. Stop," I begged. "Please tell me you made some of this up." I plopped my face back into the pillow.

"Nope." She pushed me over and sat on the bed. "One of the guys there was just your type and—"

"I don't have a type," I mumbled.

"Yes you do. Your type is anyone who lets you do whatever the hell you want and gives you lots of space and doesn't get too close for you."

I was too hung over to contemplate the meaning of that statement. Maybe later.

"So, in summary, the mighty Ms. Molly Davis, showcased her hip-hop dancing skills, rode a frat boy like a mechanical bull, and loved every minute of it."

I wasn't loving right now. Talk about embarrassing myself, ugh.

When the thought of food no longer made me want to hurl, I ordered room service and didn't leave the room until it was time to check out.

The drive back home was somewhat disquieting, though I should've been in a zen-like state. My body was spent and I let loose with alcohol like never before. I wasn't worried about any of our group spreading around what I did; I had dirt on everyone in our group, which ensured that no one would dare gossip. In the years we've been going up north to hit the slopes, I've witnessed cheating on boyfriends, minor drug use, and other embarrassing drunken episodes. We had a what-happens-here-stays-here code. I was bummed because I kept thinking about what Katie said: That my "type" was a man who let me do whatever I wanted, gave me a lot of space, and didn't get too close.

Of course she was right, she knew me better than anybody. I'd had plenty of boyfriends, but I never wanted to be with any of them for the rest of my life. Or even for more than six months. The ones that got too close made me uncomfortable and I pushed them away. More than one boyfriend dumped me for refusing to move our relationship from casual to serious. Part of me was jealous of my married friends. Most of me couldn't fathom the notion of letting a man so thoroughly into my life. As close as I was to Katie, there were the rare things I never let even her see.

I was home and unpacked by Christmas Eve night, and in bed early with an ice pack to my knee. Holy cow, did I really ride someone like a mechanical bull? No wonder my knee was still swollen.

Sir Mix-A-Lot rapped from my night stand about his love of large backsides, so I knew Katie was calling. "What's up?" I answered.

"Hey, I was just thinking," she said. "Since I'm not going to Brett's family until dinner tomorrow, want me to come with you to your mom's for lunch?"

I wiggled up to a sitting position. "In other words, you have no food to cook yourself meals?"

"And the grocery stores will be closed since it's Christmas."

I laughed. "That's fine, my mom always makes too much food anyway."

"Plus I'll be that buffer between you and your mom's awkwardness. Are you ever going to have a talk with her?"

I took a deep breath and tossed the ice pack onto the floor. "Totally. Just not tomorrow."

She huffed into the phone. "Mol, you have got to talk to her instead of letting your feelings build up inside of you."

"What kind of dessert do you want me to make for tomorrow?"

"Good Lord, you are the queen of deflection. Brownies?"

"Brownies," I agreed before we hung up.

I knew I needed to have a talk with my mom and ask her questions I've had for years. Why didn't she ever talk about Holly, my twin sister who died at ten months old? Did she and my dad have a strong marriage before Holly's death? Katie's mom, Mama, had been like a second mother to me, and it had been Mama's love for me that got me through those tough teenage years unscathed. Did my own mother realize that?

One day, when I got the nerve, I'd ask her these things. But not on Christmas. Or any holiday. I needed a nice, neutral time to make us both uncomfortable. February? No, that's her birthday. March? Nope, too close to Easter. That scratches April too. May, June? I'm too stressed out with the end of the school year.

I'd hate to ruin her Fourth of July, so . . . never. I will pencil our talk in for never.

Disgusted with myself, I laid back down and threw the covers over my head. How in the hell could I have spent the last ten plus years playing guitar and singing back up to Katie in front all sorts of crowds, but couldn't get the courage to have an important discussion with my own mother?

Sometimes, just, ugh!

Chapter 4

New year, clean slate. Well, not exactly clean since problems didn't magically disappear. Maybe erased slate was more fitting. The old stuff was still there, just smeared to the point of unrecognizable. This allowed brand new stuff to take its place. Better stuff. I was going to be like an erased slate. I'd smear the old, unpleasant parts of my life, and write over it with . . . anything I wanted.

Wreckers Weekends would never get erased.

Brett met us out in the back alley to say hi and see if we needed help (eye roll) then gave me a big smile.

Josh and Courtney had hopped out of the van, so I climbed in with Katie. "You told him didn't you?" I whispered, but not quietly enough.

"Tell me what?" Brett called to us.

"God damn it, Katie—"

"Mol, pipe down. I told him what happened, that you got really drunk one night of our trip. End of story." She turned her head and whispered so no one else would hear, "I swear that is *all* I said."

We hopped down with the cables and walked toward the back door of the bar.

Brett followed. "Molly Davis, drunk as a skunk. Now *that* was probably a sight to see. Damn it's cold out here, Katie give me that." Brett took what she had in her hands then hurried inside to set it down.

I stayed behind him so I didn't have to look him in the eye. "No not really. I, ya know, drank too much and passed out." *La la la, no big deal, please shut up.*

Despite the cold temperature outside there were a lot of people in Brett's. Wreckers Weekends were always his best two days of the month.

We played our show, people drank to keep away the chill, then we packed up our stuff and loaded it in record time so we wouldn't turn into a band-sicle.

I always took my guitars home with me instead of packing them in the van. I hurried to my Jeep and opened the hatch. When I set the first guitar in I heard a slight crunching sound.

"What the hell?" I murmured to myself. I pulled my guitar out and looked in the hatch. The space was full of flowers. "Mother fucker!" I yelled.

I set both guitars on the ground as the others came running.

"Molly, what's wrong?" Katie asked. Although I did tend to curse a lot, she knew I would scream those words only if I was seriously upset.

I stepped aside so they could see. "My hatch is full of flowers."

Everyone stood there, silent.

My hands clenched into fists. "God damn it! Who the hell is doing this?" I yelled again. I reached in and started throwing the flowers to the ground. They were roses and still had the thorns on them, so as an added bonus I got tons of little cuts all over my hands, even through my mittens. I could've slowly and carefully removed them, but I was too furious.

"Is there a note?" Heather asked.

I finished getting all of the flowers out and ran my hand over the entire surface of the hatch. Nothing else. "No. No note."

Katie picked up my guitars. "Heather, Josh, Courtney—go home. I'll handle this. Molly, come inside with me."

Katie and I walked inside, got Brett from the front bar, then marched into his office. While Katie told him what happened, I pulled a tissue off his desk. I threw myself down on the couch then blotted the pinpricks of blood from my hands.

Brett stood, hands on hips and lips pursed, clearly mad. Katie sat on the edge of his desk, and he took his place next to her. Katie crossed her arms over her chest and glared at me, almost daring me to protest, while Brett called 911 to report what had happened.

When he hung up he asked, "Molly, how did this guy get in your car?"

I finished with the tissue, wadded it up, and threw it into the small trash can next to his desk. "I was wondering the same thing. I know I locked my car like I always do."

"Is it possible you forgot tonight?" Brett asked.

I opened my mouth to answer but Katie beat me to it. "She didn't forget. I was standing right there when she pressed the lock button and shut the door."

"I want to go out and have a look at your car. Hold on a sec." Brett left his office for a minute and came back in with a flashlight. "Ok, let's go. Do me a favor and don't touch your car. I want to see if there's any forced entry marks anywhere on your hatch or doors. Did you check it out at all?"

"No. I opened the hatch from the remote, put one of my guitars in, took it back out, and threw all the flowers out." We waited for Brett to put on his coat, then walked out to the alley together. "I also felt all over my hatch looking for another note. Other than that, I haven't touched anything."

Brett aimed the flashlight at my Jeep and slowly walked all around it while Katie and I stood watching our breath in the cold. It was almost one o'clock in the morning, and the temperature was in the single digits. I was shaking, both from the cold and being freaked out.

"I don't see any damage," he said. "Are you sure you locked your car, Molly?"

I was freezing, I was tired, I wanted to go home. "Positive. Come on, Brett. Do you really think the police are going to come out here at one in the morning because someone left flowers in my car? This is hardly pressing stuff."

He walked back to us. "This isn't Detroit, Molly. It's Southgate. And yes, I think they'll come out here since there have been two other incidents and now your car was broken into. Stop trying to act as if this is nothing."

The crunch of the gravel indicated a vehicle turning in to the alley. The three of us watched the police cruiser pull up near us. A uniformed man stepped out of the car then introduced himself as Officer Czarnowski. He then took my statement and had a look at my Jeep.

When he was done with his inspection he told us, "Looks as if whoever did this slim-jimmed your car. Slim-jimming rarely leaves prints, and the guy or girl was probably wearing gloves in this temperature. It's up to you, but I don't think fingerprinting your vehicle will turn up anything."

I held out my hand, and he shook it. "I agree. Thank you, officer. I'm sorry you had to come out here when it's so cold."

"Not a problem. Ms. Davis? I'm going to give this to the detective who was handed the case of the bear and the roses. Breaking into your vehicle is taking it up a notch. You need to be careful at all times. Make sure you know your surroundings, try not to go places alone if you can help it, that sort of thing."

I nodded. "Got it. Thanks again."

When the officer left, Brett, Katie and I walked back into the bar to warm up.

We stood there for a minute in Brett's office and let our body temperatures return to normal. I sat on the arm of the couch while Katie leaned into Brett, and he put his arms around her.

"Molly, I'm going to do something about this," he told me.

"You've done enough, Brett, thank you. I don't think there's anything else you can do."

"Bullshit. First off I'm going to have cameras installed in the alley as soon as possible. I know a guy who can set me up with whatever we need. He can also tell me what else we should do. I'll call him tomorrow morning. I'm going to follow you home tonight. You" he pointed to Katie, "can ride with me then I'll bring you back here to your car."

"Good idea," Katie said at the same time I said, "Not necessary."

Katie opened her mouth to bitch at me, when I cut her off. "Listen guys, thank you. Really. I appreciate the concern but I'll be fine. I'll drive straight home into my garage, close the door, and lock myself in my house." I put on my hat and mittens.

Katie told Brett, "Good Lord, tell her okay, let her leave and we'll follow her anyway. She's stubborn as a mule and hates feeling as if she's putting anyone out, so just let her think we're not gonna follow her home."

With a huge, exasperated sigh I threw my hands up in the air and walked out of the bar and to my Jeep. About five seconds after I pulled out of the alley so did Brett and Katie in Brett's truck. I hated that I breathed easier knowing they were behind me.

Chapter 5

I should've told Brett not to call his guy to have cameras installed, but I doubted he'd listen to me. Plus he was doing this for Katie, Heather, and Courtney's safety as well as mine. I felt guilty for making people worry and for making Brett think he needed to put up surveillance cameras. Those wouldn't come cheap. At the same time, I was comforted. Maybe the idiot who'd left me those gifts would do it again and get caught. It also put me at ease when I considered the other girls, especially Katie. If some creep was doing this to me, what was to stop him from doing it to someone else?

I made it home and washed the bar smell off of me, but sleep wouldn't come. My mind wouldn't stop racing, so I grabbed a journal and wrote really nasty song lyrics to relax me. I still haven't found words that go well with "you fucking dirt bag piece of shit."

I'm not sure what time I eventually fell asleep—late obviously, because I was not ready to wake up when Katie came waltzing into my house at nine the next morning to take me on a surprise, I'm-showing-my-support-by-doing-something-I-hate-but-you-love run. We had keys to each other's house and generally came and went as we pleased.

After our run, I came home, showered, straightened my hair then went back to bed. We had to play later that night, so I needed a big nap. I should've worked on a few songs I had started, but it was the end of the semester and I had a ton of essays to grade, so that was what I did until it was time to finish getting ready, warm up my voice, and leave.

Brett's was its usual rowdy self, and normally I took comfort in the craziness. But when we started playing that night, two men in the audience alarmed me. I had never seen them before, and they alternated between watching me with intense eyes and visually searching the room. They sat at a table, dressed like everyone else in jeans and T-shirts, trying to blend in. Their body language was casual; their faces were not.

I tried unsuccessfully to ignore them. I couldn't help glancing in their direction every few minutes. They occasionally spoke to each other. As far as I could tell, they weren't drinking alcohol. There were two bottles of water on their table. Several women walked slowly by, trying to get their attention, but they hardly seemed to notice.

As we played our last song of the first set I noticed they were gone. Crap. They weren't out "decorating" my car, were they?

During our first break I grabbed a bottle of water from the fridge behind the bar then headed to Brett's office. As I reached to push the door all the way open, I stopped. Brett was talking so I stood silently and listened.

He told someone, "Once, maybe twice I could overlook as a prank. But this is three times now, and I don't like that the first time the bear had a stick coming out of its back. Then the second time fake blood was used, and Molly cut her hands up on the thorns last night. This is too fucked up for me to ignore."

"You think it could be a guy she took home from the bar and then dumped?" an unknown man responded.

What the hell? I didn't do that! Man, that pissed me off, so I shoved the door open and barged into the room. "I don't take guys home from the bar!" I blasted at them. "Brett why aren't you sticking up for me?" Then I froze. The same two men who spooked me from the audience were in the room with Brett.

"Because you didn't give me a chance," Brett replied. "Molly Davis I want you to meet Cooper and Ram," he said, gesturing to each of them as he said their names. "Gabe Cooper is the guy I told you I was calling about the surveillance cameras, and Ram is one of his employees."

First I shook Cooper's hand. Gabe Cooper had that mean son-of-a-bitch look about him. Maybe he looked more serious than mean. Whatever, there was a hard edge to him. The Bad Boy. He looked as if he was in his late thirties, about six feet tall with dark brown eyes and short, dark brown hair. There was a touch of gray at the temples. He had a few wrinkles on his forehead, as if he spent a lot of time deep in concentration. There were some old holes in his earlobes where there used to be earrings. He was decently built; both of the men were.

Next I shook Ram's hand, and I hated that I could feel my pulse quicken and face turn red as soon as our hands touched. Ram looked younger, closer to my age. He was about the same height as Cooper, maybe an inch taller. Ram had blond hair—I mean *blond* blond hair—and piercing blue eyes that drew me in. No doubt about it, he would've been safe in Hitler's Germany. He didn't have the same edge as Cooper; still, there was definitely something about him. Like, he gave off vibes that were . . . calming. I don't know how else to explain it. He didn't have the Bad Boy image going on like Gabe Cooper, yet he radiated the same confidence and control. He also looked as if he could cause serious damage if need be. Shaking Ram's hand, compared to Cooper's, was much, *much* nicer. Even with my irritation.

But because I was irritated, I had to educate these gentlemen. "For the record I have been playing in bars for a decade now, and I have never, *ever* gone home with a guy from the bar. Nor have I ever even dated a guy I met from the bars I've played at. For that matter I barely even date—"

Gabe Cooper put his hand up to cut me off. "We didn't mean to offend you. We need to see this from every angle."

"Yeah, well me being a slut is *not* an angle."

Ram opened his stupid mouth. "There's no reason to get all Angry Princess Barbie on us, Ms. Davis. We just need to cover everything."

Fucker. Why do the hottest men have to be assholes? I took a second to remember if there really was an Angry Princess Barbie (there's not), and rolled my eyes instead of making an issue out of his stupid ass comment.

Screw that, he needed to be called a name too. "Shut it, Blondie," Really, I couldn't have come up with anything better? "So are you guys the camera installers?"

Ram snorted, but Cooper said, "No, we're not camera installers. Please, sit down and we'll talk for a minute."

"No thanks. I'd rather stand." That was a big, fat lie. I was wearing three-inch-heeled cowboy boots, and my feet were starting to hurt. I would've loved to sit down, but I wanted to be stubborn even more.

Brett put his hand on my shoulder. "Molly, please. Sit down. These guys are here to help, and your being pig-headed doesn't help."

I sat. Because my feet needed it, not because they wanted me too. "So if you're not camera installers what are you?"

"Mainly we're bodyguards," Cooper said. "I own a company called 3D Protection." He handed me a business card. "We service clients in all types of personal protection. Like I said, mainly we act as bodyguards, but we also do surveillance when the client needs it, and we also do private investigations as it applies to the client's needs for protection. Most of my employees are licensed private investigators as well as bodyguards."

I surged up to glare at Brett, but pointed at Cooper and Ram. "You hired babysitters for me?"

Ram answered. "We're not babysitters, Princess, we're bodyguards. And a simple thank you to Brett would be more appropriate instead of an ungrateful attitude. From what I understand you have someone out there who wants to scare you. Or worse."

"Stop calling me stupid names," I shot back and dropped my arm. "And what the hell kind of name is Ram anyway? Were you named after the truck or the animal?"

"Neither. It's short for Ramsey, my last name."

"Oh." I had no smart comeback for that, so I put on a nice fake smile and shoved the business card in my back pocket. "Well listen, I really don't need a babysitter." I turned to face Brett. "Brett, thank you. I appreciate what you're trying to do, but I think it's overkill." I turned to glare at Cooper and Ram. "Gentlemen, nice meeting you. I'm gonna go. I have another set to play and I have to scan the crowd for a guy to take home with me tonight." And with that I walked out.

During our second set, Cooper and Ram once again sat in the audience and alternated between glaring at me and scanning the room. At least I wasn't freaked out by them anymore.

We had this song that, over the past year since we wrote the song, our diehard female fans made up a dance to it. It's a song about moving your butt around and shaking your hips to make the boys happy, and the moves did the song justice. Those same diehard ladies did that dance up on the tables. The rest of the women did it on the dance floor. It was popular with everyone. Right before we played the song I called Jenny, one of the table dancers, and directed her to hop up onto Cooper and Ram's table for the song. She took one look at them and agreed.

I stepped up to my mic. "Before we make the men in here *very* happy, I would like to dedicate this song to the two new friends I made tonight." I smiled big. "This one's for you, guys!"

Katie looked at me with her eyebrows raised. "I'll tell ya later," I mumbled.

The expressions on Cooper and Ram's faces when Jenny hopped up and did those moves were priceless. They acted as if their table held nothing out of the ordinary. Cooper looked irritated; Ram looked amused. I felt vindicated, though it would've been nicer if Cooper and Ram weren't there at all.

I walked into Brett's office during our second break and was glad to see no one else in there. I sat on the couch and put my head in my hands and rubbed my temples. A stress headache had started, and playing guitar and singing with a headache really sucked. Ten seconds later the door opened and in walked Brett, Cooper, and Ram. Ugh.

I looked up at Brett. "Why are they still here?"

"Princess, this isn't your decision. Brett hired us, not you." Ram said.

First I narrowed my eyes and pointed at Ram. "Don't call me Princess." Next I slid my glare and finger to Brett. "I'm going to go tell Katie on you."

"Katie agrees with me on this, Molly. She's scared for you and for the others too."

"Is the bar doing so well that you can afford to throw money away? If I'd known, we would've asked for a raise." Not that any of us really cared about the few bucks Brett paid us to be there.

"I've known Cooper for a while now. He's giving me a hell of a deal." Brett said.

Great. Now I'm a charity case. "Okay so what? Now I get babysat every Wreckers weekend?"

Cooper answered me. "First, we're going to install more lights and motion sensor cameras along the alley that will start recording whenever they sense movement. And because we don't know what this person may do next, we'll have a bodyguard or two stationed at the alley upon your arrival. They'll stay for the entire show, watching for any suspicious behavior. Then when you're done playing, they'll be with you in the alley while you get your stuff put away. Our men will be there before you get there and will be there until you all safely leave."

I sat forward, on alert. "So you think whoever is doing this is hanging out in the bar?" I asked.

"That's the most logical conclusion," Cooper said.

Ram added, "If there's something you need to tell us, now's the time."

"No. I was thinking the same thing," I told them. "Maybe it was someone who hit on me that I blew off." My face heated at my conceitedness.

"I'd like to talk to you more in depth. My feeling is that the person who is doing this is a patron of this bar, but I want to cover every angle."

I nodded, and began to rub my temples again. "Can we do it another time? Right now I have a headache. I just want to pop two Advil and be alone."

"What are your plans for tomorrow?" Cooper asked.

I ticked off my plans on my fingers. "Sleeping in, working out, cleaning my house, working on—"

"Can you squeeze some time in between being a smart ass and making sarcastic comments?" Ram asked, cutting me off.

I lowered my head and rubbed at my temples to hide a smile. "Possibly. When and where?"

"I want to check out where you live," Cooper said. "Can I meet you at your place around one o'clock?"

"Why do you want to check out where I live?"

"I want to see how secure it is."

"And if I say no?"

Ram answered, sounding exasperated. "Honestly? We'll go to your house when you're not home and check it out anyway."

My head popped up. "Like break in? You can't do that!"

Ram smiled. Cooper stood there, staring at me.

Ugh. "Fine. One o'clock. Can't wait. No offense, but can I please be alone now?"

"This is my office," Brett said.

"Yes, however *you* need to help the good citizens of this city get wasted. It's busy out there, they need your help."

"I know, I'm going." Brett looked at Cooper and Ram, then smiled. "I'm leaving her with you. Good luck." With a happy whistle he walked back to the bar area.

I stood up and went to Brett's desk drawer where I kept my purse. "Do you two have to stay in here with me? I really don't want to play the last set with a headache." I put two Advil in my mouth and swallowed them with the water I had left from the last break.

"We'll be out in the hall," Cooper said.

Ram turned to Cooper. "I'll be out in a minute I want to talk to Princess here for a minute."

Cooper left with a nod, shutting the door behind him. I looked at Ram, and he crossed his arms over his chest.

"I have a real name, you know," I told him.

"Why are you being so difficult?" Ram asked. "This is for your safety."

I plopped down on the couch with an exaggerated sigh. "I'm not trying to be difficult, but I hate this." He raised his eyebrows indicating he wanted me to continue. "I hate that some idiot is messing with me. I hate that I'm causing Katie and Brett and the rest of the band to worry. I hate that people are feeling the need to look after me. I hate that my problems are causing Brett to install cameras and hire babysitters." He narrowed his eyes at me. "Sorry. Bodyguards. I just want this to all go away."

"And you think ignoring it will make it go away?"

"There's nothing wrong with ignoring things you hope will go away." I should know.

"So if this happened to one of the other women in the band?"

"I would—" call on the National Guard to protect them and hunt the bastard down myself. "—allow them to deal with the situation as they see fit, not interfering a single, itty-bitty bit."

Ram pinched the bridge of his nose as if he knew I was full of shit. "Pri—Molly, let us look out for you. I'm sure this guy will try something stupid with your car again soon, and we'll catch him. Then Cooper and I will leave, and your life will return to normal."

I leaned forward and put my head in my hands. He assumed this creep would strike again. I worried about that too, and hearing Ram confirm it made it worse.

He sat on the couch next to me, and the tension in my shoulders eased. He was his own scented candle, the scent being "lusty tranquility." Ingredients: large muscled male, whatever deodorant he wore, another scent I couldn't identify, piercing blue eyes, and a take charge attitude mixed with a fair amount smart-assness.

I mean, really. Of all times for my girly parts to tingle, it had to be from a man who thought I was a brat, but had to be nice to me because he'd been hired to protect me from The Creep.

I knew Ram was right, and admitting it sucked. "Fine," I said, without taking my head out of my hands. "Have you met the rest of the band yet?"

"No."

"Well I'll go get them. You should meet them too. After all you'll be guarding *all* our bodies, right?" So long alone time.

"Yes."

I retrieved the others from the front of the bar. Once everyone was in Brett's office, Cooper and Ram introduced themselves to the band and explained what they would be doing. The others agreed having some protection was a good thing, and they were happy Brett had done this, blah, blah, blah.

"Well I hate to end this meet and greet but we've got one more set to do," Katie said.

I smiled. "By the way, how did you like 'Shake It Out Loud'? You know, the song with the dancer on your table?"

Cooper looked at me, completely unimpressed. "Don't do that again."

"Dude, you sure don't know Molly," Heather told him. "You just guaranteed a dancer on your table every time we do that song."

Katie threw her arm around my shoulder and led me out of the office. Our last set went well. I was glad to be rid of the headache from earlier. By the time we sang the last note of the last song, Cooper and Ram were at the hallway that went from the back of the stage to the back door. I could've pretended that they weren't there except that they tried to help us girls carry the equipment. And it's not that we don't appreciate the offer to help, it's that we've been doing this for so long it's easier when we do it ourselves.

I set them straight on the issue of helping us. I was irritated with the whole getting babysat situation, so I added, "Please. Stand there, look pretty, and guard our bodies," to be a smart ass.

"You got it, Princess," Ram shot at me.

The rest of the band and Brett laughed at the stupid nick name. Traitors. We loaded everything in. Josh and Courtney left, then Heather drove off. I went back inside to grab my guitars. When I came out Cooper tried to take them from me.

Katie stopped him. "I wouldn't do that, Cooper."

Cooper backed off. Ram shook his head.

I couldn't resist one more wise crack to Cooper and Ram. "So are you going to follow me home, read me a story, and tuck me in?"

Ram looked at Brett. "Brett, is that what you want?"

Fucker! "No! I was kidding. Do *not* tell them to do that!" I squeaked out a goodbye to Katie and Brett, hurried outside, put the guitars in my Jeep, then sped out of there. I glanced in my rearview mirror right before I turned left out of the alley and saw a split second of Ram smiling like he was the cat who caught the mouse.

Chapter 6

On Sunday, at one o'clock sharp, there was a knock at my door. I unlocked and opened it. Cooper stood on my porch. "Hey, come on in. Let me take your coat."

"Do you always open the door without looking to see who it is first?" he greeted as he took off his coat and handed it to me.

"No, but I was expecting you at one, so when there was a knock on my door at one I knew it was you."

"You should still look first anyway."

I hung up his coat on a wall hook in my small foyer. "Fine. Have a seat. Do you want anything to drink?" I asked.

"No thank you," he said, still standing.

Here's what I was learning about Gabe Cooper: The man was all business. I don't think I'd seen him come close to smiling. If he wasn't talking about the business at hand, he wasn't talking at all.

"My furniture doesn't bite, I swear. Feel free to sit."

He ignored me. "I had a look around the outside of your condo unit. I like the style. Access to your windows is higher off the ground than a typical ranch."

I lived in a condo complex of raised ranches. Our homes were all ranch style, with six steps leading to the front door. Even if you entered through the garage, you'd have to walk up six steps to enter the small mud room. There were four condos in each building with twelve buildings total. I lived on an end unit in the very back of the neighborhood. My backyard was private, backing up to a long stretch of woods. I'd paid a premium to have an end unit with privacy, and the price was worth it.

"That's good."

"*That's* good," he agreed. "The rest is a concern." He walked toward the kitchen, which was at the back of my condo. I followed.

We stood in the middle of my kitchen. "Like . . ." I prompted.

"Like your backyard bordering the woods. That makes it easy for someone to hide. The sliding glass door into your kitchen has nothing covering it for privacy. That makes it easy for someone to look in here, see what you're doing, get a feel for the layout, that sort of thing." He paused and turned around to look at me. "I'm not trying to scare you—"

"You sure about that?" I was beginning to feel paranoid.

"I was hired to keep you safe. Whoever is harassing you has shown that he will escalate his behavior to get your attention. He's already broken into your car. I don't want your home to be next."

"You and me both. So you keep calling this person 'he'. You think this is definitely a man?"

He nodded. "Makes the most sense."

"I agree." I motioned to the large view outside. "So you'll feel better if I get window coverings for the glass door?" I asked.

"Yes. And I'm going to bring over a board to put down here." He crouched down and waved his hand the length of the left side of the tract where the glass door slid open. "Someone would have to break the glass to get inside here when it's in place."

"Well, I'm just feeling safer by the minute." My sarcasm wasn't going to help anything so I apologized. "Sorry. What else?"

"I saw from the outside that there's basement access through a window slider. Can we go down to your basement? I want to see how secure the window is."

"Sure." The stairs to the finished basement were off the kitchen so I took him down. My basement had hardwood floors and not too much in terms of decoration. One of the corners was set up as a music station. There was a huge cork board hanging on the wall, posted with the lyrics to various songs that I was working on, both Wreckers songs, and songs I'd been writing that weren't right for The Wreckers. There were also a couple guitar stands with my guitars on them. A table and two comfortable chairs completed the music corner.

The rest of the room was my dance space. There were several large mirrors hung on one wall, a fan, and miscellaneous dance gear stashed against another wall. Another small table held an iPod speaker station.

Cooper took a look around and headed to the one window that was required for fire code. He opened it, climbed out, then came back in. "Pretty easy for a body to fit through here, which is the point in case of fire. I want another board for this window, too. Again, someone will have to break the window to get in here. Let's go back up so I can assess the rest of the house."

We headed back upstairs and I walked him around the rest of the house, which was the master bedroom with attached bathroom, guest bedroom and hall bathroom. Those passed his inspection. Finally we went back to the kitchen.

"So what's the final verdict?" I asked.

"Since you don't have a security system installed, make sure everything stays locked, even when you're home. Especially at night. Can we talk now?"

"Sure. Let's go back to the living room. I'm going to get a drink for myself. Sure you don't want anything?" I grabbed an iced tea from the fridge and held it out for him. Surprisingly he took it and gulped some down. I did the same, and we walked into the living room.

I sat on the couch while Cooper sat on a chair adjacent to it. "Okay, ask away," I told him.

He took another sip. "Hold on a minute. Let me make a quick phone call." He dialed, waited, then spoke. "I need you to go to Home Depot, measure the length of a standard glass door wall tract and bring me a board that fits in the half space the door opens into. Then bring me another board eighteen inches in length." He then rattled off my address (which I had never given him) and hung up.

Cooper returned his attention to me. "When Brett contacted me about the stalking—"

"Stalking?" I didn't like that word.

"So far that's what it looks like." He carried on without further explanation. "When Brett contacted me about the stalking, and I asked him questions about you, he didn't tell me much. He gave me the basics, your name, age, and that you play at his bar once a month.

"I'm a private person. He knows that. Did he at least tell you about my sparkling personality?"

No reaction. Not even a hint of a smile.

Cooper continued. "If yesterday is an indication of your normal behavior, then you don't hang out in the bar during your breaks?"

"Once in a while, but usually I hang out in Brett's office," I said. "Listen, I was serious when I told you I don't hook up with guys from the bar. Never have. I get hit on and asked out occasionally. So do the others."

"I believe you. Has anyone ever hit on you that gave you a bad feeling or got angry that you turned them down?"

I thought for a minute. Yeah, men pay some attention to me. Let's face it, girls who play guitar are hot. Random fans have asked me out. Then there's Adam, the drummer from Crawling Home After Midnight. However, he has no problems getting attention from women—during Wreckers Weekends at least—and never wasted more than a few minutes on me. "Not that I can remember. I'm not a bitch about it. I make up a lie, usually that I'm involved with someone, smile, and move on."

He nodded as if he believed me. "All right. Let's look at the other parts of your life. I'm assuming you have a real job? One that pays the mortgage?" He pulled out a small memo pad and pen from his front pocket.

"It's a good thing you're taking notes, there's a quiz later." Again, nothing. "That was a joke. I'm a teacher at Brownstown High school. Social studies."

He wrote that down. "How long?"

"This is my eighth school year there. Besides subbing before I was hired into Brownstown, I've spent my entire career there."

"So we've got several years' worth of past students. Anyone in the past eight years you think could be behind this?"

"I don't think so." I took a minute to reflect. "There have only been two former students I can think of who I didn't have a cordial relationship with while in my class. They were the kind of kids who didn't really get along with any authority figure. One of them, Brendon Smatcher, had to repeat my Government class three times. He finally passed after the third go around. The other one, Kelly Adams, was smart as hell. Passed with an A+. Just didn't like school or teachers. I think the classes were too easy for her."

"How long ago were these two students?" he asked while still taking notes.

"Let's see . . . Kelly was my student two years ago and graduated last year. Brendon was my student for the last time five years ago I think." I might have been off a year on Brendon, but I was almost positive the timing was correct.

"So that would make them how old now, approximately?"

"Kelly should be 18 or 19. Brendon, about 23."

"Brendon is over 21 so he can get in Brett's."

I shook my head. "I would recognize him. I would know if I saw him at the bar." Would Brendon, as I knew him, be capable of this? He did have a fairly troubled past. His mother and I had many lengthy conversations, and she'd told me all about his mental and legal troubles.

"Is there any part of you that thinks Brendon might be capable of this?"

At least we were on the same wave length. "I was thinking the same thing. My gut says no. He was no fan of mine, don't get me wrong, but he was so relieved to finally get out of my class and graduate I think he wanted to run and never look back." I shrugged. "I guess it's possible. I will tell you this about him—he was a troubled kid growing up. His mother told me a lot of things about him that I don't feel comfortable repeating, so check him out if it makes you feel better. I haven't heard anything about him since he graduated."

"What about colleagues? Any possibilities there? Have you dated any of them? Do any of them give you extra attention or come to the shows?"

"Are we really going to get into my dating past? Because if so this will be a short conversation." I wasn't ashamed that I didn't date all that much, but I didn't want to get into the reasons why. Cooper didn't seem like the type to care about my intimacy issues unless it could help him figure this out, which it couldn't.

"Anything you tell me is going to help. If you choose to not share information with me then I can't do my job as effectively." He set his notebook on the coffee table. "Your call."

With a sigh I told him what he wanted to know. "There's a small group of teachers from work who come to the shows, none that are there every single month, and they're mostly women. The men that come usually bring their wives or girlfriends. A couple years ago, I dated another teacher. John Sarkowski, Language Arts. We dated for the last half of the school year and part of the summer. The relationship ran its course, and we ended it." I paused to think about the timing. "We broke up two summers ago. He's the only colleague I've ever dated. I've had a few dates here and there, none lasted more than two dates. This past summer I dated Owen Simmons. That lasted two or three months. I broke it off in July."

"Why did you break it off? Was he mad about it?"

"I broke it off because he didn't do it for me, and he was only mad that he dated me for so long and I wouldn't sleep with him. I really don't think Owen would do this."

"Owen was the last man you dated?"

"Yes."

He picked up the notebook and started writing, then asked: "What about bartenders from Brett's?"

"Never dated any of them."

"Have any of them asked you out or do any flirting with you?" Cooper's tone changed when he asked this question, so I assumed he noticed Johnny, Brett's resident flirt, smiling and winking at me. I considered him harmless, I loved his charm, and he made me feel pretty, so I don't discourage him.

"A couple have asked me out over the years. None who still work there. Johnny flirts with me on a regular basis. He's a flirty guy. He does that with a lot of women."

"Is there anyone you think it could be? I'm sure you've scrutinized this a lot."

To the point of insanity. "I honestly have no idea. That's part of what is so frustrating."

Someone knocked on my door. I stood up, made a point of looking to see who it was, then let Katie in. "Hey. What are you doing knocking?"

"There was a truck in your driveway. I didn't want to walk in on, you know, like a date or something." She smiled, no doubt giving herself a mental high-five, while she took off her coat and hung it up on a coat hook. "Sorry. I tried to keep a straight face while saying that. Hey, Cooper. What's going on here?"

Cooper nodded his head in acknowledgement of Katie. "I wanted to check out how secure the premise is and talk to Molly about who the stalker could possibly be."

"*Stalker?*" Katie asked in the exact tone I did.

"That's how I see it," he said.

She suddenly went from happy to serious. "Dang. That freaks me out even more." She joined me on the couch.

"Would you please relax? What did you come over for, anyway?" I didn't want Katie to get any more upset over this. She and Brett were already too protective of me.

"It just started snowing and isn't supposed to stop any time soon. I wanted to work on the songs we've been stuck on then hit the hills tonight. You interested in sledding later?"

"Hell yes!" Katie and I still loved sledding.

"I'm pretty much done," Cooper said. "I'm waiting for Ram to bring me a couple things. He should be here soon."

"Out of curiosity," I asked Cooper, "what is Ram's first name?" *Please* let it rhyme with something vulgar, like Vic or Buck.

"Caleb."

Damn. I still needed to get him back for calling me Princess. Blondie didn't seem to bother him.

I wanted to talk about our upcoming sledding excursion, but Katie sat on the couch and looked at Cooper. "So Cooper, do you have any idea who this creep is?"

"Not yet. I was talking to Molly about men she's dated and I want to explore that."

Katie gave a sound of disgust. "Well that's a seriously short list so it shouldn't take long,"

"Excuse me for being selective." I shoved my shoulder into her. "Don't start on my dating life, please."

Katie continued talking to Cooper. "Can you believe my girl Molly hasn't had a date since the summer? And before that," she looked at me, "Who was before that? That guy from work?"

Ignoring us, Cooper broke in on our conversation. "Katie, can you think of anyone who might possibly be doing this?"

She scrunched her face to think. "I don't know. I don't think Owen has it in him." She turned to me. "Who was the guy from work?"

"John."

"Oh yeah, John. He didn't seem the type either. I don't know. Sorry."

Cooper continued writing in his little notebook, while Katie and I discussed which sledding hill we would go to. Finally Ram showed up. Of course, I identified the knocker before I opened the door.

"Here's your stuff, Princess," Ram said, handing me the boards while stepping inside so I could shut the door.

I put on a nice sarcastic face. "Some girls get flowers, I get a man with wood."

Katie burst out laughing.

I cringed. "Shut up, Katie," I warned. She didn't.

I held up the longer piece. "Where does this wood go?"

Katie laughed harder.

Ram smiled, and had the cutest dimples I ever saw. "The longer one is for the sliding glass door. I don't know where the other one goes."

"Basement window," I told him, trying not to stare at his cheeks. How did he make dimples look manly?

"Well then, that one's for the basement window."

He still smiled, and his liveliness was contagious because I was smiling too. "Okay. Well is there anything else?" I forced myself to look away from Ram to Cooper.

Cooper answered. "No. We're done. We'll see you next Wreckers Weekend. Remember what I said about making sure everything's locked. Make sure you always have those boards in unless you're using the door. Then make sure you put them back in when you're done. Cover your kitchen door, too."

"Got it," I said. "And thanks. You too, Ram."

"You bet," Ram said. "You need me to put the wood in for you?"

My face went bright red, I could feel it burn from my neck to my hairline.

The second he realized his double entendre he threw his head back and barked a laugh. "Never mind. See you next month. Bye, ladies." Cooper and Ram took their coats off the hook then left, but Ram turned to me at the last second with that cat-and-mouse smile.

As soon as the door closed, I yelled, "Katie, shut up!" She was still laughing.

Chapter 7

I woke up Monday, ready to go back to work, and thankful I had sustained no injuries from our sledding excursion the night before. Katie and I had the brilliant idea to try and sled standing up. Turns out it is harder than you think and is nothing like snowboarding.

Katie called me on my way home from work. "Hey, Brett told me the cameras were going to be installed tomorrow. I just wanted to let you know."

Okay, the cameras were a good idea, which meant I wasn't going to give Brett a hard time about it. Any alley in the back of a bar should have them. What bothered me was the cost. "So how much is Brett spending on all this?"

"The cameras? I don't know, didn't ask. Molly, the cameras are going in. End of story. Don't call him and bug him to not put them in."

"I won't. I actually think the cameras are a good idea for everybody. I'm talking about the other stuff. Gabe Cooper and Ram. Their bodyguard and private investigation services. That can't be cheap. I did research online for 3D Protection last night. It seems like they are *the* place to go for any type of personal protection anywhere in the state. It's a pretty good sized business. How much is Brett is putting out for this?"

I heard Katie sigh on the other end. "I don't know, Molly, really, and I don't want to know. Listen, if Brett wants to do this then let him. He's really bothered that this happened *and* that it happened at his bar. You wanna go grocery shopping later in about an hour? If I don't go, I won't be eating anytime soon."

"I'm gonna dance for an hour or two when I get home. Pick me up at six so we can go hungry. I get a lot more food that way. Listen, I'm going to talk to Brett about letting me share the cost of this."

"You can try but I'm sure he won't let you. I gotta go, I'll pick you up about six. Later." Katie signed off.

"Later." I clicked my cell shut, as I pulled into my driveway.

I waited until Wednesday afternoon to check out the cameras. I drove straight to the bar after work knowing it wouldn't be busy. I wanted to talk to Brett without Katie around so the two of them couldn't tag team me. When I walked in, Brett was behind the bar trying to look busy by wiping everything down. "Working hard or hardly working?" I asked him.

"Funny," he replied, then looked up, concerned. "What's up? You don't come in here on weekday afternoons."

I took a seat on a stool and threw my purse on the bar. "I want to have a look at the cameras and talk to you for a minute. Can you show them to me?"

"Sure, give me a minute. I'll get Heather to watch the front." Brett left, and in a minute he and Heather came back out front.

"Hey, Heather, how's it going?" I asked.

"Good. Man it's weird seeing you in a suit. I almost forgot you have a real job. You look all professional. Dude, you're a grown up!" She pretended to cootie spray herself. "What are you doing here?"

I smiled and answered, "I wanted to see the cameras." I turned to Brett. "Ready?"

"Yup. Let's go. Call me if you need me, Heather. I'll be in the alley."

"Okay."

I grabbed my purse, and Brett and I went around the bar to the back. He gestured to his office, and we went in. The first thing I noticed was a new table against the back wall with two monitors and other box-like equipment on it.

"These are the new monitors," he explained. "There are two of them that record when the cameras sense motion. If more than two of the cameras catch images to record, the monitors turn into split screen. I'm assuming they're going to record a lot of trips to the Dumpster and smoke breaks. Probably some animals. But hopefully the idiot who's doing this to your car will get recorded, too."

The monitors were about fifteen inches and flat screen. Looked pricey. Nothing was moving outside because they were not recording. "Nice." I said.

Brett gestured toward the door. "Let's go to the alley." We walked outside. "There are four cameras total. Here, here, here, and here," he said, pointing to each one. "See the light under each one?" I nodded. "Both the lights and cameras cover the entire alley and roughly three feet beyond. The picture is actually pretty clear."

"Seems pretty in-depth."

He stood looking at the cameras. "It is. I wish I had done this a long time ago, to be honest. I can't believe I didn't, and it took you getting harassed to get them put in." He turned and looked me straight in the eye. "Molly, I'm sorry I didn't have these things in a long time ago. If I did, this may have never happened, or whoever did it wouldn't get away with it."

His statement confirmed the guilt I suspected was eating at him.

"Is that why you're doing this? Because you feel guilty? Brett, this is *not* your fault."

"Maybe not," he agreed. "I still should've had cameras put out here by now. Or, at the very least, better lighting."

I took a very deep breath and slowly exhaled, then got right to the point. "Brett, I don't know crap about camera systems, but I can tell that this system isn't cheap. Plus Gabe Cooper is providing his bodyguard and PI services. How much are you paying for all of this?"

"I told you, he's giving me a hell of a deal."

"Why?"

He leaned against the building. "I've known Gabe for a while. When I came out of the Army, he recruited me to work for him. That's how he gets his employees. Obviously, I turned him down and bought the bar, but we became friends, sort of. I've actually helped him out a couple times over the years, so in his mind he owes me. When I told him what was happening, he agreed the cameras were needed regardless of anything weird happening or not and didn't hesitate to offer his services. He's pretty sure this guy will make contact again, and we'll catch him soon."

I put my hands on my hips, which Katie told me I always did when I needed to get my point across. I preferred the other person to be sitting down; however, that wasn't an option here. "And what if he isn't caught soon? Then what? How much do you plan on shelling out? This may damn well get expensive." I took a second to get a good stare in before I demanded, "I want you to let me share the cost of this."

"No. Absolutely not."

"Why? The bodyguard and PI crap is for me. I should pay for it."

"No. The bodyguard service is for the entire band, especially you and Katie. You guys play exclusively at my bar. I am going to pay for it."

My hands were still on my hips, and I took a couple steps toward him. "What if it gets too expensive? Will you let me help then?"

He pushed himself away from the wall. "Stop doing your intimidation stance thing. You're not my teacher, and I'm not your student. It won't work on me. And stop worrying about the financials of it."

"Then let me help," I told him.

"No."

"Yes."

"No!"

"Yes!"

"Molly," he said, rubbing his temples. "Will you please let this go?"

I stood there for another several seconds, trying to look intimidating. Clearly my mean face wasn't working on him. Shit, was I losing my touch? Once again, I was giving in, which was frustrating beyond belief. "All right. For now. But this isn't the end of this conversation if this thing drags on. Do we understand each other?"

He sighed. "Yes Ms. Davis. Can we go out for recess now?"

"Smartass. I'm freezing. Let's go back inside."

We went back inside, where I talked to Heather at the bar while Brett went to his office.

"Hey, Molly, what would you think about a karaoke night here? Our numbers are low for the weekends during the winter when it's not a Wreckers weekend. I thought if we advertised it out front and spread the word online and stuff, we would get a decent crowd in here. What do you think?"

I personally didn't have a Facebook page, but The Song Wreckers did. Courtney kept it updated. We had 332 friends. Go us. "Sounds like a good idea to me. I love that stuff." Really, I only liked watching other people do it. Especially really drunk people.

"Um, here's the thing. I want you and Katie to help advertise and make it clear that you guys will be here. That's what is going to help bring people in," she said.

"It's not like we're going to be playing."

Heather smiled sheepishly. It made her look twelve. "No, but maybe you and Katie and anyone else doing 80's and 90's songs would be cool. I think it would go over really well. I think if you and Katie talked to him about it he'd do it."

Ah. She wanted Katie and me to do her bidding. "I'll talk to him, *and* I'm telling him it's your idea." I went around to the side of bar so Brett could hear me yell, "Hey, Brett! Get out here. I need to talk to you!"

"Maybe Katie should ask," Heather said.

I sat on a barstool. "Well if he doesn't say yes to me, we'll have her do it. It's a good idea, Heather."

Brett came to the bar and sat on the stool next to me. He faked annoyance. "What now?"

"Heather has a good idea that will help drum up business in here, which you need during the winter. You should get a karaoke system. Then you could have, like theme nights—80's night, 90's night, that sort of thing. Katie and I will help put the word out, and at least we, if not the rest of the Wreckers, will show up, sing some karaoke, have some fun." I paused for a few seconds so he could comprehend what I said. "So, what do you think? Do you want to do this, or should I call Katie and tell her to persuade you by withholding sex until you agree?"

Brett looked at Heather. "If this was your idea, why aren't you the one pitching it to me?"

She shrugged her shoulders. "I figured you'd be more receptive to Molly or Katie. So?"

"Can I get a system in here in the next week, learn how to operate it, and do this thing the last weekend of the month?"

Heather smiled. "Yup. I have info on several different systems. You can look at them and choose the one you want. I'll print it out and bring it in tomorrow."

"Sounds like a plan," he said. "Can I go now?"

"Yeah. I have it handled out here," Heather said. "Thanks, Brett."

Brett went back to doing whatever he was doing; probably trying to master the surveillance system. I went home.

Chapter 8

On the last Friday of January, Brett's had its first karaoke night. Brett and Heather didn't need to theme it. People came to the bar to warm up with drinking, singing, and dancing.

Katie loved the idea. Anything where she could perform and be the center of attention was perfect for her. I wasn't overly thrilled with the idea of doing karaoke, but I could suck it up if it meant good business for the bar. I was really attached to the place, and to Brett. He was like a big brother to me. Every Wrecker worked like crazy to spread the word. Josh and Courtney said they'd try to stop by for at least an hour or so if they could find a babysitter.

I even called Kyle, and he got his band to come since they weren't playing that night. Katie and I arrived around seven o'clock, though karaoke didn't start for another hour. We rode together so she could drink. I was driving, so my drinks were limited to iced tea (which I had to convince Brett to stock when we started playing there regularly) or water.

Eight o'clock came and Katie jumped up to the microphone. Heather was managing the whole karaoke system and signups for singers. The crowd was respectable for a night with temps in the twenties.

"Hey, y'all," Katie twanged. "I am proud to be the first karaoke-er of the night, and shut up, Molly, I don't care if karaoke-er isn't a word."

She knew me well, as I had opened my mouth to tell her that, in fact, karaoke-er was not a word.

Katie lost a bet on the way to Brett's, so her punishment was that she had to sing like me (no twanging allowed) for every song she sang that night. She hated to mimic a Midwestern accent. I didn't see what the big deal was. As her back-up vocalist I'd been mimicking her southern twang from the get-go, from our early days when we used to Wreck songs—take any popular song and turn it into a rockin' country version—to current times when we perform almost all originals. My fake twang matches her genuine twang perfectly.

As the night wore on, the crowd grew bigger. People danced, and people drank. Even Kyle and his band showed up around nine-thirty. I took my turn at the mic alone and then with Dave, Midnight's lead singer. We did a pretty humorous version of "Don't You Want Me?" It seemed as if everybody in there took a turn on the stage at some point. All in all, Heather's idea was a success.

At midnight, Katie kissed Brett good night and we left. He was going to her house after the bar closed. I dropped Katie off then drove myself home. Since I drove straight into my garage I didn't notice the front porch until the next morning when I got the newspaper.

As I stepped out of my front door, my attention was drawn straight down to a dead, bloody something, partially covered with rose petals on the middle of my porch.

There weren't a lot of petals, but they were there. January was typically windy in Michigan so there might've been more that had blown away. A couple dozen were stuck in the blood from whatever animal was stuck to the cement. I didn't look too closely, because the body was bloody and mutilated, but morbid curiosity wanted me to find out what was killed. With the glimpses I stole, it looked stabbed or maybe whacked with a shovel. Both perhaps. Parts of it were separated from itself. Exact cause of death was hard to tell, since I had to keep looking away so I wouldn't heave. I think it may have been a squirrel. It was the same color and same size as one. Its tail was gone so I couldn't be positive.

The snow was gone except for a few stubborn spots that refused to melt, so there were no footprints leading to or from the porch.

God, this was disgusting, and I wanted nothing to do with it, but I couldn't leave it there. I tiptoed down the porch steps and into the front yard to minimize the coldness to my feet, and took a quick look around my condo. There were a few petals stuck in the bushes near the side of my unit, nothing else. I ran back inside for shoes and an old towel, making sure not to pause so I wouldn't lose my nerve. Once I was back on the porch, I took a deep breath and held it, then as fast as I could, I picked up the squirrel with the towel and ran to the woods behind my condo and tossed it. When I was finally forced to inhale, I gagged at the grossness of the squirrel and the fact that this creep had done this to me.

I raced back to the porch to grab my newspaper, then launched my ass inside and locked the door. I leaned against the door. My foot tapped a million times a minute and I squeezed the newspaper like one of those stress relieving hand balls. What do I do? Should I alert anyone? Who? If I tell Katie, she'll tell Brett, which means Cooper and Ram will find out. Then they'll smother me even more. Calling the police was an option, too.

I should do all those. But that would be like admitting that some sicko lurked about, actually, officially stalking me. I wasn't ready to do that. I mean, this could still be a harmless prankster trying to be funny, right? Monkeys . . . ass . . . yeah. If The Creep was trying to scare the hell out of me, it was working.

I took a quick look around, although I didn't believe anyone had come in my house. I was so grateful to Cooper right then for those boards in my slider door and basement escape window. Knowing they were in place made me feel more secure.

I was satisfied that I was alone both inside and outside my house, so I poured a cup of coffee then sat down to think. Things were left on my porch, not at the bar. That meant whoever this was knew where I lived, and that there were cameras watching the alley of Brett's. Even when I wasn't there as the entertainment, I still parked in the alley out of habit, and this person knew that too. Because of all the word of mouth we did about going to Brett's, my whereabouts for several hours the previous night during karaoke was no secret. I was not home. The Creep could've checked that my car was at the bar before coming to my house. Was leaving a dead animal on my porch escalating behavior, or did the person just not want to be caught on camera? Mutilating an animal was definitely escalated behavior.

I didn't want to stress the others out, particularly Katie, and I didn't want Brett, Cooper, or Ram to get all fired up, so I made a deal with myself: if anything else happened I'd speak up. Until then, I'd make sure to keep my eyes open and be well aware of my surroundings.

The week between karaoke night and February's Wreckers weekend yielded no more disturbing gifts. I pulled into the alley on Friday at eight twenty five and saw Ram outside waiting for the band.

"Princess," he greeted me, once I stepped out of my Jeep.

"Caleb," I replied. It felt oddly personal using his first name since I had never heard anyone call him anything other than Ram. He smiled and I stopped to stare. God, the man was gorgeous.

Seconds later I was still staring, but at least I hadn't drooled. He hadn't taken his eyes off me either. I threw my thumb over my shoulder. "I gotta go get my guitars," I said, before our staring began to feel weird.

I went around to the back of my Jeep and lifted out my guitars. "Man, it is cold! I'm going to wait inside until Courtney and Josh get here. You gotta stay out here?" I asked.

"Yup."

"Sucks for you," I said with a cocky smile, trying to change the vibe to playful.

"Thanks for your sympathy. I owe ya."

I jogged to the back door, then to Brett's office to set down my guitars. No one was in there, but the cameras were recording since Ram was on the monitor. I took a minute to admire him, until Heather pulled up and ran into the building after waving at Ram. In a few seconds she joined me in the office.

Cooper walked by the office with another man. He saw us and came in. "Molly, Heather, this is Nick. I want to introduce the band to him since he'll be filling in for me or Ram occasionally. He'll actually be here in my place tomorrow."

Heather shook his hand first, then I did. Like Cooper and Ram, he looked like a bodyguard—built, confident, and aware. He was younger, though. Mid-twenties I'd guess. "Nice to meet you." I said. "Why don't you go by your last name like everyone else?"

"My last name is Faulkowlowicz. A bit of a mouthful," he answered.

"Good choice," I agreed.

Everyone's gaze went toward the monitors, and we watched Katie pull in. She did the same as Heather—the wave and run—then joined us in the office.

As soon as she came in I did the introduction. "Hey, Katie, this is Nick. He'll be guarding our bodies when Ram or Cooper can't."

"Nice to meet you," she said, shaking Nick's hand. Turning to Cooper she said, "Ram's gotta be frozen out there. It's cold enough to freeze the balls off a pool table. Shame on you."

Everyone snickered. Not Cooper, he said, "I was about to relieve him now. Nick and I will trade with him so Nick can meet Courtney and Josh." They put on their gloves and hats while heading out. We watched them on the monitor. Cooper said something to Ram, Ram nodded in acknowledgement and disappeared through the door.

"Geez, Ram, you look cold," I said, once he was in the office.

I felt the softest ice cube on my neck. "Aahhhh!" I jerked forward. Chills went down my spine.

He pulled his hands from my neck. "I told you I owed you, Princess."

Katie and Heather laughed at me. "Could you please stop calling me that?" I mumbled to Ram, embarrassed that the chills were more from his touch than from the cold. Not to mention his stupid nick name for me.

He cocked his head to the side, pretending to think. "I don't think so, it fits you too well. And besides, Angry Princess Barbie is too long. Just easier to shorten it."

My face heated from embarrassment at his implication that I was a spoiled brat. "Well at least stop calling me that in front of other people. It's embarrassing."

He shrugged. "Fine. *Molly*."

Surprised, I said, "Thank you."

Our attention once again turned to the monitors when we saw Courtney and Josh pull up. "Time to brave the cold, ladies," Heather said, and we headed out to unload.

After Nick had met the entire band he left. We played well that night, as always, but I was on edge. I kept wondering if The Creep was there, watching me. Without a doubt, I was safer with two capable men watching out for me. I hated that.

During the second set, a beer dropped on the floor near the stage. The crash it made was loud. I jumped, missing a few notes of the song. Katie and Heather glanced at me, so my reaction was noticeable. Obviously I was pretty edgy.

Both Cooper and Ram made eye contact with me when that happened. I smiled and mouthed the words *I'm fine*. They each gave a small nod. Cooper went up to the bar to talk to Brett, and I could feel them talking about me. God, that was annoying.

As we were finishing loading our gear into the van, Cooper reminded us that it would be Nick with Ram the following night. Once we all said *okay,* Ram walked up to me, arms crossed. He spoke quietly. "You got jumpy tonight. Anything you need to tell me?"

"Nope. I didn't take a nap after work like I usually do when we play on a Friday. Being tired makes me jumpy. No big deal." I smiled big to cover my lie.

He held out his hand. "Give me your cell phone."

I automatically felt the back pocket where my phone was. "Why?" I asked.

"So I can program my and Cooper's numbers in there."

"Why?"

"Just in case."

"In case what?"

"In case you need me or Cooper. Princess, please." He waited, his hand still out.

"You said you weren't going to call me that, *Caleb.*"

"No one can hear me. Now will you please—never mind," he said, then pulled out his cell phone. He dialed my number, let it ring once and then hung up.

"How did you get my number?" I hadn't given it to him or Cooper.

He put one finger up, indicating for me to wait a minute while he made another call. After a few seconds he spoke. "Do me a favor. Call Molly's cell, let it ring, and hang up . . . Because she won't hand over her phone so I can program our numbers into it. If you call, she'll get your number. I just did the same . . . Yup, bye."

Ten seconds later my cell rang a couple times then stopped.

"You have two missed calls on your phone. When you get home take those numbers and store them into your contacts list. Remember the first one is mine and the second one is Cooper's. And I got your number because I'm a private investigator. There isn't much information out there that I can't eventually get."

I pointed to his chest with my phone. "You know what? You earned yourself an insulting ringtone." Ha!

He cringed. "You know what else? It's scary how obvious it is that you spend a large amount of time around teenagers."

That may be true, but, all I could say was, "Bite me." Ram turned serious again and gave me his I'm-not-messing-around look. "Molly, I have a feeling you're hiding something, so I'm telling you: Be. Safe.

I put my hand to my forehead and saluted him. "Aye, Aye, Captain."

He pinched the bridge of his nose for a second, then let the issue drop. I turned away and went home. The first thing I did was program Cooper and Ram's numbers into my phone.

I wished I could've crawled into bed and drifted off to sleep, but I'm a horrible sleeper. My mind was on overdrive. That was another reason I loved to workout so much; to make myself so tired that I could sleep for as long as possible before I started waking. I never slept through the night without waking several times. Then the tossing and turning began. To make it worse, every little thing woke me up. The heat or air conditioning kicking on has been known to wake me. Outside noises were the worst: dogs barking, loud cars going by, a cricket burping. I didn't think I'd ever slept through a thunderstorm.

Since I couldn't sleep, I got out of bed and checked every window and door. I hadn't yet gotten window coverings for my slider door, so I made it a point to get them the following day. Since sleep wasn't coming any time soon, I grabbed the latest journal I'd been writing in and headed back to bed. I'd been writing songs like crazy recently. None of them were really Song Wreckers material so I'd been thinking about trying to sell them to a record company.

An hour or two later I finally fell asleep.

Saturday, I worked out, got ready, then called Katie. I wanted to take her to get the window coverings with me since she was so much better at coordinating and decorating than me. I rarely made any decorating decisions without consulting her first.

Katie picked up the phone as I was about to hang up. "Hey, Mol, what's up?"

I heard Brett talking in the background. "Sorry, I didn't know Brett was still there."

"What does that matter?" she asked.

"I was going to see if you wanted to go shopping with me. I need to get curtains for my kitchen slider door. I'm afraid of getting ones that won't look good."

Luckily Brett didn't have to go in until six o' clock on Saturdays. I agreed that I would spring for lunch if they would measure, pick out, and hang curtains for me.

A few hours later, I had privacy and a lot more style in my kitchen.

I pulled into the alley energized that night. I'd taken a good nap, and I loved the way my new curtains looked.

Heather was in her car, waiting, and Katie's car was there so she must've been inside, probably making out with Brett. Ram and Nick were waiting for us. As soon as I stepped out of my car, Courtney and Josh pulled in. I waved to Ram and Nick, and Nick jogged over to the van. Heather did the same.

"Ram told me to help you bring stuff in," Nick said.

I shot Ram my *you're asking for it* look. Before I could give Nick the usual spiel about helping—it's easier if you don't, but thanks—Heather said, "And can you believe he's standing over there not even offering to help?" She turned to Ram, "Hey, Ram! Dude, get your butt over here and help us!"

Ram let out a quick snort and came over to the van. The women let the guys haul all our equipment to the back of the stage. Ram and Nick made a small mess of things, but that was okay. Their help meant I could sit in the warmth while they did all the work in the cold.

When they were all done Ram hopped on the stage next to me. "Carrying the microphone stands bruised up my shins and I pinched my finger on . . . I don't know. Something over there," he whined, holding up his finger.

I grabbed his finger and gave it a quick kiss. I turned on the sarcasm to cover my shock at doing something out of character. "Poor thing, you want me to get you a bandage? Maybe drive you to the ER?"

He crossed his arms over his chest, going from mortally wounded to world protector.

I rolled my eyes and continued putting equipment where it belonged.

Ram and Nick went off to do their bodyguard thing, and The Song Wreckers did our rocking-the-place-out thing. I was in a good mood all night. From the time I showed up until the time I left, I had a smile on my face. My glass was half full. Ram and I had a good rapport going on. Nothing set my creep detector off. Maybe The Creep was done. Maybe I wasn't worth it anymore. Maybe my life would go back to normal, or as normal as it was before this crap started. Maybe world peace was finally achievable.

Stop me it you've heard this one: Right. And monkeys will fly out my ass.

Chapter 9

I hated February for two reasons: the weather was brutal, in Michigan at least, and Valentine's Day. Blech.

Valentine's Day was on a Saturday that year. Katie and Brett were celebrating before he had to head to the bar, and I was sitting on my couch grading papers. When the doorbell rang, I assumed Katie had come over and that she forgot her key. But when I peeked out my window I saw a strange man holding flowers. Shit.

Was this the asshole who was messing with me?

Damn it. I should call 911, or maybe even Cooper. I didn't, though, because seeing him there made me mad and if he was The Creep, I wanted to beat the living shit out of him.

My foot began tapping as nerves crept in. I didn't even try to sound nice. "What?" I yelled.

"I have a flower delivery for Molly Davis. I'm from Westwood Florists," the man replied.

Yeah, right. I unlocked my door and opened it quickly with my left hand. I had my right hand cocked back ready to hit if he took even one step toward me. He wasn't very big and he couldn't have been older than twenty. If I took him by surprise I would have the upper hand.

The look on my face must've been all kinds of crazy because his eyes got huge and he took a step back. "Uh . . . Molly Davis?" His voice wasn't very steady.

"Who are you?" I demanded.

"I'm Steven from Westwood Florists. I have a delivery for you. Here." He shoved the flowers at me, quickly turned then went to his van and took off.

I shut the door and took the flowers to the kitchen table. There was a card so I removed it. Did I really want to know what it said? Yes. If The Creep made contact with me again, I needed to know. I'd made a deal with myself to go to the police if anything else happened. I slowly took the card out of the envelope and read:

Happy Valentine's Day!
I miss you.
Call me! I have great news!
Love, Alan

I let out the breath I'd been holding. Relief. Complete, utter, relief. Oh hell, he'd scared me with that one.

I felt bad for scaring away the delivery boy without giving him a tip, but I was also thankful to get flowers from someone other than The Creep. I ran to the phone right away and called Alan, my oldest friend. We met in the dance studio when our ages were still in the single digits. I quit dancing right after I turned eighteen. He moved to New York to find work as a professional choreographer.

His boyfriend, Garrett, answered after the first ring. "Hey, Molly, how's it going?"

"Hey, Garrett, it's good. What's the big news?"

"That I get more handsome with every passing day," he joked.

"Wow, that *is* great news."

"Hold on. Alan's coming into the room now. If I tell you, he'll kill me. Here he is."

Garrett handed the phone to Alan, and I immediately heard a screech. Then excitedly he asked, "Guess who landed a music video for Candy Delight?"

"Oh my God, are you serious?" I asked. Choreographing a music video for a pop star was a huge deal.

Candy Delight had burst onto the music scene less than a year earlier, and her videos were burning up the MTV charts. Candy Delight was everything I hated: overly produced, overly made up, and overly stupid. However, her videos got a shit load of play time and being part of one could make or break a career.

"Alan, I am so happy for you! I can't say I'm all that surprised. You rock! Congratulations! Thank you for the flowers by the way." No need to tell him he scared the bejeezus out of me.

He squealed again. "You're welcome. Molly, I'm so excited and freaked at the same time." I heard the tremor in his voice. "We start rehearsals in two weeks and then make the video immediately after that. So about two weeks and two days. I wanted to come home for a visit anyway and thought since I was coming home, I'd show you what I have and you could give me your input. What do you say?"

Wow, that was flattering. "You really want my input?"

"Yes! When it comes to dance, I completely trust your opinion, you know that. Plus I know you'll tell me the truth. Molly, we've been dancing together forever. I need you."

"Well, you have me. Absolutely. I'd love to see what you have. When are you coming? Do you want to stay at my place?"

Yay! I love when Alan comes to town. We dance like the old days, and I pretend I'm as good as I used to be.

"I get in this Friday afternoon, and I leave early Tuesday morning. We're staying at my parents' place."

"So Garrett's coming too? That's pretty big." Alan's parents had long ago accepted their son was gay, but he'd never brought a man home to meet them.

"Yeah. I'm nervous, he's nervous, and I'm sure my parents are nervous. It will be interesting, to say the least." He gave a short, nervous chuckle.

"Garrett's a good guy," I told him, even though I've only talked to him on the phone. "Your parents will love him."

"Let's hope."

We talked for a while about the particulars of his trip, when we'd meet up, when we'd dance, that sort of thing. He was bummed his visit wasn't during a Wreckers Weekend, so I told him we'd hang out at Brett's one night, and he could meet Katie's man.

Of course he asked about my love life. "So is there anybody *you're* going to introduce me to?"

"Nope, and don't start. Katie does that already."

"Okay, okay. I'll see you Saturday. We'll do all our catching up in person."

"Sounds good. And I'm excited to finally meet Garrett in person."

"He's excited too." Then he added in a serious tone, "And Molly?"

"Yes?"

"You better stretch or do whatever you need to do, because I'm going to work your ass off."

He wasn't joking. If you let him, he'd burn so many calories from you you'd be skin and bones. "Looking forward to it. See ya Saturday," I said, and we hung up.

Since I had my basement set up mostly as a dance space, Alan and Garrett agreed to meet at my place Saturday afternoon. We planned to get Katie later in the evening and go to Brett's.

I spent the days before Alan and Garrett's visit practicing old routines. Any time Alan visited we always did what we considered our best stuff. Although I wasn't as good as I had been at eighteen, I was still good. I'd kept up my flexibility and hadn't lost much of my stamina. I'd gone up a size in clothing when I quit dancing, but I'd maintained that size for twelve years. Alan and I couldn't do the same caliber of lifts that we used to, but he could still toss me around pretty well.

I was so excited to see Alan again. I must've looked out the window for half an hour waiting for them, and the minute I sat down to pee, I heard a car pull into my driveway. The doorbell rang simultaneously with the flush of the toilet. I verified it was Alan and Garrett, then wretched open the door. Before I could get out a single word, Alan picked me up and swung me around.

"Man, I missed you!"

"I missed you too! Come on in. It's freaking cold."

He set me down, and we walked into the living room. Very few people get a true hug from me, and Alan is one of those few. I went up to Garrett and gave him one of my elbows-in-so-you-can't-get-too-close hugs. He hadn't earned the real kind yet.

"It is so good to finally meet you in person and put a face to the voice." I took their coats and a bag that Garrett was carrying and hung them up.

I truly was thrilled to meet the man Alan held in such high regard. Garrett was a successful photographer and videographer, which I suspected as half the reason Alan was initially smitten with him. Garrett loved to take pictures; Alan loved to be photographed.

"You too," he told me. "I've seen pictures, but you are much more beautiful in person. How are you not married?"

"Oh God, not you, too! You know, I liked you up until about three seconds ago. Now? Forget it." I was joking, but ugh . . . not him too!

He cringed. "Sorry. Alan put me up to that. It's the end of it, I swear."

We spent the next hour touring my house, and catching up. After that, we headed down to the basement. Alan and I stretched and warmed up, while Garrett went upstairs. He returned with a camera.

"Molly, do you mind if I take pictures of you and Alan?" Garrett asked.

I stood up from a stretch. "Depends on what you plan on doing with them."

"Nothing public, I promise. It's just for you and Alan."

"Sure." Snap. Apparently the man didn't waste any time.

We easily spent three hours down there. We danced; we laughed. Garrett took pictures. We laughed. I told them about my drunken episode in Traverse City; we laughed so hard we almost peed our pants.

When Alan showed me the routine he choreographed for the music video, I was blown away. He taught me parts of it, and I loved it.

I have always been proud of Alan. I spent a lot of time being sarcastic and joking around with the few people I'm close to, but it was time for me to be completely serious. He was still nervous about the Candy Delight video, and needed reassurance. "Alan, this is really going to launch your career. Everything you've shown me is fantastic. I don't know a lot about what you've been doing lately, but this has to be your best work yet. I hope you're ready for the big time, because you're about to be there. You should be really proud of yourself." At this point I barely had the strength to wipe my sweat with a towel.

"Do you really mean that?" He tried to hug me, but sweaty dancer hugs are gross. I pushed him away.

"Yes I really do. I'm not kidding, Alan. This video is only the beginning for you."

Garrett finally spoke up. "It smells so bad down here I'm going to die. Seriously. Can we please go upstairs and you two take a shower. What time are we going to dinner?"

I threw my sweaty towel at him. "I told Katie we'd pick her up around six-thirty and go out to dinner then. After that, we'll head to Brett's."

Garrett threw the towel back.

Once Alan and I were clean and stink free, we piled in my Jeep and picked up Katie. Katie and Alan had always gotten along, and she and Garrett hit it off immediately. Garrett fell in love with her southern charm, and of course her twang. She poured it on thick, though she's lived in Michigan far longer than she lived in Mississippi. We had a great time at dinner. We kept Garrett entertained by telling him funny stories about ourselves in our teens. The three of us laughed ourselves silly when Katie reminisced about Alan's awkward year which included a home perm and love of spandex bike shorts.

We made it to Brett's at eight-thirty. There was a decent crowd. Katie introduced Brett to Alan and Garrett while we sat down for drinks. I was driving so I stuck to drinking iced tea.

Once Katie was tipsy, karaoke became her agenda. Heather was working, so she set it up for us.

"Molly, Alan? If I sing a song will you two dance to it?" Katie asked.

Alan jumped up. "Yes!"

I stood up and put my hand in the *stop* position. "Wait. What type of dance?" Seriously, my body couldn't take the vigorous dancing we did earlier.

Katie shrugged, "Whatever. I think it would be cool if I sang and you two danced. Do you dance at all, Garrett?"

"Hell no," Garrett answered.

Katie sang, and Alan and I danced. We did this kind of ballroom-meets-dirty-dancing number for a while, then switched to two-stepping-meets-hip-hop. Amazingly, it went well together. In our minds anyway. Brett had been watching, and I don't know which shocked him more: Katie singing songs that weren't country or me dancing.

"Holy shit," Brett said. "Molly, I had no idea. And Katie! It kind of freaks me out hearing you sing a song like that."

Katie sang a few more songs, and Alan took me in his arms and led me around the dance floor like I was the belle of the ball. I loved every second of it.

After we left the bar, I dropped off Katie at her house and said my goodbyes to Alan and Garrett. I wouldn't be seeing them again before they left, as they wanted to spend as much quality time as possible with Alan's parents.

Having Alan come to town and dance with me was exactly what I'd needed. I'd barely thought about The Creep all weekend. My optimism was back and it held for days.

I felt good, and I was looking forward to seeing Ram again. I loved Wreckers Weekends, but for the first time wished they were more than once a month. Creatively, I was on a roll. My jumbled mess of emotions were coming out in lyrics that, unexpectedly, just worked. Alan and I had talked about when he came out to his parents, and that convinced me to stop being a wimp and finally talk with my mom. Really talk to her. Ask her about my dad. Ask her about my dead twin, Holly. Connect with her. Find an activity we both enjoyed and then doing it together.

I made a mental note of things we might do, such as seeing a movie or taking a class together.

Michigan's weather tends to be interesting. Even those of us who have lived there all our lives can talk about it as if we're fascinated and truly surprised. I have learned not to put away my winter gear until the end of May, and may have to get out the spring jackets well before the spring season came.

There was an odd break in the weather for March's Wrecker's Weekend so I busted out my lighter jacket, hoping it didn't smell too much like it hadn't been washed before being worn.

Friday night, Ram was by himself at Brett's. Cooper and Nick were stuck on a job, Ram had told me. Saturday, they would switch places.

During the breaks, Ram kept me company in Brett's office. He stuck to me like glue, which was nice for me and probably boring for him. He was used to this sort of thing, being part of his job, but still. I enjoyed his company. I didn't want him to feel that he had to shadow me. I wanted him to *want* to shadow me.

He sat on the couch, throwing scrap paper balls into the trash while I sat cross legged on Brett's desk keeping score. "Hey, I'm sure I'm totally fine in here by myself. Why don't you go out in the bar area and at least enjoy yourself for a few minutes? There are a couple dozen women out there who would love to drool over you some more." It was kind of funny noticing the women trying to get his attention. He and Cooper both acted as if they didn't notice these women, which was hard to believe. Several of them were gorgeous.

I'd be a big, fat liar if I said Ram leaving wouldn't wound my ego.

He took another shot. "Are you trying to get rid of me, Princess?"

"No. Come on, babysitting me can't be very fun for you. I feel bad you're stuck here with me. That's twenty points." Ten paper balls had made it into the garbage.

"I don't mind being with you. I never do." We looked at each other and fell silent. Then he shrugged and spoke again. "Anyway, it's my job to keep you safe. If I was out there while you were in here by yourself, I'd worry about you the whole time. If you want, I'll wait outside the door."

"I didn't mean to imply that I wanted you to leave," I told him. "I just wanted to give you the option."

What I meant was, *Please don't leave!*

See, here's the thing. The first time I met Ram I was attracted to him. Yeah, he may have irritated me, but I got over that. He was hot. He was nice. I loved the way I felt when I was around him. It bugged me that I had no idea if he was attracted to me. We talked a decent amount, and he seemed genuinely into our conversations, but he'd never hit on me. Maybe he conversed with me to pass the time and avert boredom. I was like, his client. Asking me out would be in poor taste. So would me asking him out. (Not that I would ever ask him out. I was a total chicken shit about those things.) Whatever, he had to be counting the minutes until The Creep made his move and he could quit babysitting me.

I wanted to be near him, and I wanted him to *want* to be near me, too. To not think of me as an obligation. I was safe with him around. My mind even seemed to slow down when he was around, as if my brain knew he was there, so I didn't have to take on everything myself. I knew I was safe with Cooper too, but he didn't radiate the same feelings in me as Ram did.

Ram gave me butterflies in my stomach, and a slew of feelings that, frankly, scared the hell out of me. No man had ever affected me like Ram did.

That was why I ignored my attraction to him, or at least didn't push to see if he felt anything for me. I didn't want to mistake his kindness for interest and make an ass out of myself. See, my plan was that when this whole Creep mess was over, I would call him to thank him and then maybe he'd ask me out. And if he didn't I would write in my journal about what a butt-head he was.

That would teach him.

I changed the subject before things got weird. "So do you at least like our music? If you don't, you should have the decency to lie and say you do."

He barked a laugh and threw a paper ball at me. "Of course I like it, but to be honest I was surprised. I saw you guys set up and get ready to play and wished I had earplugs." I stuck my tongue out at him. "As soon as you started playing, I was bowled over. You guys have to be the best band around."

I beamed. "I'd like to think so. The Song Wreckers have been playing for eleven years now." I slid off the desk and sat on the opposite end of the couch, my legs stretched out, crossed at the ankles. I laced my fingers behind my head. "Katie taught me to play guitar and sing in high school. Then, in college, we found Courtney, Josh, and our first bass player. We've been playing together a long time, although Heather's only been with us the last couple of years. Feels like she's always been part of the band."

I was giving him the short version of the History of Molly and Katie when Katie knocked on the door and opened it at the same time. "Hey, Mol. Time to play. Hey, Ram."

I joined the rest of The Song Wreckers on the stage, and Ram took his seat in the bar. Lucky for him, Brett always had a small table reserved for the babysitters; otherwise, they'd have stood all night.

We played our three sets, packed up, and I went home. I thought about Ram once I was settled in bed for the night. I wished when it came to men I was one of those confident women. I knew I was fine in the looks department, but I was no fashionista, like Katie. I wasn't glamorous like Katie either. She was polished; perfectly make up (bottle) blond hair, hazel eyes, hourglass figure. She was pretty much my physical opposite. I was . . . average. Brown eyes, brown, naturally curly hair I almost wore straight and in a ponytail, average height, thin, athletic body. But I hadn't been stretched out by kids, and I had a healthy cholesterol level. That counted for something, right? God, I would even settle for not being a complete fucktard. Note to self: find out if Caleb Ramsey liked fucktards.

Chapter 10

Was I dreaming? I couldn't make sense of a single God damned thing. My body was weighed down, and my mind was dizzy. No, more than dizzy. Like my brain was buzzing, and the buzzing was keeping me from focusing on anything else. I wasn't sure if I was awake, but I made an effort to . . . I don't know . . . figure out why I couldn't get up and out of my bed.

Except I wasn't in my bed, because mine was much more comfortable. People around me were talking quietly. Farther away, people were walking. Somebody was sniffling as if they were close to crying. There was a constant, low-key noise level.

What the hell was going on?

Unable to put the pieces together yet, I laid there, dazed. I struggled to open my eyes but they were weighted closed. I needed to know what was going on. Fear kept me from falling back into the sleep that my body desperately wanted. I put all my effort into opening my eyes. They fluttered for a while, but eventually opened.

Then my mind registered pain. Sharp, stabbing pain. Shoulder. Ear. Arm. Stomach. Face. Knees. Back. Hand. Pretty much everywhere. I'd been chewed up and spit out.

Panic mixed in with the pain, and I learned it hurt to take anything more than a shallow breath.

"Her eyes are open." Katie's voice. "Molly, can you hear me?"

I turned my eyes toward her. She sat on a chair on my left side. "Molly, you're okay. Do you understand me? Molly?"

Katie had been the one I'd heard sniffling.

My voice came as barely a whisper. "Katie? What's going on?"

She put her hand on mine. Luckily she put it on my left hand which was one of the few places on me relatively unhurt. "Don't you remember?" she asked.

I looked around as best I could, but turning my head hurt. I was in a hospital room. I noticed the ugly décor that seems specific to hospitals and saw usual hospital machinery. There was a bandage on my left arm and an IV in my right. My hospital gown covered another two bandages. I closed my eyes to think. I breathed as deeply as I could.

Oh God. Images started flooding my head. That night my life almost ended.

We'd rocked out Brett's on Saturday. Cooper and Nick were my designated babysitters. I spent both breaks out in the bar with the rest of the band and Nick. I was feeling social, probably due to the unseasonably nice weather. Cooper was in a back corner watching and making phone calls.

Before we were about to go on for our last set, Cooper walked over to our table, phone in hand. "I just got a call. There's an issue at the office, and I need to be there. Are you all right alone or should I call in Mitch?"

Nick shook his head. "No, I'm good."

"Fine. You know the routine. Keep your eyes open, be the last to leave." Cooper looked at me. "Would you feel safer with someone else here with you guys?"

I waved him off. "Cooper, I'm fine. Go deal with whatever you need to do." I really was fine, and I didn't want to insult Nick by telling Cooper I wanted Ram, or this Mitch guy, here to keep me safe. Nick could do the job himself.

"All right, I'm leaving. Call if you need anything." Cooper rushed around the bar and toward the back alley.

We played our last set then began to pack up. "Hey, Nick, wanna help?" Heather asked him.

"Uh . . ." He didn't want to look like a jerk by saying no.

Courtney saved him. "She's kidding, Nick. Relax."

Equipment loaded, Heather, Courtney, and Josh left. Katie went back inside to hang out with Brett. I put my guitars in my Jeep then remembered I'd forgotten my jacket. I turned to go inside and noticed Nick next to his truck, talking to a girl from the bar. And by talking I mean whispering in each other's ears while getting gropey. I had noticed Nick had a harder time ignoring the hotties at Brett's, and after Cooper left, Nick had been getting flirty with a woman I'd never seen before.

"Hey, Nick, I forgot my jacket. I'll be right back," I said and started to walked inside.

He said, "Uh-huh," but I wasn't sure he even registered what I'd said. The girl had her hands somewhere that made him moan. Those two were definitely getting lucky later. I'd be lying if I said I wasn't jealous.

My jacket was in Brett's office, along with Katie. She had draped it over her arm, intending to bring it to me. I took it from her, and we talked for a few minutes. Then she went into the front bar area, and I headed to my car. Nick and his truck were gone. I had no doubt that the girl was with him, and they were on their way to a body slamming good time.

As I put my hand on the door handle to open it, I saw a person out of the corner of my right eye approaching me. I turned my head to see a young woman. I breathed a sigh of relief since it obviously wasn't The Creep.

She didn't have a nice look on her face, though. She sized me up and down and looked at me with disgust. I didn't recognize her. She wasn't a regular at Brett's, and if she had been there that night, she'd kept a low profile.

We stared at each other for a couple seconds, then, "Hey!" she yelled, her voice as unfriendly as the look on her face. She took a few steps toward me and stopped about ten feet away.

Instinct took over. Playing in bars for so many years has unfortunately earned me my fair share of fights. Whether I was defending myself from an angry, drunk girlfriend of some guy who was too friendly with me, or defending Katie or Courtney from the same, I could handle myself in a fight. I widened my stance for better balance, with my left leg slightly forward of my right. My purse slid off my shoulder and my right arm was ready if needed it. I was wearing my three-inch heeled cowboy boots, which could be problematic for me, but taking them off would either send a hostile message or keep my hands tied up when I might need them.

"Can I help you?" I asked. Maybe I was taking her the wrong way.

"Yeah. You can help me by staying the hell away from my boyfriend." She took another step forward.

"Excuse me?" Who was her boyfriend? She had to be mistaking me for another woman.

"You heard me, bitch. The guy you hang all over even after he tells you he's not interested? He's mine, and you need to stay away from him."

I truly had no idea who she was talking about. I hadn't been hanging over anyone in a very long time. There was no one from the bar I could think of. Johnny had innocently flirted with me and several others, the same as any other night.

"Why don't I help you stay away from him?" She closed the distance between us.

Here we go again. Why me?

She swung at me, and I blocked it. Shit, fighting with a leftie was harder. I needed time to run back into Brett's, so I pushed her hard in the shoulders to get her away from me. But she grabbed my shirt, and we fell together.

She was on her back, and I was on her. I tried to scramble away from her. She kept hold of my shirt and started hitting me on my side and back. Not enough power to keep me in place, though.

I slid my knees forward and got to a straddling position. I held her arms down with my knees. She spastically wiggled her body to get out from under me, so I punched the bitch in the face, giving her a nice shiner as souvenir of her bad judgment.

She cried out but kept moving. I couldn't hold her arms down any more. They flailed every which way. She wasn't a fighter, but she was pissed. Pissed because she thought I was after her boyfriend or because she was failing to dole out a quick ass kicking? Who knew? I hopped off to let her up, hoping to reason with her since I wasn't who she wanted.

Once steady, I yelled, "Listen to me, I don't know who you want, but you have the wrong person!"

She pushed herself up and came at me full force. Her hands reached out to grab my hair or possibly even strangle me. I stepped to the side and pushed her face first onto the gravel. Since her arms were out, her head didn't hit the ground.

I stayed in my spot and let her get up again. Stupid. I had it in my mind that she would see reason. Stop her assault. She staggered upright, swung, and hit me in the jaw.

The last ounce of patience I had vanished.

She swayed off balance so I punched her in the face. She stumbled back a few steps. I punched her again. She fell backwards to the ground, and I jumped on her. I punched her again. And again. And again. And again. Adrenaline and rage had taken over. I was completely out of control, punch after punch, grunting with each hit.

My fist hurt. I paused, ready to block anything she threw out. Only she wasn't fighting back, much less defending herself. She was unconscious.

Shit. I scrambled off her and bent over with my hands on my knees, trying to get my breathing and thoughts under control. I needed to get into the bar and call the police. I wanted the safety of being indoors, so calling on my cell phone out here didn't seem like a good option. I didn't even know where the damn phone was since I dropped my purse. Obviously no one was in the office paying any attention to the cameras since they'd assumed I—and the rest of the band—was long gone.

My right hand hurt like hell and my knees were torn up from straddling my assailant on the gravel of the alley. I took a deep breath. The adrenaline was already wearing off and I felt shaky and weak. I straightened out my body to clear my head.

As I raised my head, I saw another person running at me. A man.

The Creep. Had to be.

In an exaggerated disguise. Wig, ball cap, partially hidden face. Smeared with dirt? Wearing lots of clothes.

Knife in his hand, almost to me.

I froze. Damn it, run, Molly! He raised his knife hand, and only then could I move, but not fast enough. He plunged the knife down the back side of my right shoulder. I opened my mouth to scream, but no sound came out. He pulled out the knife, the blade slicing me up to the base of my hairline behind my ear, then the back of my ear as well. I fell to my knees.

I was finally able to speak. "Stop! Why are you doing this? Please!" The words were shaky. I had started crying without realizing it.

He backhanded me on the side of my head. I fell sideways, landing on the shoulder he had stabbed. My head smacked the ground. Stunned nearly senseless, I watched him study me. Or maybe taunt me.

He never answered, never spoke at all. He merely smiled and shrugged. He waved the knife back and forth, like a hypnotist trying to put me under his spell.

The Creep's calm scared the shit out of me. I was barely able to yell, "Get away from me!" then started scooting my body back while trying to kick him at the same time.

He watched me, a smile twisting his mouth, and I was almost sorry the alley had better lighting allowing me to see his facial expressions. He enjoyed this.

We both knew I was weak. He dropped to his knees and grabbed my leg to keep me from scooting back any more. Before I could kick him, he raised the knife. I shielded my face and he slammed the knife into my left arm, halfway between my elbow and wrist, and kept it in.

I scrambled back several inches while choking out sobs. He grabbed my leg once more, and I hurt too fucking bad to do anything. There was a knife in my arm and his hand on my leg. Any attempt I made to get away wasn't working. "There are . . . cameras back here," I gasped out, hoping to scare him. "Someone's . . . going to see you and call . . . the police."

He finally pulled the knife out and, despite the pain I was in, felt a second of relief. Blood ran down my back from the stab to my shoulder, down the side of my neck, and down my arm too. My body was shaking. I was so God damned unbelievably exhausted, and he knew it. He shook his head at me as if I was stupid. I kicked to knock the knife out of his hand, but was too slow. He moved his hand out of my foot's reach easily.

I made a poor attempt to wiggle out of his grasp. He jumped off me, and as he did, he swung his knife down and sliced me above my left hip. I screamed and rolled to my side. The fresh pain made me want to vomit. Basic functions became difficult. I could hardly see, hardly think.

I turned my head and spit at him, which broke his composure for a brief moment. His face flashed rage before he caught it and forced himself back to calm.

As I lie there, helpless, he pushed my hip with his foot so I was on my back again and lowered himself until he covered my body with his own, doubling my pain. He covered my mouth with his hand. I tried screaming, so he clamped down harder on my mouth. I could hardly breathe which made me weaker.

He wasn't much taller than I was. With his head bent, we sprawled head to head, legs to legs, and hips to hips. He stayed like that for a moment, breathing heavily, moving his hips ever so slightly against mine.

The movement of his hips was the slap in the face I needed. I had to pull it together. If not, he was going to kill me, rape me, or both. I was absolutely sure of it.

With every ounce of strength and concentration I had left, I shoved my knee into his groin and screamed.

He took his hand off my mouth and pulled himself to his knees, and I kicked the arm the knife was in before he had a chance to expect it. He didn't drop the knife, but in his attempt to keep hold of it, he was no longer pinning down any part of my body. My legs were now free and I could breathe a little better. I screamed and kicked like crazy.

He leaned forward to try to get control of my legs again, and I hit him in the chest with the heel of my boot. He stumbled for a second, holding his chest. With my last speck of energy, I kicked so he couldn't fight me off and hold the knife at the same time.

Finally he stood. The Creep took a couple seconds to look at me, as if trying to figure out what the hell he should do with me. The fighting and screaming, the pain and blood loss, it was too much. I tried to get up, but couldn't. I tried to scream again, but it was barely audible. My whole being sagged, almost lifeless. I had nothing left. I rolled my head to the side. The Creep was not the last thing I wanted to see before I died.

I saw the shadow of his raised knife on the packed down gravel, and waited for the slosh of a knife tear into my body. Instead I heard the back door to the bar slam open and fast footsteps. The Creep, ready to strike again, sputtered out a curse and ran. It was the only word I'd heard him say.

Katie screamed my name. Brett did too.

I turned my eyes to watch The Creep run away.

Still on my back, I attempted, uselessly, to get myself up.

"Stay down, Molly! An ambulance is coming, just stay down!" Katie yelled at me.

"Where's the girl?" I mumbled. I'm not even sure how I was able to remember her. I think I was trying to do anything to take my mind off of the pain I was in. The back of my shoulder where I was stabbed first was pressed against the ground, but I didn't even have the strength to take my weight off of it. I hurt everywhere.

"What girl, Molly?" Brett asked from the other side of me.

"Girl first." I stopped to catch my breath. Talking wasn't easy. "Unconscious now I think."

Katie stayed by my side, while Brett stood up and looked around. "She's over here," he called. "She's breathing."

Brett came back to my side, took out his phone, and called 911 again. He told the operator there was another person who needed medical assistance. I lay there with nothing to concentrate on except how badly I hurt. My eyelids were heavy. I was being pulled under by an invisible force. Fight it or give into it?

"Katie, talk to her. Keep her conscious," Brett told her. He sounded far away.

She was crying. "Molly, listen to my voice. Help is on the way, Okay? Open your eyes, Molly."

With a lot of effort I did. Brett dialed again. He was frantic, running one hand through his hair and holding his phone in the other. "I'm calling Cooper. What the fuck happened to Nick?"

"Hurts." A huge wave of pain and nausea gagged me.

"I know, Molly. I'm so sorry. Hang on, I can hear the sirens."

I must've blacked out because I was suddenly in the ambulance without having any recollection of being transported there. People were working on me. A woman was talking to me. I had no idea what her calming voice was saying.

The next time I opened my eyes I was in the hospital.

Chapter 11

"Hi, Ms. Davis. I'm Dr. Ahmed. Can you tell me how you feel?"

I looked at Dr. Ahmed standing at the foot of my hospital bed. Late fifties, well put together under his doctor's coat, and an idiot. How the hell did he think I felt? "Not great." I told him.

He gave me a sympathetic smile. "I bet. What I mean is, how much pain are you in? Do you need more pain meds?"

"Yes, please on the pain meds."

Dr. Ahmed stepped out of the room.

Katie gave my hand a gentle squeeze. "Molly, I'm gonna go call your mom and let her know what's happened and that you're going to be all right. I'll be back in a sec."

She started to get up, but I grabbed her shirtsleeve to keep her down. My grasp was weak, but she paused. "Katie, stop. She doesn't need to know about this." There was nothing my mom could do for me. Why worry her?

Katie sat back down. "Mol, your mother has a right to know. You have to tell her."

"No. I don't. Not now, anyway."

Katie didn't know what it felt like to not be close to your own mother. She might have disagreed with my decision to not tell my mom, but I knew she'd respect it and not say anything.

The nurse came in with pain meds for me, and I took them. When she left, the doctor came back in. "Ms. Davis, I'm going to talk to you about your injuries and then the police are going to want to talk to you. Okay?"

"Yeah."

"You have four lacerations, or more accurately, puncture wounds. All of them required stitches. The one behind your ear isn't deep and doesn't concern us. The other three are a different story. Nothing is life threatening. You'll have physical therapy ahead of you for the wound to your shoulder. The knife tore into the deltoid muscle somewhat, but mainly your rotator cuff is what most concerns us. When you get up you are not going to want to move it for a while. It's important that you actually use it as much as the pain will allow. Lack of movement can lead to complications. At this point we don't think surgery is necessary, however if it has not healed the way we anticipate, surgery will be necessary to connect the muscle tissues back together. You are right handed?" he asked.

I nodded, or tried to anyway.

"You will have to start doing more with your left arm for at least the first month or so; brushing your teeth and hair, things like that. In the other two injuries you were quite lucky."

"Yeah. Lucky is the word I was thinking."

"Sorry, Ms. Davis. Lucky in the sense that your attacker didn't slash directly down." Using an imaginary knife, he pretended to stab himself in the left forearm and across an imaginary stomach to make his point. "The cuts in your arm and abdomen went in more of a slicing motion. They are fairly deep wounds but they could've been much worse had your attacker gone straight down. Your forearm will be sore for a while. Since nothing major was hit, you will be able to use it fine. As for your abdomen, nothing major was hit there as well but because of the location of the wound," he paused to indicate on himself where the wound was, "it will make getting up and down and your everyday chores challenging for a while. In short, you are going to have scarring, maybe surgery. You are going to be physically fine. I am going to recommend physical therapy for your shoulder. The other injuries—the bruising to most of your body, and the cuts on your knees will be the first to heal and shouldn't cause you any future trouble. We have you started on antibiotics to ward off any infection. We started pain medication through the IV, but want you to continue them orally." He stopped and gave me that sympathetic smile again. "I'm sorry for what you went through Ms. Davis, but this really could have ended very differently."

Dr. Ahmed picked up my chart and flipped through it. He nodded to himself and left.

Katie came back to my side. "Brett is here, and so are Cooper and Ram. They all want to see you. Are you up to it? The police are going to be in here to talk to you, too. Say the word and I'll tell the guys to go home."

Katie was worried but at least she could see I was going to be all right. Brett had always watched out for me, kind of like an older brother, so I owed it to him to see for himself that I was going to be fine.

"Are the police here yet?"

She shook her head. "Not yet."

"Then let the guys come in, but would you cover me with a blanket first?" I was vain enough to not want to be seen looking like a beat up rag doll in a hospital gown.

She did, then invited Brett, Cooper and Ram in. They met her at the door, and all walked in together.

Brett had red eyes. Had he been crying? He looked uncomfortable, as if he didn't know what to say or if he should say anything at all.

Cooper looked angry but in control.

Ram surprised me the most. He radiated fury and was having a hard time controlling his temper. His eyes were almost scary, very intense. He couldn't stand still. He was breathing heavily. For the first time, I didn't feel calmer in his presence.

Cooper spoke first. "Molly, what happened? I've been trying to call Nick, but he isn't answering his phone. Was he there?"

Katie sat back in her chair trying to look like she was okay. I don't think she was.

"I left my jacket in the bar," I said. "He was gone by the time I came back out." I wasn't going into detail now about how he was rushing to get laid simply because I didn't care at the moment.

My answer upset Ram even more. He sat in a corner chair and put his head in his hands. He raked his fingers through his hair a few times, then stood and began pacing.

Cooper continued. "The police will be here shortly, so we don't have much time to talk. Did two people attack you? Brett said there was a woman unconscious, and he saw a man run away."

"The woman attacked me first. No weapons or anything." Talking was difficult. "Once she was down I was trying to catch my breath and go inside to call the police, but a man came at me with a knife. He would've killed me if Brett and Katie hadn't come out when they did."

Brett stepped forward and put a hand on my bed. "Molly, I'm so sorry. I didn't think to watch the cameras because I figured you were gone. Me and Katie walked into my office, and we saw you on the ground with him. I called 911, and we ran out there. Damn it Molly, I'm sorry."

"Brett," I said, looking him in the eyes without turning my head. "I know you are. I'm okay thanks to you two. This is not your fault."

Ram's head popped up. "No, it's not. It's Nick's fault. I'm going to kill that son of a bitch for leaving." He stood up and resumed pacing.

Cooper didn't even tell him to cool it. Instead he said, "As soon as I find Nick, he will no longer be working for me."

"And he may wind up in this same hospital if I find him," Ram said, then cocked his chin side to side like boxers do before a fight.

"Ram, stop," I told him. He stilled, and looked at me. "I can't handle your manic anger right now. You're pissed. I get it. Calm down."

He stood there as we continued to stare at each other. He didn't resume pacing, his breathing slowed down and he unclenched his fists. His eyes lost most of their intensity.

Three quick raps on the door interrupted us. Two men walked in. One was Officer Czarnowski, the officer who came to Brett's when the roses were left in my hatch. The other man wasn't dressed in uniform and introduced himself as Detective Lindsmere.

Cooper and Ram told me they'd see me later and left. No doubt they were going to go hunt down Nick. I didn't know what they were going to do to him besides fire him. I really didn't care.

I asked the officers if Katie and Brett could stay while they questioned me, and they said yes. I looked at Katie. I wasn't sure if she wanted to hear the details. "Katie, if you don't think you can handle hearing this you should leave. You know I won't be upset."

"I'll be fine, Molly."

Before they started, I wanted to know about the woman who attacked me first: who she was and how badly she was hurt.

Detective Lindsmere answered. "Her name is Belinda, Lindy, Nord. She says she's the girlfriend of the man who attacked you. She gave us the name of Bill Smith. We think it's a fake name, but we don't know if she's making it up or he gave it to her. Her story is that he kept telling her that you won't leave him alone, that you continuously hit on him and ask him out despite him telling you that he isn't interested. Said he was getting freaked out by you, so they came up with a plan for her to catch you alone, where she would beat you up so you would leave him alone. She claims she had no idea he planned on attacking you as well. She did admit to starting the fight. Believed she was justified."

My body tensed. *Justified?* I clenched my fists, noting the dulled pain in both. I relaxed, not wanting to make any injuries worse since whatever the hell they gave me for the pain was starting to work. "That's bullshit. I never saw her before she came at me. I didn't recognize Bill Smith, or whatever his name is. He was in a disguise. Fuck her. I'm glad I beat her ass."

Both men looked shocked at my statement, but Detective Lindsmere smiled.

Then he continued. "You definitely did that. And if you didn't recognize her before, you definitely wouldn't now. You did a real number on her face—gave her a concussion, a broken nose, a split lip, and an entire face full of bruises."

"I didn't mean for it to be that bad. I actually gave her two chances to get up and stop, but she wouldn't. Am I going to get in any trouble over that?"

"No. I need to get the entire story from beginning to end. Are you up to that now? It's usually better if we get it fresh so you remember the details."

I didn't feel up to doing it now. I wasn't sure if I would ever be up to it though, so I told him what happened from the time I went back into the bar to retrieve my jacket, to Katie and Brett running out to save my life. My head was a bit fuzzy, but I still had perfect recall of what had happened. By the time I finished recounting the story, Brett had hold of Katie's hand, and she leaned into him for support.

I could take a deep breath since the pain pills were really doing their job. Really. Pain. That's a funny word. It rhymes with . . . whoever designed the hospital room had really bad taste.

I was happy that Katie had Brett, because he was really good for her. Caleb was really mad. Was there more to it than wanting to kill Nick? *Nick, Nick Bo Bick, Banana Fanna Fo Prick.* Ha, that's funny. Why did I keep thinking of Ram as Caleb lately, but I always called him Ram? Do rams have horns?

It must've been obvious that my mind was wandering because Detective Lindsmere said: "Ms. Davis, we can continue this tomorrow—well, later today—or even Monday. You should rest. Any idea of when you're going home?"

"I don't know. I want out now." My speech was slightly slurring. I looked at Katie. "Katie, take me home please."

"I can't just take you out of here, Molly. I'll go see what I can find out. Bye officers." Katie gave a wave to the men and left the room with Brett.

Detective Lindsmere put his card on the side table/tray thing. My new mission in life was to find out what that was called. "Ms. Davis, call me as soon as you feel up to continuing. We need to get a description of your attacker as soon as possible. I know you said he was in disguise, but we still need to get what we can. If you can, write down anything you need to before you forget it."

Ten four, good buddy. Over and out.

I woke up alone in the hospital on Sunday afternoon. I really needed to use the bathroom, since I hadn't peed since the night before. Getting up was very slow and difficult. Not only did I still have an IV in, I was stiff and pain was shooting from several spots on my body. I could tell I was going to have to do everything without the use of my right arm. My feet inched along the floor as I held on to the IV pole. I made it to the toilet without looking in the mirror. When I finished peeing, I stood at the sink and looked at myself in the mirror.

Saying I looked like hell was an understatement. There was a huge bruise on the right side of my face that went from just below my eye up to my forehead. That was where

The Creep backhanded me. At least there was no bruise from getting punched in the jaw by Belinda Nord. Puffy eyes looked back at me and saw blood caked around my hairline.

Slowly, and very carefully, I peeled off the gauze from behind my ear to look at the stitches. Tears started rolling down my face. Then I took the coverings off the other stab wounds and stared at them for a long time. After replacing the gauze, I wet a washcloth to remove the blood, but I wasn't strong enough to apply the pressure needed to wipe it off. It was too caked, and there was a lot of it.

I didn't care about the pain so much—that, I could handle, no matter how much it sucked. What I cared about was the scarring, the visual reminder of what happened that I would see on my body every single day for the rest of my life. Would I be able to continue being a Song Wrecker? Oh God, if he took playing guitar away from me . . . No. I refused to entertain that thought.

I stood there, staring at myself, until I heard a nurse call my name. I grasped the IV pole for support and slowly walked back to my bed.

"You should've called us for help getting around. You must be in a lot of pain," the nurse told me.

"I'm okay." I sat on the bed and she helped me lay down. I pinched my eyes shut from pain. "Maybe not. Can I have more pain pills please? I needed to use the bathroom and get a look at myself. Can I go home soon?"

She adjusted my blankets while trying to convince me that staying another day was best. I insisted that I wanted to go home, so she left to find the doctor to sign me out. Another nurse came in and handed me pills and a cup of water. I took the pills then closed my eyes but didn't sleep.

My head played a continual loop—the first bear left on my Jeep, rose petals, dead animal, The Creep, bear, petals, animal, Creep.

Then The Creep's image was by itself. I concentrated the best I could on his features, but they had been so obscured by dirt and a wig. Eventually, his face became the dead animal's and I gave up trying to get a picture of who he might be.

Chapter 12

Luckily, the hospital wasn't busy and the doctor signed me out in under an hour. I called Katie. My IV was taken out. I received instructions from the nurse on the follow up for my injuries and prescriptions for pain medication and antibiotics. Several hours later, I was home.

Katie helped me to my bathroom, and I let her scrub the blood off me. There must've been more than I realized because she muttered, "Good Lord," a few times, and "Sorry!" when she touched a sore spot and I flinched. She even took the time to run a wash cloth over sections of my hair to strip the dried blood out of it. When I was as blood free as she could get me, she helped me back to the living room. I needed to eat, but had no appetite so I had her grab me a box of crackers from the kitchen. I was as comfortable as I could get on my couch while Katie settled herself in a chair.

"Do you want me to stay the night? I don't like the idea of you being alone."

It wasn't that I didn't want her around, but I had a lot to think about. Plus I had to call my department head at work to let him know I wouldn't be in for a few days, talk to the police . . . and Cooper. God, when he and Ram found out about the dead squirrel, or whatever it was, on my porch I didn't tell them about, yeah. I wasn't looking forward to that admission. Maybe I'd just keep my mouth shut.

"I love you Katie, but I'm going to spend the rest of the evening talking to people. Go home. I'll call you if I need you. Maybe you could stop over after work tomorrow."

While dusting cracker crumbs off me she said, "Yeah. I'm going to stop by later tonight anyway,"

"Katie?" She looked at me and tears pooled in my eyes. "Thank you."

Tears pooled in her eyes too. "That's what best friends are for." She made sure I was comfortable and that everything I needed was nearby, then left.

First I called my department head. The last thing I wanted was for it to be common knowledge that I had gotten stabbed, so I told him that I was in a car accident instead. I didn't know if any of this was going to make the news, so I lied. I'd worry about what to say if the truth ever came out. When I told him the extent of my injuries, he convinced me to take the entire week off.

Next I called Cooper. I owed it to him to give him the story as soon as possible. He told me he'd be at my place in an hour, so I took the time to take a get the rest of me cleaned up. Katie had taken care of my face and hair, but my body felt dirty. I still wore the clothes I was attacked in.

Getting undressed was a slow, painful process, especially with all the bandages. My body's protest at doing the simplest activities was another reminder of The Creep when I wanted nothing more than to move on and forget him. I threw everything I was wearing in the trash.

I began crying. This was so unfair!

I desperately wanted to step into a hot shower, but wasn't allowed to. My sutures needed to stay dry. Damn it, that psycho wasn't going to interrupt my life to the extent I needed help with the very basics.

Once in the bathroom I grabbed a square of toilet paper and dried my tears. I sat on the edge of my tub and used a washcloth to clean my entire body, for the most part. The dirt and gravel of the alley felt permanently imbedded on my skin. I shaved my legs, or the bottom halves anyway. Afterward, I even sprayed dry shampoo on my roots and brushed it through to freshen up my hair. I did most of it with my left hand, but I did it. It took forever, was difficult, and it hurt way worse than I'd anticipated. As I finished getting dressed in comfortable sweats, my doorbell rang.

It took a while for me to get to the door. Washing and getting dressed had taken a lot out of me, and my whole body was tired. I looked out the window and saw Cooper and Ram. At least Ram looked in control.

I opened the door and panted, "Hey, guys, come on in." I didn't offer to hang their jackets because I wasn't physically able to do it. Plus I really didn't give a shit about hospitality at the moment. Even through the pain pills, I throbbed from head to toe. Cleaning myself and getting dressed had been too much. I inched my way to the chair and sat, giving them the couch. Cooper set a bag by his feet.

I noticed Ram's swollen hand. "Looks like you found Nick."

"I did. I didn't give him even half of what he deserved," he said.

"He's not going to have you arrested or anything is he?"

"Hell no. He knows what happened was his fault." Technically, my attack was The Creep's fault, but telling Ram that would be a waste of time. His eyes then turned softer, and he asked: "How bad are your injuries?"

I told them everything the doctor had told me. I even lifted my sweatshirt to show them the knife wounds on my abdomen.

Ram's whole body tensed. He clenched his jaw and fists, then took a deep breath as if to get himself under control.

Cooper seemed to be angry, too, if the slight furrow of his brow was any indication.

Cooper finally got down to business. "Molly, I want you to tell us everything that happened. If you can't remember something, tell us you don't remember. Don't reach for details."

Once again, I recounted the entire story in graphic detail. Cooper wasn't taking notes and his face wore the same expression it always did. Ram tried to stay cool, but the skin around his eyes kept tightening. He was still clearly angry, but doing much better than he had the previous night at controlling himself.

"Your story matches what we saw on the security cameras," Cooper said.

I'd forgotten about the cameras, and didn't know how I felt about them watching the attack. On one hand, the tapes would prove that I hadn't started anything, that I was the victim. Even though The Creep was disguised, maybe someone would recognize and identify him. That was good.

On the other hand, *there was a recording of the minutes I was almost killed* and people could watch it. I could watch it. The whole freaking world could watch it. That sure as hell did not sit well with me.

Chapter 13

I felt light-headed for a second, but forced myself to get a grip. "Who's seen the tape?" I asked.

"Only Brett, myself, and Ram. Then Brett gave it to the police, so I'm sure they've seen it," Cooper said.

"Shit." That was all I could think of to say. Just . . . shit. I leaned my head back on the chair. Luckily it was soft, so it didn't make the huge bruise on the back of my head hurt any worse. A tear ran down my cheek. One thing I hated more than crying was crying in front of other people, so I kept my head back for a minute.

Ram laid his hand on the arm of my chair. "Molly, this being on tape is a good thing. It will help us catch this guy. There's nothing on that tape for you to worry about."

I still looked at the ceiling. "Won't the police know how to catch this guy after talking to the woman—Belinda? She was his girlfriend."

Cooper answered. "Apparently not. She swore he told her his name was Bill Smith. We don't think that's his real name. She said she doesn't even know where he lives, that they always hung out at her apartment because he was ashamed that he still lived with his parents. We—and the police—have no idea who this guy is or where he lives."

"So in other words, he used her to wear me down so he would have an easier time killing me or . . . whatever he was going to do with me." I was sick of crying. I wiped my tears and looked at the two men sitting on my couch.

"That's what we're thinking, yes," Ram said.

"So what's going to happen to her? Legally, I mean."

"The police are charging her with assault. She can't deny anything since her actions were recorded. Well she can try, it won't do her any good. If this is her first offense, and she helps the police, she'll probably get a slap on the wrist. She's swearing that she didn't know he was going to attack you, too." Cooper stopped, acting as if he had more to say, but wasn't sure if he should. His mouth would open to talk, then close, then open, then close.

"Say it," I told him.

Cooper tilted his head. "Judging by the way you handled yourself, this couldn't have been your first fight."

If the situation wasn't so messed up, I would've laughed. Instead I said, "Nope," and left it at that.

Cooper asked if I minded if he and Ram stayed while the detective came over to get a description of The Creep. I told them that was fine. That way, I'd only have to do it one time. I called Detective Lindsmere. He arrived at my house about twenty minutes later.

The doorbell rang and I automatically lifted to get up to get the door. Ram stopped me. "I'll get it," he said, getting up. I was grateful.

Detective Lindsmere came in and settled himself on the other chair. I could tell that the three men were already familiar with each other as they said their hellos.

He took out a mini-notebook and pen. "Ms. Davis, I saw the tape, but I still need as detailed as possible description from you. I took a description from Belinda Nord, and I want to compare it to yours. The attacker may still be in disguise, so I want both likenesses."

"Okay. Can you three stand up, please?" I asked. I wanted to compare The Creep's height to theirs. They stood. All three were too tall. Once they sat back down I continued. "He's shorter than all of you. How tall are you, detective?"

"Five-eleven."

"I'd put The Creep at five-nine."

"The Creep?"

"That's what me and Katie refer to him as. So, five-nine. Small to medium build. He was wearing several layers on his top half, maybe to make himself look bigger than he is? I don't know, so most likely he's a smaller build. Dark sweatshirt on top, dark ball cap, dark jeans, dark tennis shoes. He wore an obvious wig, dark. It looked more like Barbie doll hair." I used my left arm to indicate the length of the hair. "It came down to his eyebrows in front, covered the sides of his face, and not quite to his shoulders in back. He had dirt smeared over his face. Maybe it was makeup, I don't know."

Still writing he asked, "Were you able to ascertain his eye color?"

I closed my eyes to concentrate. "No, sorry." I looked at the detective again and laughed humorlessly. "Probably dark, just like everything else. Even though he was disguising himself he seemed . . . I don't know, average. I didn't recognize him at all."

Detective Lindsmere continued to ask me questions and take notes. Cooper took notes too. Many of the questions were the same thing, just asked differently. When the detective was finished writing, he put away his notebook and stood. "Ms. Davis, you have my number. Call me if you have anything else to add."

Detective Lindsmere left. Cooper reached down by his feet and picked up the bag he'd brought with him, then dumped the contents onto the coffee table. He and Ram sorted the pieces into two different sized rectangles.

Cooper grabbed a handful of pieces and left the room while Ram explained what they were doing. "This is a temporary alarm system for the night. They'll be mounted to each door and window like this." He held one small and one medium piece side by side. "The sides that face each other have magnets in them. When they're turned on, they'll create a very loud alarm if the magnets are separated more than an eighth of an inch. Tomorrow we have the alarm company 3D uses coming to install a real alarm system."

"You didn't think to ask me first?" Not that I would've said no, but I should have at least been asked as a courtesy. It irritated me that I wasn't.

"Princess, don't. This is non-negotiable." He walked away and started mounting an alarm on my front door.

"So screw whatever I want and do whatever you want? Why don't you camp out on my couch with your gun at the ready all night?" I didn't care that I was being unreasonable. My privacy was going to be invaded. People were going to be traipsing all over my house and no one even asked my permission.

Without stopping what he was doing he answered, "If I thought you'd let me, I would."

Cooper came back and grabbed more alarm sets then headed toward the hall. He was obviously going to do the bedrooms and bathrooms. I watched Ram work. He was completely unapologetic.

I had no fight in me, not about this. "So what time do I need to be decent tomorrow?" I asked.

He walked to the back of the house. "I'm not sure, I'll call you first. It should definitely be before noon."

They continued putting up the temporary alarms while I went into the kitchen and took more pain pills. I didn't let the doctor prescribe the same pills I'd received at the hospital, because they made me feel too loopy. I hadn't done much more than sit on the chair and still I was hurting and tired and quite irritable. Once in a while, to break up the monotony of sitting on my ass I would get up for a drink, and Ram watched me out of the corner of his eye whenever I moved. I walked like a hundred-year-old lady.

Once finished, Cooper opened my front door with the alarm turned on so I could hear the ear-piercing screech that sounded when the magnets were separated. Since I'm already a light sleeper there was no doubt they would wake me up if they went off. And possibly the neighbors, too.

Ram and Cooper left. I was grateful to have some protection covering every possible entrance into my house. Since I hadn't really eaten, and didn't want to be alone, I called Katie to see if she wanted to eat with me. She came over with a pizza and turned on the TV. Katie didn't hover over me, and we didn't talk all that much. I told her about getting an alarm system installed and she was relieved. Her company was nice. She probably had a ton of questions she wanted to ask me, but left it alone for the night. Around ten-thirty I kicked her out and went to bed.

I slept like crap. I knew I would. The Creep knew where I lived and was still out there. If he broke into my house, how fast could I move to defend myself? It would take forever to grab my phone and dial 911 even with my cell sitting next to me on the night stand. Knowledge of the cameras hadn't stopped him, so why would a piercing alarm?

By seven a.m. I was done lying there. I slid out of bed—so freaking irritatingly slow—and made myself coffee and breakfast and took another pain pill. I was getting annoyed all over again at the way I was now forced to do things. I could barely do all my normal personal things for myself. I couldn't drive, for a while at least. I was going to have to depend on other people for a good week or two. I hated that. God damn it, the fucking asshole who did this to me did so much more than hurt me. He temporarily took away my independence. He made me paranoid and scared.

School was about to start for the day, so I called into my classroom to make sure my sub for the week understood my lesson plans. I gave her my cell number and told her to call me if she had any questions. This woman had subbed for me before and did a great job, so I wasn't anticipating any problems for the week.

I cleaned up using the same method as the day before, and got dressed. I felt better even though I still looked like shit. I was standing in the middle of my bedroom when it hit me, I was already bored. I couldn't dance, couldn't workout, couldn't play my guitar. I could only write left-handed, so writing in a journal was out of the question. My choices were reading and watching TV. I chose TV, which turned out to be a good choice, because even that tired me out.

After about a half hour of channel surfing, Ram called. "I'm on my way over," he told me. "Don't forget to shut off the alarm on the front door before you let me in."

I shifted my weight to my other butt cheek so numbness wouldn't set in. "Hallelujah. I am bored out of my mind."

"It's not even nine o'clock."

"I know. I'm in for a long week. See ya in a few," I grumbled, and hung up.

Ram showed up alone. I expected him to arrive with the alarm company people. "So you're a bodyguard, a private investigator, and the alarm company?" I asked.

"No." His hands hovered around me while I walked back to the couch, as if he was prepared for me to fall. "The alarm installers will be here in a little while. I wanted to talk to you about a couple of things first." He stole a glance at the bruise on the side of my head.

"About what?"

He motioned for me to sit. My face scrunched in pain as I lowered myself. He sat only after I was settled.

"I think there's a detail or two you're not telling me."

"I told you every single detail about the attack. What the heck do you think I left out?"

"Not about the attack. Something else. It doesn't make sense to me that he left things at your car a few times and then nothing else until the attack." He stared at me, waiting for me to fess up.

I stared back at him. There was no reason not to tell him, except he'd be really angry, and he would have every right to be.

He raised his eyebrows as if to ask, "Well?"

I let out a sigh and told him. "The last weekend in January I came home from Brett's late."

"It wasn't a Wrecker's Weekend, right?"

"No. We convinced Brett to get a karaoke system, and it was the first time we used it. We advertised as best we could that we—The Song Wreckers—were going to be there doing karaoke so anyone could have known that I wouldn't be home. So anyway, the next morning I went out to get my paper and there were rose petals on my porch."

I stopped for a few seconds. His eyes were already tightening, so he really wouldn't like the next part. "And a dead squirrel. I think it was a squirrel. It could've been something else."

He closed his eyes and pinched the bridge of his nose, but said nothing.

"It looked like it had been stabbed or . . . I don't know, smooshed. It made me sick. I wrapped it in an old towel and threw it out in the woods. I didn't tell anyone, not even Katie."

He dropped his hand and looked at me like he wanted to yell at me. He didn't. Instead, he took a deep breath and calmly said: "If we'd have known, Cooper never would've left you guys with just Nick. Damn it, Molly, why didn't you say anything?"

I looked away, mostly from embarrassment. "I don't know. I didn't want to worry anyone more. I told myself if anything else happened, I would go to the police. You don't need to tell me how stupid I am. I spent a good deal of last night doing that myself." My foot was tapping a million times a minute. Ram gently put his foot on mine to stop the tapping. I looked at him.

"I think you're the furthest thing from stupid. You just put everyone else's feelings ahead of your own. You think you can handle everything yourself."

"Usually I can."

"Is that it? Is there anything else at all you haven't told me yet?"

"No. I swear that's it." I was done with this topic. I felt so stupidly irresponsible for keeping my mouth shut. "You said 'a couple of things', what else did you want to talk to me about?"

Ram needed me to set up a series of passwords and alarm codes. He wanted obscure numbers and names from my past that no one would reasonably connect with me.

"Did the police get a description of The Creep from Nord?" I asked.

"Yeah. Cooper would have that information. Want me to call him?" He took out his phone.

I was too tired right now to get into all of that. "No, not now. I'll call the detective later. How long will it take to get the alarm system installed? Will it be difficult to work?"

"It will take most of the day. You're getting an excellent system. It shouldn't be too difficult to learn how to use. Most people do set the alarms off accidentally for the first month so keep the instruction manual out."

"Oh, yay," I deadpanned. "I needed something to read. Is there any good smut in it?"

"Well you could put on mood music while reading it and pretend that pressing buttons turns you on. I read in *Cosmo* some women get turned on while reading stuff like that."

I didn't know whether to laugh or gag. "You read *Cosmo*? I don't even read *Cosmo*."

"I have sisters, and they leave it out when I visit," he said, sounding defensive.

"That doesn't mean you have to read their magazines, you loser." I was trying not to laugh because it would hurt.

"Be nice, or I won't share my subscription with you."

Unable to hold it in, I burst out laughing. "Ow!" I pressed a hand over the cut on my stomach. "You mean your sister's subscription?"

He looked away. "Uh, yeah. My sister's. Anyway, the alarm company should be here soon."

I gave out a snort and then gasped. "Ouch. Nice subject change."

He fiddled with the papers in front of him and avoided eye contact, probably embarrassed.

I couldn't let it drop. "Big, bad Caleb Ramsey reads *Cosmopolitan*. What is the world coming to?"

He shifted his body toward mine and leaned slightly into me. "That magazine is a wealth of information about women. Would you like to go out with me and see the things I've learned?"

His question was more of a dare than anything, but still, it shut me right up. I was a couple days out from being viciously attacked, and I there I was, laughing with him? That he could make me forget, if only for a few minutes, freaked me out. Actually, it terrified me. I sat quietly for a while, not knowing how to respond. The silence grew uncomfortable. "So when are the alarm people gonna get here? It's been more than a little while."

Ram leaned back on the couch and took a few seconds to study at me. "Hmm. Nice subject change."

Touché.

Luckily, he let the subject go. He took out his cell and made a call. When he finished he stood and said, "It should be about fifteen or twenty minutes. I'm going to get these temporary alarms off."

When someone knocked on my door, Ram put up his hand, indicating I should stay seated while he let in the alarm people. There were five uniformed men. *Ryder Security* was stitched on their shirts.

They spent the rest of the day installing and testing the system. Being in my own house with strangers moving about was weird. There was nowhere I could go since I couldn't drive, and Katie was at work. I alternated between eating and watching TV. I moved so slowly, most of my time was spent walking between my kitchen and living room. When they left for lunch—all except Ram, who'd taken his lunch break before everyone else—I napped. Then I watched a *Ninja Warrior* marathon, which killed a lot of time.

When the new alarm system was installed, Ram walked me around the house to explain everything to me. Every window and door was secured. I had a key pad near my front door, the kitchen slider door, and in my bedroom.

The tour took quite a while since I still moved with the speed of a snail. The alarm system didn't seem too complicated to figure out, but it was intricate enough to need time to learn it. Sometimes, Ram would gingerly put his hand on the small of my back as he led me to the next place we had to be. Other times, he would gently hold on to my arm, as if I were going to fall. Every time he touched me, I became more relaxed and anxious at the same time.

He turned to me with the instruction manual. "Do you want me to tell you how everything works or do you want to read it?"

"You can give me the brief version then I'll read the manual tonight." He was very detailed in his instructions, so I doubted I'd need to do any reading, which was too bad. Studying would've helped bore me to sleep.

Chapter 14

The rest of the week was rough. I spent a lot of time making adjustments just to be able to do everyday tasks, and they took much longer. I hurt a lot, but pain was nothing new to me. I'd spent my entire life being uber-active. Knowing what my body was and wasn't capable of was pretty instinctual.

Mentally, the week was hell. I had too much time to think and no way physically to work out my issues. Usually I would go for a nice long run, do yoga, or go to the batting cages. Nothing beats the batting cages for those times when you want to hit the crap out of something. I was pissed I could do none of those things.

The detective called me to tell me Belinda Nord gave him a description of Bill Smith. I heard him turning the pages of his notebook. "She says he's two or three inches shorter than me, short brown hair, brown eyes. Average build. Good looking." He made a sound of disgust. "That part doesn't help us any. He sounds like your everyday guy for the most part."

Fan-freaking-tastic. "Thanks, Detective."

"We're trying, Ms. Davis. We really are," he told me.

"I know. Thanks again," I said. Her description didn't help anything as far as I was concerned.

Katie stopped over after work each day. The rest of the band and Brett had stopped over during the week as well. Even though Katie had called them and told them what had happened, I had to recount the story first to Courtney and Josh, and then to Heather. Everyone pretty much had the same reaction—horror, pity, and sympathy. They all told me to call them if I needed anything. I wouldn't. Being dependent on Katie was bad enough.

Cooper stopped by a couple times, and Ram stopped by every day. Cooper would make sure I was okay then leave. Ram would stay for while to keep me company. He quizzed me on how to use the security system, watched TV with me, and never talked about the attack or got too personal. I think he understood now was not the time to see if we had anything. I could tell he cared, but I couldn't go there. Not then.

I called Alan to see how the video went. He was ecstatic about the whole thing. Filming had gone better than he'd expected. I wasn't surprised. He was the most talented dancer I had ever seen. When he was done telling me about the video, I told him everything that happened to me regarding The Creep, even the car and porch stuff. He didn't get as detailed a version as the police, but he got the point.

"Oh crap, Molly." That's all he said for a long while.

"I know. Listen, Alan, I'm okay. Really I am. I had a state of the art security system installed, and there are a lot of people watching out for me. I'm going to heal soon."

"Promise me you'll let Katie take care of you."

"I will, Alan. I'm going to be fine." Physically at least.

"Did your mom totally freak out?" he asked.

"I didn't tell her, and I don't plan to. I know you'll tell Garrett, but don't tell anyone else, please."

"You know I won't. Will you call me if you need to talk?"

"You know I will. I gotta go. I'll call you next week. Tell Garrett I said hi."

"Bye Molly. Love you," Alan said.

"Love you, too. Bye."

I survived the week. I was able to move about more freely and took myself off prescription pain medication, switching to over-the-counter pills. I was ready to go back to work with my fake car accident story. I probably should've taken another week off, but needed the normalcy of my job. My right shoulder was healing better than expected. I was able to lift my arm straight out, so I was pretty sure the doctors overestimated the extent of the injury. I would still have to write on my whiteboard with my left hand for a while. My students had better not complain since I had to read their chicken slop handwriting all the time.

I spent a lot of the first day back at work fake smiling, saying I was fine, and telling everyone my fake story. Everyone heard I had been hurt in a car accident, so they went out of their way to accommodate me. It helped. Either a teacher or student was always there to open my door or carry my stuff.

A neighboring city had suffered a large fire at a strip mall that had taken out a couple businesses and damaged another the same night as the attack. My horror story was nothing more than a quick blurb that was easily overlooked and forgotten. My secret was safe.

Life slowly returned to normal. I called my mom to see what she had been up to. I made up excuses as to why I hadn't gone for a visit in a while. I promised her I would soon.

After a couple weeks I started exercising, very lightly. I worked what I could of my injuries; mostly I worked around them. I didn't go to a physical therapist for my shoulder because I was sure I could rehabilitate the injury myself.

Ram came by for more visits until I told him to stop. I couldn't put my finger on why I didn't want him around me. The same feelings I always had when he was with me were still there: comfort, serenity, security, sexual attraction. I think the attraction I had for him since before the attack made me uncomfortable. I didn't know how to deal with it.

I couldn't deny that I was still attracted to him, but I let the attack push it from my mind.

How could we even start anything, assuming he even wanted to? Would he think he had to constantly be mindful of my mental health because I was a fragile little princess who wasn't capable of handling my attack? Maybe he was simply being nice, maybe the coming-by-and-seeing-how-the-client-is-doing-after-a-traumatic-experience routine was what he did.

Hell, I didn't even know what to think of my, or his, feelings. Okay, I was pretty sure he had feelings for me. He wasn't pushy with them, but they were there. I wasn't ready to deal with them. I needed to think of him as Ram, not the more personal Caleb. He honored my wishes by keeping his distance and switched to calling to ask how I was.

Everyone assumed there wouldn't be a Wreckers Weekend for a couple months. Katie, Courtney and Heather were at my house for dinner a few days before April's first weekend, and their jaws hit the floor when I told them I wanted to play our normal show. My shoulder wasn't healed completely, but playing in April was the proverbial middle finger in The Creep's face. He was determined to screw up my life; I was determined to continue as normal.

As soon as she was done chewing, Katie said: "I had a feeling you'd wanna play. This is just like you. I gotta call Mama when I get home. She said you'd do this."

"Molly, no one cares if we take a month or two off. We did it after Lilah was born. Take the time to heal," Courtney said. We'd used the time after Courtney and Josh's daughter was born to practice and work on new material.

"It's Molly's decision. If she wants to be a dumbass, let her," Heather said. She really needed to stop saying that about me.

I told the half truth. "Guys, I feel a lot better. I've been playing my guitar, and I know I'll be fine."

Katie huffed. "Don't piss on my leg and tell me it's raining. Good Lord, you know damn well there's a difference between sitting in your basement playing a few songs and standing up on stage with an entire band for a good forty five minutes at a time. Don't be an idiot."

I took a deep breath. "Okay, then let me tell you why I really want to play this weekend: I need to. I need my life to go back to as normal as possible. I feel like The Creep is winning if I don't play. I need to get control of my life back."

That was the total truth. Playing so soon after the attack was going to hurt like hell. I would struggle, and the quality would probably suffer, but I didn't care. I wanted my life back. All of it.

Heather shrugged. "You know it's fine with me."

"I'm not going to tell you no. I just don't think it's smart." That came from Courtney.

I looked at Katie. She was the person I really had to convince. If she didn't want me to play she would tell Brett, and he would cancel our show.

She looked me right in the eye and said, "You win. Do what you need to do."

With the issue of our next show out of the way, we were able to talk about other stuff. Brett and Heather had another successful karaoke night. Courtney and Josh were talking about having another baby. Katie asked if I was ready to go out and get a pedicure. I was.

Chapter 15

I was really nervous as I pulled into the alley behind Brett's. Could I pull this off? Was I really about to play a show a month after being stabbed?

Yes. I had to.

Ram and Cooper were there waiting for me. Cooper probably didn't trust anyone else to guard us after the Nick fiasco. No one would let me carry anything, either, also as I'd expected. Ram saw me staring at the location where my blood had shed—thankfully I couldn't see any traces of it—so he ushered me inside while Cooper helped with the equipment.

Once we were in Brett's office Ram made sure I sat down. "You sure about this?" he asked, leaning against Brett's desk with his arms crossed over his chest. He was making an effort to keep a distance from me, and I felt bad for that.

I gave him a smile that I hoped looked genuine. "I am. Please don't get on my case about it. Everyone else already has."

His body was rigid, and his face stayed unsmiling. "God forbid people who care about you get on your case and try to talk sense into you. Moving on, if you see anyone in the bar tonight that resembles The Creep *at all*, you have to signal one of us."

"How? I left my bat-signal at home." Sometimes I'm funny.

"This is not the time to joke, Molly. If this guy comes here tonight we need to get him. We don't know what he's going to do. He might be sick enough to show up here, especially since he knows he hasn't been identified yet."

He'd called me Molly when no one else was around. Maybe he was upset with me or maybe I wasn't as funny as I thought. "Fine. How do you want to be signaled?"

"If there is even the smallest chance that someone you see is The Creep, you need to make eye contact with me or Cooper. Once eye contact is made, move your eyes to the possible suspect. We'll take it from there. Got it?"

"I got it," I said. He was in Cooper mode tonight, total business.

Man, I was nervous up on that stage. I was having serious doubts about performing. The whole bar was staring at me and whispering so I guess word had gotten around about the attack. Either that or I was being paranoid.

I had to take ibuprofen and rest during the breaks, but I played fine. I scanned the crowd constantly for The Creep. I didn't see anybody I thought he could be. There were several men who may have had the same build, but they were too tall. Or they were the same height, but fifty pounds too heavy. I didn't signal anyone to Cooper or Ram the entire night, or the next night either.

I was proud of myself for being able to play that weekend. Of course, not having to load and unload our stuff was a big help. Cooper or Ram now followed me home after the shows and called me once I was inside to make sure the alarm system was set.

Spring break started the following weekend. With the extra week to rest, I was pretty sure I would be able to start using my right hand to write on the whiteboard at work again. The stitches had been out for a while, but the scars were pretty noticeable, especially the one on my left forearm. I'd have to wear a long sleeved shirt to cover it. The mark behind my right ear wasn't too bad, noticeable only if you looked right at it. The ones on my shoulder and stomach I wouldn't have to worry about until the time came to wear summer clothes.

Katie's mom had moved back to Mississippi after we graduated from college, and Katie was going to visit her for Easter. She invited me to go with her, but I needed to see my mom. I had been avoiding her since the attack.

My mom and I spent Easter like we spent the other holidays: friendly with emotional distance. I think I was waiting for her to make a first move. She had to see the difference between us and other mothers and daughters. I mean, come on already.

She noticed the scars on my hairline and left arm, so I gave her the car accident story while eating lunch. I couldn't bring myself to tell her the truth about really happened.

"Oh honey, why didn't you call me?" she asked.

Adequate time had passed that I could answer casually. "Mom, it was no big deal. I got banged up and cut with some glass."

I think it made us both sad that we weren't close enough for me to be comfortable calling her when something bad had happened to me, but that's the way our relationship was. We finished eating, and she suggested we go to the couch to talk. That was odd.

She put her hand on mine and gave what was meant to be a reassuring squeeze, which wasn't normal. At first I took it as a gesture of comfort toward me, maybe for the "car accident," until then she asked, "Have you talked to your father lately?" I knew then her behavior was more a sign of nerves.

The question took me by surprise. I hadn't seen or heard from him in years. "No, why?"

"Believe it or not, he called me the other day. He asked about you and then told me he was getting married." Mom's gaze went from me to the floor.

This news hurt my mom. I honestly didn't care anything about his life, especially that he was getting married. "Good for him. I hope he's happy." I said, feeling unexpectedly bitter. So maybe I did care. Or maybe I didn't want him to have a good life without us.

She continued. "He wanted to know if I thought you would come to the wedding. I told him I didn't know, and that he'd have to ask you himself. Then he apologized for everything, and we actually had a nice conversation. He sounded happy." She shrugged. "So what do you think?"

"About what?"

"Going to the wedding. I think he wants to start over or start to have a real relationship with you."

I pulled my hand from hers. You know what ticked me off? That my own father didn't even have the balls to call me himself and ask me first. He used my mom as a go-between. "We'll see," was all I could think of to say.

My mom put her hand back on mine. She looked determined to be pleasant. "He's the only father you'll ever have. One day he won't be here any longer. I don't want you to have regrets."

Here's what I wanted to say: *Too late for that! I have a ton of regrets! I regret that you and I were never that close. I regret I still don't have the nerve to ask you questions that I need answered. I regret not having a father. I regret that I never knew my twin sister. And, oh yeah, some psychotic ass tried to kill me last month!*

Instead I changed the subject. I asked about other family members, their children, their health, anything that steered conversation away from talking about my father or me.

I spent the rest of Spring break angry. Angry at The Creep, angry at Belinda Nord, angry at my father, angry at my mother, and angry that I couldn't beat myself down physically to deal with it.

I deserved a good old fashioned pity party all by myself, so one evening I went to the store and bought myself a bottle of quality vodka. Before I got good and drunk, I called Katie and talked to her and Mama for a while. I told her the news about my father and that we would talk about it when she came home.

Then before I knew it, I was—to use a Mama phrase—walking on a slant. I was sloppy drunk when the phone rang, and Ram's number came up on caller ID. "Yo, Caleb," I answered.

"Uh, hey, Princess. I was just calling to make sure you were okay."

I smiled because he called me Princess, but then remembered this was my night to be pissed and immediately wiped the smile off my face. "I am *freaking* great."

"What's wrong?"

Everything. "Nothing."

"Are you drunk?" he spat.

"Damn, Ram." Ooh, that rhymed. "You are good. I hope Cooper pays you the big bucks." My words were coming out sloppy, so I began overcompensating by over-enunciating everything, which was a sure sign of drunkenness. "Which reminds me—why haven't I gotten a bill for the security system yet?"

"I don't think you'll ever be getting a bill for the security system. Cooper's taking care of it."

"Great!" I exclaimed with a lot of sugary, fake happiness. "I'm a big fucking charity case these days! Brett wouldn't let me help pay for anything, Cooper's not letting me pay for my own fucking security system, and everyone around me is trying to do everything for me. I am *such* a lucky girl."

"Molly, are you okay? Do you want me to come over?"

Molly, huh? "Nope. I wanna be alone and celebrate my awesome life all by my awesome self. Was there anything else or can I get back to celebrating?"

"No. You're not gonna go anywhere are you?" he asked.

"To bed. Alone. Bye Ca—Ram." Click. I hung up before he could say anything else.

Now I added being angry with Caleb Ramsey on my list. Why did he have to be so . . . great? Why wasn't he married with a hundred kids and a dog? Well, maybe he had a dog. I never noticed a wedding ring—I checked the first night I met him—or even an indentation of where a wedding ring was supposed to be. Maybe he had the kids. I really didn't know all that much about him, and he knew a lot about me. Guess what? That made me angry too.

I woke up the next morning with a killer headache and horrible breath. I swallowed two Advil and drank a cup of coffee. A half an hour and a bowl of cereal later, the brain fog wore off. I cringed when I remembered being a bitch to Caleb. Damn it, Ram. I was still as angry at the world as I had been the previous night, so the alcohol didn't help.

I went for a run for the first time since the attack. I had been doing gentle yoga and very light weight lifting, but no cardio. After getting dressed, I grabbed my new can of pepper spray, compliments of Katie, and headed out.

I walked for a mile, then went into a light jog. After about a half mile of slow jogging, I could only walk the rest of the way home. I had expected problems, but my performance still disappointed me. I knew when to push myself and when not to. Just then, pushing myself wasn't smart.

I had made it into my condo complex and was two units away when Ram's black GMC Yukon drove past me from behind and turned into my driveway. As soon as I stepped foot into my tiny yard, he flung himself out of his truck and stomped toward me.

"What the hell are you doing?" he asked me.

"Mostly walking," I told him.

He threw his hands up in the air. "Alone?"

"I have pepper spray." I showed him the can.

He held his hands out, and they shook like he was about to strangle me. "Do you have any notion of personal safety? Any at all?"

"I have pepper spray," I repeated, waving the can in front of his face.

He dropped his hands. "Prin—" He stopped himself. "Molly. You *should not* be out here *alone*. What were you thinking?"

"That I have pepper spray."

"So you think pepper spray is going to keep you safe?"

Since he had gradually been getting louder, I started walking to my garage. I didn't want my neighbors to hear me arguing with Ram. Plus it was mid-April, and the air had a chill to it. "I was hoping. What do you want me to do? Have a chaperone every time I step out of my house?"

"Yes!" he yelled.

"Come on, Ram. That's not possible, and you know it. If you think I'm going to stay locked up in my house like a prisoner then you don't know me very well."

"You have a gym membership. Why not use a treadmill there?"

I'd never told him I belonged to a gym. "Because I wanted to be outside in the fresh air."

He let out a big sigh and crossed his arms over his chest. "How are you feeling? Any pain?"

I entered the code in the garage remote and waited for it to open. "Not too much. I walked the first mile and that was okay. After a short jog, my shoulder started cramping up and pain shot through the spot on my stomach so I went back to walking. Did I mention I had pepper spray with me?"

He followed me up the steps and into my kitchen.

"You're attempting to be funny, so does that mean you're not mad at me anymore?" He was, of course, talking about how I'd treated him on the phone the previous evening.

Turning away so he wouldn't see my face turn red in embarrassment, I said: "I'm sorry about last night. I was . . ."

He leaned against my kitchen counter. "Mad at me?"

I took a glass from the cupboard, filled it with water, and took a big drink. "Mad at everyone. Everything. You called at the right time—well actually the wrong time—and became an easy target for me. Don't take it personally; anyone who called at that moment would've gotten the bitch treatment."

"Even Katie?"

"I called her before I started drinking so that wouldn't happen."

"Did the one night drinking binge help?"

I put the glass in the sink and faced him. "Not even a little bit. That's another reason why I went out today," I said, shrugging with my uninjured shoulder. "Are you guys watching my house now?"

"Not officially, but everyone at the company has been instructed to drive by your house when they're in the area, so if you notice lots of dark colored SUV's drive past, don't freak out," he said.

"So why are you in the area?"

He looked at me without saying anything for a while. He took a deep breath and then admitted: "Because I was taken off my previous bodyguard cases when you were attacked. I've let Detective Lindsmere know what I'm doing so we can share information. Surprisingly, he's agreeable. He really wants this guy caught." He paused. "Okay, let's hear it."

So I had a police detective and a private detective working to catch The Creep. Plus the private detective was acting as my sort-of bodyguard. I had a very nice security system in place. And I was paying for nothing. "If I fight you on this, does it change anything?" I asked.

He smiled. "Nope."

"Well then what's there to say except thank you?"

Chapter 16

By the time May rolled around, my emotions were running hot and cold. For the most part I was fine. There were no problems at work, the talent show went off with no more than a few minor hitches, and the anticipation of the end of the school year put students in a good mood. My injuries were healing nicely. I wasn't in constant pain, and the pain I did have was very manageable. Sometimes, I would have moments when the glass was half full; I knew that everything was going to be okay. Then I would have moments where the anger would resurface, and I wanted to hit and kick and scream. Why couldn't they catch this asshole? Why did my stupid father have to remember he had a kid? Why couldn't I tell my mom the truth?

May's Wrecker's Weekend went much better for me. I was able to play as well as I always played. Kyle, Dave, and Mike from Crawling Home After Midnight, and Mike's girlfriend were at the show on Saturday night. I hadn't seen them for a while, so I joined them in the bar during our breaks.

I told them about the attack to get that topic out of the way. I assumed they had heard about it, and I didn't want any awkwardness about it lingering in the air.

They each said their version of "I'm sorry" then I waved it off with a few flicks of my wrist so we could move on. "So what's up with you guys?" I asked. "I'm surprised you're not playing tonight."

Dave leaned back in his chair. "Yeah. Notice who isn't here."

"Adam." Their drummer.

Dave continued. "He can't keep himself out of trouble. He keeps getting arrested for stupid stuff. Being drunk in public and mouthing off to the officer, drugs, and his latest—domestic violence."

Heather gave out a snort. "That's not surprising to me since I dated him a while back. He can be a real jerk. I never would've guessed domestic violence, though."

"So what's going to happen to him?" I asked.

This time Kyle answered. "Don't know. He's been spending time in jail off and on, and it's really screwing with the band's schedule. As far as I'm concerned we should start looking for another drummer."

"I wanna give him one more chance. But he'll know, one more arrest, and he's done," Dave said.

Kyle took a swig of beer. "Whatever, man."

Adam's antics were obviously a source of tension within their group. Mike kept silent the whole time and shook his head slightly every once in a while.

And unfortunately, there was no Creep at the shows.

Katie called me Sunday morning. "Guess what?" she asked.

"Do you really want me to guess at random stuff or will you just tell me?"

"After you left last night a man approached me at the bar—" she started.

"Did Brett kick his ass?"

"No Mol, not that kind of approach. Listen. He hands me a business card, says his name is Kent Adler—"

"Too bad his last name isn't Ucky. Get it? Kent Ucky? Kentucky?"

"Uh-huh. Funny. Anyway, he tells me he's a talent scout slash agent for Crystal Records, and he's interested in possibly signing The Song Wreckers. I guess they had a couple of scouts here the last couple of months, and Kent wanted to see for himself if we were as good as they said we were. Cool huh?"

"Very. I wonder what the heck took so long." This sounded arrogant, but we always knew one day we'd be approached about a record deal. Yes, we're that good. It's one thing we talked about early on—what would we do when it happened? Another reason The Song Wreckers got along so well is that we were all happy with our lives as they were. Maybe if we had received an offer while still in college we would've taken it. Not now. We all had careers, and Josh and Courtney had a child and were trying for another one. Heather was the only one who might have been attracted to an offer, but she couldn't go without the rest of us. The rest of us weren't interested. We liked being a hot, local band.

"Can I have his number?" I asked Katie.

"Wow, that's pretty forward for you," she said.

"I don't want a date."

"Of course not."

"Shut it. I don't want a date. I want to talk to him about selling the songs I wrote that aren't Wreckers material."

She gave me the number, and with slightly shaky hands I called immediately after hanging up with Katie.

"Kent Adler," he answered.

"Hi, Mr. Adler. My name is Molly Davis. I'm a Song Wrecker. I play guitar and sing backup vocals," I said, hoping he'd remember who I was. Silence. "You came to at least part of our show last night. At a bar called Brett's."

"Hi, Ms. Davis. What can I do for you? I was under the impression the band had no interest in trying to get signed."

"That's true," I said. "I want to talk to you about music I've written. Do you have a few minutes? If not, I can call you back when it's more convenient."

"Now's as good a time as any, Ms. Davis. Let's hear it." He sounded intrigued. I hoped that was a positive.

"Please, call me Molly. I've been writing music for a long time now. For years, it was all Song Wreckers stuff. The last few years, I've been writing a lot of material that's really good, but not right for The Wreckers. I actually have a group of songs that would make a damn good country album. So, to cut to the chase, I am interested in selling what I have. For the right price that is."

He was again silent for a few heartbeats.

Damn it, I should've made cutesy small talk. I feared maybe I offended him until he spoke.

"Well I can tell you this right now—I'm interested in hearing your stuff. If this other music is of the same caliber as your Wreckers songs, we may be able to work a deal out. Maybe."

We talked about the details. He was not the person who dealt with song acquisition, but he was about to sign a young singer who was a fabulous performer who had only done cover songs in bars. He believed with the right original songs, she could have a hell of a career. Her name was Gina Swinger, she was 19 years old, and Kent thought she could be a big star. He insisted I call him Kent, and told me about George Masonberry, their go-to guy for song acquisition at Crystal Records.

Before we hung up, he asked me about myself—what I did for a living and if I played any other instruments—then he said that he would call George and tell him about me, and that George would call me so we could talk, and he could hear samples of what I had to offer. He sounded sincere, but what did I know? He could have been selling me a line of crap, and I would have no idea. I would have to wait and see.

I did research online about Crystal Records. They were a newer, smaller record company based out of Nashville. They had made good choices in their artists and enjoyed a respectable amount of success for the size of their company. So far, they'd dealt exclusively in country music.

I was surprised when I came home from work the next day and there was a message from George Masonberry on my machine asking me to call him.

"George Masonberry," he answered.

"Hi, Mr. Masonberry. It's Molly Davis returning your call."

"Well, hi there Ms. Davis. I'm glad to hear from you." George Masonberry had a deep voice with a slight southern drawl most women would find sexy. Not quite like Katie's; but slower, charming. Katie was more "Hey, y'all!" while George was more, "Heeyy, y'aaaal."

He wanted to know about my songwriting past, so I told him all about how it started with Katie at age fourteen. I told him how it had only been the last few years that I'd been writing stuff that wasn't Wreckers material, but every bit as good. He told me that since he'd never heard any of the Wreckers stuff, my opinion didn't mean anything to him.

"So what I want you to do, Molly, is go grab your guitar, put me on speaker phone, and let me hear what you got for me," he instructed.

So I did. I assumed he'd want to hear pieces of a few songs to get a sample of what I had. I ended up playing every song I wrote that I considered commercially sellable, which was fifteen songs. We were on the phone for a long time.

After I was done playing, I swear I heard him smile. "Molly? I think you and I are going to make each other very happy."

"That's good to hear," I told him. "What's our next step?"

We talked more about the song acquisition process, when we'd discuss the financial end of it, and contracts. The phone call was a huge success.

I called Kent to thank him. "George called me today, and it went well. Looks like Crystal Records may have a new songwriter."

Kent had the slightest of accents, as if he'd worked hard to get rid of it, but couldn't mask it entirely. "That's good to hear. Sounds like you'll be spending time in Nashville here with me."

"And Gina Swinger," I said, though I couldn't imagine I'd have to spend much time in Nashville.

"Of course," he said.

I had been on the phone for hours and was dying to be off of it; nevertheless I had to call Katie and tell her the highlights. She was happy for me, as I knew she would be. If I could earn money as a songwriter, she would get a huge ego boost since she was the one who taught me how to play guitar, sing back up, and write songs.

"You know, if I can turn this into a second career it will be all thanks to you, right?" I told her.

"So long as you acknowledge it," she said. "What do you think would be an appropriate thank you gift for me?"

"A Happy Meal?"

"Keep thinking 'bout that one, Mol."

"I gotta go, I'm sick of the phone. When I get a big, fat check in my hand, I'll go jewelry shopping for you. Deal?"

"Deal."

Not five minutes after I hung up with Katie the phone rang again. Detective Lindsmere. "Hi Detective, did you catch him yet?" I knew his capture was a long shot, but I could still hope.

"Sorry, Ms. Davis, no. I called to tell you that Belinda Nord is being arraigned in a few days. She's expected to plead guilty."

"That's good," I said.

"She's agreed to work with the police to catch Bill Smith, or whoever he really is, in return for probation and community service."

My feelings were mixed at that point. On the one hand, she was being punished and helping catch The Creep. On the other hand, she meant to beat me to the point of not being able to fight off The Creep so he could kill me. Of course, she maintained she didn't know he was going to do that. I couldn't say whether I believed her or not.

"Ms. Davis?" Detective Lindsmere asked.

"Yeah, sorry. I don't know how I feel about that."

"I figured. I've talked to her at length, and I got to say I think she's telling the truth. I think that son of a bitch manipulated her to be able to get to you. From what she told me, that night wasn't the first time they'd waited for you to be alone. They actually watched from a distance a couple of times, but your bodyguards were always there."

"So they figured if they kept it up, I would eventually be alone. Did she say she knew about the cameras?"

"She said she didn't know the cameras were there and didn't think to check for them. She also said our suspect wasn't in disguise before she approached you, so he must've done a quick job of it." Detective Lindsmere sighed. "Ms. Davis, this young woman is naïve, and she got played like a fiddle. I really don't think she deserves to be in jail, and I also think that she learned a valuable lesson."

I'd told the detective once that I was glad I beat Belinda Nord's ass. I really wanted to express those sentiments again, but held my tongue.

I took a deep breath. "Do you need anything from me?"

"I need for you to let us know if anything, and I mean anything, happens or you remember anything else. And be careful."

No shit, Sherlock.

Chapter 17

I spent more time on the phone over the next week than I had in the past year. As it turned out, Kent had big plans for me and this Gina Swinger chick.

I assumed I would sell Crystal Records my music, get a check, and be on my way.

Not even close.

Upon learning I was a teacher, and therefore not working over the summer, Kent proposed I spend that time in Nashville with Gina Swinger, acting as her mentor. Since Gina was young and relatively inexperienced, he thought I should teach her the songs and help guide her. He didn't seem to think it mattered that I had no experience in professional music making. That I had been playing in a pretty successful band for years and was used to working with teenagers was worth a lot to him.

I had a feeling he didn't want to be the one to deal with her, and so was passing her off to me. That didn't bother me because I had something to offer her. And I insisted on being paid handsomely for my time. The bonus in all this was getting away from my problems for the summer. This was good for me on so many levels, I wasn't going obsess about why they were taking this chance on me.

I was clear that I would not miss a Wreckers Weekend, so I would have to fly home a couple times. He was clear that Gina Swinger's success was almost entirely in my hands and that Crystal Records was taking a huge risk on me. But no pressure.

Since I was going to spend most of my summer out of Michigan, I called Katie and Ram and asked them to come over so I could tell them in person and only have to explain my plans one time. I should've called Cooper, but Ram was easier to talk to.

Ram sat on the arm of the couch. "What's the rush?" he asked, when I finished.

"The record label wants her album out well before next summer hits. I guess Kent scouted another Gina-like singer before he found Gina. They were in talks to sign her when another label came and took her from right under his nose. Offered her more money. His contacts at the other label are telling him that Abigail Stinerson—the artist who was stolen from him—her album is coming out around next summer, so Crystal Records wants Gina's album out by March. That way, they can have a couple of hit songs on the radio by the time summer concert season rolls around and get her to open for a big name act on one of the summer tours. Kent said they always saved a spot or two for the brand-newbies."

Katie gave me the stink eye. "So you'll be spending the whole summer in Nashville?"

"No, not the whole summer. I'm still going to Mississippi with you in June. You know Mama would kill me if I cancelled out on that."

Katie's face relaxed.

"I'll be in town for Wreckers Weekends, of course. But I'll be going back and forth between here and Nashville for the summer."

We talked more about the details. Ram pushed himself off the arm of the couch and began pacing. His eyes were slightly narrowed and his jaw was clenched. He wasn't happy about this. "Who all knows about this—your traveling plans for the summer?"

"So far, just you and Katie. I'll tell my mom. And Kent of course," I answered.

Ram went into planning mode. "I want to keep it that way. Don't tell anyone else where you're going this summer. The more people who know, the more likely it is that The Creep could find out. I don't want him following you there or knowing your house is going to be empty for long periods of time."

Katie, who had been comfortable on the chair, stood next to Ram. I guess this was a show of solidarity between the two of them. "He's right, Mol. You need to listen to him."

I rolled my eyes at the two of them. "You guys don't have to go on the offensive with me on this one. I actually agree. I wasn't even planning on telling my mom the details of my travels, just that I'll be out of town for a while over the summer."

Ram, still planning, said, "I'll tell Cooper, obviously. One of us will escort you to and from the airport when you fly."

"Whatever. We'll work out those details later."

He took a step closer to me, crossed his arms over his chest, and looked me in the eyes. "Yes. We will." Then he added, "I have to get back to the office and let Cooper know, and work on other cases I have." He stared at me for a few seconds then headed for the door. "Bye, ladies," he added on his way out.

When he left, Katie sat back down and told me to do the same. "What?" I asked.

"Ram cares for you."

"Duh. I had that figured out a long time ago."

She pretended to investigate her fingernails so she wouldn't have to look at me. "And you care about him. So what's the hold up?"

I shrugged. "I'm not ready to go there. Can we leave this topic alone?"

She dropped her hands and looked at me. "You know what, Mol? No. We can't. Don't think I haven't noticed you're shutting me out. I knew you needed space, but now I'm getting pissed." She huffed. "This sucks, you know that?" She stood up to leave.

"Katie, sit down. I'm sorry."

She turned around and sprawled on my couch.

I stood up and started folding the blanket on the back of the couch so my hands were occupied. "Okay. There's nothing going on between me and Ram, but there's something kinda there, you know?"

"What do you mean, 'kinda there'?"

"Like . . . I think he's interested in me."

Katie sat up. "And what about you? You interested in him?"

I shrugged.

"What do you mean?" She mimicked my shrug. "You don't know if you're interested in him?"

I draped the refolded blanket on the back of the couch. "Well, I'd be lying if I said I didn't think he was gorgeous, had a nice body, was nice, and that I genuinely like him."

"And you think he might be interested in you, which he is by the way. It's obvious as hell. And you like him. So for craps sake what is the problem?"

I really didn't want to voice this next part out loud, so I waited to answer. After a minute of silence, and after Katie pulled me down onto the couch with her and hugged me, I told her. "I don't know. I can't explain it. Okay, part of me wants him. Badly. But Katie, there's such a big part of me that is scared shitless. I'm not ready. It's like. . . like I don't have anything to give him. Or anyone. I have to work out issues in my head first. I'm sorry."

Katie stayed there and hugged me for another minute. "Don't be sorry. I'm sorry I pushed. Don't shut me out. Okay?"

"Okay."

I spent the next month getting ready. Mama really wanted me and Katie to come for a visit when the school year let out, and I had agreed. Between planning for Mississippi and Nashville, I needed to get everything in order.

I was still cautious, always on the lookout for The Creep, but at least I had other things to occupy my mind. I spent a lot of time via email working out the details of what, exactly, was going to go on with Gina Swinger in Nashville.

Out of the fifteen songs I had, George and Kent wanted nine of them for the album. Other songwriters would supply the rest of Gina's tracks. Crystal Records also purchased a few other songs from me to keep on the back burner for other artists. Two they wanted nothing to do with.

I was told that this was highly unusual: very few new songwriters have so much of their music used.

The one item we still had to work out was how much I was going to be paid. This was one area neither George nor Kent would discuss with me over the phone. I had done as much research as I possibly could, but still had no idea what to expect and was extremely nervous. After consulting a lawyer about the basics of what I should expect, I was going to act on my own behalf. From the research I had done, and from talking to Kent and George, Crystal Records had a fairly laid back vibe to it, so I didn't want to go in all balls-to-the-wall with a cutthroat lawyer. I had gotten my hands on sample contracts, so I wasn't going in totally blind. And God bless the Internet, because it had a lot of information I was able to absorb and make myself at least seem knowledgeable.

I had to make a day trip to Nashville in early June for the negotiations. The people at Crystal Records would discuss money in person only. I used my last personal day at work and hopped on a plane. I had worked out what I wanted to say and went over it a hundred times on the flight. I really wanted to make a good deal for myself. My main concern was whether or not I should accept, or say forget it if they offered me crap.

Kent insisted on picking me up from the airport and driving me to Crystal Records. I walked into the place hoping I looked like a woman of confidence and so much talent I was worth shelling out the bucks. Luckily, the place wasn't intimidating. Everything looked elegant yet comfortable. Tiled floors and modern furniture mixed with a touch of greenery, coupled with employees wearing clothes on the more casual side eased some of my tension.

Our meeting was catered. I liked these people already. We ate first, which gave me a chance to go over everything in my head again. We all talked. They told me about the brief history of the company and they grilled me about, well, almost everything.

The negotiations included founder and President Bubba (no, I'm not kidding) Guthrie, Kent and George, plus Michael, Crystal Records's lawyer. Their secretary joined us, too, probably so I wouldn't be the lone woman.

We ate while we exhausted all of our topics of discussion except one. Finally, it was time to get down to business.

"Gentlemen," I began, hoping my voice hid the fact I was nervous as hell. Everyone's attention was on me, as they sat up a fraction straighter as if remembering, *oh yeah, we're here with this chick for a reason.* "Before we get to the nitty gritty, I want to say a few things." God, my gutsy speech was either going to go very well or very, very badly.

I smiled. "I don't want the bullshit. I want your best offer. I know I'm good, you know I'm good, and you want me to deal with a nineteen-year-old so you don't have to. If you have any hope of continuing a future business relationship, don't screw with me. I will have no trouble jumping ship,"—that was a lie—"if I think I'm going to be treated better somewhere else. Do we understand each other?" I smiled, but only to cover my fear of vomiting all over the floor.

Everyone was silent until Bubba let out this weird snort-laugh thing, then everyone else chuckled, and we got down to business.

As it turned out, my speech went very well for me. I negotiated an amount of money that made me almost pee my pants. I sounded knowledgeable and fairly professional, which was good, considering I'd feared I was going to hyperventilate almost the entire meeting. And the times when my breathing was actually under control I'd worried I'd puke from nerves.

When we were done, Kent walked me to his car. "Do you have any idea what you just did in there, Molly?" he asked, as he opened the door for me.

"I believe it's called negotiating a deal." I climbed in and buckled my seat belt. "Was that not what I did?" Although the afternoon still seemed surreal to me, I was cocky. I'd earned the right to be.

"You did that all right. I think Bubba actually likes you, and considering you resemble his last two ex-wives, that is quite an accomplishment. Well played." Kent slid in beside me.

"I wasn't playing, Kent. I meant every word I said in there. I hate game play. I need you and this company to be straight with me all the time, or I'm out. Remember that."

He started the car. "Believe me Molly, I will not forget. What hotel are you staying at?"

"I'm not. I have a flight in . . ." I checked my watch. "Two hours. To the airport, please. I have to work tomorrow."

Kent raised an eyebrow. "Not after the deal you made."

I smiled even wider. I almost pumped my fists in the air several times and yelled, "I'm Queen of the World!" but kept myself in check. I wanted them to know me as cool and professional, not a total goober. "Believe it or not, I love my job, and I'm good at it. I have no intention of leaving it."

He pulled out of the parking lot. "Woman, I have no doubt you're good at everything you do."

He looked me up and down as he said it, more like he was trying to figure me out instead of trying to check me out. I was still feeling high on myself, so I said, "You're damn right I am."

Chapter 18

School let out for the year on the second Thursday in June, so Katie and I planned to fly to Mississippi the following Monday morning. Mama suggested the visit, and since I hadn't seen her in so long we were long overdue for some face-to-face time. I loved her a ton, and she had always been there for me. Katie said she really worried about me after the attack and wanted to see for herself how I was doing.

I was excited about going. And really, the more time I spent away from home just then, the better.

Mama now lived outside Jackson, Mississippi. Her sister was diagnosed with breast cancer after Katie and I graduated from college, so she moved to Jackson to be near a better cancer hospital, and Mama took an early retirement and went with her to take care of her. Luckily, her sister beat the cancer. Mama stayed since she'd missed home so much. She found a part time job and was happy.

I hadn't been to that area of Mississippi for several years. It was beautiful. Not that Michigan isn't beautiful and scenic, but the south is a different kind of beautiful. So many of the people take pride in the area; as if they were the ones responsible for it. And it's not flat like Michigan, which is kind of neat.

Mama lived in a cute little ranch house. She loved gardening and it showed. Both Katie and Mama had a great sense of what colors work well together. I always wished I was interested in plants and flowers. Sadly, I only like to look at the end result without putting any of the work into it. That's part of the reason I moved into a condo.

We plunked our bags down in the spare bedroom. I took a deep breath and teased, "Ah, land of hillbillies." Katie punched me in the arm.

Without unpacking, we walked outside to enjoy the gorgeous Monday afternoon. I looked around at how picturesque everything appeared and was so glad to have an entire week there. The temperature had me breaking a sweat already, and I uselessly fanned myself with my hands for a minute before giving up. Mama followed us out and stood between Katie and me, one arm around each of us. After she declared us "so pretty we could make a hound dog smile" and hugged us, she motioned for us to sit at the patio table and went inside to get us lemonade.

What is it that made some women seem to not age at all? Mama looked great. Naturally slender with a touch of meat on her bones that made her the perfect amount of curvy, like Katie. Her bottle blond hair always looks perfect, too, like Katie. Screw them both.

Mama came back out carrying a pitcher and three full glasses. We all took a drink then Mama blurted out, "I have a guest coming to dinner tonight."

Oh, hell no. I swear to God if she tried to find me a boyfriend I'm leaving right now. I did not come here for this.

"Mama, Molly's gonna kill you," Katie said.

Mama looked surprised. "Why?

"Because she came here to relax, not get set up on a blind date."

Mama patted my hand. "I'm not fixing you up." Then she looked at Katie. "Your daddy is coming over."

Katie's eyes went wide. Clearly this surprised her. The news surprised me, too. I'd never met Katie's dad. "Daddy? What is he doing here?" Katie asked.

Mama took a breath and told us the whole story. "You know, after your daddy's divorce several years ago, he started calling me to talk. Wanted to figure out what went wrong, that sort of thing. We talked every once in a while, no big deal. About a year ago Bob-See finally moved out on his own and your daddy started calling more and more. He was glad for Bob-See to be out on his own, but he was tore up about it too. It got so that we were talking every week or so. Then after a while we finally realized that we fell back in love with each other. He moved back here about a month ago. Bought himself a duplex and got your Grandmama to move into the other side."

Spelled Bob-See but pronounced Bobsy, Katie's half-brother was fairly unknown to her. His real name was Robert Seeten Culver, Jr. Since her dad was already Bob, Bob-See got stuck with the nickname. I swear, only in the South.

Mama stopped talking. Katie and I stared at her. It was like the era of dad surprises. First my dad popped up and wanted to be a part of my life again, and now Katie's dad hooked back up with Mama. Our lives were becoming a damn soap opera.

"Say something, Katie," Mama said.

"I was just here for Easter, and you didn't think to tell me any of this then?"

This was fascinating. My head swiveled back and forth between Katie and Mama.

"I know," Mama said. "I wanted to. I guess I didn't want to say anything until I knew our getting back together was gonna last. Didn't wanna jinx it or anything. I'm sorry, baby. So what do you think?"

"I . . . I . . ." Katie stopped for a minute to undo her brain scramble. "I'm happy for you Mama. I'm surprised, that's all. So where does he live now?"

"About five miles away, over on Petunia."

I laughed, ruining the moment. They both looked at me. "Okay, how many kids ask Santa or Jesus for their mom and dad to get back together?" I looked at Katie. "And yours did!

It's a Christmas miracle!" I laughed alone, but at least they each cracked a smile.

Katie pulled a Molly: not wanting to talk about it anymore until she'd had a chance to mull it over. So we moved on.

Even though I had talked to Mama on the phone a few times after the attack, she needed to talk about it more to be sure that I was fine. She looked at each of my scars, and tears started dripping down her cheeks. Then she gave me a big hug, while I held my own threatening tears.

Mama released me, but held my shoulders at arm's length and looked me in the eye. "You would tell me if you weren't okay, wouldn't you?"

I gave her one of those smiles that doesn't reach the eyes. It was the best I could do. "Yes. Really, I'm fine, Mama. Swear. I still get mad. I still get weirded out that this guy is still out there, but I have people looking out for me. Seriously, between Katie and Brett and Cooper and Ram, and the rest of the band too, I'm doing good. I promise." That really wasn't a lie. A good deal of the time I was almost back to normal. "Did Katie tell you my big news?"

Katie smiled and said, "Molly's pregnant, Mama."

I slapped her in the arm. "I am not! Katie Scarlett, you're an idiot!"

Rubbing her arm, Katie said, "Ow! Mama knows I'm kidding. Calm down."

Judging by the expression on her face, Mama about had a heart attack. She even held her hand over her heart.

"Oh, that's right," Katie continued. "It would be. . . what's that called when you get pregnant without having sex?"

"Immaculate conception." Mama and I said together.

"Right. That's what it would be, 'cuz Molly hasn't seen any action in a loooooong time."

"Maybe I have and didn't tell you," I said.

"I doubt it. A girl can tell when her best friend has been laid. And you have not been laid. In a really looooooong time."

I winked at Mama. "Shame on you. You raised a rotten daughter."

"Don't I know it," Mama said, and we slapped high fives, while I stuck my tongue out at Katie.

Because I'm so mature, I got Katie back. "Do you want to know how Katie and Brett saved my life the night of the attack? Because she and Brett went into the office for a quickie. Instead of getting lucky, they noticed on the monitor what was happening to me in the alley."

Katie opened her mouth and sucked in a lung full of air. "I never told you that!"

"You didn't have to. Why else would you and Brett have been going into his office on a Saturday night when he had a crowded bar to run? Huh?"

Katie opened her mouth to lie then closed it and shrugged instead. "At least I'm getting some."

"True," I said. "And for the record, I'm sorry for getting in the way of your bah-chick-a-wha-waaaaaaaah." I sang the last part.

"All right," Mama choked. "Enough. I don't need to hear any more about my daughter having . . . let's just be done with that."

I finally told Mama my news about selling my music. I told her all about how I was writing most of the music on the album of a new country singer and how I'd be spending most of the summer traveling between Michigan and Nashville.

Since Katie inherited her musical talent from Mama, although Katie has surpassed anything Mama has ever done musically, she took partial credit. I was happy to give it to her. She gave out what I assumed was a rebel yell when I told her about the deal I negotiated. Then she told me she was proud as punch, which I was pretty sure was good.

Katie, Mama, and I had dinner with Mr. Culver, Katie's dad, and his mom. Then the three of us lounged on the back porch and talked about everything and anything, simply catching up and enjoying being together. Katie learned the family gossip. It was nice to sit and listen to the dramas of other people for a change.

Katie trudged downstairs the next morning a couple hours after Mama and I had already been up a while. "Dang, Molly, you still sleep like crap. Your tossing and turning kept waking me up last night."

"Sorry," I said.

She poured herself a cup of coffee and sat at the kitchen table with me. "You wanna hit the beach today? It's gonna be hot."

I said, "Sure, whatever," trying to sound nonchalant. Really, I was apprehensive about wearing swimwear. My scars wouldn't be covered with a bikini. I had a one-piece suit that covered the scars on my right shoulder and stomach, but who wanted to wear a one piece to the beach on a hot day?

After a long, lazy morning we went upstairs to shower and change. I stood in front of the bathroom mirror in my bikini, angling my body different ways, seeing how bad my scars looked. They were only a few months old, so they were still raised and red. They definitely stood out.

Katie came in, saw me staring at my reflection and said, "Molly, any guy who sees that face and that body isn't going to notice those scars."

I officially rescinded my offer to sell her.

That girl could always be counted on to make me feel better and I loved her for that. "Thanks," I said. "Let's go before I change my mind."

The beach was crowded, so no one paid much attention to us. The temperature was in the low nineties with the occasional cloud offering shade. Hot and perfect for the beach. No one gawked at me as if I were a circus freak, so my scars were as horribly noticeable as I feared.

Chapter 19

Bob-See and Mr. Culver came over for dinner Wednesday evening. Bob-See was nice; pretty much your typical young man. Dressed in designer jeans and a button down shirt, he was clean cut and decent looking with zero resemblance to Katie. He must've gotten his looks from his mother's side of the family. He told us about his new job and apartment with a confidence all guys his age had when they finally started making their own way in life. He told us about Deena, his girlfriend of six months. She was a waitress, aspiring singer and actress, and in his opinion, she was pretty good.

After dinner Mama and Mr. Culver sat outside. Still in the kitchen, Bob-See approached us. "Hey, you girls want to go out tonight?" he asked in a whisper.

Katie whispered back, playing along. "Where? Is it a secret?"

Bob-See looked at his dad and Mama to make sure they couldn't hear. "Okay, here's the truth. Deena came up here with me, but she's staying in a hotel 'cuz no way Grandmama would approve her staying with me at Dad's, and me staying at a hotel would hurt Dad's feelings."

"Okaaaaaay . . ."

"So I hoped we'd head out to the Rusty Nail tonight and meet her there. They got karaoke, and she wants to sing."

"We can do karaoke," I said. "Let's go, Katie."

"Fine with me," Katie said.

We spent a couple more hours with Mama and Mr. Culver. After a quick freshening up, and an outfit change, we left to meet Deena at the bar.

As soon as we walked in, we were waved down by a pretty young woman with really long blond hair. She was dressed to impress in black dress pants and a peasant blouse that was a bit too open at the chest, allowing the world to see her medically enhanced cleavage.

"That's her," Bob-See told us, so we wound through the crowd and made our way to her table. Standing next to her, I felt plain in my jeans and Bon Jovi concert T-shirt. We did the usual getting-to-know-you chitchat, and I was relieved she acted so nice. She and Katie looked over the karaoke menu and were excited about taking their turns to sing. We watched others sing for a while, and the performances were exactly like karaoke anywhere. Some were okay, some were pretty good, and some you got embarrassed for because they believed they were hot stuff, when they weren't.

While I normally enjoyed watching drunk people belt out tunes the most, and the drunker the better, I anxiously awaited Deena's turn since she was an aspiring singer. A woman in her forties sang a mediocre version of Dolly Parton's "Jolene" and then Deena was called up to the stage.

Wow. What a surprise, and unfortunately not in the good way. Deena reminded me of when a new season of American Idol begins and you watch it to hear the really bad people audition, but there is that one particularly horrible singer who gives their heart and soul to the judges. They believed in themselves so much you wanted them to get a pity pass to Hollywood. They get rejected then cry and make a big scene because, God, they really believed they were going to be a star. Then a brave soul finally tells them the truth: honey, you suck.

That's what it felt like listening to Deena sing. She had the heart. She really believed in herself. Oh ugh, no one should have to sit there listening to her without the benefit of a mute button.

About halfway through her song I turned to Katie. "If you so much as even hint to her that I'm now in the songwriting business or have any connections with a record company whatsoever, I will tell this whole bar about the time you farted in biology class and it stunk so bad that Derek Karski got blamed for letting off another stink bomb."

She ignored the threat. "Good Lord, she's so bad. I'm not sure she could carry a tune in a bucket. What if she asks us what we think? She knows we're in a band."

I'd be lying if I said I never lied, but usually I advocate not lying. Not this time. "We lie."

"Agreed," she said.

Katie sang a couple songs and knocked 'em out of the park, as usual. I did a song and sounded pretty kick-ass. Instead of country, I went with 80's rock. I do an awesome Pat Benetar. "Hit Me With Your Best Shot" and "Love Is A Battlefield" are my best numbers.

A few other singers, along with Katie and me, received quite a few compliments, which did not go over well with Deena. Bob-See telling us how good we were didn't help either. She started acting snotty toward us and making passive-aggressive comments. We lied and told her how talented she was. We even sounded sincere, but our assurances weren't good enough for her. I guess she wanted to be the shining star.

Katie went to get a round of drinks for our group. She would have to carry four drinks back to the table herself without help, so I started walking to the bar to grab a couple from her. When I was almost there, Katie turned around with the drinks in her hand, and I saw that Deena was already there. I assumed she was going to take some of the drinks to carry. Instead she bumped right into Katie, spilling the drinks onto her shirt. Deena tried to make it look like an accident. It clearly wasn't.

The bartender saw what happened and started to re-make the drinks.

I snapped. I went from fine to furious instantly. I walked right in Deena's face. "If you can't act like a grown up, you shouldn't go to grown-up places," I growled.

She raised her chin in bratty defiance. "It was an accident."

"Bullshit," I said.

Katie took the remade drinks. "Molly, take two of these, and let's go back to the table."

I really wanted to hit the bitch. I didn't, I took the drinks, and we returned to the table where Bob-See was waiting for us. Katie put down the drinks and told him, "You need to take your little girlfriend back to the hotel."

He looked between the three of us. "Why?"

"Because your sister and her friend are jealous," Deena said from behind us.

Katie choked in that *are you serious?* way, and I just glared. We had to let the incident go and leave. Thank God we drove separately from Bob-See and Deena, because I didn't think a car ride together was a good idea. Somebody might have gotten their ass pummeled in the back seat.

When we were settled in the car, Katie started laughing. "Good Lord, I was waiting for you to hit her," she told me.

I finished programming the GPS toward Mama's then pulled into the street. "Not gonna lie. I wanted to. I still have anger issues and hitting her would've felt really good, but I think I would've re-injured my shoulder."

"Plus you don't want to land in jail," she said.

Oh yeah, that too. "Sorry if I made your relationship with Bob-See weird," I said.

"He's my half-brother and I hardly know him. It's already weird. And you didn't do anything, she did."

We sang along to the radio on the ride back. When we were almost at Mama's, Katie asked, "What do you mean you still have anger issues?"

"I get angry more often, and little things tend to set me off. Stupid stuff. About a month ago I got really mad because every time I went to close my freezer door it would pop back open, and I couldn't figure out what was making it do that. Next thing I know I whipped a bunch of stuff out of it and started slamming the door like, repeatedly. I snapped out of it after a minute." I shrugged.

She didn't say anything so I continued. "Over Spring break, Ram called me to see if I was okay, and I went off on him. He didn't deserve it. I was drunk."

"You got drunk on Spring break? By yourself?" she asked.

"Yeah. The night I called you and told you about my dad."

"Have you talked to him yet?"

"No. He's called me twice. I let the machine get it."

I pulled into the driveway. We went inside as quietly as possible, since Mama was sleeping. When we were lying in bed, Katie said, "I think you should call your dad."

"I know. Do you think your parents will get remarried?"

She propped up her head with her hand. "I don't know. It would be weird, right?"

"No, not weird. I think it's sweet."

"I guess," she said.

Both of us drifted off to sleep, but only one of us had visions of ass beatings dancing in her head.

All in all, the trip to visit Mama was nice. We hung out at the beach, went shopping, and ate dinner with Mama, Mr. Culver, and his mother a couple more times. My time in Mississippi was relaxing and unexciting for the most part, which was the point, since my summer was going to be very busy.

Bob-See wasn't mad at Katie for the bar incident. He called Katie and said he was able to cool Deena down after telling her how good she was. He told us she took another turn singing that night and felt better. I was grateful he never asked us our opinion of her, and that no one told them about my new music connections.

Katie and I flew home on Monday afternoon, and I was flying out again Thursday. That gave me a week and a half in Nashville before coming home for a Wreckers Weekend. I left myself two and a half days to get ready for my new adventure. I had to unpack, do laundry, and repack. Yuck. Katie would keep an eye on my house and get my mail, and I pay almost all of my bills online, so no worries there.

I called Ram to make sure he had the details of my flight numbers, departure times, and the hotel I where I was staying. I wanted to hear his voice, so I didn't email him. For once he didn't answer his phone, so I left the information on his voicemail. About an hour later he knocked on my door.

"Hey, what's up? Come on in," I said opening the door. "I just left you a message with my flight and hotel info."

"I got it. I wanted to stop by and see how your trip to Mississippi went." He walked to the couch and sat down.

I sat on the chair. "My trip was good. Except for almost knocking someone on her ass, it was rather uneventful and relaxing."

He gave a half smile. "Glad to hear it. Especially the part about not knocking someone on her ass."

"How was everything around here? How was your week?" I asked.

"Okay," he answered. There was an expression on his face that let me know he had more to say.

"So explain 'okay'. There's obviously more to that statement."

"Well, there was a stabbing at Smarty's bar, the one on West Road. We thought there was a chance the suspect was The Creep. It wasn't," he said.

"How do you know?"

"He doesn't seem to fit with the guy from the video surveillance. We also took his mug shot to Belinda Nord, and she said the man in the picture wasn't him. I'm only bringing it up because I want to show it to you to be sure." He took out a photo and handed it to me.

I studied the picture for about ten seconds. "It's not him. This guy's face is too . . . big. His features are bigger. I can't say with a hundred percent certainty that it's not him, but I don't think it is."

He took the photo back. "We wanted you to have a look anyway." He stood up. "I'll be here Thursday morning at seven a.m. to pick you up for the airport."

"Okay." I stood up too. "Hey, I was about to make myself dinner. If you're hungry, feel free to stay and eat."

He went from looking at me in the eyes to looking off in the distance. "Thanks, but I have plans. I need to get going before I'm late."

It hit me then that he wasn't dressed like he normally was. When he was at the bar he wore old jeans and T-shirts to fit in with the crowd. When I saw him during the day he was usually in casual business attire, occasionally jeans and T-shirt. That evening he was wearing nice jeans and a nice shirt, the kind of outfit that showed he was making an effort to look nice without being too formal. He was clean-shaven and smelled really good. He always smelled really good, but coupled with the way he was dressed . . . oh my God, he had a date.

"Sure. Just wanted to offer. No big deal, I was going to make dinner anyway, and you're always so nice to me, and I thought—never mind. I'll see you Thursday morning." I cut myself off from babbling.

We said goodbye, and he left. To his date. I wondered if this was a first date or an I'm-going-to-spend-the-night-at-her-place level of date. Wow, I really didn't know all that much about Caleb Ramsey. Did I have any right whatsoever to be jealous? No. Was I anyway? A little. A little and a half. Okay, a lot. Damn it.

Chapter 20

I spent as much time as I could with Katie because I was going to miss her. We'd keep in touch daily, or close to it, but still, she wouldn't be a short drive away.

I wanted to get the call to my dad out of the way. I was still irritated with him for calling my mom and asking her if I'd come to his wedding. I was secretly hoping that when I called he wouldn't be home. He answered on the second ring.

"Molly?" he said. It's weird how nobody answered "hello" anymore because of caller ID.

"Hi. Mom said you wanted to talk to me." Was the irritation coming through in my voice? I didn't know.

"I do. How have you been?" he asked.

"Great. Same as always." Which he would know was not true if he had bothered to be a father to me for all those years.

"How's the teaching going?"

"Great. Same as always." At least this was actually true.

Silence. I wasn't going to break it. He was the one who wanted to talk to me, so I was going to make him take the initiative in the conversation.

He let out a big sigh. "Okay, we have issues between us. I want to talk to you in person. Can we meet for dinner? I have a lot to tell you."

"Like what? You're getting married? Congratulations," I said, knowing for sure my irritation was shining through in all its glory. "I don't even know where you live."

"Yes, I'm getting married. I live in Bowling Green. It's just over an hour—"

"I know where it is." God, how long has he lived so close?

"Can I take you to dinner? Please? I really want to see you."

"Bad timing. I'm going out of town tomorrow morning and won't really be back until the end of August. Anything you need to say has to be now or wait for a couple months."

"Well I'll tell you this now. I'm getting married in October to a wonderful woman named Joy. I also want to say I'm sorry for everything and wanted to know if we could start over."

This was pretty much what I'd expected him to say, so I didn't respond right away. Part of me wanted so say, *too little, too late,* and hang up. Part of me wanted to hear him out. "Listen, I don't want to get into this now. I have a lot on my plate. I'll call you at the end of August, and we can go out to dinner then. That's all I can give you right now."

"I understand. Despite what you think, I love you, Molly. Please call me when you get back. We really need to talk."

"Yup, bye," I said and hung up, glad that was out of the way. I didn't want to deal with those feelings right now.

I had a new challenge waiting for me.

Thursday came, and I was all ready for Nashville. I was nervous as hell. There were so many variables that could make this deal a disaster. What if Gina and I didn't get along? What if Kent and I didn't get along? What if Gina hated my music? What if I hated Gina's singing? The only thing for me to do was hope for the best and remember if I tried really hard, I mean, really dug down deep, I could get along with anybody. Probably.

At five minutes to seven Ram came to pick me up and loaded everything in his truck without letting me carry a thing. Being overly gallant was his way of making up for not being able to take Katie and me to the airport when we flew to Mississippi. I wasn't taking my guitars with me since I could use the studio's instruments. We buckled in, and he headed for the airport.

I couldn't resist. "How was your date the other night?" I asked.

"How did you know I had a date?"

"I could just tell."

"It was fine. Are you nervous?"

Believe me when I say I noticed how he quickly changed the subject to avoid talking about his date; I was the queen of subject switching. "Very. I feel like I did my first day of teaching. Almost like I'm gonna puke. Don't worry, I'm not. I think."

"How can you be that nervous? You've been writing songs for a long time."

"This is *so* different." He didn't say anything so I assumed he expected me to explain. "Okay, first, a freaking lot of money was paid for my work. There's a huge weight on my shoulders for this to be a success. You can be the best singer in the world, but if your songs are crap, no one is going to listen to you or, more importantly, buy your music. Second, writing songs and then performing them is like . . . how can I explain this?" I took a second to think of a fitting analogy. "It's like reading your diary out loud. Before, I always hid behind Katie because we wrote most of the songs together. She performed them, ya know, so the assumption was that those words were her feelings, her thoughts. Everyone working with this album will know these words came from *me*. That scares the hell out of me."

He glanced at me for a second. "You mean—" dramatic gasp "people might actually feel they know you? Oh no!"

Smart ass. I ignored him. "And sometimes you write because you feel something right at *that moment,* but once you finish the song you don't feel that way anymore, but you did at the time. Or sometimes you can write about someone else's life but they don't know that it's not your life in those words, or sometimes you start writing about stuff you've been through and realize it doesn't flow very well, so you have to, like, make stuff up or borrow from someone else's life but mostly it's *your* thoughts and *your* feelings that everyone is going to hear and judge." Whew. I felt better getting that out. Wait, I had more. "I mean, I seriously don't know how these people who write and perform their own music do it." I looked at Ram. "Could you get up on stage and tell everyone what you think, dream, desire? Could you let people in like that?"

He looked at me as if to answer, but I cut him off. "And did I mention the money part? If these songs don't deliver, I'll be a complete failure. A complete failure with a big fat bank account is still a failure."

"Are you done?"

I let out a big sigh, leaned forward so my elbows were on my knees and rubbed my forehead. "Yeah. I think I just gave myself a stress headache."

"Well first, I don't think you're capable of failure. And second, you're not going to perform the songs so unless people read the fine print the general population won't know it's you."

Still massaging my forehead I said, "I hope you're right on both counts."

He reached over with his right hand and rubbed up and down my back, probably to be soothing. Instead, it made the butterflies worse. "You're going to be fine, Princess."

The plane ride was uneventful. I had no trouble getting my rental car or finding my hotel. Everything was going as planned except I still felt Ram's hand on my back, even hours later. I called Kent once I was settled into the hotel and told him I'd be at his office within the hour.

I arrived at Crystal Records without problem, thanks to GPS. The building housing the recording studio was next door to the record company. Convenient, which I guess was the point. Kent wanted to show me around since I would be spending so much time there with Gina. I'd meet Gina and her mother the next day.

I toured the record company and the recording studio, then was introduced to a bunch of people. Once done, we headed back to Kent's office and he explained to me how Crystal Records was finally making a bigger name for themselves and that they were counting on Gina to help them. Again, no pressure.

"You ready?" he asked.

"Of course."

"Great. Tomorrow we'll all meet here at nine a.m., get to know one another. When you're ready, I want you to head to the studio and show her what you have for her. We're working on getting her band together, still deciding between a couple people. All that will be finalized by the beginning of next week. For the next few days, I want you getting familiar with each other. You two are going to be spending an awful lot of time together."

I gave my best reassuring smile. "Kent, I got this. We're going to get along fine. She's going to make a great album, and you're going to make a lot of money." I had no idea if any of this was true, but he seemed to need to hear it.

He nodded. "That's what I wanted to hear." He slapped his hands on his desk. "So, you hungry? I would like to introduce you to the nicer restaurants here."

"Generally I'm always hungry. How nice? Do I need to go back to the hotel and change first?"

Kent stood, and I followed suit. Then he looked me up and down and smiled. "You're good the way you are," he said.

I wanted lunch, so I ignored the appreciative look in his eyes. "Fine. I'll follow you, so don't drive like an idiot."

"No need. I'll drive us. I'll bring you back to your car afterward," he said.

He took me to a nice restaurant, which irritated me. I was wearing a very casual sundress, whereas the other patrons wore nicer attire, including Kent. My initial reaction was, *oh well, I'll never see these people again*. Then I remembered I'd be spending a lot of time in Nashville for the next couple months so I might. Ugh.

We were seated, given the menus, and asked what we wanted to drink.

"Wine?" Kent asked.

"Help yourself. I hate wine. Keep in mind if you have more than a couple glasses, I'm driving myself back to the hotel." I looked at the waiter and said, "Iced tea please."

"Make that two," Kent said.

I was apprehensive sitting there with Kent. Being together in a nice restaurant had a date vibe to it, thanks to our not knowing each other very well.

"So, Molly. Tell me more about yourself that didn't come out at the slaughtering," he said, referring to the negotiations meeting. "What else is there? Is there a boyfriend?"

I really didn't want to spend the next hour talking about myself. "You first," I said. "All I know about you is that you work as a talent scout and agent. What else is there? You married?"

He smiled. "Divorced. Two teenage girls. My ex-wife and I believed the love we had as teenagers would last forever. After two kids, we found out that wasn't the case. With us anyway."

"Hmm. I never would've pegged you as having teenagers." He didn't look that much older than me.

"We had them real young." He paused for a moment. "Your turn."

"Not married, no boyfriend, no kids, no pets," I said.

"So what does the rest of the band think about what you're doing?"

I shrugged. "They don't care. They're supportive, of course. They all have their own lives and aren't overly concerned with mine." Except when it came to The Creep. "Katie loves it, since she's the one that taught me everything I know. Musically that is."

We sat in silence. A couple times it seemed as if he was going to say or ask something, but didn't. Finally, our food came, which was a nice distraction. The first bite had me in heaven. "Oh yum," I said.

Kent raised an eyebrow. "You sure do have a way with words, no wonder you write songs."

We engaged in superficial conversation during dinner. I cleared my plate and cringed. I wished I'd checked out the hotel exercise facilities. If I was going to keep eating like that, I'd need a new wardrobe before I returned to work.

"What's wrong?" Kent asked.

"Nothing. I'm hoping the hotel has a good gym. I don't want to leave here double the size I am now. I just spent a week in Mississippi and barely worked out there at all, and I couldn't workout at all for a while after—" *the attack* "—my car accident."

He gave one of those *oh geez* expressions. "So you're one of those women afraid of getting fat?"

"Well . . . kind of. If I eat like a pig and don't burn it off the results will not be good." I realize I sound like one of those stupid, weight obsessive women. I wasn't neurotic about my weight, though. I simply felt ten times better after a good, strenuous, beat-my-own-ass type of workout.

Kent gave me a funny look, then cleared his throat. Apparently this was the opening he'd been looking for. "You know, I have a nice gym at my house. Treadmill, elliptical, stair stepper thing, free weights, dumb bells, other machines."

"Good for you," I told him.

"That you can use."

"Uh, thanks. I think the hotel gym will get me by," I said.

"Well what I meant to say was that you can stay with me instead of a hotel and use my gym while you stay."

Whoa Nelly, where did that come from? Was this like, some sort of sexual proposition? Oh my God, was Katie right and others could sense that I hadn't had sex in a really long time? Was he hitting on me, or was I being high on myself again? Did he actually think I would agree to this?

"I'll pass, thanks anyway. Are you ready?" Not only did I not want to finish that conversation, I wanted to leave. Badly.

Kent reached over and put his hand on my arm, then yanked it off. "Molly, listen. I have a big house with extra bedrooms. It makes no sense for you to stay in a hotel when I have plenty of room for you. You'd be more comfortable in my house than you would in a hotel anyway, with the length of time you're staying."

How naïve did he think I was? "Oh, gee, how would I ever repay you for your generosity?"

Kent raised an eyebrow. "It wouldn't be like that. It would be strictly professional."

"So what's in it for you?" I asked.

"I'd be able to keep tabs on you." He put his hands out as if to say *wait*. "Tabs on how the album is coming along. You know we want to rush this album out without compromising quality. I won't micromanage you, but I need to know how everything's going all the time. It's a win-win."

I had to clear the air on his intentions. "Nothing else? Because I get the vibe from you that you... you know..." *Want to see me with my clothes off and you on.*

"This arrangement would be strictly business. No inappropriate behavior, I promise."

I raised my eyebrows, letting him know he still hadn't answered the question.

"You are a beautiful, smart, talented woman. I'd have to be gay to not be attracted to you."

The woman in me blushed at one of the best compliments I had ever received.

I sat there for a minute. I hated the idea of staying in a hotel. He was right about a house being more comfortable. But if he thought this was a way to get in my pants, he needed to think again.

He continued trying to convince me. "I even have another car you could use instead of a rental. And did I mention I have one of those lap pools? The kind where you stay in place and can still swim? I think it's one of the stupidest things I've ever seen, but my oldest daughter is a swimmer so I had one installed a few years ago."

Lap swimming? Continue on, good sir.

"Plus I have a top of the line security system so you'd be totally safe."

Bam, that was where it hit me. Kent asking me to stay in his house while insisting he would keep his paws to himself was odd. The whole conversation reeked of Caleb Ramsey.

I put up a finger. "Hold on a minute," I told him, then dug my phone out of my purse to call Ram. A waiter walked past as I was dialing and gave me a disgusted look. I stuck my tongue out at him.

"What's up, Princess? Are you okay?" Ram greeted me.

In my typical cut-to-the-chase fashion, I asked him, "So living with Kent for the summer was your idea so he could keep an eye on me? You want him to be my pseudo-bodyguard when I'm in Nashville?"

"Yes," he said.

That was one thing I loved about Ram—he told the truth right away. He didn't pussyfoot around anything. I totally respected that even though his decisions frustrated me sometimes.

"Let me guess: You had him checked out, and when he came out clean you called him and set this up?"

"Yes," he said again.

I sighed loudly. "Is there a reason you didn't come to me with this?"

"Because you're so pig headed I didn't think you'd agree to it if I brought it up with you. If it makes any difference, we would feel much better with you at Kent's house. It would be safer."

"Who are *we*?" I asked.

"Me. Cooper. And I assume Katie and Brett would like this better as well."

I cupped my hand over my mouth and whispered, "Did you tell him what happened?"

"I didn't tell him anything, just that I was concerned for your safety."

I stood up and walked away from Kent so I could have privacy. Still whispering I asked, "You don't have any qualms about going behind my back to set me up to stay at a man's house who I barely know? How do you know he's not a sicko pervert?"

"I had him checked out, and I talked to him several times on the phone. I was considering threatening him if he did anything that made you uncomfortable. I knew if you actually agreed to this then you'd threaten him yourself, so I didn't bother." In a serious tone he added, "Princess, don't turn this down to be stubborn. At least think about it for a night before you say no."

"I was about to say I can't believe you did this, but I can."

"I told him to play up the workout equipment. Did that work?"

"Duh, of course it did."

"Here's a free tip: thirty-year-olds shouldn't be using the word *duh* anymore."

Fucker. "So let's see . . . you want me, while I'm in Nashville, to live with a single, rich, good-looking man?"

The amusement left his voice. "Princess, I want you, while you're in Nashville, to *be* safe and *feel* safe."

"So you really think staying with Kent is better for me?" I asked.

"Duh," he said.

I snort-laughed. "Okay, I'll think about it. Ram, if I do this and don't like it, I'm going back to a hotel, and I don't want any crap about it. Deal?"

"Deal," he said.

We hung up, and I went back to the table. Kent was sitting back in his chair with his hand on his chin. Thinking mode.

"So Ram called you and bullied you into letting me stay with you?" I said to him.

"He didn't bully me into anything. I'm completely fine with it. It really would help me feel better about the album. I wasn't lying about that. I want to shove this album in the Record Company Whose Name I Won't Speak's face."

I sat there staring at him for a while. I think I was trying to see something in his eyes that would lead me to think he was a slime ball. All I saw was a set of eyes that stared back at me. Finally I said, "Okay. We'll have to set ground rules if I'm going to stay at your house."

"Such as?" he asked

"Well, I don't want to walk in on like, a big orgy going on in the middle of your living room, or anything like that."

Kent raised an eyebrow. "Fine. I'll conduct all my wild orgies in my bedroom. I'll even lock the door. Satisfied?"

"You know what I mean."

"What the hell kind of man do you think I am? Damn, woman."

"So no wild parties or . . . whatever?"

He sighed. "No. Occasionally I have a woman spend the night. That's it. And although I can't say I'm real big on the idea of you bringing any strange men into my home, I'll allow it. I don't expect you to abstain for the summer."

"I didn't come here to man hunt, so don't worry about me bringing anyone home."

"What else?" he asked.

I looked him in the eyes and gave him a look that was meant to imply I was dead serious. "If you hit on me, or put your hands on me, or 'accidentally' walk in on me naked or anything like that I will *beat you senseless.* Are we clear on that?"

He smiled. "Quite. Don't think that rule applies to you. Feel free hit on me, put your hands on me, or walk in on me naked any time you choose."

I leaned back into my chair and let my arms flop down. "Okay, now see, you're ruining it."

He raised one eyebrow. "I'm kidding, Molly. I won't do anything inappropriate. I do have two daughters that stay with me once in a while. Are you okay with that?"

"Yeah. Why wouldn't I be? How old are they? What are their names?"

He told me briefly about his daughters. Haley was fifteen and was the swimmer. Riley was thirteen and was more into books than sports.

We finished dinner and he drove me back to Crystal Records so I could get my rental car. I got all my things together at the hotel and loaded them in the trunk. I refused to checkout just yet, though, in case Kent proved too awkward to live with. Or in case I was a pain in his ass and he kicked me out.

Chapter 21

Thanks to the lady on the GPS, I didn't pay attention to directions to Kent's place. I was too busy studying the grandeur of homes leading me to where I was going to be staying.

When the lady told me my destination was on the right, I looked right, and almost hit a tree because I accidentally pulled the steering wheel right as well. I screamed and slammed on my brakes, then slowly pulled into the garage Kent had open and waiting for me.

Kent's house was beautiful. The neighborhood homes were all architecturally different, but equally breathtaking and *huge*. His house was easily five thousand square feet by my guesstimation. There were five bedrooms and five and a half bathrooms, a dream family room with a huge flat screen, and a kitchen that made me want to stay in all day and cook. Every room was obviously professionally decorated.

He and his daughters took up three of the bedrooms, so there were two guest rooms. I chose the one that was farthest away from Kent's. There was no denying that I would be way more comfortable at his house. Once I'd unpacked, I checked out his exercise room in the basement. It had everything I could possibly need to get in a good workout, even the floor space to do yoga.

If Kent's exercise room wasn't enough to convince me that staying at a hotel was not the way to go, my spacious and elegant bathroom was. It had a custom shower that spoke to me. *Come to me, Molly,* it said. The shower was a big walk in and had three different shower heads: one removable shower head in the traditional spot, one at the back and one coming from overhead. A small silver box inset into the wall let me program it for a custom shower experience.

Loooooove me, the shower said. I started falling in love with it right then.

I woke up the next day excited and nervous. The day I would officially start to share my music with the rest of the world outside of Brett's was here; the day that would lead to my music writing career being successful or going down the toilet. I took an extra long shower to help rid me of the nerves.

The bed in the room I claimed as mine was comfortable, and I was able to actually get several hours of sleep that first night, which was a pleasant surprise. Luckily for me I'm used to sleeping like crap, so even if I didn't get eight hours, I would be able to get through my day perfectly fine. Surprisingly, I was over the weirdness of sleeping in an almost-stranger's house.

Kent had left before I did, so I met up with him at his office. I walked into Crystal Records and had barely told Kent good morning when two women walked into his office: Gina Swinger and her mother Cindy.

Gina was a pretty young woman, with long, black hair and blue eyes—though I suspected the color came from contacts. I was surprised to find out that they were from McComb, Ohio, which was only about an hour and a half from where I lived in Brownstown. You could get there by taking I-75 straight south. So Kent and the other scouters got to see both Gina and The Song Wreckers without having to fly into different airports. Convenient.

I needed to learn all I could about Gina so I would know how to best work with her. This was where my teacher skills would come in handy. I'd had to learn to work with all types and to adjust my teaching style to different learning styles.

Kent left us alone and went and did whatever the heck head talent scouts did all day. I interviewed Gina.

"Kent said you don't play guitar. Do you play any instrument?" I asked.

"No. Is that a problem?"

"No, but I'm going to teach you to play guitar. If you're going to be a singer, you need to be able to play, if for no other reason than chicks who play guitar are cool."

That made her smile. "Okay."

I'm fairly young. I'm hip. You could even say I'm jiggy wit it. I'm also extremely disciplined and take what I do seriously, and I have zero tolerance for drugs. Take care of your body and it will take care of you. I gave Gina my modified version of the "Just Say No!" speech, except I added at the end that if I suspected Gina was doing drugs I would kick her ass and tell her mommy.

Cindy smiled while Gina grimaced like only a teenager could.

We made plans to talk more over lunch. I texted Kent to let him know what we were doing and to recommend a restaurant. Instead of texting back, he walked into his office and told us he would take us to lunch and then over to the recording studio to get set up so we could start working.

After eating entirely way too much again, which I justified by thinking of Kent's workout room, we made ourselves comfortable in the studio. Cindy took to being part of the background, which I appreciated. It seemed like she wasn't going to be a pushy stage mother.

The first thing I did was ask Gina to sing *a capella* so I could learn her voice, her style, even see how often she had to take breaths while singing.

Hot damn, she was good. Really, really good. I sang harmony with her to see if she would lose any of the melody line. She didn't. I took the melody line and told her to sing harmony with me. She could. I picked up a guitar and played while she sang. She was fantastic.

This was going to work.

I played her the songs I wrote that were going on her album. She liked them, if the foot tapping and head bopping were any indication. We ordered dinner delivered to the studio and kept working. Finally, around ten o'clock, I called it a night because we were all obviously tired.

We agreed on a schedule for the next week and a half. Gina was to come with her voice all warmed up to the studio at nine a.m. each day. We would work on the songs by ourselves until her band was finalized. I would spend about an hour every day teaching her how to play guitar.

The first thing I did when I got back to Kent's that night was to call Katie.

She answered the phone, "Well?"

"I don't know if I should be making predictions like this, but I think we got a winner here."

"Tell me all about it. Brett says hi," she said.

"Hi back to him." I paused so she could tell him. "Gina is young, pretty, and talented as hell."

"More talented than me?"

"No one is more talented than you," I said. "And so far, I like her attitude. Her mother is here with her, and she seems okay too."

I told her all the details of my day and found myself almost falling asleep on the phone. She told me she was proud of me and to go to sleep, to which I happily agreed.

Chapter 22

Working on the Gina Swinger album kept me completely busy. I woke up early every morning to workout, then spent the day with Gina and her new band until I was about ready to collapse at the end of the day. The schedule was perfect for me. I barely remembered anything else existed.

Kent had put together first rate musicians. Those people were true professionals. I found myself respecting Cindy Swinger for the way she'd raised Gina. Gina was a hard worker, she never complained, and had no hint of a diva attitude . . . to that point, anyway.

Kent and I got along surprisingly well. I think he liked having another body in his house, and I know I certainly liked staying in his house versus a hotel. My showers every morning were heavenly. I'd worried he'd have different bimbos parading around every night, but he didn't. He brought home one woman, and I only saw her in passing as she was leaving.

One morning Kent joined me for breakfast. As we started eating, he turned to me. "My girls are coming to stay for a few days."

"Okay. When?" I figured our times in the house would overlap eventually.

"Well, they're supposed to come tomorrow."

"Soooo . . ." I prompted.

"When I told my ex-wife about you staying here, she threatened to not let them come without meeting you first."

"Smart woman," I said. "When do you want me to meet her?"

He looked surprised. "You're okay with this? I worried it might offend you."

"Why wouldn't I be okay with this? If I was a mother, I wouldn't let my children stay in the same house with some strange woman. For all she knows, I'm a psychopath."

Kent's body relaxed. "This is a huge weight off my shoulders so thanks. My ex and I have actually been getting along the last few years, and I want to keep that going. Why don't you end early tonight, and I'll have the three of us here for dinner."

"Sounds like a plan. What time?" I asked.

"How about six-thirty?"

I was curious as to what Kent's ex-wife would act like toward me. Bitter shrew? Happy housewife? Whatever, I could handle her. But hopefully, I'd win her over too.

When I returned to Kent's that evening, he and his ex, Lisa-Anne, were in the living room talking. I said hi to Kent then walked up to Lisa-Anne and shook her hand.

I gave my best I-have-your-child's-best-interest-at-heart smile. "Hi Lisa-Anne. Molly Davis. Nice to meet you."

Caught off guard by my forwardness, or maybe my firm handshake—I couldn't help it, I hate when women give those wimpy, limp-wristed handshakes—she frowned. Being southern, she recovered quickly, presenting me with a warm smile. "Nice to meet you too," she said. "Kent told me you're staying here while working for him?"

I sat on the couch and indicated for her to do the same. "That's right. I avoided staying at a hotel, and he gets to keep tabs on me to make sure I'm earning what he's paying me. I'm sure you have more questions so fire away."

Lisa-Anne gave me a strange look, then looked at Kent questioningly.

Smiling, Kent said, "Molly's subtle like a bag of bricks upside your head to get your attention is subtle, Lisa-Anne. You get used to it eventually."

"Oh," said Lisa-Anne. "Well, Kent says you're a teacher?"

Kent obviously played up the parts of me he knew would win points with her. "Yes. I teach high school, but I'm also a songwriter. It just worked out that his company liked my music for a new artist he's representing. And with me being used to working with teenagers, not to mention that I've been in a band for all of my adult life, he thought it would be a good idea to bring me on board to help her out—be a mentor, coach her through the songs, things like that. And he's also hoping to forge a professional relationship that will make him a lot of money in the future." I smiled at Kent with that last statement.

"Like I said, bag of bricks."

Lisa-Anne didn't say anything for a while. When she finally spoke, her tone held a note of suspicion. "I don't mean any disrespect, Molly. Why do you need to stay here instead of at a hotel?"

When Kent told me his ex-wife wanted to meet me, I figured she'd be racking her brain to figure out why I wasn't staying at a hotel or renting a house like Cindy and Gina. My staying with Kent certainly wasn't the norm and wasn't professional in any way. I'm sure it had *I'm screwing your ex-husband to get into the music industry* written all over it. So I intended to tell them both the truth. If either one of them didn't want their daughters there with me, that was okay. I could stay at a hotel while they were there.

I sat up straight. It didn't matter that I hated talking about what happened to me. I gave a half smile that I knew looked forced. "Okay, there's a reason why I agreed to stay here." I looked at Kent. "Kent, remember when Caleb Ramsey called you to set this up?"

"Yes," he said, apprehensively

"Well, he did that because he's kind of my bodyguard. Sort of. And he's a private investigator working on a case involving me." I took big breath and continued. "Last summer, I started getting unwanted attention from a psycho. The Creep. That's what I nicknamed him."

I definitely had both their attention now. "What kind of attention?" Kent asked.

"He started leaving me creepy things, always having to do with flowers. At first, I hoped it was a joke. After several times I knew it wasn't. The highlight was when he left rose petals and a dead, mutilated animal on my front porch."

Lisa-Anne had a look of disgust on her face. "Oh my goodness," she said.

"Yeah, it gets worse. This past March he attacked me after a show. He stabbed me a few times." I stood and showed them the scars. Lisa-Anne put her hand over her mouth. "Luckily, as he was getting ready to stab me again, my best friend Katie and her boyfriend Brett ran out to help me. They saved my life. But The Creep ran away and was never caught. Ram—that's what everyone calls Caleb Ramsey—is convinced it will be better if I stay here since it's in a gated community with a good security system. He thinks I'll be safer here." I stopped to let everything I'd said sink in.

Finally Kent spoke. "Damn. I knew there had to be a good reason why he wanted you here. I had no idea it would be something like that." He had clenched his pants in his hands as I was telling the story and now had two wrinkled spots, one on each leg.

I wanted to ease any fears they had. "Only a few people know where I'm at. We wanted to keep my traveling this summer on the down low." I looked directly at Lisa-Anne. "If you're not okay with your girls being here with me, I totally understand. It really is no big deal for me to go to a hotel. In fact, I would love to not have to look at your dog of an ex-husband every morning." I was kidding with this last part, but I wanted Lisa-Anne and Kent to know that there would be no hard feelings if they didn't want me there any longer.

Kent and Lisa-Anne looked at each other. "She needs to be here," Lisa-Anne said.

"I agree," Kent said.

"Are you sure? I don't think The Creep will follow me here, but I can't be sure of anything. I can't even identify this guy since he was in disguise that night. I have no idea who he is, if he knows me, nothing."

Lisa-Anne came over and put her hand on mine. "I'm sorry that happened to you, and I want you to stay here when you're in town."

Her voice rang with sincerity. I gave her a smile of gratitude. "Thank you," I said. "That means a lot. Kent, I'm sorry I didn't tell you this before. I really don't tell anyone."

"I get it, Molly. I do."

Lisa-Anne, Kent, and I then had dinner together. I really liked Lisa-Anne. She told me all about Haley and Riley. She told me that Haley was fifteen, boy crazy, and had lots of attitude and that Riley was thirteen and a bit of a loner.

I reminded her that I dealt with those situations every day at my real job, and that nothing her kids would do could faze me. She also told me about her husband, Beau, but not too much since it made Kent squirm.

Poor Kent didn't get many words in edgewise while Lisa-Anne and I talked. Having dinner together must've squashed any misgivings she had about letting her children stay at their father's house while I was there.

Lisa-Anne and I hugged good-bye, and she left. I was pretty sure we'd be friends going forward. After shutting the door behind her, I turned to Kent. "I really should have told you why Ram set it up for me to stay here with you. I honestly don't think you're in any danger. Again, I'm sorry."

"Don't be. I'm going to bed. See you tomorrow."

I couldn't quite read Kent's words to tell if he was mad or not. I also couldn't read the emotion on his face. "Kent, it's okay to not want me here." He stood there looking at me.

He didn't say anything so I assumed he was angry. Maybe he didn't want to say he didn't want me staying with him in from of Lisa-Anne for fear of looking bad. "Listen, I'm going to stay at a hotel until I leave for the weekend. Let me pack."

"No. Molly, I don't want you to go, I want you here with me. I feel kind of . . . I don't know."

"Mad at me for not telling you earlier?" I asked.

"Not mad at you. More like mad *for* you—at the guy who did this to you. Your ordeal was kind of a lot to take in. Do you really think he was going to kill you?"

I plopped down on the couch. "Yes, I do. When Katie and Brett came screaming out of the back door, he had his knife up like this," I held my hand up how The Creep had held his. "He was going to stab me again. At that point, I was done. Fighting back wasn't possible anymore."

"Damn."

"Yup. That about sums it up. And to be honest, it's part of the reason why I agreed to come to Nashville. I really needed to get away for a while, find something to keep me busy. You coming to the bar interested in us, me wanting to sell my music and Gina needing me was perfect timing. Almost makes me believe in karma, like I was getting a break for such a shitty thing happening to me."

"Well, I'm glad I know now. I don't know what to say to you. You know all men aren't scum, right?"

I chuckled. "It didn't make me a man-hater, Kent. I'm fine. I've dealt with it. I'm moving on. Okay?"

"Okay. Well I really do need to get to bed. Just so you know I'll be leaving the office early tomorrow to get my daughters. They'll be staying through the weekend. Goodnight, Molly."

"Night, Kent."

After he went upstairs, I stayed on the couch for a few minutes to clear my head. I'd once again told the story of the night that changed my life. I wasn't furious while telling it, merely anxious. Luckily Kent and Lisa-Anne took it so well because if not, my life would've gotten that much more complicated. My mind wandered to Ram and what he was doing, then I went to bed as well.

The next day I left the studio early enough to meet Kent and Lisa-Anne's daughters. Haley and Riley lounged in the family room watching a movie when I came in to introduce myself. Their hellos were weak and apprehensive. I could tell they didn't know what to think of me. After all, they were used to having their dad's house to themselves, and there I was, invading their space. If I wasn't so used to teenagers I might've felt awkward around them, too.

I wanted to get to know them better, so before heading up to bed I engaged them in light conversation. They really did seem like nice girls. I had a lot in common with both of them. Haley and I talked about the sports she participated in, especially swimming. Riley and I were able to talk books. Thank God she'd read the best books ever written—Harry Potter—so at least we had one thing we could discuss. I was pretty sure that we would have no problems getting along after our talk.

As I stood and gave a stretch before going upstairs, Haley blurted out, "So are you my dad's girlfriend?"

I sat back down and faced the girls. "No, I work for him. That's it. Didn't your mom tell you that already?"

"Yes, she did," Riley said. "Haley didn't believe her." She turned to Haley. "See I told you. Mom wasn't lying."

"I'm a songwriter working with an artist your dad is representing. Since we're rushing out this album, and I'm going to be spending a lot of time in Nashville this summer, it made sense for me to stay here." I looked at the both of them. "Okay?" I asked.

"Okay," they said.

I left it at that and went to bed. I had one more day with Gina and her band before flying home for the weekend.

I became giddy thinking of being home. I missed Katie, I missed The Song Wreckers, I missed my house.

I washed up for bed, then crawled under the covers and tried to read. My eyes skimmed the words, but my thoughts had locked onto seeing Ram again. Just thinking about him gave me butterflies. What the heck would happen if he ever kissed me? I'd probably pass out, and then die of embarrassment.

I must've fell into a deep sleep because suddenly I opened my eyes and the bed-side clock read two twenty-three a.m., and I was still on top of my covers, flat on my back.

Chapter 23

I glided down the airport's escalator stairs expecting to see a blond haired, blue eyed, dimpled hunk waiting for me. Instead I found a dark haired, dark eyed, serious looking man with his arms crossed scanning the crowd. Cooper. We made eye contact, and I waved. Since I didn't check any luggage, he took me straight to his SUV.

Cooper only engaged in conversation when it was necessary, I'd learned, and though there was nothing pressing to discuss, I wanted to be polite.

"So how's everything?" I asked.

"Everything's good. Unfortunately nothing new on your case," he said.

"Gotta be honest, I didn't expect there to be." I turned my body to look at him. "Cooper?"

He gave me a quick glance. "Yeah?"

"Do you believe this guy will ever be caught?" I didn't think so. Deep inside me truly believed that I would never know who did this to me.

"Hard to say." That's it. That's all he said.

"Care to elaborate?"

He shrugged. "If he tries something again, then yes, I think we'll get him. If not, I think there's a good chance we won't ever find out who he is. But you have to remember that this is a sick individual we're talking about. Chances are he'll start another obsession, either with you again or someone else."

That's what I'd figured. It still made me sick to think of another woman going through what I did. The actual attack was only part of my hell. The prolonged fear, not knowing if or when he would strike next, or if The Creep was someone I knew, all added fuel to my anger. My small circle of friends worried about my safety, making me feel like a burden. I hated that.

Cooper dropped me off at home, and I practically ran into my house. I walked around the entire inside to make sure everything was as I remembered it, not that I was expecting anything different. My God, it felt like I'd been gone a month and a half, not a week and a half.

I had two hours to get ready and leave for the show. I called Katie to let her know I was home and that I'd be at Brett's at our usual time. Then I sat on my couch and gave myself a moment to breathe. Lately everything was rush, rush, rush. Not that I was complaining. After all, I had signed up for this. However, I needed time to be able to change gears.

As I pulled into the alley behind Brett's, Ram stood by the back door waiting for everybody. My heart rate sped up at the sight of him. I'd pushed him away after the attack, but I had the urge to go up and wrap my arms around him right then. Unfortunately that wouldn't exactly be appropriate behavior for us, not to mention uncharacteristic behavior for me. What are Ram and I? I wasn't his employer since I didn't hire him. I guess I was his client. I think we're friends. Well, whatever we were, we shouldn't be hugging. I'd have to settle for regular conversation.

I stepped out of my car, unloaded my guitars to take inside, then walked up to him. "Yo, Caleb. How's it going?"

He chuckled at the phrase I'd used when I was drunk. "It's going good. How was Nashville?"

I smiled at him, and nodded toward the door. He opened it for me. "Nashvile was good."

I set my guitars up on the stage, and we went back outside to wait for Courtney and Josh. We leaned against the wall next to each other. There was a light breeze going, which helped it feel more comfortable in the high humidity of the night. For a minute we didn't say anything. The quiet was peaceful. I usually felt like that anyway when I was around him, and I appreciated it that much more since I didn't feel like that often. I wondered if Ram and I were a couple if I'd feel as serene all the time.

Ram broke the silence. "So staying with Kent is working out?"

"It is, thanks for that by the way." We talked for a few minutes. I described Kent's home gym and told him about meeting Kent's ex-wife and daughters.

Ram replied with "hmmm" and "huh". He was unusually close-mouthed. What was that about?

I almost asked him if he was still dating the same woman, or any other woman. The question sat on the tip of my tongue the entire time I stood there with him. I chickened out. Eventually the other Song Wreckers pulled in, we unloaded, and rocked out Brett's as if we were famous. I suppose in the confines of that one bar, we were.

The rest of the weekend passed in a blur. I spent most of the day Saturday with Katie. We had manicures and pedicures and engaged ourselves in retail therapy. At night was our show, and Sunday morning and early afternoon we held band practice. Then, before I knew it, Ram was at my door to take me back to the airport. It hit me on the way that I was going to be gone much longer than a week and a half this time.

He opened my door and I tossed my carry-on bag on the floor. Thinking out loud I mumbled, "Wow, I'm not coming back for an entire month." Ram glanced at me and didn't say anything, just shut my door after I got in, and went around to the driver's side. "I hope my house doesn't smell funny when I get back."

He started the engine. "That's what's going through your mind at the thought of not being home for a month?"

"I have about a hundred things going through my mind right now." Like, will you miss me? Do you feel the sexual tension in the air or is it me? "That happens to be what popped out."

"You can be a strange one, Molly Davis."

"I know."

Ram pulled his SUV to the curb for departures and let it idle while I grabbed my bag and he walked me to the doors. It took damn near everything in me not to hug him or kiss him or do something that would make my body press against his.

Instead, I smiled and told him thank you, then in a blink I was back in Nashville.

I walked into Kent's late Sunday night feeling airplane icky, so a quick shower was definitely in order. I had spent almost the entire plane ride thinking of Ram. His strong jaw that gave him a hard edge mixed with his dimples that softened him was the perfect combination. No one appreciated a muscular physique more than me, and he had a lot for me to appreciate.

A flash of Ram kissing an exotic beauty crossed my mind. Someone like him could have anyone he wanted, why would he want an average Jane like me?

I turned on the three shower heads then undressed and stepped into the spray. I could not get the image of Ram out of my mind. His face, his body, his smile, the way he looked at me—sometimes exasperated, sometimes playful, and sometimes intense—the whole package. God, why couldn't he be in here with me right now?

I was so turned on just by my mental pictures of him. And that removable shower head looked pretty nice with its many tension control settings. I reached up and took the shower head out of its holder. Holy shit, was I actually contemplating this?

I played with the different pressure settings, testing them on my hand. I spread my legs and tested them . . . lower. When I found my favorite setting, I went for it. It didn't take long for the convulsions to start ripping through my body because I fantasized about Ram the entire time, and I hadn't had an orgasm in . . . what year was it? And although I would much rather have had Ram doing this to me, I felt better when the deed was done.

It was official. I loved that shower.

I replaced the shower head and peeked my head out of the shower, afraid someone was close by and knew what I did. I could count on one hand the number of times I've masturbated, and it always made me feel self-conscious afterward. Plus I was in Kent's house; that added another level of oh-my-God-I-can't-believe-I-just-did-that. But it took the edge off my new sexual frustration. Though it could in no way could replace a man, I'd needed the release.

Monday morning came, and I was back at it. Not the getting-off-in-the-shower thing, but the music thing. We worked non-stop from the time we woke until quitting time.

The month of July was crazy and exciting. Gina, the band and I found our groove and made my songs better than I ever could have hoped. Every last one of us worked our asses off. If you didn't know how an album was put together, you couldn't realize how much work it was. And when people had their dreams on the line, they never wanted to stop working. I came back to Kent's feeling like the walking dead every night. It was awesome.

I obviously wasn't keeping track of the days very well because I didn't even realize it was July twenty-fifth, my birthday, until the calls started coming in. Shortly after I woke up, Katie called to give me birthday wishes. The rest of the band texted me during the day, then my mom called in the early evening.

Then—surprise of all surprises—my phone rang while I was getting into bed for the night, and Ram's number came up on caller ID.

"Hey, what's up?" I answered, crawling under the covers.

"Just wanted to say happy birthday, Princess."

My heart rate accelerated. "Thanks. How's it going?" I was giddy at the sound of his voice.

"It's good. How is the album going?"

"Very good. Better than expected, actually. Gina is going to be a big star."

"With you behind her, I don't doubt it for a minute."

I couldn't stay still, so I hopped out of bed and paced the length of my bedroom. God, how old was I? Twelve? "Your confidence in me is appreciated. You have my flight info for this weekend, right?"

"Yes."

"Well, I'm bringing Gina home with me, so let whoever picks me up know."

I heard a knock in the background, the sound of the door opening, and a woman's voice tell Ram hi. My heart sank right into the ground. "Well I can hear you have company. I'll see you this weekend."

We said goodbye, and I collapsed onto my bed. My mood went from great to crappy in a matter of minutes. Happy fucking birthday to me.

I really, really tried not to let the knowledge that Ram had a girlfriend, or was at least dating someone, affect my work for the rest of the week. I thought I hid it well, but in the mornings when I had time to think, I thought. About Ram. Which soured my mood.

"Someone been pissing in your Wheaties, Molly?" Kent sat at the kitchen table, drinking coffee and eating a bagel while reading the news on his iPad.

I sat across from Kent with my coffee and bowl of cereal. I was not going to discuss my confused Ram feelings with Kent. "No."

"Anything you want to talk about? Is there something going wrong with Gina or the band you want to tell me?"

"Nope. Everything's good on the Gina and band front."

He took a few bites and left me alone for a minute. I ignored him as he pretended to read, but his eyebrow raised as he glanced at me several times.

"PMS extra bad this month?" he asked.

I looked up and gave him the stink eye, ready to tell him to shove it up his ass, but he was smiling at me. He'd said that to get a rise out of me, to get me to talk to him. Instead, I rolled my eyes. "Yes, my period is extra heavy this month and I think I'm low on super absorbency tampons." Ha, that ought to get him. "So maybe I should wear a pad as back up." I waited for him to tell me to stop—I said the T word *and* the P word. "And I think I need Midol, too." There. The M word.

He sat looking at me with that stupid smile on his stupid face, as if I'd barely fazed him. "Why the heck haven't you gone running out of the room with your hands over your ears yet?"

"Woman, I was married, and I have two daughters, both of whom have their periods. I became immune to period talk years ago."

"Ooh, let's talk more about periods." Okay, that was a stupid thing to say. I was trying to deflect.

It didn't work. "So you going to tell me what's wrong or keep it bottled it inside?" he asked.

Damn it. I was finished with my cereal—not Wheaties by the way—and put my bowl in the sink. "I'm going to keep it bottled inside. It's no big deal, stuff I have on my mind." I turned around from the sink to look at him and he shrugged.

"Suit yourself then. Thought maybe you'd want to talk about it."

"Thanks, Kent. FYI, I'm not really a talk-about-my-feelings type of girl, ya know?" I may write about my feelings and eventually put it in a song, and then be part of a performance for others to hear those feelings, but I'm not going to talk about them beforehand.

"I know." He stood and cleared his section of the table. "If I don't see you before you leave tomorrow have a safe trip and I'll see you Sunday night."

Chapter 24

Kent went into the office early, so I didn't see him before I left for August's Wreckers Weekend. I took a cab to Gina's the next morning to pick her up, and we went to the airport. I was really excited for her to see the Song Wreckers play. Gina Swinger was already a good singer and performer, but Katie was the ultimate performer. She knew how to play to the crowd and really work her magic. Gina could learn from that. Plus it would do her good to get away from her mother and from Nashville for a couple days.

Cooper picked us up from the airport again. Part of me was disappointed it wasn't Ram, and part of me was relieved I wouldn't have to spend the whole car ride with him with a million questions on my tongue.

I made the introductions between Gina and Cooper. He drove us to my house and nodded in agreement occasionally while I explained about the area I lived in. Gina thought I lived in a city called Downriver, because I usually referred to where I lived as Downriver, when actually I lived in Brownstown. Downriver was the name of a bunch of suburbs south of Detroit and west of the Detroit River. No matter where you were Downriver, you were a few minutes away from another suburb. In the span of a five minute drive you can cruise through three different towns—if traffic is light. Brett's was in Downriver, but in the city of Southgate. And although Katie and I both lived in Brownstown, our houses were in different school districts.

I had asked Katie to stop by my house and make sure the guest bedroom was set up so it didn't look like it had been neglected for a month. Everything else had a layer of dust on it. I took time to make my house look lived in again, and explained the highlights of my security system to Gina.

Several hours, a nap, and a shower later, Gina and I were at Brett's. Both Cooper and Ram were waiting outside for us when we pulled into the alley. I introduced Gina to everyone and made her help us take the equipment in. If she was going to make a living in the music industry, she needed to know as much about what goes into it as possible, including behind the scenes stuff. Once inside, I introduced her to some of the women who were regulars at our shows so she would have people to sit by and talk to. I even spent the breaks out in the bar with everyone else. Go me.

Kyle and Mike from *Midnight* and Mike's Girlfriend, Julie, eventually made their way into Brett's. They'd joined our little group during our last break.

"What, not playing tonight?" I asked Kyle and Mike.

Kyle answered. "We haven't been playing in a while. Adam got his sorry ass thrown in jail, and now we are minus a drummer. So now my nights are spent becoming the Wii baseball world champ." He threw his arms up in the victory pose.

Katie perked up. "Ooh, then you might have to challenge Brett. He thinks no one can beat him at that." She turned toward the bar to yell at Brett. "Hey, honey, Kyle says he can whoop you at Wii baseball!"

Brett gave her an *I have no idea what you just said because I can't hear you* look and hand gesture, so Katie went over to tell him again and probably taunt him about it.

I was a schmuck. "Sorry guys, I had no idea this was going on. I've been wrapped up in my own stuff lately. Any prospects on a new drummer?"

Mike answered, "Not really." He motioned to Josh. "Josh doesn't have the time. We checked out a couple of other guys, but they didn't want to leave the bands they're already in. Another drummer will come along. We'll have to wait, I guess."

"Seriously, Molly," Kyle said, making ass-smacking motions with his right hand, "If you ever need to get spanked in Wii baseball, let me know."

He was trying to goad me because he knew first hand I had a competitive side. When he was our bass player, we had a couple of minor episodes that were competitive in nature, and which ended with the best (wo)man, me, being declared the winner. He'd never gotten over it, the big baby, and I knew he wanted a rematch.

I goaded back. "Ooh, Wii baseball. Uh-huh, well that's fine for a wuss like you. I'm not a wuss. If you wanna play real ball, then we'll talk."

Our whole group became interested in the conversation now.

"You gonna let her talk to you like that?"

"Haven't you learned your lesson by now, Kyle?"

Kyle glared at me. "Oh, little Molly, just because you got lucky a couple times in the past don't think you can beat me at ball. I'm a guy. I grew up playing baseball."

I glared back. "Well, I'm a girl, and I'll smear your face into the ground with any sport, pig."

The others were still, on alert waiting to see where this smack talk was going. Kyle stood up, put his hands on the table, and leaned forward. A big smile stretched across his face. "Good golly Miss Molly, I do believe we need to settle this. You and me? Baseball?"

I stood up, matching his pose, smile and all. "You and me. Baseball. How about you and your pathetic band,"

"Hey! Not cool," Mike complained in the background.

"Put a team together, and the Wreckers will do the same. What do you say?"

Ram and Cooper gathered at our table, along with Katie and Brett.

Ram stood to my right, almost touching me. "What's going on?" he asked.

Kyle and I remained in our poses, waiting for the other to back down.

Gina answered him. "I think they challenged each other's band to a game of baseball. I'm not sure if it's Wii baseball or real baseball."

"Oh, it's real baseball, right, Molly?" Kyle said.

"You're God damn straight it's real baseball. So you accept?"

He leaned forward more to put his face in mine, attempting to intimidate. "Prepare to go down."

We still smiled and glared. "Not likely." My face started aching. "Get your five best men and five best women. May the best team—mine—win."

"Dream on. When is this game taking place?"

I knew the baseball coach at work. He would let us play on the school's ball field. "How about the Sunday of Labor Day weekend? I'll arrange a field for us to play on."

"Done. No recruiting anyone from each other's band. Our band members play for us only." His smile must not have felt good either because now he looked constipated.

"Last chance to back out." I warned him. "I won't even make fun of you. Much."

"Never." He held out his hand. "Let's shake on it."

I shook his hand, and we finally broke the God awful smiles. I took a look around, and everyone appeared quite amused. Even Cooper, who had one corner of his mouth raised.

Kyle heckled us the rest of the night. That was okay. Let him feel like he'd win. It would be that much sweeter to rub his nose in it when I won.

Before I left, Kyle and I agreed we'd establish the rules over the next couple of weeks via email.

Ram and I didn't talk much during the Wreckers Weekend. We were friendly with each other and cracked a few jokes, but I was preoccupied with Gina and trying to figure out who I was going to ask to be on my ball team. Ram and I met in a messed up circumstance. Not a way to start a relationship. Plus he was obviously with someone else. The sooner I accepted that we weren't meant to be together, the better. Except, damn. I needed him on my ball team.

I used the plane ride back to Nashville to finalize my players. It had to consist of people I knew were athletic. By the time the plane landed, I was mostly settled on who I wanted, and if any of them said no, then I would I would badger, bribe, or otherwise coerce until they gave in. For my five men I wanted Josh, Brett, Ram, and Cooper, and God, who else? I needed one more man.

My women would be me, Katie, Heather, Courtney, and Lori, one of the *Scream It Out Loud* table dancer girls. I offered a spot to Gina. She told me she'd never played and didn't want to mess up my chances of winning.

I think Gina genuinely enjoyed herself that weekend. I hoped she'd picked up tips about performing by watching Katie.

When I walked into Kent's family room on Sunday, he was spread out on his couch with his eyes glued to the TV.

Ohmygod, Kent! He could be my fifth guy! He was in good shape—he actually used his gym.

"Hey, do you play baseball?" I asked immediately after finding him. He was watching, of all things, a baseball game. Fate.

He didn't even look at me when he mocked. "Hey, Kent, how was your weekend? Did you do anything fun? So good to see you again."

Okay, I forgot about the pleasantries. Sue me. "Sorry. How was your weekend? Did you do anything fun? It is so good to see you," I said, trying to sound interested.

I think he forgot I was there.

"Come on," he told the TV, "just hit it far enough to let the runner on third get across the plate."

I sat next to him to get his attention. "So, do you play baseball, Kent?"

"Why?"

"Because I have to put a team together of five men and five women to play a baseball game over Labor Day weekend, and I'm short one man."

"Run! Run!" He stared at the screen and waited. "Yes! One to one." He spared me a quick glance. "Is this like an annual thing that you do?"

"No. This is an I-got-challenged-by-this-guy-who-actually-thinks-he-can-beat-me-at-sports thing. We agreed on a ball game, and I have to put together a team that will allow me to rub his face in the dirt of my victory." I said, complete with hand motions of me pushing a head in the dirt and smearing it around.

Kent pulled his eyes away from the TV to look at me for more than a split second. "Consider me out."

"Why? You can't play?"

"I can play. I'm just afraid of what you'll do to the players on your team if you lose."

I stood and put my hands on my hips. "I'm going to win, so there's nothing to worry about." I shifted from foot to foot, worked up at the idea of playing a real ball game, which I hadn't done in a while. Plus, I had to settle once and for all that Kyle was a suck ass.

"All the same, I'll pass." He turned his attention back to the TV.

"Please?"

"No."

"Please?"
"No."
"Please?"
"No."
"Kent!"
"What?"

Time to work it. "What are you, a pansy? Afraid of a little ball game? Huh?"

No response. "Afraid of getting dirty, pretty boy?"

He gave a quiet snort but otherwise continued to ignore me. It was time to pull out the big guns. "Afraid you can't measure up to a bunch of Yankees?"

That did it.

Kent once again turned his gaze to me. "You better watch it, woman."

Hell no, I wasn't going to watch it. Had he learned nothing about me the last couple of months? I did a stupid dance in place and sang, "Kent's afraid of Yankees! Kent's afraid of Yankees!"

Instead of getting mad, he laughed. "You are ruthless, you know that?"

"So does that mean you're in?"

"No."

"Come on! Why not?" God, I so thought I had him.

"You expect me to fly to Michigan to play a stupid baseball game so you can rub it in some guy's face if you win?"

"Yes! And *when* I win. Not if. And I'll pay for your ticket. And hotel room. And food. I'll even spring for a hooker, Kent. Please!" Yeah, I was getting desperate.

"I don't think so, Molly," he said, without conviction.

But it wasn't a definite no. "Yay! I have my fifth guy!" I jumped up and down and clapped my hands in joy. My team was set.

"I did not say yes!"

"You will, or I'll drive you crazy! So crazy you'll do it to shut me up! Thanks, Kent!" He started to protest, so I ran out of the room so he'd know I wasn't going to listen to his excuses.

Over the next week I called everyone I wanted on my team and convinced them to accept the challenge. To my surprise, Ram and Cooper agreed without much prodding. I asked—okay demanded—everyone get to the batting cages whenever they could, and promised we would schedule a practice before the game.

Kyle and I set the rules of the game through email. We gave each other the names of our players and agreed to seven innings of softball. We would find two people to act as umpires and would play rain or shine.

Whichever team lost would have to pay for a pizza dinner that night and would have to announce their team sucked and the winning team ruled to all the bar patrons at the next Wreckers Weekend. For me, the best prize of all was bragging rights.

Kent finally resigned himself to being part of the team. He grumbled about it, mostly because he had to fly out of state to play.

The five percent of my mind that had been obsessed with organizing a ball game, could now go back to obsessing about Gina Swinger. I had enjoyed mentoring Gina, and her hard work showed. Crystal Records had set it up for her to sing a few songs at local bars, and her voice was phenomenal. Both her stage presence and handling of fans were top-notch. She didn't need me anymore, and I was happy to be going home soon. I was anxious to get back to work and have my life return to normal.

In the little down time I had, I thought of The Creep and how his actions dropped Ram into my life. How messed up is that? The man I want to forget more than anything led me to the man I can't stop thinking about. And the man I can't stop thinking about, is thinking about someone else. Ugh.

Chapter 25

The day I returned to Michigan for good was bitter sweet. For the most part I was glad to be home and resume the life I'd once had, even though it seemed like forever ago. I would to miss working on Gina's album, though. The hard work, the late nights, the new friendships, even the stress, were all therapeutic for me. I was coming home a new person, or rather the person I was before The Creep came into my life. I felt better than I had in a while.

Kent and I had formed a pretty solid friendship. We respected each other, worked well together, and were able to live together without killing each other. I was pretty sure we would work together in the future, and if I ever needed something he would be there and vice versa. I was really going to miss living in such a nice place, and would especially miss his shower.

Cooper picked me up from the airport and dropped me off at home. I immediately dove into unpacking and laundry and cleaning. A clean, organized house helped me think better, so even with a million other things for me to do, the first was to get my house in order before I started any of it.

While scrubbing, organizing, and laundering, I made my mental to do list. One, I needed to talk to everyone on my ball team and schedule a practice or two, and make sure everyone took a trip to the batting cages at least once.

Two, I needed to touch base with my department head regarding the classes I was going to be teaching for the upcoming school year. He had left a voicemail telling me things had changed since we'd last talked.

And last, I needed to call my dad.

Avoiding my dad made me feel like a wuss, so I sucked it up and dialed his number. After a few rings a woman answered.

"Hi, this is Molly. Is this Joy?"

"Hi, Molly. Yes, this is Joy. I'm so glad you called. Your father is in the other room. Let me go get him."

I wanted the hang up while waiting for him to come to the phone. That would be cowardly. I might as well talk to him and get it over with.

There was a scuffling sound, and then a man's voice, "Hello, Molly."

"Hi, Dad. I'm back in town. You wanted to talk?"

"I think we have a lot to talk about."

I let out a snort. As far as I was concerned *we* didn't have all that much to talk about. *He* needed to do the talking. "So talk."

He didn't say anything for a minute. Then, "You're so angry, Molly. I understand, I do. Can we . . . will you meet me for dinner? I really want to see you. Just you and me?"

I owed him nothing. I agreed anyway. "That's fine. When and where?"

He'd been living in Bowling Green, Ohio for several years. The fact that he had lived so close to me for a while, and just recently contacted me, did not win him any points in my favor.

Despite wanting to throw a large object at his head, I agreed to meet him for lunch in Toledo since it was roughly the halfway point. I called Katie immediately after hanging up with my dad, and she said I did the right thing. She also told me to go easy on him, he was taking a big step in trying to get back into my life, and trying to connect with me was actually pretty brave of him.

I was pretty sure I should wash my hands of him as he'd done to me. My life so far had been fine without him. Okay, so when you got past the surface I had a semi-fucked up life, and I definitely had relationship issues. Would letting my dad back in my life change any of that? Doubtful.

When I walked into The Olive Garden and checked in, the hostess led me to my dad's table. He stood when I arrived. I stared for a moment, taking him in, then sat.

My father had the same generic quality I did: brown hair, brown eyes, average height for a man. I vaguely remembered him as being handsome, but that was when I was six. He was softer and balder, but still recognizable. I hung my purse on my chair, folded my hands on the table, and gave him a look that said, "Well?" I was not going to be the one to start talking.

He gave me a warm smile, as if he mistook my entrance as welcoming. "You look great."

"Thank you," I said, as neutrally as I could. I picked up the menu and studied it. My foot tapped under the table, the only outlet for my anxiety.

The waitress came, and we ordered our drinks and meals at the same time. As soon as she left, my dad got down to business. "I guess I should start out by saying that I'm sorry."

"For?" We both knew, I just wanted to hear him say it.

"For not ever being there for you. For not being the father you needed and deserved. It was wrong of me, and I'm sorry, and I regret it."

I was not going to make this easy on him. "The things you're sorry for aren't minor things, Dad. I don't know if I can forgive you. To be honest, I don't know if I even want to forgive you."

"I can understand that. Do you want to hear my reasons of why I did what I did?"

"Do I want to hear your excuses for having a child and then abandoning her?" Did I? "I don't even know if it matters at this point. What's done is done."

He nodded, "I know. Still, I'd like to explain."

"Well I'm not leaving because I'm starving, so say what you need to say."

The waitress set our drinks in front of us and left without saying a word. It must have been obvious that we were there to talk and didn't want her interference.

He took a deep breath. "I loved your mother very much when I married her. Having you. . . and Holly. . . were the best things that ever happened to us. We were really happy. Then when Holly died something happened inside of me. Looking back now, I'm sure I suffered from depression. Severe depression. I'd lost the ability to feel. My life was never going to be the same. Everything I had planned for the future was going to be different, and not in the good way. Or that's what I believed at the time. Your mother was having a rough time, too. We were in so much grief we couldn't even be there for each other. We either ignored each other or we fought. Eventually we gave up, and I left."

He looked at me, waiting to see if I was going to comment. I stared at him without any expression, so he continued. "I know I shouldn't have stopped visiting you. Part of the time after I left is a blur. I think I convinced myself you would be better off without me around much. Then later, I moved out of state for work and never really looked back. Time had healed some of the wounds, but not all. I knew I should have visited you, I just didn't. I kept telling myself that you were fine. That your mother was a good one. That's true, isn't it?"

I shrugged. "Sure."

"Good. That's good." The waitress came with our salad and bread sticks and once again set our stuff down without a word. She pointed to her parmesan cheese grater and when we shook our heads, she left. We ate in silence for several bites before he started talking again. "I did think about you over the years."

Whoop-de-fucking-doo.

I again kept silent, so he carried on. "About five years ago I relocated to Bowling Green. Soon after I met Joy. She's a secretary in the College of Fine Arts at the University. We were friends at first. I ended up confiding everything to her. She convinced me to get help, and I did. And somewhere along the way we also fell in love."

I was pretty sure he expected me to comment about his little speech. I didn't give him the satisfaction. I wanted to make him squirm. There was no part of me that felt bad about that. I didn't care if I was being immature, selfish, or whatever.

If Katie were there, she'd want me to give him the benefit of the doubt and be forgiving. She wouldn't necessarily expect it. I admit, for a minute I wavered. *Only* a minute. Here's my dad telling me how he really screwed up by abandoning me, and, golly gee, the fault wasn't his because he was depressed. Oh, he's sorry too.

Instead of feeling all warm and fuzzy, I was plain old pissed.

We ate, awkwardly avoiding eye contact for a while. Then, "I wish you would say something, Molly."

I didn't. I looked up and watched him get fidgety with me glaring at him. Finally I said, "I hope our food gets here soon."

"You know that's not what I meant."

The waitress strolled up to our table with our orders. "Here you go. Cheese?" We each shook our head. "All right, enjoy."

I took a couple bites. "So what exactly do you want from me, Dad?"

He kept his gaze on his plate. "I want to be in each other's lives. I want you to come to my wedding in a couple months. I want you to forgive me." He looked at me. "I want to know if that's even possible."

Was it? Did I want those things too? Shit, I couldn't even answer that question. I took a few minutes and answered him honestly. "I don't know. Sorry. I need time to think, I guess."

He nodded, and we finished our meal in silence.

Since the drive home was long, I called Katie and filled her in on our conversation.

"Wow, Mol. I'm actually proud of you!"

"Seriously? Why?" Because, let's face it, my behavior was not all that great.

"Well, you didn't curse him out or hit him. That's a big step for you."

"Ha ha. And anyway, you know I never throw the first punch. So what do you think?"

"You already know what I think. I think forgiving your father and letting him into your life will be good for you, but I'm not the one who has to deal with the fact that my father abandoned me. You know I'm there for you no matter what."

I smiled. "I know, and that's why I love you."

"That and because I'm talented and beautiful and smart," she added.

"And humble."

We both laughed. Katie made me feel better, as always. I was still angry at my dad, but the tension was gone. I still wasn't sure how I felt about my father. Meeting with him ignited feelings of abandonment I didn't know I still harbored.

Chapter 26

The week before the big softball game I corralled everyone, except for Kent, together for a practice, despite our different schedules. Cooper and Ram were the muscle hitters on the team, cracking the ball well into the outfield, while Brett hit power grounders. Lori was our pitcher. She had played in high school and still had the ability to whip balls just outside the strike zone, tricking batters into swinging. I put myself at short stop. Brett wanted catcher, Ram wanted first base, Courtney wanted second base, and Josh took third base. Katie, Heather, and Cooper made up the outfield, and that's where I put Kent as well. He probably wouldn't care what position he played. Everyone swore they would get to the batting cages at least once.

Our team looked good. Everyone was in at least halfway decent shape, of course. I wouldn't have had them on my team if they weren't. We all knew each other fairly well so we got along. And almost as important, everyone seemed to enjoy themselves. Seriously, how could you not enjoy yourself while playing ball? I haven't seen Kyle's team in action, but there's no way he had better players then me.

I was looking forward to the actual game which would take place after I had to go to work in a few days. Teaching staff were required to report back to work the week before the students so we could get our classrooms in order, attend curriculum meetings, and do the menial tasks like make copies of the first week's assignments. Right now though, my days were open and I didn't know what to do with myself. Cleaning only took so long. I had spent the last couple of months being so busy I pretty much collapsed at the end of every day, and now I didn't have that schedule anymore. Boredom was bad. A lot of free time meant too much opportunity to think over matters I'd rather keep shoved in that spot in my brain labeled: To Do Later.

And boy, did I think. I started out the week thinking about The Creep and trying to figure out who he could be. Still not a clue. I even called Detective Lindsmere to see if anything new developed. Of course there wasn't. Once again, the fact that no one could identify that asshole made me mad.

To keep myself from thinking about The Creep, I thought about Ram. We acted like friends at ball practice, but the thoughts stirring in my brain weren't exactly friendly. Watching him play was a total turn on. Especially when he would lift his shirt to wipe his face and I stole peeks at his body. And then even more so when he ditched the shirt because of the heat. Not looking wasn't an option. He was all firm and toned and muscled without the ripped six pack that screamed, *I spend too much time in the gym and not enough time eating!* All man. I should've offered to wipe his sweat off for him. After all, that's what good coaches did, right?

Now my anger was aimed right at me. Maybe I should've opened myself up to dating him. What the hell had I been so afraid of? He was a great guy and now I had to face the fact that waiting, plus pushing him away, equaled no Ram for me. Sometimes I was so stupid.

To keep myself from thinking about Ram I thought about my dad and everything he'd told me. He'd said all the right things, so why was I still so angry? Maybe I was more hurt than mad, but those feelings were still strong. I was actually upset that he was happy with another woman. How dare he? How dare he let himself be happy after acknowledging that he'd basically crapped all over me and my mom?

I putzed around my house, picked up my guitars and played a few times, and tried to read. Concentration was a no-go, so I admitted defeat. I needed to hit something, or kick something, or go run a million miles. I didn't want to do anything calming like yoga or swimming. My mind raced. My blood was beginning to boil.

I changed into workout clothes when my phone rang. Ram. "Hey," I said.

"You okay, Princess?"

"Yeah, why?"

"You sound. . . kinda stressed."

"Well I kinda am. I think I'm going to head to the batting cages again. I really need to hit the shit out of balls right now." Ugh, not what I meant. Mental forehead slap. "So what's up? Why did you call?"

"I wanted to see how you were doing. Want any company at the cages? I need to go anyway so you'll stop pestering me about it."

"I don't pester. I merely threaten to do away with your firstborn if we lose, and it so happens you didn't get batting practice in." Which reminded me. "Do you already have a firstborn?" I'd wanted to know that for a while, and since I was already kind of on the subject . . .

"No. So do you want company or not?"

"If you can put up with a pissed off woman who may be premenstrual and will have a bat in her hands then you're more than welcome to join me. If not, I suggest you stay home. I'll be there in half an hour." I assumed he knew to get to the cages closest to my house.

When I parked my Jeep, I saw Ram waiting for me. He held up a plastic cup filled with tokens, so I skipped the token line and headed toward the bench he was on. He stood when I approached. "Let's get started," he said.

We walked with our bats and helmets, and he waved his hand toward all the cages. "Which one?"

"Fast pitch softball would make the most sense. Go ahead," I said.

He took a step back. "Princesses first."

We took turns in the cage several times without really speaking beyond "good job" and "nice hit." I was in total concentration mode. My goal was to hit the living daylights out of as many balls as it took to make me feel better.

During my third round I swung really hard, and missed. A jolt of pain shot down my right shoulder. The one that got stabbed.

"Aahhh . . . God *damn* it!" I grumbled. I took a step back because there was no way I was going to be able to hit another ball for a few minutes.

Ram opened the gate. "You okay?"

"I will be. I just tweaked my shoulder." I dropped the bat and wrapped my left arm across my body, grasping my hurt shoulder. "Here," I said stepping toward the gate, "take the rest of my turn."

"Come and sit down for a minute." He put his hand on my lower back and steered me toward the bench and sat next to me. "You're hitting out of anger and throwing your body positioning off."

I dropped my arm and stretched my shoulder. "Ya think?" I pinched my eyes closed for a second. "Sorry. I'm not trying to be a brat."

"Don't be sorry. You warned me beforehand, remember?"

"I remember. Still, I meant to take my issues out on the balls, not you."

"Have you ever considered taking up boxing?" he asked.

"I can't afford to have sore hands. It makes it too difficult to play the guitar." Because, believe me, the idea of being able to go at it on a punching bag or another person was really appealing. However, the way I knew my hands would hurt afterward wasn't.

Ram took another turn in the cage. When he came out and indicated that it was my turn, I told him to go ahead again. I still needed a few more minutes.

He took another turn then sat next to me. "Princess, don't take this the wrong way, but what about talking to somebody?"

"I talk to people all the time."

"I mean a professional." I must've had a *huh?* look on my face because he clarified, "A psychiatrist."

My eyebrows shot up. "You think I'm crazy?" I admit, more than one person has called me that. It stung coming from Ram.

"You're not crazy, but you obviously have feelings from your attack that you need to work out. Maybe talking to a professional could help you with that."

I hoped he was joking.

He wasn't. His voice was soft when he spoke, and there was no sense that he anything but serious.

I was shaking my head no when Ram put his hands on either side of my face and turned it toward him. We stared at each other for about five seconds before he said, "Well?"

I pushed off his hands as I stood up, not knowing what to say. So I went back into the cage to hit a round of balls. It hurt, but the pain was worth it as long as I didn't have to look at him.

I came out but he didn't go in like I wanted him to. Instead he continued talking. "It's okay you know."

No, it wasn't okay. "You think I need a shrink? You think I'm so stupid that I can't work out my own problems and need to go complain to somebody?" I mock-whined, "Poor me. . . somebody hurt me . . . boo hoo . . . what am I ever gonna do?"

I tossed my bat onto the grass, and shut my mouth before I started rambling about other shit that was affecting me. If I kept going, I'd make an ass of myself. I took a deep breath and slowly blew it out through my mouth. "I know you think I'm this weak, pathetic, little girl, but I'm not. I can handle my own problems. This," I said, pointing to the cages, "is my shrink. Running is my shrink. Going down in my basement and dancing is my shrink. Writing is my shrink. I *don't* need to go talk about it. I'm not a wuss."

He stood up and stared me down. "Why would going and talking to a professional make you a wuss? And where did you get that I think you're a weak, pathetic, little girl?"

I threw my hands up and let them fall, ignoring the pain the motion caused in my shoulder. "Oh please, Ram. You've been calling me Princess since you first met me. You even referred to me as a Barbie doll. Well guess what? I'm not this delicate, fragile thing that's going to break."

Ram pulled his face back in confusion. "You think I call you Princess because I see you as weak, pathetic, delicate, and fragile?"

"Why would I think anything different?"

He pinched the bridge of his nose and closed his eyes. "For someone so smart, you can be so clueless."

I snorted at that then hopped up to do another round in the cage.

"What the hell did you mean by that last comment?" I asked him when I finished.

"It means that, although you seem to be highly intelligent, you came to a really stupid conclusion. Duh."

I gave him the look that said, *explain please.*

"You think I called you Angry Princess Barbie because I viewed you as, let's see, fragile, weak, pathetic, and delicate. Is that right?" I didn't answer, so he continued. "I called you that because you barged into the room mad as hell. You were bossy and brave. You're so damn perfectly beautiful you made me think of a Barbie doll. I don't know. You reminded me of royalty or something, so Princess slipped out." I crossed my arms over my chest while he paused, seemingly to gather his thoughts. "And honestly? The more I was around you the more it fit. You're incredibly brave, bossy as hell when you want to get your way, and the most beautiful woman I have ever laid eyes on. And you have to admit, you are pissed off a lot."

Wow. Huh. Wow. I plopped down on the bench, shocked. Ram went in the cage and batted again. Three more rounds, actually. When he came out, I was still sitting on the bench. He gathered his bat, helmet, and batting gloves. "I gotta go. It's a Wreckers Weekend so I'll see you Friday. And Saturday. And at the game on Sunday."

"Okay," was all I could manage to get out, because seriously, *what the hell?*

Chapter 27

The next several days were going to be packed, and I was relieved. Friday and Saturday was a Wreckers Weekend, plus I was determined to get in even more batting practice. Then Sunday was the big game. Or as I liked to think of it: The Day Kyle Went Down. That also meant that I had to pick Kent up at the airport on Saturday. He was staying at my place since it would be easier. His accommodations would be nowhere near as nice as I'd had it at his house, but they would be better than a hotel. He'd go to Saturday's show, and on Monday, Labor Day, I was taking him to Josh and Courtney's for a cook out. The next day was the start of a new school year. That left no time to wallow in self-pity, which I was ashamed to admit I'd been doing. I was seriously pathetic.

Friday's show came and went. Ram and I were distantly friendly with each other which really bummed me out. Now that I could fully admit to myself that I wanted him, it was damn near killing me that I couldn't have him.

Saturday, I was able to busy myself by going grocery shopping, cleaning, and getting in more batting practice before I picked up Kent from the airport. I went easy on myself, concentrating on making contact with the ball. I didn't want to do anything that was going to leave my shoulder under one hundred percent.

I met Kent at passenger pick up at Detroit Metro Airport and gave him a friendly punch on the arm. "Hey, there. Welcome to my neck of the woods," I greeted him.

He shook his head at me. "All right. Let's get this over with."

We began walking toward baggage claim. "Don't act like you're not excited to play a ball game this weekend. Come on, man up."

"I know I'm going to regret getting suckered into this. You owe me, you know."

"Yeah, I know. Thanks for this, by the way."

We grabbed his suitcase from baggage claim then headed back to my place. After warning him about the alarm system, he got settled in my guest bedroom and took a nap. I freshened up and warmed up my voice for the show.

Once we arrived at Brett's, I introduced Kent to the rest of the band, and then to Cooper and Ram, as the fifth man on our team. I could tell no one knew what to make of me and Kent. Their faces wore masks of fascination. They wordlessly looked between Kent and me, presumably wondering if we were an item. Katie knew there was nothing between us so I guess that's all I cared about. And really, I could've taken the time to explain that we were friends and colleagues only, but why bother? Who cared what everyone else thought. Even Ram.

Game day! Suck it, Kyle!

Start time was two o'clock. My team was there by one fifteen to stretch, warm up, and start talking smack. Kyle and I took several minutes to size up each other's team. His team consisted of himself, Dave and Mike from *Midnight,* and two guys I'd never met before. Apparently Adam was still in jail or maybe out of the band. I didn't want to ask. The women consisted of Dave's girlfriend, Mike's girlfriend, two *Shout It Out Loud* girls, and Kyle's sister. Unfortunately we looked pretty evenly matched.

A coin toss determined Kyle's team would take the field first, leaving my team to bat first.

The first few innings were rough. Everyone was finding their groove. Both teams were good, though I still believed mine was better. By the start of the fourth inning the score was two to two. That was when Kyle's team really stepped up their shit talking.

Fourth inning, my turn to bat. No outs, Kent on first. I'd squared up to the plate when Kyle yelled, "Hey! Since when do they let little girls play ball?"

The pitcher pitched, I swung and missed. Strike one.

Ooh, that cock sucker. "Good one!" I yelled. "I hope you don't cry when we kick your ass!"

Kyle yelled out to his team, "Everyone move in a few steps. If she actually hits the ball, it ain't going far." His team came forward.

That did it.

Katie talked to me from the bench. "Don't let him get to you, Mol. You got this."

The next pitch came and I hit it as hard as I could, aiming it toward third base where Kyle played. It obviously came as a surprise that I hit it right to him because he wasn't ready for it. Kyle brought his mitt up a split second too late and the ball nailed him in the forearm instead going into his mitt. It dropped to the ground, and for a second he looked at it before picking it up. He was so intent on getting me out that, instead of throwing it to second like he should've, he threw it to first. God damn it, he got me out. That's okay because now we had a runner on second that wasn't a forced run.

Since our hitting orders were boy-girl-boy-girl, Cooper was up next and Kent made it to third. Then Courtney was up and got out at first which helped Kent make it in to score and break the tie. I was so excited I ran up to Kent and jumped on him to give him a hug.

I didn't think anything of it, and I don't think Kent did either, but Ram deliberately turned his back on us. I wondered for a brief moment why he did that. His girlfriend came to the game to watch him, so why would he care if I hugged Kent?

The rest of the game was intense. Kyle's team scored, then we scored, and at one point they were up by one, then us again.

We were up by one point at the bottom of the seventh inning, so we didn't have to bat our last turn. I was so proud of Katie—she actually scored in the sixth inning. I took partial credit because I made her wear two sports bras to keep her big boobs from slowing her down. It must've worked.

Once Kyle's team was done batting, and we knew we had won, I hugged everyone on my team without caring that this level of affection was very unlike me. And maybe I held on to Ram for longer than was necessary, and maybe I pressed my body against his in a way that wasn't really appropriate for a social hug, but I didn't care about that either. We'd won!

Kyle and I had talked so much shit to each other from the moment we agreed on this game I think we were both done. For the time being, at least. I told him good game, and that his team played really well and had me worried until the very end. He gave me a one-armed hug, a kiss on the head, and told me good game too.

We all went home to shower then met at Pizza Hut. This was going to be the best tasting pizza I had ever eaten. We were done with all the smack talk toward Kyle's team, and they were actually pretty good sports about the whole thing, so dinner was quite enjoyable. We talked too loud, ate too much, and harassed each other. It felt good. Seeing Ram's girlfriend show up to watch him play put a slight damper on my mood, but I pushed that to the back of my mind. At least he wasn't all touchy-feely with her. That would've been too much for me. In fact, I didn't even see him kiss her, thank God.

Kent and I came home, almost dragging our bodies through the door, and went straight to the living room. We both plopped down, him on the couch and me on a chair. Kent grabbed the remote and started flipping through channels.

"Tell me you didn't have fun," I told him. "And how annoying is it that you don't know what any of the channels are?"

"Fun. Annoying."

I stretched my legs and nudged him on the arm with my foot. "Come on, Kent. Did you have fun? Tell me the truth."

Still flipping through channels he shrugged. "Uh-huh."

Oh, man, now I started to feel bad. I'd dragged this man several states from home for him to do me a favor. "That's it? 'uh-huh'? Oh my God, you hated it, didn't you?"

He smiled. "No, woman. I actually had a lot of fun. I haven't played ball in a long time."

I shoved him harder with my foot. "You jerk. I was starting to feel all guilty that I made you do this, and you were miserable. I hope you have sore muscles tomorrow."

Kent found a sports channel to watch. Yuck. I didn't want to fall asleep so early, so I went to the kitchen and loaded the dishwasher, sat at the table with my laptop and checked email, then scooped two bowls of ice cream.

I walked back into the living room and handed Kent a bowl. "Here. Chocolate."

"Thanks," he said.

The only sound for five minutes were our spoons clinking against our bowls. "Ugh," I moaned as I set my bowl of the coffee table. "I'm going to explode."

I waited for Kent to finish his ice cream, then announced I was going to bed.

"Molly?" he asked, handing me his bowl.

Oh shit. Okay, here's the thing. Kent and I were colleagues and pretty good friends. But there was a small part of me that was always waiting for him to confess he had feelings for me. Conceited, I know. I had friendly, comfortable feelings for him, but not I-wanna-screw-your-brains-out feelings.

"Yeah?" I answered.

"Is the whole band going to be at this barbecue tomorrow?"

"Yeah. Why?"

"Including Heather?"

My face lit up. "What? You're hot for Heather?"

He shrugged. "She's cute."

"She's also a good fifteen years younger than you."

He looked at me, as if to say "So?"

"She'll be there at least for the beginning of it. I don't know if Brett has her working that night or not. She's pretty much the assistant manager."

Kent gave a single nod.

I walked back over to stand in front of him. "Listen, Kent." I shoved him with my foot yet again to get him to look at me. When he did, I continued. "Heather is in my band, and I consider her my friend. Do. Not. Hurt. Her."

"Is this where you threaten to kick my ass?"

"This is where I promise to kick your ass if you hurt her."

He gave me another nod. "Understood."

Kent wasted no time sniffing up Heather's behind once we arrived at Josh and Courtney's place on Labor Day. I should've called her to warn her beforehand. Oh well. She was a big girl. I hung around Katie sans Brett since he was at the bar. I told her about Kent asking about Heather, and I think it took about two seconds before she started making plans to enact her revenge on Heather for all the comments that Heather made to her and Brett before they started dating.

Katie and I walked around and munched on the food. The weather was gorgeous, and everyone was in good spirits.

Those of us who had played in the previous day's game were still talking and analyzing every move made, especially every mistake made by Kyle's team. We reminisced about how awesome we were and how we should plan another game next year because beating them again would be every bit as fun.

After we ate, Katie and I sat down in lawn chairs. A continual breeze made the full sun less stifling. I stretched my legs out and closed my eyes, intending to relax. I did—until Katie mentioned Ram.

"Was that Ram's girlfriend at the game yesterday?" she asked.

My eyes popped open. Caught off guard by her question, I sat up straight and stared at my shoes for before answering so annoyance wouldn't show on my face. "I guess. I didn't ask. He's been seeing someone for a while, I think."

Katie leaned forward with a serious face. In a mock Dr. Ruth (I'm guessing) voice she asked, "And how does that make you feel?"

In an equally fake voice I answered, "I could give two shits. Ram is a grown man and can date whomever he wants."

"I think the two shits you could give are what you're full of Ms. Davis. What do you have to say to that?"

I broke character by smiling. Katie knew me too well. I relaxed back into my chair. "You're right. Like the old saying goes, you snooze, you lose. I made it pretty clear to him that I was unavailable, and he lost interest and moved on. Shit happens."

Katie stayed in character. "He may have moved on but he didn't lose interest."

"You know the worst part about his girlfriend—or whatever she is—showing up yesterday? I was having a hard enough time when I knew he was seeing someone because

I kept picturing him sleeping with a faceless woman who wasn't me. Now I have a face to put with it."

Katie put her arm around me and leaned her head on my shoulder to comfort me. Her chair was too far away from mine to pull that off, so she tipped into me, falling almost completely down. I caught her—barely—then pushed her upright. It was the thought that counted.

After we finished laughing, she continued, thankfully without the horrible accent. "You know, Molly, if you went up to him and told him how you felt about him, he'd dump that girl in a heartbeat."

There were two problems with her suggestion. One, I didn't think I had the nerve to do that. Two, purposely stealing a woman's man from her is just plain wrong. If that was done to me, I'd be royally pissed. And I'd want to kick her ass.

"Can't do it," I said.

Heather and Kent walked over to us, so I was spared having to talk more about Ram and how I screwed up.

"Have a seat, guys," I said, while pulling over another couple of lawn chairs for them.

If I read Kent and Heather's body language correctly, she wasn't romantically interested in him, and he had given up on her. The four of us lounged for another hour before accepting that we had to leave. Heather had to work the bar, Katie and I started the new school year the next day, and Kent had an early flight back to Nashville in the morning.

Chapter 28

So another school year began. For most people, their New Year's Day is January first. As a teacher, the first day of the school year is your New Year's Day. I had a list of things in my head that I both needed and wanted to accomplish that year.

I needed to talk to Cooper about ending the babysitting/body guarding/whatever service and letting me pay for my own alarm system.

I needed to decide whether or not I was going to forgive my father and let him back into my life.

I needed to have a real conversation with my mother.

I wanted to continue writing songs for Crystal Records, specifically Gina Swinger.

I wanted to try for a relationship with a man where I wouldn't toss it aside after a while.

I really fucking wanted the police to catch The Creep.

After a couple of weeks the craziness of the new school year wore off, and I planned a trip to 3D's offices after work. I called Cooper, and once I found out he was at the office, I told him to stay there because I was coming in to see him.

3D was located in downtown Detroit. I rarely went into the city, so I didn't really know my way around. Between construction projects closing off streets and business men and women continually darting in front of my car it took me longer than expected to get there.

The offices of 3D were quite nice. I guess when your clients are the who's who of Michigan, you make sure your base is as nice as it can be. The floors were gorgeous hardwood, instead of marble like you'd expect in an office building, making the space feel warm and inviting. There were four leather chairs circled around a table, and three huge landscape portraits of the Detroit skyline, Mackinaw Bridge, and the capitol building hung on the walls. The reception desk and the woman behind it screamed professional and competent.

There was no need for me to go to the receptionist because as I walked in, Cooper was waiting for me.

He led me down a long hallway. I looked around, trying to see if Ram was there. He wasn't, not that I could tell. I saw, like, three people. Cooper ushered me into his office and closed the door. I took the seat meant for clients. He sat in the chair next to me instead of behind his desk, crossing his leg the way men did, and stared at me, waiting for me to begin.

I was nervous because things were going to go one of two ways. First, if he agreed to stop the babysitting/body guarding thing, that level of personal safety wasn't going to be there anymore. Or second, if he didn't agree to stop, I wasn't getting my way and that idea really irked me.

"Hey," I started, "this is a nice place you have here."

"Thank you. What can I do for you, Molly? I'm a little worried that you wanted to meet me here. Anything wrong? You know I would've come to your house."

"Nothing's wrong, I just wanted to talk to you about," deep breath, "ending your services." I didn't want to sound ungrateful for everything he'd done, so I added, "Not that I don't totally appreciate everything you've done for me. Because I do, I just think it's time to be over."

I must've surprised him, because he raised his eyebrows and leaned back into his chair. "Is this because of Ram? Did you two split up?"

Huh? He thought Ram and I were a thing? "There's nothing between me and Ram."

"Really?"

I wished. "No. Honestly, I feel like I'm taking advantage of you. There's been no more threats against me. I'm fine. I have the alarm system on my house, I'm being careful, everything's fine. Which brings me to why you haven't been letting me pay for said alarm system."

Cooper stared at me. "So you came here to sever ties with my company?"

"No. Yes. Kind of." That didn't come out like I wanted it to. I put my hand up in the *wait* position and continued. "I don't think it's fair. You've been doing too much for me. Brett and Ram have basically told me to shut up about it, but I—"

"But you don't like it when other people do things for you. It makes you uncomfortable. Ram told me this about you. He also said you'd eventually try to get us to back off or to let you pay. Sorry, no."

I shot out of my chair to stand over him. Now I was kind of pissed. "No? What do you mean, 'no'? You can't tell me no. You're fired!" Take that, Cooper!

He stood up, put his hands on my shoulders and pushed me back into sitting on the chair, then sat down himself. "You can't fire us. You didn't hire us," he told me, all calm, cool, and collected.

"Fine. Brett fires you then."

"You can't fire someone for someone else, Molly. And it doesn't matter anyway, Brett doesn't pay us."

I shot up again. "What?"

"Sit down," he demanded.

"No."

He spoke in a manner meant to intimidate the hell out of me. "Sit. Down."

Good thing for me I don't intimidate easily. "En-Oh. What? You took me on as a charity case?" I half yelled at this point because I was humiliated. I did *not* want to be a charity case.

"Molly, sit down. I don't want to talk to you if you're going to go off half-cocked."

He didn't say anything else. He waited for me to calm down and sit. It took a while.

When I sat, I leaned forward and put my head in my hands. I'd had no idea he was doing everything for free. And it wasn't like I couldn't pay. I had a great job and a lucrative side job. I could totally pay!

"Molly, look at me," he ordered.

"No."

Without even so much as a sigh of annoyance, he grabbed my chair and turned it so it faced him directly. Then he took my wrists in one hand and pushed my forehead up with the other hand so I had to look at him.

Once he was satisfied that I would remain in place, he explained. "This case is personal for me."

"That doesn't make any sense. You didn't even know me before anything started happening."

"Try to look at it from my point of view. At first, Brett was paying us—which is no big deal because it's a write off for him, and I gave him a deal anyway. Then an employee whom I not only personally recruited, but trusted, doesn't do his job, and you end up almost dying because of it. Don't interrupt." I had opened my mouth to tell him it wasn't his fault that Nick left early. "You know what they say in the military right? When people don't follow orders, people die. Nick knows this, he was military. He didn't follow orders. You know the rest."

I pulled back so he was forced to let go of my wrists and take his hand off my forehead. "Okay, you feel responsible or guilty because Nick screwed up. So what? You're going to act as my bodyguard until this guy is caught? What if he's never caught? Cooper, this is ridiculous! I don't blame you or your company for anything! You don't owe me anything!"

Cooper turned my chair back to its original position and stood. "My answer remains the same. You can get in my face and complain all you want to. We're doing this by my rules, and my rules say until this guy is taken care of, you're stuck with us. Are you sure this has nothing to do with Ram?"

I stood too. "No! There is nothing between me and Ram! Or me and anybody for that matter! And everyone needs to leave me the hell alone about it, too!" I pointed to his face. "I don't like this you know."

He pushed my hand down. "I know. I don't care. Goodbye, Molly."

And with that I grabbed my purse and left. Jerk.

That fuck-knob. I stewed all the way home. I changed clothes then grabbed my pepper spray for a nice, long run. I should have run all the way to 3D to give one Mr. Gabe Cooper a peppery squirt smack dab in the eyes. The fantasy made me feel better.

After a quick shower, I called Katie to tell her what had happened. I needed her sympathy, but she didn't give me any. Zip, zero, zilch. She said she was glad that Cooper stood up to me and loved how he dismissed me. She told me that I was being an ungrateful shit, and I told her to fuck off. Then we agreed I would come over to her house for dinner the next day, and we left it at that.

I grabbed my current journal and started writing. I'd been pretty good about writing every day, even if it wasn't much. And the more pissed I was, the more I wrote. The makings for a lot of good songs were in my pages. I wondered if I could write a song called "Cooper Sucks, And Ram Does Too, So I Should Kick Both Their Asses." Hmmm . . . what rhymes with asses?

Chapter 29

After a couple of days, I was over the whole episode with Cooper. At dinner, Katie and Brett managed to make me understand his perspective. And I got it, I did. That didn't mean I had to like it. I was thirty-one years old, and had people looking out for me as if I were a toddler who might not look before crossing the street. It was demeaning.

So next I had to start concentrating on my father. In the month since we'd had dinner, he'd pretty much left me alone except for a phone call the previous week. I wasn't home and he left a message to call him. Forgive him? Forget him? Forgive him? Forget him? I couldn't choose yet.

Okay, if my mom called saying he'd died, how would I feel? Would I feel like *good riddance?* No, that was harsh. After all, as far as I knew, he wasn't a burden to society. Maybe it would depend on how he died.

Like, I would feel really bad if he got hit by a bus, but didn't die right away and lay there in agony while no one noticed and then the bus backed over him, squashing him like a bug, before he finally died a slow, painful death all by himself.

Would I feel as bad if he was whacked over the head with a frying pan (had just read that in the book I was reading) and died almost instantly? No wait. In the book, it took the victim a while to bleed out.

Damn it, I was getting off course.

And double damn it, I would feel bad no matter how he died. Because, regardless, he's my father. Even though he wore his ass as a hat for many years, at least he recognized he'd screwed up and was trying to make amends.

Looked like I had a phone call to make.

His wedding was the third Saturday in October, which, thankfully, wasn't a Wreckers Weekend. The nuptials were going to be a small affair in a church in Columbus, where Joy's family was from. My dad emailed a list of nice hotels nearby, since Columbus was over three hours away. Thankfully, he and Joy didn't ask me to be a part of the wedding ceremony. I don't think I could've handled acting like the undamaged daughter.

A couple of things made me anxious. Mainly, this was the first real step in starting to mend the relationship between my dad and I. I was pretty sure I was doing the right thing, and God knows Katie let me know every chance she could that, yes, I was doing the right thing. Then the evil part of me popped up and didn't want my dad to think that he could get away with abandoning me as a kid. I still wanted him to pay for what he did. And I know those kinds of feelings aren't healthy, but I couldn't let go of them.

I was also nervous because I started thinking about the smaller details. What should I give them for a wedding present? Did they really need anything at this point in their lives? Did old people even register somewhere?

Should I bring a date? I didn't want to go alone, but I wasn't dating anyone. A wedding wasn't an event you bring a first date to. I didn't have any male friends I felt comfortable bringing, except Alan, and that wasn't possible.

I had to call Katie.

After I told her about my dilemma she started brainstorming.

"Hmm . . . there's no way you'd call Ram and tell him to ditch the bitch so you could take him?" she asked.

"That's mean! Kinda funny, but mean. And no, I will not do that."

"Kyle? It would be funny if you brought a guy with all those piercings."

Maybe. "We're friends, I don't know. I don't think I'd be comfortable with him for that kind of situation. He's a possibility, I guess." It would be fun to watch my dad's reaction to me bringing such an "alternative" looking guy.

She named a few other guys, all of whom I shot down.

"I could get one of Brett's friends to go with you. There are three or four really cute ones. Some you've seen at the bar."

"I don't want to go with a stranger."

Katie gave an exasperated sigh. "Well, then I don't know what to tell you, Mol. Good Lord, go alone."

I moaned. "I think I'm gonna have to."

"Wait!" she yelled.

"What?"

"What about Cooper?"

"Cooper? Why on earth would you suggest him?"

"Well, you know him well enough. He's good looking. And if you don't ask him, then you really have no other choices besides Kyle. And I think Kyle has a girlfriend now anyway."

I gave it a second of thought. "I don't know, Katie. I think I'll go alone."

We talked about all her choir stuff happening this time of year, how Gina was doing on her album, then hung up.

I really, really did not want to go to this wedding alone. Cooper was looking like my only option. Ugh, I'd have to work up the nerve to ask him. This would take almost two days out of his schedule. We'd have to leave early on a Saturday, then we'd either have to get hotel rooms for the night, or drive home very late on Saturday. Since I wasn't comfortable with making the long drive home so late at night, reserving a couple of rooms and not heading home until Sunday made the most sense.

That man did so much for me already and asking him to go with me would make me feel as if I were taking advantage of his generosity. The more I thought about it, he really was the perfect choice. I was fairly comfortable with him. Not nearly as comfortable as I was with Ram, but still, comfortable enough. We could hold a conversation. I wouldn't have to worry about him pawing at me all night. He was totally professional, and I highly doubted he would get rip-roaring drunk and make an ass of himself. He would act exactly perfect for the occasion, which was good because I wasn't really sure about myself.

I couldn't find the nerve to ask him, though, so my chicken-shitness decided for me. I would go alone.

I didn't see Katie much because work demanded a lot of her time, so I didn't tell her I decided to go solo to the wedding until October's Wreckers Weekend. She huffed, but left the subject alone.

That is, until our second break. I was sitting in Brett's office reading when Cooper walked in.

"Katie said you wanted to talk to me?" he asked.

I looked up, confused. "What? No I don't." Then it hit me, that little shit. "Sorry, Katie's being an idiot."

He crossed his arms and leaned against Brett's desk. "She also said to not leave you alone until you spoke to me."

I could not believe Katie opened her big, fat mouth. "No, Cooper. Don't worry about it." I smiled to reassure him.

"Katie seemed worried about you, so I'm not leaving until you tell me what's wrong. Is it The Creep? Has he made contact again?"

"No. Forget it."

Cooper stood there, in the exact same position, glaring at me for like, two minutes. Two minutes is a long time when someone is glaring at you. And God damn it, it's effective. I know because I do it all the time to people. I turned my attention to my book and read the same paragraph over and over. Damn it!

His glare wasn't like most people's glares. His was super penetrating. Kind of freaky. Finally I couldn't take it and gave up. In a snit I told him, "Fine! My dad—who I don't really know—is getting married in two weeks—from tonight actually—in Columbus, and I don't have a date. And I don't want to go alone because I'm afraid I'll go bat shit crazy being there by myself without knowing anybody. And when I was talking with Katie about possible dates, she said I should ask you. But I decided not to, because you already do way too much for me, and I don't even know if you have a wife or girlfriend or whatever, and it would take two days away from you, and I feel so stupid right now I can't even tell you."

Where was a hole for me to sink into?

Cooper looked at me as if I was crazy for a few seconds and then whipped out his cell and dialed. "Hi Beverly, this is Cooper. When you get this message clear my schedule for, hold on." He must've checked the calendar feature on his phone. I couldn't say for sure because I was hiding my eyes to avoid looking at him. "October seventeenth and eighteenth. Reschedule or reassign any appointments or details I have for those days." He snapped his phone shut and continued staring.

I peeked at him. "Seriously, just like that?" I asked. I'd never really considered that if I asked him he'd say yes. Come to think of it, I technically hadn't even asked him.

"See, here's the deal. I do this for you, and you're never going to ride me about your alarm system, or the body guarding services, or the PI services."

"So you're doing this to shut me up?"

"Absolutely. I'll be your date to the wedding, and in return you never mention stopping my services ever again."

I stood up, put my hands on my hips, and tilted my head to the side to think. I stuck out my hand. "Deal," I said.

We shook on it. "Good. Call me this week with the details."

I agreed, so he went back out into the bar.

Hot damn, I had a date for the wedding. A pity date mind you, but at least I wouldn't be alone. He was going with me so I wouldn't bug him about his free services, but at least I wouldn't be alone. And it wasn't with Ram, which really bummed me out, but at least I wouldn't be alone.

Now all I had to do was refrain from killing Katie for her little stunt, because I needed her to go shopping with me so I'd have a dress to wear.

Chapter 30

Looking back, my naivety was embarrassing. To my credit, the signs were never there, but still.

I lay in bed alone and came to grips with what I'd done. I wasn't ashamed. I wasn't love-struck by any means. I didn't regret it, not then anyway. I did feel a tad bit guilty, though.

Cooper picked me up Saturday morning, as planned. I had offered to drive, but he turned me down. I tried to give him gas money, but he glared at me until I put the money back into my wallet. I rolled my eyes and let him drive us to Columbus on his dime. We then checked into our respective hotel rooms and got ready for the wedding.

He was supposed to meet me at my hotel room at four-thirty. I needed a drink before I could brave this thing, so I called his room at ten after four, telling him to meet me at the restaurant downstairs in twenty minutes.

The hotel had a small restaurant on the main floor that, thankfully, had a small bar. I ordered a vodka and cranberry juice and was halfway through it when Cooper came down and found me.

He walked up to me, gave me the once over, but said nothing.

"You want a drink?" I asked.

"No, thanks. I didn't think you drank."

"Hardly ever. I feel like I need liquid courage tonight, ya know?" I downed the rest of my drink. "Listen, do not let me drink more than two drinks at the reception. If I go for a third, you have my permission to do whatever you need to stop my drinking. Not that I'm some sort of alcoholic or anything. I'm, ya know, really nervous. And when I start drinking when I'm nervous, I have been known to go overboard. Oh my God, this one time when me and Katie went snowboarding—never mind. Two more drinks. Period."

He nodded. "Okay. You ready?"

I took a really deep breath and blew it out slowly. "I'm ready. Let's go."

See, most men in that situation would inquire about my nervousness. Not Cooper. He didn't give a shit about emotional stuff like that. Which was good, because if he'd asked I would have to tell him that my anxiety stemmed from the fact that attending the wedding was the first step in the process of forgiving my father for abandoning me and my mother so many years ago. That, although I had decided to forgive him, not all of me was okay with that decision.

So I was glad I didn't have to rehash my feelings, because then I might regret being there. Or possibly I might feel better about the whole situation.

The ceremony was nice. Not so short that the long drive was a waste, but not so long that my butt was numb from the hard church pews.

After the ceremony and during the receiving line, both my dad and Joy hugged me. I didn't respond with the same enthusiasm, but I pulled off polite and caring, I thought.

Then we were off to the reception, where we joined about fifty people who had also gone to the wedding. There were a few members of my dad's family present, but mostly Joy's family and the friends they shared.

My dad's sister and brother, my aunt and uncle, were there and introduced themselves to me. Sadly, I didn't even recognize them. That was awkward. Several of my dad and Joy's friends came up and introduced themselves to me as well. I introduced Cooper simply as Cooper. I didn't say "This is my friend, Cooper," or "This is the man who's here so I won't bug him anymore, Cooper." I simply said, "This is Cooper," even though his name is actually Gabe.

After dinner, we sat at our table. Mingling in a crowd of people I didn't know wasn't my thing. My foot began tapping. I looked around to avoid staring straight ahead like an idiot. Finally I turned to Cooper. "You have to either talk to me or dance with me because this is where the going bat shit crazy is going to happen. I'll just sit here and think and stew. What's it gonna be?"

"I don't dance," he said.

"So then tell me about yourself."

"I'm forty years old and run a business that keeps people safe." He gave me a sardonic glance. "Or tries to anyway."

"Well, duh. I already knew that. Well, I didn't know your age. So I'm assuming you're not married. Do you have a girlfriend?" I asked.

"No."

"Kids?"

"No."

"Hmmm. It's like pulling teeth. Gay lover?"

This earned me a "Really?"

"Chill out. That last one was a joke. Okay, so you don't want to talk about yourself. What do you like talk about?"

"Sports is good."

"Ew."

He turned toward me and put one arm on the back of his chair. "You're probably the most athletic woman I know, and you say 'ew' to talking about sports?"

"I like to play them. I don't follow professional teams. That's . . . boring."

We chose to get up and get drinks to break the monotony of our attempt at small talk. Neither one of us drank any alcohol at the reception. I stuck to water. Cooper drank pop.

Once we sat back down, I continued our conversation. "So you said I'm *probably* the most athletic woman you know. What other women do you know who are athletic? Are they more athletic than me? Tell me who they are so I can kick their asses."

"Are you serious?"

I rolled my eyes. "Of course not." I should've answered yes to see if it led to a more interesting conversation.

Cooper stood up and held out his hand. "Let's dance."

I put my hand in his and let him pull me up. "What brought this on?"

"Honestly, Molly? If we don't dance I'm afraid of what bizarre thing you'll say next."

"So you're dancing with me to shut me up?" I should have been offended, but wasn't.

Instead of answering, he led me to the dance floor, put one hand in mine, and the other on my lower back.

"You know I was a dancer for fifteen years, right?" I informed him. "And I still dance on occasion. So I could mop the dance floor with you." I threw my head back and laughed because, really, I *was* funny sometimes.

Cooper raised his eyebrows. "I'm glad you humor yourself."

"Well, somebody has to."

We danced a couple of songs here and there throughout the night. When I would badger him with conversation too much, he grabbed my hand and led me to the dance floor. Slow dancing with Cooper was pleasant, nothing fancy. More than what you'd think him capable of. He caught on early that I could follow any lead and stepped up his game, so his "I don't dance" comment was a lie. There surely was a story as to why he could slow dance, but I wasn't going to bother asking about it. We'd go back to the table, sit in silence for a while, then I'd try to get him to converse with me again.

I was surprised that typical traditions of a wedding were kept. Especially the garter and bouquet tosses. Cooper was in total agreement with me that we should find a place to hide while those God-forsaken activities took place. I hated them. I'd learned a long time ago to sense when the bride was gearing up to toss her bouquet, and made myself scarce before the DJ called all the single gals to the floor. Because if they made me go out there, I would do what I had to do to catch the stupid flowers. Then I would beat everyone over the head with it to teach them all a lesson.

Was it me or was I getting more violent in my old age?

At the end of the night, I said my goodbyes to my dad and Joy with promises that we would get in touch soon. Surely, his version of soon and my version of soon differed, but that wasn't the time to get into semantics. I snagged Cooper, and we left.

He walked me to the door of my hotel room.

I pulled my key card from my purse, and we stood facing each other. "Cooper, I want to say thank you for doing this for me. I really appreciate it. And I promise I won't say anything about your misplaced sense of guilt. I mean the services that you are providing me free of charge even though I am completely, totally capable of paying." I gave him a sincere smile. "No, really. Thank you."

"You're welcome. And Molly?"

"Hmm?"

No verbal response. Instead, he leaned down and kissed me. A regular kiss at first, no tongue. He pressed his mouth to mine for a few seconds then pulled back to look at me. I leaned back slightly to look at him too. I had *not* seen that coming.

He kissed me again. But this time when he pulled back, he kept his forehead pressed to mine. I didn't pull away, so he went for it. He kissed me for real. Slowly. His lips parted. Automatically, mine parted too. Then his tongue touched mine very gently, as if testing to see if kissing me was okay. My tongue responded to his, and we really, *really* started kissing.

Oh my God. Cooper? Wow.

Katie would freak out if she knew.

Ram would . . . nope. Not going there.

Should I be doing this?

I pulled back a few inches. I needed a breath or two to clear my head. Cooper didn't say anything. He waited for me to make up my mind. He was staring at me, so I looked into his eyes. Then I looked at his whole expression. It wasn't a look of impatience at having to wait; it was a look of lust. Cooper wanted me. I wanted to be wanted. I hadn't had a man inside of me, pleasuring me, in so long. I needed what he was offering.

And I knew the score with Cooper. He wouldn't want anything from me except sex. I didn't want anything from him except sex. We were just two people who found each other attractive and wanted to act on that attraction. Before he kissed me, I'd never, ever thought of Cooper in a lusty way. But now I was turned on and didn't want to deny myself any longer.

I still had the room key card in my hand. I opened the door, and he pulled me inside. Without any hesitation, I tossed my purse on the floor and put my arms around his neck and resumed our kiss, letting him know that, yes, we were going to do this.

He ran his hands over my back, my hips, and up my stomach. I hadn't been touched like that in so long, and my body shivered. I put my hands inside his suit jacket and slid it off him. Then I un-tucked and unbuttoned his shirt and ran my hands over his bare skin.

He felt good.

His hands were the slightest hint of rough on my skin. Ram's hands were probably smoother, his kisses softer. No, maybe firm, totally passionate.

Stop it! No more thoughts of Ram.

Crossing this line with Cooper was my acknowledgement that Ram and I would never be.

I snapped back to the present with Cooper, and he was unzipping my dress. He pushed the dress off my shoulders so it fell to the carpet. I slid his shirt off, and we stood there partially dressed, checking each other out. We were both blemished: him with tattoos and me with scars. I could tell his tattoos were old. One looked relatively new, as if it had been done to cover an older one. Both of his upper arms were covered in tattoos, which stopped a couple inches above his elbows. He had one that started on his stomach and went to his side. The newer one was on his chest.

I stood there in my bra, panties, thigh-highs, and heels. Cooper was in pants, socks and shoes. He kneeled and removed my heels. Then he peeled off one thigh-high, followed by the other.

When he stood again, I noticed how aroused he was, and my heart beat quickened. I pressed myself against him and kissed him again before I made quick work of his belt, pants, socks and shoes.

He walked forward, backing me into the bed. When we couldn't go any further, he gently pushed me onto the mattress and then followed, crawling over me. I scooted up while still on my back, until my entire body was on the bed. Cooper lay so his legs were between my mine, upper body propped by his elbows. He kissed me once more, then pulled himself up so he was kneeling, still between my legs.

He didn't say anything. His gaze roamed over my body. He leaned slightly forward so I took the opportunity to run my hands along every part of his chest, stomach, and arms, appreciating the work he obviously gave to his body. He reached behind my back, then undid my bra and tossed it on the floor. His hands went right back on me, stroking up my stomach to cup my breasts, then ran his thumbs over my nipples. His mouth followed his hands. He kissed his way up my stomach until he reached my breasts.

I let him have his fill, then took his face in my hands and guided his mouth back to my mine. While we kissed, I slid my palms slowly from his shoulders to his chest, down his sides, and into his boxers. He helped me get them all the way off, then did the same to my panties so we were both, finally, naked.

We took another moment to stare at each other. I worked hard on my body, so I knew I looked pretty good, but the intensity of his glare made me self-conscious, especially when he took his thumb and ran it over the scar on my stomach. I propped myself up on my elbows, ready to ask him if he changed his mind when he practically pounced on me.

Cooper's hands and mouth were everywhere after that. So were mine. At one point, I was able to flip him over and straddle him. I wanted to touch him, torture him, and tease him. I leaned back and trailed my fingernails from his ankles, up the sides of his legs, over his hips, up his stomach and chest, and into his hair where I got a good grip and pulled. When I leaned down to kiss him, he turned us around again.

Once he had me on my back, he darted off the bed and rifled through his pants. He took a couple of condoms out of his wallet before joining me again. He knelt between my sprawled legs.

I froze.

He leaned forward and nuzzled my neck. "What's wrong?" he whispered.

"Nothing," I whispered back.

"Molly, if you're changing your mind tell me now."

Was I changing my mind? Hell no! Still whispering, I told him: "I'm not changing my mind. I'm just nervous."

His body was supported by one arm. His other hand started feeling me up again. "Why?"

Because this was the point of no return. "It's been a while," I answered. Then I pulled his mouth to mine, but instead of kissing him, I told him, "Cooper. Fuck me."

I didn't have to tell him twice. The condom went on, and he went in. He was unhurried at first, maintaining control of himself. After a minute he became frantic. There was heavy breathing and soft grunting from Cooper, and maybe a squeal or two from me.

Just when I was thinking he wouldn't last long at that pace, he took a shaky breath then slowed down and rolled us over so I was on top and could set the pace. I rode him nice and slow for a while, letting his hands once again go anywhere they wanted. Then, keeping him inside of me, I lay down and changed from straddling his hips to aligning my legs in with the rest of my body. Shutting my thighs to make myself as tight as I could, I slowly rocked my body, forward and backward. He must've liked it because his eye rolled back into his head and a weird noise came out of his throat.

He grasped my hips to stop me. I laid my head on his chest and felt his chest rise and fall. The first several breaths were deep, then changed to normal. I lifted my head. He kissed me and slowly rolled us over so I was on my back yet again. He stayed very still for a minute and kissed along my collar bone. Then, finally, he drove into me fast and hard.

I dug my fingers into his arms and let the convulsions rip through my entire body. He came shortly thereafter. After his final thrust, he rested his head next to mine while his breathing went back to normal. Then he pulled out, tossed off the condom, and collapsed next to me. Neither one of us said anything for a long time, and without his body on mine, I started getting cold. I reached under the pillows to grab the edge of the blankets. Before I yanked them down I asked him, "Are you sleeping here or going back to your own room?"

He yawned. "I should go back to my room. I have some calls to make." He got off the bed and dressed.

"Toss me my bra and panties please." He did, and I put them on while he watched. "Check out is at ten tomorrow morning. I'll be at your door at nine-thirty."

"I'll be ready. Good night, Molly."

Now I yawned. "Night, Cooper."

It didn't say much for me that my first thought after he left was, *thank God I don't have to share the bed.* I was tired and wanted to simply fall asleep right where I lay, but I had to get up to take my birth control pill anyway. Since I was getting up to do that, I might as well do the rest of my nighttime routine, so I brushed my teeth, washed my face, peed, and put on my pajamas.

I crawled back into bed and pulled the covers up to my chin. *I just cheated on Kent's showerhead.*

I laughed myself to sleep.

Chapter 31

The next morning I lay in bed trying to convince myself to get out from under the covers and into the shower. I replayed the previous night. I'd finally ended one hell of a dry spell.

The guilt came when I thought of Ram, which was stupid because he'd probably done the same thing last night with his girlfriend.

The drive home was the same as the drive there. The weird thing was, there wasn't any regret or uneasiness between Cooper and I. We weren't ignoring what happened. The vibe was like, *so what. It happened.*

He dropped me off, and I called Katie right away. She'd be dying to know about the wedding, my dad, and how I'd behaved. I wasn't going to tell her about having sex with Cooper.

I told her all about the wedding, minus the nakedness, and she gave her usual best friend responses. She was proud of me, I should feel good about taking this step, blah, blah, blah.

"So you and Cooper really slept in separate rooms?" she asked toward the end of the conversation.

"Of course. We each had our own room and spent the night in those rooms." Not a lie.

"That's too bad. I was kind of wondering what he looked like naked."

Damn good. "Shame on you, Katie Scarlett. You better hope Brett didn't hear you."

"I already told him that if you two did it, I was getting full details."

"Please tell me his response to that was asking you to stop using the phrase 'did it'." I made fake gagging noises.

"He doesn't care what I call it as long as he's getting it."

We hung up with Katie disappointed, thinking Cooper and I didn't do it. But boy, did we.

The last weekend in October was a karaoke weekend at Brett's. Yes, Heather's idea was still going strong. It had been too long since I'd gone. Feeling guilty about that, I joined Katie and belted out a couple songs with her.

We had fun. For once, I was the more relaxed, laid back one. Katie was on edge.

While other patrons were taking their turns butchering classic songs, I nudged Katie away from our seats by the bar and toward the back, where we had privacy. "Do you wanna tell me what's wrong?" I asked her.

Whereas Katie usually had to pry my problems out of me, one question from me was all it took to open the gates for her.

She leaned her head against the wall. "Molly, why don't you think Brett has asked me to marry him yet?"

I loved very few people, and Katie was top on my list. My heart sank at her sad expression. Her face dropped all its happy pretenses, and she looked miserable.

I stated the obvious. "He's a man. Doesn't it take them, like, forever to decide this stuff?"

"But we're both over thirty. We love each other, we practically live together, we both want kids. What's his hold up?"

"I don't know. Have you asked him?"

"No. I keep waiting and waiting and waiting. It's been over a year. Hasn't he had plenty of time to decide if he wants to spend the rest of his life with me? I mean, he's been getting the milk for free. It's time he bought the damn cow!"

I laughed. "For the record, you said that, not me." She half-smiled. I hugged her. "Katie, you should know by now that my understanding of men and relationships is practically nonexistent. You have to suck it up and ask him."

She bumped her hip into mine. "You really stink at giving advice."

"So love me for my looks." I made a kissy face toward her. We were still laughing when Heather joined us. "Dudes, what's going on?"

Katie told her the story about Deena's hissy fit while we were in Mississippi. Then we imitated her awful singing voice. That kept us laughing for a while, and Katie visibly perked up.

Thank God, because I loved Brett like a brother. But if he hurt Katie I might have to punch him.

The next weekend was a Wreckers Weekend. The band was excited because we had two new songs to debut.

They went over well, of course; I mean, who didn't love a song about going to hell or killing the bastard who cheated on you? Like I always said, we had songs for everyone.

After Saturday's show, Cooper followed me home. Instead of waiting for me to go inside, turn on the lights then wave to him from the window, he asked if he could come in. He obviously wanted a repeat of the after-wedding festivities.

I let him in. I'd be damned if I'd suffer another couple of years of celibacy. I was thirty-one years old. I should be able to screw whoever I wanted and not feel bad about it. Almost getting killed made me realize I only had this one life to live, and it could end at any time. Therefore, if I felt like screwing Cooper without any form of relationship, then so be it.

Our first time together repeated itself. We had hot sex and he left. We both got what we wanted and didn't pretend to want anything more.

I hadn't seen my mom in a while, so on Sunday I called her and we made plans for dinner. I figured I would test the waters for having the talk I've wanted for so long by bringing up my dad's wedding. If it went well, I would move on to other topics.

I grew up in Temperance, Michigan. It was a nice suburb with good schools that had changed over the years with more subdivisions, more commercial businesses, and more people. I totally understand progress, but seeing your hometown change so much was weird.

My mom's house was in the middle of a side street. All of the houses were different, and some of the neighbors took advantage of the fact that there was no home association to set standards for their lawns. Still, most of the street was well kept.

I knocked and walked in, drawn by the smell of my favorite meal. My mom made the best chicken cordon bleu I have ever tasted. She knew I loved it, so that must've been why she made it.

"Hey, Mom. I'm here," I called out.

She came from the direction of her bedroom into the kitchen. "Hey, Molly."

This was where things went weird. She hugged me. Not one of her usual half-assed hugs, but a real wrap-your-arms-around-me-and-squeeze-while-gently-rocking-side-to-side hug. I hugged her back. We held on to each other for way longer than normal.

"You look good," she told me when we finally let go of each other.

I waited, half expecting *Twilight Zone* music to start. "Uh, thanks. You too. So what's going on?" I asked, sounding as if nothing unusual had just happened.

She took my hands in hers and smiled. When people did this it usually meant they were about to tell you something significant.

"We have a guest today. His name is Victor. We've been seeing each other for a while now, and I wanted you to meet him. He's joining us for dinner. He should be here in—" she looked at her watch. "ten minutes or so."

What hell was it with parents and surprises? First Mama and Mr. Culver got back together without telling us, then my dad popped up, now this. When your children are grown, is there a rule that you spring stuff on them? Were they trying to make our hair turn prematurely gray?

It's not like I cared if my mom was dating. Couldn't she have mentioned it to me over the phone and then *asked* me if I cared if he joined us, though?

Mom's surprise totally ruined my plans to try and talk to her about my dad's wedding and my dead twin sister. I'd finally worked up the nerve but lost the chance.

Victor arrived, and we exchanged pleasantries. He wasn't at all what I expected him to look like. I'd imagined tall, charming, and handsome. In reality, he was short, plump, and charming, and he seemed like a really nice guy. Their affection for each other was obvious. Hell, maybe they were in love with each other; I wasn't going to dig that deep.

Mom made apple crisp for dessert and even had vanilla ice cream to go with it because she knew that's how I liked it. She usually only made it for Thanksgiving.

"Wow. My favorite dinner and your Thanksgiving dessert. What gives?"

"Well, I'm spending Thanksgiving with Victor's friends, so I won't be here to make my apple crisp for you. Is that okay?"

"Uh . . ." I stammered. "Of course it is."

"Will you be okay? Do you have somewhere you can go?"

"Yeah, Mom. I'll be fine. Don't worry."

So I didn't get to have the talk I wanted to with my mom, and she dropped two bombshells on me. She was happy, so who cared? I was glad for her. She needed love and laughter and contentment in her life. What was weird was that when it came to my dad, I merely *accepted* that he'd moved on. My mom, I was happy for. Though it would've been nice for her to invite me to wherever she would be, or at least set aside time for me.

My dad called a few days later to invite me to Thanksgiving. Coincidence? I doubted it.

I lied and told him I already had plans. Maybe I'd go snowboarding. I'd have to look into how full or empty the ski resorts were for holidays.

It looked as if Thanksgiving was going to be an ordinary day for me. Katie would go to Brett's family. She invited me along, but I declined. My nametag would've read: Molly Davis, Loser Third Wheel. No thanks.

Gina and I had kept in regular contact since I'd left Nashville in August. She was great, getting along with the band, and singing for a living. The last time I spoke to her a cold virus was working its way through the band. I'd worried that if she caught it, she wouldn't give her voice the proper time to heal. I dialed the phone to check on her, perhaps threaten to tell Kent on her if she wasn't taking good care of herself.

She didn't answer, so I called Kent instead.

He told me Gina was doing really well and everything was going according to plan. The album would be finished in the next couple of months, then she would do the cover shoot for the album and start publicity.

He asked about my plans for Thanksgiving, so I told him how I was spending it—with no one to bother me.

"That's stupid," he told me.

"Why is it stupid? And anyway I might go snowboarding that weekend."

After a pause he said, "I'm calling in the favor you owe me for playing the softball game."

"I'm not having sex with you."

He snorted. "Get over yourself."

"I was kidding! What are you going to make me do?"

"Lisa-Anne invited me over her house so I could spend Thanksgiving with the girls. I couldn't say no, even though the idea of spending it with her husband made me want to."

"So?"

"So you're going to come to Nashville and spend Thanksgiving with me, Lisa-Anne, the girls, and Beau."

"You expect me to come the Nashville and have Thanksgiving with you?"

"Like you expected me to go to Michigan and play ball with you."

Well, he had me there. And I had told him I owed him one, which I would never back out of. And I knew and actually liked Lisa-Anne and their girls.

I whined anyway. "Don't you have a flavor of the week you could take instead?"

"Not really."

"Fine. You know, this is a bigger favor than what I had you do."

"How do you figure that?"

"Because I have to fly on the busiest flying day of the year! You're lucky you pay me well and I don't back out of favors. Get my damn room ready."

So I had plans for Thanksgiving. I wasn't exactly looking forward to going, but at least I wouldn't be all by myself. That made me slightly less pathetic, right? Kent had mentioned Lisa-Anne was an excellent cook, so at least I'd eat good food. And what better to go with good food than being someone's date just so they had you to help ease the discomfort of spending the day with their ex-wife and her husband. And the fact that I had nothing better to do than be Kent's date?

Ugh, I didn't want to go there.

Chapter 32

The hustle, bustle, and general craziness of the airport didn't bother me. Despite the ridiculously long lines, the madness of parents frantically herding their children to the correct gate, and the God-awful crowds, I wasn't irritated. Cooper had come over the night before and spent a good hour all over me, so I was pretty non-frustrated. I was so sexually satisfied I wouldn't even bat an eyelash at Kent's showerhead.

I arrived at Kent's Wednesday afternoon and planned to stay until Sunday morning. The weather was nicer in Tennessee than in Michigan, plus I didn't want to rush into town and then rush right back out. Kent and I were pretty comfortable around each other, so I wouldn't feel awkward. He could go do his own thing, and I would hang around and do mine.

I really wanted to see Gina, but she and her mother went home to Ohio for Thanksgiving and were staying for a week.

If I got bored, I could start my Christmas shopping.

Kent and I showed up at Lisa-Anne and Beau's at two o'clock. Dinner was supposed to be at four. Why is it when people hosted holiday dinners they weren't at proper meal times? It forced everyone to starve all day so they could gorge themselves.

As it turned out, several members from Lisa-Anne's family were also there. A sister, her husband, and kids, and an elderly aunt and uncle. No one acted as if Kent being there with a date was odd.

I caught up on Haley and Riley's lives. They were such good girls. Haley was all about the dramatics. I saw Riley emulate her a few times, so she wasn't not too far behind in that department.

I think Kent was able to relax since I was there. When he talked to Beau, he was glaringly uncomfortable, so I would step in and join them. It helped, I think.

I had a nice time. The people were pleasant. I ate enough to make up for all the calories I burned having sex with Cooper.

I noticed Kent watching Lisa-Anne toward the end of the night. He looked at her in a way he doesn't look at other women. I didn't say anything until later.

Back at his house I told him, "So you're still in love with your ex-wife."

We were tired and full, so we'd changed into comfy clothes and were plopped on the couch watching a movie. *Forrest Gump*, one of my all-time favorites.

He ignored me.

"Kent."

"What." He still wouldn't look at me.

"Do you still love Lisa-Anne?" I asked him.

"Does it matter?"

"I don't know. Does it?"

"Nope. It doesn't."

I wouldn't let him drop the conversation like I knew he wanted. Kent was my friend. If I could help him feel better, I was going to do it. Plus I'm nosey.

I nudged him on the side of the leg with my foot. "So you still love her, but she's married to Beau, so it doesn't matter? Or is this a case of I don't want her, but I don't want anyone else to have her?"

He looked at me and mimicked one of Haley's sayings. "Are you for real?"

"Oh, my God! You sounded exactly like Haley when you did that! Come on, Kent. Spill."

"I don't know, woman. I find myself missing what we had when times were good. My daughters are being raised more by their step-father than by me, and that's not right."

"So why don't you talk to her and arrange it so they come here more?"

Kent stood. "I'm getting myself a beer. You want anything?"

"You have any vodka?"

"I got vodka."

"I'll take vodka mixed with something. Surprise me. Oh, and I'm a lightweight, so make it nice and girly."

He left and came back with a beer and my drink. I sipped. Whoa! I jogged to the kitchen and added more orange juice, then joined him on the couch.

"That drink wasn't even strong," he said.

"When I said I was a lightweight, I wasn't kidding." I took a big drink. "So? You going to get your girls more or what?"

"I don't know. I haven't thought about it."

"Liar."

"Listen. Lisa-Anne and I have been getting along lately. I don't want anything screwing that up. I don't want to start fighting again."

We finished our drinks and poured more. By the time the movie was over, we were both drunk, him more so. The more Kent drank, the more he opened up to me about Lisa-Anne. I didn't know if he was still in love with her, but I do think he missed being a family.

The credits started rolling, and I was tired.

"Molly, do you think I'm pathetic?"

"Maybe, yeah," I answered.

"Gee thanks." He let out a huge belch.

"And that's why I don't drink beer. You're not so much pathetic, more like a little lost." I had a few more swallows of my last drink left, so I took a sip. "Oh, wait. I think I described myself." Screw it, I chugged the rest. "No you're fine. Talk to Lisa-Anne about seeing your girls more, and stop going from woman to woman to have a body to sleep with. I don't think it's Lisa-Anne you really want. I think you're ready to move on from all your flavors of the week into a meaningful relationship." Wow. "Damn, I'm insightful when I'm drunk."

He laughed as I stood because I spilled some of my drink down my face and shirt, and took several attempts to wipe it off with my hand.

"You're probably right," he finally said.

I settled myself again. "I usually am." I wished.

"So why are you pathetic and lost?"

I stared straight ahead, mouth closed.

"Oh come on, Molly. I opened up to you," he said, and waited.

I took a dramatic breath. "Well let's see. A year and a half ago my life was a lot less complicated. In the past fifteen months, I feel like it's gotten. . . surreal. I pushed away the man I think I might be in love with, and now he's moved on." And I started screwing that man's boss. "I'm always looking over my shoulder like a paranoid freak. I feel like everyone is moving in the right direction except me. I'm stuck in my life, waiting for it to go back to where it used to be, even though I know it will never be that way again. I have father issues, mother issues, relationship issues, and escaped attacker issues. I'm a train wreck."

When I looked at his face, it read *oh shit, sorry I asked*. Once he realized it, he relaxed his features and smiled, albeit sympathetically. "Well, at least you write good music."

"Yeah. Professionally I'm great. Just not personally. Wow. Huh."

"What."

"That was the first time that I allowed myself to admit all that crap." Equal parts freeing, and terrifying.

"Do I know the man you may or may not be in love with?"

My face burned bright red. "No."

"Now who's the liar?" he asked. I said nothing. "All right then. I'm going to bed. We can have sex, and I'll start working on my meaningful relationships tomorrow. What do you think?"

I stood up and grabbed a throw pillow. Then I whacked him with it a few times. "Kent!" *Whack.* "I like you. Don't." *Whack.* "Ruin." *Whack.* "It!" *Whack, whack, whack.*

He had his arms up to protect his head. "God damn, you're freakishly strong! You know I at least—" *Whack!* "—had to try."

I stopped hitting him. "Kent. You know if we went there it would ruin everything we have now. Admit it, I would drive you crazy."

He crunched his face in thought, then exhaled loudly. That was a yes.

"You want someone more permanent, and I'm the easiest thing for you to reach for right now. Is having sex with me—knowing that we would never work out as a couple—worth losing our friendship *and* professional relationship?" I jabbed my finger into his chest to drill in my point. "Remember, Kent, I am going to continue to make you a lot of money. I'm working on a lot of new stuff that's really good."

He slumped down, admitting defeat. "Huh. You are insightful when you're drunk. It's kind of annoying."

I whacked him with the pillow once more for fun, then we went to bed. Alone.

I returned home to Michigan and unpacked. Seeing Christmas decorations already up put me in the holiday spirit, so I went out and braved the crowds in the stores for a few hours.

I had the people I buy gifts for every year: Katie, Mama, my mom, Alan, Heather, Josh, and Courtney. That year I added Kent, Haley, and Riley. I wondered if I should add my dad. I mean, I was being a big girl deciding to have a relationship with the man, so I should add him to the list. Which meant I added Joy to the list. And if I added Joy then maybe I should add Brett, since he and Katie were serious, even without a marriage proposal.

Oh hell, gift buying pressure sucked the Christmas spirit right out of me. Thank God I found a few great things for myself, and the coolest bracelet for Katie since I'd promised her jewelry months ago, so shopping wasn't a total waste.

I called my mom to find out how her Thanksgiving with Victor went, with the selfish hope that she didn't have a good time and I'd have to comfort her. Then that would lead us into the serious topics we needed to discuss.

Nope. She was unusually talkative and sounded happy. And I continued to be happy for her. I still had a lot to discuss with her, but the time wasn't right. I was afraid of ruining the continuous good mood she was in whenever we spoke.

December came and brought the kind of cold that chilled me to my bones. The anticipation of going snowboarding with Katie kept me from hating the weather. When you lived in Michigan you either embraced the winters, or let it kill your mood for months.

But it did kinda suck having to haul the band's equipment from the van to the stage when the wind was so frigid and fierce it took your breath away.

Kyle showed up to the Wreckers Weekend with his new girlfriend, Shannon, and was quite smitten with her. She seemed pretty nice. I actually hung out in the bar with the rest of the band during our breaks to talk to them.

I had a great time telling her about the softball game Kyle had lost, and I had won. He challenged me to a rematch next summer; I accepted.

Eventually I asked Kyle how his band was doing since he hadn't mentioned them at all.

He shook his head. "Shit man. I don't even know anymore."

"What do you mean?" I asked.

He took a long swig of beer. "So get this. Adam gets out of jail like, two weeks ago, and guess what he does?"

"Asks for you to take him back?"

"Yup," he says, making a popping sound on the P.

"And?"

"And I'm the only one who thinks it's a bad idea. Everyone else thinks that because we haven't found a replacement yet we may as well take him back. They don't think we'll find a drummer who fits. Never mind that he's a worthless piece of shit."

Damn. There must have been more between Kyle and Adam than just being band mates. "What are you going to do if the rest of the band lets him back in?"

In a cute, reassuring gesture, Shannon started rubbing his back.

"I don't know," he said. "Suck it up, I guess. He's a really good drummer. This band really has something good going. This might be my chance to make it, ya know? I mean, I know it's a long shot. Hey, you never know, right?"

"Right," I said, and eye-balled the rest of The Wreckers. Turning down a possible record deal gave me a case of the guilty squirms. No one must've said anything to Midnight because Kyle seemed oblivious. "For what it's worth I think you're right. That man is going to be nothing but trouble for you all. Maybe I'll try and talk sense into the rest of the band the next time I see them."

"Won't do any good," Kyle mumbled.

Ram was there by himself the entire weekend. I didn't get to talk to him much on Friday since I hung out with Kyle and the rest of the band. He followed me home, and I found myself wishing he would ask to come inside instead of driving away once I gave him the wave to let him know I was okay. Of course, that didn't happen.

At Saturday's show, Ram and I hung out more. I had fun. We talked and joked around. I couldn't help but wonder if he knew about me and Cooper. I'm pretty sure he remained in the dark. I didn't think Cooper shared anything personal with anybody. And I'd like to think Ram would care enough to be jealous if he found out about our affair.

Cooper never came over since Ram was assigned to us for the weekend. Maybe he was out screwing someone else. Should I have been bitter with that thought? I wasn't.

Chapter 33

A week and a half later I got a text from Kyle asking if I was home and if he and Dave could come over. I texted him back *yes* and gave him my address.

I had just gotten back from the gym, so I took a quick shower, put on sweats and a sweatshirt, then heated up leftovers for dinner. As my microwave dinged to let me know my food done, the doorbell rang.

With dinner in hand, I let Kyle and Dave in. Dave's right arm was in a cast.

"Oh my God, what happened?" When you play guitar, a broken arm was your doom. I motioned for them to have a seat on the couch while I sat in one of the chairs and started eating.

Kyle let out one of those fake laughs you do when the topic isn't the least bit funny.

"Broke it," Dave said. He was in about as good a mood as Kyle.

"I see that. How?"

Dave told me how Adam was helping him install a new countertop in his house when Adam let his side drop, which caused Dave to drop his side as well. The counter landed on Dave's arm and broke it. Apparently Adam was doing a lot of ass kissing to everyone in the band, so when Dave asked if anybody could help, Adam volunteered without hesitation.

I expressed my sympathies, then asked, "What does this have to do with me?"

Kyle leaned forward. "We finally got some gigs back. We start playing this weekend."

"How are you guys going to perform without a guitar player?"

They waited for me to figure it out.

"Oohhh. You want me to be your guitar player." I took a bite of my dinner to think for half a minute. "Why me?"

"When we sat down to talk about what we were going to do, I knew you'd be our best option," Kyle said. "I remembered how quick you were with picking things up; hear it, play it, know it." Adam had played bass for The Song Wreckers after our original bass player left, and before Heather joined us. "When it comes down to it, you're the only one we know who could learn our songs super quickly and be able to perform 'em no problem. We need you for about six to eight weeks, starting this weekend."

I let that sink in. He was totally right. I have a kick-ass memory. It has served me well in life, and I didn't like to flaunt it, but I was surprised Kyle had caught on. I could learn those songs in a heartbeat and be able to perform them easily. I couldn't let them put their band on another hiatus when they were finally, hopefully, getting back on track, provided Adam kept his act together. I didn't enjoy the idea of anything that kept me in proximity with Adam, but saying no wasn't an option. They needed a break.

"Do you guys have gigs lined up through Christmas and New Year's?" I asked, hoping the answer was no.

"We do," Dave said. "We have dates through February, as of right now."

Damn. If I did this, it meant no snowboarding trip. Katie would be mad at me for that one. I hated to miss it. Double damn.

"I'm in," I told them. I had to help them out.

I instructed them I wouldn't play the Wreckers Weekend, but that any other night would be okay. I'd have to play on some weeknights, which might make me tired for work, but that was no big deal. Years of crappy sleeping prepared me yet again.

Since I didn't have anything going on that week, I told them I could rehearse after work each day. I made a mental note to reset my alarm clock to get up earlier to workout before work.

I needed courage to tell Katie that I was bailing on the snowboarding trip. Then I was going to need a lot of caffeine for the next couple of months.

The guys were pretty psyched that I said yes, and that I wanted to start immediately. I scarfed down the rest of my dinner and led them to my basement so we could get started. Since I had been to a few of their shows, I was familiar with most of their songs.

Crawling Home After Midnight was a four piece band. Dave sang lead vocals and played guitar, though Mike was their lead guitar player. I would be playing Dave's part of guitar while he sang. Kyle played bass and sang backup vocals along with Mike. Adam played the drums.

I learned as much as I could before kicking them out to go to bed. I told Dave to email me details on all of the gigs. I debated with myself for a minute whether or not to tell Cooper or Ram, but they'd end up finding out somehow, and telling them also gave me an excuse to call Ram. He called me whenever to see how I was doing because looking out for me was part of his job. I couldn't do that with him. I needed a reason to call him and now I had one. Slightly adolescent, but oh well. Him having a girlfriend didn't mean I stopped wanting him.

I had all the information emailed to me by the next morning, and after work I decided to tell Katie the bad news.

I sat in my car. My foot started tapping. Maybe I'd call Ram first.

"Princess," he answered.

"Hey. Got news for you," I said.

"Let's have it."

"I finally found out how many licks it takes to get to the center of a Tootsie Pop."

He didn't say anything for a few seconds, then, "For real?"

"No. I actually agreed to be a fill-in guitar player for the band Crawling Home After Midnight for the next couple of months, and I'm going to be playing in a bunch of bars all around town. Most are north of the city, but two are in Ohio."

He gave a big sigh. "What kind of bars?"

"The kind that will give you a heart attack when I tell you."

He cursed. "Can I ask *why* you're doing this?"

"Because it's Kyle's band, and I consider him a friend." I gave him the run down on what happened, and why they needed me. I started to rattle off the bars and dates, but he stopped me.

"I'm driving."

"So?"

"I'll never remember every bar and every date."

"How about I email you everything? It's not like I'll need you guys there for me. I'm sure the guys in the band will look out for me. I just wanted to tell you because . . ." I wanted an excuse to talk to you. "I didn't want to hear your complaining if you found out without me being the one to tell you."

I hung up with Ram and pulled out of the parking lot. At the first red light I called Katie. She wasn't very pleased with me. She understood why I wanted to help Kyle. She didn't understand skipping the trip up north, which meant practically skipping her birthday.

"Well, if you're not going up north, I don't want to go," she said.

"You have to. We already paid for our rooms." I was basically throwing away the money I had spent on my hotel room, since we had to book our rooms pretty far in advance. I wasn't happy about it, but the lost expense wasn't as big a deal for me financially as it was Katie. I was going to see if there was anyone else who wanted to go in my place so I could recoup at least a portion of the cost. "See if Brett will go with you," I suggested.

"Not enough advanced notice. This sucks."

I felt really bad. "I'm sorry."

"Yeah. Heaven forbid you tell them no."

"Don't get pissy. Look, I'll talk to you about this later. I gotta go." I snapped my phone off before she could say anything else.

I sped home and changed clothes before heading to Dave's house so I didn't have to play in the suit I wore to work, then got right back in my Jeep and drove off again.

Dave lived in a city that bordered Detroit. It was a working class area, with more emphasis on receiving welfare than actually working, but he could afford his own home there. Although the houses are fairly close together, Dave said his neighbors didn't care that they played in his garage, as long as they didn't play too late.

Oh God, I had band practice in a garage where the next door neighbor's house was so close, I could sneeze and my spit would land in their yard. I was determined to be a good friend, so I sucked it up, even though I felt ridiculous.

Practices with Midnight were productive each day that week. I was tired from putting in all the hours, and majorly bummed about having to miss my trip in a couple of weeks. Regardless, I was ready to be an official grunge band member. Go me.

Kyle, Dave, and Mike were all really cool with me being the fill-in. Adam totally avoided me. Kyle had pulled me aside that first practice at Dave's house and told me Adam didn't think I was good enough to play with them, to which I just rolled my eyes. I've been playing guitar since the age of fourteen. Whatever.

Cooper texted me on Thursday afternoon. *Need to see you tonight. What time will you be home?*

Home at nine, I texted back. *Business or pleasure?*
Both.

I pulled into my driveway ten minutes late. Cooper sat in his car waiting for me. I opened the garage door and pulled in. He met me in the garage.

I took my guitars out of the hatch, and he went ahead of me and opened the door into my house. We walked up the stairs into the mudroom, where I set everything down, kicked off my shoes then trudged to the living room.

"Ugh," I said when I landed on my nice, comfortable couch. I plunked my feet on the coffee table and tried to rub the tired from my eyes. It didn't work.

Cooper sat down. "You taking on this favor is a total pain in my ass, you know."

"Yeah, Ram bitched when I told him. Katie's mad at me for it too. I guess you and everyone else is going to have to kiss my ass." I was tired so my politeness took a back seat, like way back in Arkansas.

He ignored the rudeness. "There'll be one of my men there at every show, but not me or Ram."

"Wow, you're going to trust other employees with my safety?"

"I don't have a choice this time, Molly."

I rolled my head to the side to look at him. "Listen, Cooper. I honestly don't need you guys for this. The guys in the band will look out for me. Seriously, I think you're going overboard."

"The bars you're going to be playing aren't nice places. And besides, even if I agreed with you, Ram would never let you go to those places without protection. I think he personally threatened anyone who lets anything happen to you. He worries about you."

I looked away, but could feel him study me, as if he was trying to gauge my reaction to that statement.

When you want to deflect, change the subject.

I shifted my body to face him. "You know, if you let me lounge here any longer I'm going to pass out."

He blinked, then stood and held out his hands. I grasped them, and he pulled me up. I raised up on my tip toes and kissed him.

After a minute of making out, he led me to my bedroom and got to the pleasure part of his trip. He didn't care that I was tired and not able to reciprocate with the same amount of energy. He worked that much harder to make sure I stayed awake. Cooper was pretty skilled with his tongue and did things that definitely kept me alert. After he concentrated down south for a while, he came up north and drew patterns on my neck with his tongue, which sounded weird, but felt good—particularly when paired with what his hands were doing—and there was no danger whatsoever of my tiredness getting in the way of a rocking orgasm.

Chapter 34

The 3D employee assigned to me during Midnight's shows introduced himself as Taylor, and followed me everywhere I went. He even stood outside the bathroom door when I peed.

Playing with Crawling Home After Midnight was quite an experience. Not good, not bad. Different.

After the band had everything set up, and we were about to start playing, I thought maybe there had been a mistake. Like maybe we were at the wrong bar or were about to play at the wrong time. Whenever the Song Wreckers played, we had a pretty good crowd right from the start. As the night went on it grew, but damn near everyone in Brett's was ready for us as soon as we hit the stage.

There were about fifteen people sitting and standing around the bar. A few, at most, cared that Midnight was there and about to go on. Dave said a few words then we began playing, just like that. There was no cheering, no yelling, no rowdy excitement like I was used to. Not one bar patron yelled out a comment about my boobs or ass. Weird.

I had been to several of their shows before. I hadn't shown up until later in the night, so there was always a crowd by the time I arrived. That night, people were there for the alcohol and because the bar fit their image. Crawling Home After Midnight played to a partially enthusiastic group of drunks.

I received a few weird looks because, even though I tried to look as if I belonged in a grungy, alternative bar, I clearly was in a place I would not normally go. I was like a cheerleader showing up at a Goth party.

During our one break—they only played two sets—Dave, Mike, and Adam went outside, most likely to smoke and have another beer. I hung out with Kyle, Shannon, and, of course, Taylor.

We sat at a table in the corner. "Not like playing a Wreckers show, huh?" Kyle said.

I didn't want to hurt his feelings with the response that popped into my head, which was: *Is it always this bad?* Instead, I said, "Different band, different bar, different crowd. It's about what I expected."

I don't think Kyle believed me, because he gave a *yeah, right* snort.

I made it through the weekend. I wouldn't exactly call it fun and I'd be glad when Dave's arm healed and they no longer needed me, but I was glad I'd decided to help them out.

Since we had gigs in the middle of the week as well as the weekends, with the exception of Wreckers Weekends, Dave, Mike, Kyle and Adam didn't feel it necessary to have extra practices. They were fully accepting of my competence as a guitar player, and since we wouldn't be working on putting together new songs, they didn't see any reason to take up more of my time. Hallelujah.

Katie was still ticked at me, so every time we talked our conversation was short, and not so sweet. I tried a few times to get her to open up about her and Brett since she had confided in me about the uncertainty of their future together. She blew me off. She didn't even want to go out with me and celebrate her birthday, which was *very* unlike her. Instead, she flew down to Mississippi as soon as school let out for winter break to spend time with Mama before she went up north to play in the snow. We exchanged gifts before she left. It wasn't one of the happier times we've spent together.

Since I was off work for winter break and home by myself, I kept myself busy by constantly writing and dancing. I spent so much time in my basement, I started to forget what daylight was.

On Christmas day I went to my mom's for a few hours. She fixed my favorite meal and dessert, and talked about the places she and Victor were planning on traveling to. Then I left so she could go to Victor's house.

Once again, she was in such better spirits I didn't even try to start any sort of meaningful conversation with her. Being Christmas, I didn't want to bring up anything unpleasant. I was glad she seemed to be getting more of a life. I was happy for her, really.

But why couldn't she include me?

Curled up in the corner of my couch with a blanket tucked around my legs, I tossed the book I had just finished onto the coffee table. Why did I have to read a story about best friends and how they journey through life together, growing up and finding love?

I grabbed my cell from the side table and texted Katie. *Miss you. Doing okay?*

Yup. Brett's on New Year's Eve like always?

Shit. She forgot I had a show with Midnight. *Playing with CHAM, remember? Sorry.*

I stared at the phone in my hands. No response. I carried it with me while I went to the kitchen and grabbed an iced tea from the fridge. I leaned against the counter and took a drink, waited, took another drink, and waited some more.

Great. Another reason for Katie to stay mad at me.

I set the tea down and stared at the phone. Ram's face (and body) popped into my head. If I called him to see how his Christmas went, would he think that was odd?

I grabbed my phone and dialed before I lost my nerve. It rang once. I lost my nerve and hung up. Damn it, I'm so chicken. I set the phone on the counter and it rang. I'd obviously popped up on Ram's caller I.D., because his name was now popping up on mine.

I felt so stupid. God, you would think that I was thirteen instead of over thirty. I picked up and lied. "Hi. Sorry. I dialed the wrong number and hung up when I realized."

Could I get any more junior high?

He could've said, "Okay, whatever," and hung up. He didn't. We talked about how my time playing guitar with Midnight was working out, and how we celebrated Christmas. He told me he had a brother and three sisters, all of whom still lived in the area. They went to his mom's to celebrate Christmas. I didn't ask him if he'd spent the holiday with his girlfriend—I wanted to—because his love life wasn't my business.

"So was it crazy there with grandkids and stuff?" I asked. We'd never talked about him much at all so hearing about him instead of talking about me was nice for a change.

He chuckled. "So far there's ten grandkids, so yeah. By the time everyone leaves, it looks like a tornado tore through the house."

"That's nice."

"Not for my mom who does the cleaning."

"No, I meant that you have a big family to celebrate with. You're lucky." He probably had lots of fun and lots of laughs reminiscing with his siblings, teasing each other mercilessly. I bet he always looked forward to the holidays so he could get together with his family.

"Yeah, I am. My dad died when I was a kid, and us kids held it together for my mom for a while. We've always been pretty close. We drive each other crazy, too."

"That must've been rough losing your dad. Was he one of those types that played with his kids and went to all of their extra kid stuff?" This was fascinating information to me. He could go on all day and I'd never get bored.

"He was," he said, then stopped. Maybe this was a sore subject or maybe he wondered why the hell he had told me so much in the first place.

I had nothing to add, the conversation was clearly over. "Okay, well I'm sorry I bothered you. Just . . . have a good New Year's."

"Princess, you didn't bother me. And you have a good New Year's, too."

Chapter 35

I was bummed having to spend New Year's Eve playing a show with Midnight. If I was going to be in a crowded bar the last day of the year, I would rather be at Brett's with Katie. I wasn't sure she'd confide in me, but at least we'd be together.

I didn't know what bug she had up her ass. She never hesitated to tell me what was wrong. I was going to give her distance for as long as I could stand it, but sooner or later she was going to give me answers.

I left her alone until January's Wrecker's Weekend. When we were loading our equipment onto the stage, I cornered her.

"We need to talk," I demanded.

She looked at me and half-smiled. "I know."

"Can I come over tomorrow? Or maybe we can go out to lunch. My treat."

She stopped and put her head on my shoulder. "That sounds good, you paying for lunch." She didn't move away, so I put my arm around her.

"Are you okay? Are you sick? Oh my God, is it Mama? Is something wrong with her?" I swung her around so we faced each other and held her by the shoulders.

She peeled my hands off her and huffed. "For crap's sake, Molly, calm down. Nothing's wrong with anybody. We'll go out to lunch tomorrow and talk, okay?"

"Okay," I said. There was no use trying to talk about what was bothering her when we were about to play.

Cooper was at Brett's by himself Friday night. After our show he discreetly asked me if he could come over for a while. Of course I said yes.

The band said our goodbyes quickly because the temperature was unbearably cold, then we all drove off. Cooper followed me in his SUV like he always did, even if he wasn't coming inside to get laid.

I had a two car garage, so I'd been letting Cooper squeeze his SUV in there when he came over. We went inside, I put all my stuff down, took off my boots, and without stopping, walked straight into my bedroom with Cooper right behind me.

I turned around and faced him. First, I took off my shirt and threw it at him. He caught it. Then I followed with every other piece of clothing I had on, and he caught all those, too.

Soon after, I had all of his clothing off, and we were hot and heavy. Down and dirty. Low and lusty.

I heard noises, clicking maybe. I lifted my head. "What was that?" Cooper didn't answer. "Did you hear something?"

He stilled for a second. "Nothing," he said, then found his rhythm again.

The noise must've been us. If Cooper wasn't concerned, it was nothing.

A familiar twang squealed, "What the hell!"

Cooper and I both froze. I lifted my head again and saw Katie's stunned face staring at us. Yup, the noise was her. She had a key to my house, and the code to my alarm.

Fortunately, Cooper and I were under the covers. He turned his head to look at her, so the three of us stared at each other, not knowing what to do.

"Um Katie? Get out please," I told her.

She gasped, "Cooper?"

I didn't give him a chance to respond. "What are you doing here? Are you okay?" The sex haze finally cleared from my mind, and it dawned on me that if Katie had come over that late, she really needed to talk.

"Uh . . ."

"Katie! Go to the kitchen and wait for me. I'll be there in a minute."

Cooper let out a sigh and dropped his head down on to the pillow.

Finally recovered, Katie smiled. "That's okay, Mol. I'm going home. I'll talk to you tomorrow."

"You don't have to do that," I told her.

"Yes, she does," Cooper mumbled into the pillow.

"No, really, call me tomorrow," she said, then turned and left.

We stayed frozen in place until the front door shut and the lock clicked back into place. Cooper resumed our previous activity. What was so important that had Katie traipsing to my house so late? She hadn't been crying, so she and Brett were fine. Had she lied earlier about nothing being wrong with Mama? That—

"Molly!"

I looked at Cooper, who was no longer moving.

"I said your name three times before you noticed. Is this a lost cause?"

Oh yeah, I was getting laid. "No no. Keep going. I'm fine."

I tried to get back into it, I really did. Ugh, but my mind was on overdrive worrying about Katie.

Cooper finished without me getting off, and to be honest I didn't care. He was slightly irritated when he left, so I threw him a half-hearted, "Sorry," as he walked out the door.

Of course I called Katie as soon as I locked up after him.

"You know I want details," was her greeting to me when she answered the phone.

I really did not want to explain me and Cooper to anybody, but since she was my best friend and had walked in on me in the middle of having sex, I figured I would answer her questions.

"What do you want to know?" I asked her.

"How long has this been going on?"

"Since my dad's wedding."

Silence. I cringed while waiting.

"You told me nothing happened between you two! You lied to me!"

"I didn't lie. You said, 'so you two really slept in separate rooms?', and I said, 'of course'. I didn't lie. We had sex in my room, he went back to his room, and we slept in separate everything."

"So you two have been doing it for—" she paused to calculate the timing— "over two months?"

"Yes."

"And you didn't tell me?"

Was she hurt that I didn't tell her, or impressed that I was finally receiving some action? "I didn't tell anybody."

"Are you two an item? Like boyfriend and girlfriend?"

I yawned. "No."

"Okay, I can take a hint. Pick me up at noon tomorrow and be prepared to dish."

Great. She was dishing, too.

Katie ran out of her front door and into my Jeep. "You first," I said.

She fidgeted in her seat as I drove, explaining she'd been thinking of breaking up with Brett because he wouldn't ask her to marry him. He'd said he wanted to get married but wasn't ready yet.

"You're seriously thinking of leaving him?" I asked.

"I don't know what else to do. What's his hold up? It's not like we're twenty five. If he doesn't want to marry me and have kids, I need to find someone who does."

"Wow. Would you want marriage and kids with anyone else besides him?" Surprised at her line of thinking, I turned toward her since we were stopped at a red light.

Her face lit up, and she wagged her eyebrows a couple

times. "No. That's why I have to make him see that he can't live without me, so he'll be dying to marry me."

Yikes. "Explain."

This is where she turned animated. "I've been so depressed lately over the fact that he wants things to continue as we are. So finally it came to me: I gotta shock him."

"So breaking up with him is going to be the shock?"

"Yup," she said, smacking the dashboard. "I'm going to break it off with him and then tell him that if he wants me back he better come asking with a ring. The light turned green."

I refocused on the road and punched the gas. Her plan was too drastic for my taste, and I wasn't sure it would work, but more power to her for having the guts to do it. "I hope to hell it works out in your favor."

"And if not then I'll know he's not the one for me, and I need to move on." She sniffled, so I knew if I looked at her I'd see a few tears run down her cheeks.

I drove the rest of the way in silence, allowing Katie to compose herself. I didn't want her to get emotional in public. She hates not looking her best.

We ordered our food, then waited in line for our order, Katie smiling in the way I knew she did when she was waiting to pounce. On me. It's a look I used to fear, but am now resigned to. After all, she's my best friend. Of course she wants all the details she can get.

Finally we sat and she pounced. "Start at the beginning," she said.

We tore into our lunch while I explained. She found it hard to believe that all Cooper and I had was sex—no dating, no romance, no commitment. I told her Ram was a lost cause since he had a girlfriend, so when Cooper made a move on me, I went for it.

She begged for the nitty gritty details of Cooper's skill in bed. I told her he knew his way around a woman's body and left it at that.

Happy with each other again, Katie and I parted in better moods. I was sure she was glad to tell me about Operation Shock Brett, but I was also sure if her plan backfired and she lost Brett, her heart would break into a million pieces. And what were the chances of her plan working, anyway? Brett was a man. If he got dumped, wouldn't he just get really drunk for a while then move on? I knew he loved her, really loved her. But he also had hot women flirting with him all the time at the bar. What if he started dating someone else? Brett hooking up with other women was bound to have repercussions for the band, not that we wouldn't be able to find other bars to play in. And what about Heather? If we had to start playing somewhere else, she was going to be stuck in the middle since she worked for Brett.

All I could do was hope for the best and prepare for the worst.

Gina called me the last week of January. She was done recording the album and ready to share the finished product with me.

I stood in front of the refrigerator where my calendar hung, looking for an opportunity to fly down to Nashville for a couple of days. Between work and both bands, I didn't see it happening. Gina was determined to be present when I heard the polished album for the first time, so made plans for her and her mother to go home to Macomb instead. That way, they could visit family before the album's release, and I could take an evening to drive down and listen.

I picked up a Sharpie and wrote *Gina's album after work* on Tuesday's square, not that I'd need the reminder. But seeing the words written made me proud. Soon, the whole country—or possibly world—could hear my songs.

Not gonna panic. Seriously. Okay, maybe a little.

Deep breaths. Try to focus on something else.

Like Dave cast. It was coming off in a few days. I figured it would take a good two to three weeks before he was able to play guitar for a show. I wasn't going to rush him. Much.

The following night I stood on the world's smallest stage in a dirty little bar, helping Midnight set up for our gig, wondering if we were all going to fit. God, I didn't miss playing in dives. Brett's had a large stage and a good sized dance floor. Lots of tables and personable bartenders.

With a sigh I ignored my surroundings—when did I become a bar snob?—and scooted the equipment as close together as I could.

Dave tried to help, but I stopped him. "I got this."

"Wearing a cast is getting old," he said, backing off. "I can't wait 'til this thing is gone."

I talked to Dave about what he should expect in terms of recovery, including that he wouldn't be able to play guitar for at least a week or two after his cast is cut off.

"How do you know about this stuff?" he asked.

"I've spent my entire life getting hurt in one way or another, so I had to learn how to rehabilitate my own injuries. When my shoulder was stabbed, it should've taken a lot longer to heal and give me a lot more problems. I knew my limits and how to work within them. Then I beat you guys at softball."

The rest of the band let out a grunt or two but generally ignored the jab.

We finished setting up and had a good fifteen minutes before we were scheduled to start, so Kyle, Adam, and Mike went to the bar. Dave and I sat with Tyler, my babysitter.

"Whatever happened with the guy who stabbed you?" Dave asked me.

I shook my head. "Nothing. The guy was never caught."

"Doesn't that freak you out?"

Only every day of my fucking life. "Yeah. Anyway, my

whole point was that I can give you tips to get your arm and hand back to normal faster."

Kyle sauntered up with a beer in one hand, and set the other hand on my shoulder. "Molly, Molly, Molly. How are you at bowling?"

Not so great, but I sure as hell wasn't going to admit weakness to Kyle of all people. "I rock at bowling. Want me to kick your ass at that too?"

He motioned to his girlfriend, Shannon. She'd been talking to some friends, but left them to join us at Kyle's signal. He moved next to her, opposite me, and crossed his arms over his chest. "Hey, Honey, I think we should take Molly here bowling soon. What do you think?"

"I think that is an excellent idea," Shannon said.

The tone of their voices made it obvious this was a rehearsed conversation. And since she spoke with an evil grin while rubbing her hands together, I'd have to be an idiot not to see that they had been waiting for the right opportunity to challenge me.

I faked surprise. "Gee, this sounds so unplanned!" Then, serious. "When and where?"

Kyle practically glowed with hope. "How about next week, Bowl-A-Way Lanes?"

Damn, that didn't give me much time to practice and get better. I tapped my foot while I thought about the timing. Mike and Adam joined us, so with the whole band listening there was no way I could turn down Kyle's offer and risk looking like a wuss. "You're on. I'll be going down to Ohio on Tuesday after work and won't get home until late, so not Tuesday."

"Wednesday, then," Shannon said. "Any partner you want versus me and Kyle."

We agreed to one game. I just had to find someone who could bowl good enough to make up for my ineptitude at that particular activity. I refused to call it a sport, because if bowling was a sport I would excel at it.

I surveyed the band for a minute. Dave was out for the obvious reason, and I didn't want anything to do with Adam. Mike didn't seem the least bit interested. Who else? Ram or Cooper? Nope, not going to go there. I didn't know anyone who bowled regularly, or bowled well enough to beat Kyle.

Shit.

At the end of the night, I smiled sweetly at Mike. "Are you sure you don't want to bowl with me?"

"Positive," he said. "Ask someone who works there."

"At the bowling alley?"

"Yeah. They probably bowl all the time."

Huh. Kinda brilliant.

Immediately after work the next day I drove to the bowling alley to beg for help. I've never been one of those women who flirted or flashed her cleavage to get what she wanted. That day, though, you could bet your ass that if showing a little boob was what it took to get someone great to bowl with me, therefore allowing me to kick Kyle's ass again, then I'd do it.

Before going in, I made sure my suit jacket was open and undid a couple more buttons on my blouse. I was prepared to lean on the counter while using my arms to squeeze my boobs together, creating an amount of cleavage I didn't naturally have. I'd even go so far as to seductively lick my lips. Obviously I expected a man.

Turns out my bowling partner would be none other than Brenda Reading, assistant manager of Bowl-A-Way Lanes and really good bowler. My feminine wiles could be saved for another day. I had to play with Midnight Thursday, Friday, and Saturday nights, so we worked out that I would come in at opening on Sunday, and Brenda would give me pointers and get me as ready as possible.

Back to being busy. Tuesday, I would finally get to hear Gina's album; Wednesday, I would show Kyle and Shannon not to mess with me; and then I would finally get to play with my own band when next Friday rolled around.

The more I thought about Gina and the album, the more my stomach twisted in knots. By the time the final bell rang Tuesday afternoon, I was practically hyper with anticipation. I hauled ass home to change my clothes and then practically burned rubber getting to Gina and Cindy's home in Macomb.

Chapter 36

After the second knock, Gina opened the door and let me in, then gave me a big hug. I stood back to look at her and noticed she'd had a makeover while in Tennessee. Before, she was very pretty. Now, she was sleeker, more glamorous.

"You look great," I yell-told her. Hey, I was excited and having a hard time keeping it contained.

She took my coat then I said hi to Cindy while Gina grabbed my hand and literally dragged me to her CD player. She pressed play, and we listened to the entire CD without saying anything. Twelve songs.

Oh my God, Good Lord, and holy shit! I was blown away by how absolutely great it all was. Gina and her band had done magic with those songs. The three songs that weren't mine were every bit as outstanding. Usually when I listened to an entire album, there were at least a couple songs, if not more, that didn't do it for me. Not on this one. Every song was a hit, as far as I was concerned. The band had taken what I gave them and made those songs ten times better.

When the last song ended, Gina was looked at me with that "well?" expression on her face.

I let my shoulders slump. "It sucks. I can't believe you ruined my songs like that."

Her face fell for a second until I yelled, "Are you kidding me? Gina, that was like the best freaking thing I have ever heard! You did it!"

She gave out a woo-hoo type yell, and we jumped up and down while she hugged me to the point of damn near asphyxiation.

Gina hit the play button again. She told me about her makeover, and that when she went back to Tennessee she would shoot the album cover and do other promotional shots.

Cindy had cooked a spaghetti dinner for us, and all we talked about while we ate was what was to come for Gina. Kent had given her a rundown of what her schedule was going to be like. She was how anyone in her shoes would be—excited, nervous, and freaked out.

I called Kent on the way home to tell him how great the album was. He was pleased, as well. The people at Crystal Records had thrown a lot of money into that album in the hopes that Gina was the next big thing. I assured him their money well spent.

I sang and danced in my seat the rest of the way home. I was more excited for Gina than I was for Alan when he landed the music video. I mean, I had been a part of this. How cool was that?

I was proud of myself. Had I not been driving, I would've pinched myself to make sure I wasn't dreaming. I mean, everything in my life was going to come together. I could almost feel it.

Instead, I felt the hard crash from my short-lived high as soon as I turned into my driveway.

"It's going to be okay, Molly." Katie sat next to me on her couch, rubbing a hand up and down my back, trying to calm me down and comfort me since I'd burst through her door madder than hell with angry tears in my eyes.

No, it's not going to be okay. Before I could voice it, there was a knock on the door. Katie let Ram in.

"You okay?" he asked, walking over to me.

"No. I'm pissed. Let me guess: no one found anything."

He shook his head. "Sorry."

I threw my head back into the cushion in frustration. I'd figured the police wouldn't find anything since The Creep had eluded them thus far.

I pinched my eyes shut to keep the angry tears away. How did he keep getting away with torturing me?

As soon as I had pulled into my driveway that night, coming home from visiting Gina and Cindy, I noticed a clump on my porch thanks to the bright as hell porch light Ryder Security had put in last year.

And I knew. The Creep was at it again.

I inched into my garage. Instead of going inside the house, I came out and walked up the porch steps. A black cat with white only on its paws was laying on its side on a pile of rose petals, with a knife sticking out of its chest.

My heart sank—that was my neighbor's cat. Obviously and grotesquely dead. A note was attached to the knife. Although parts of the paper were saturated with blood, I could still read the message.

Thinking of you

Nothing since he'd attacked me outside Brett's, then bam! Why now? Why wait so long without doing anything and then come back? It had been almost a year.

I couldn't toss this cat into the woods and ignore it again. I ran to my car and drove off. I called Ram to tell him what happened and that I was going straight to Katie's house.

I opened my eyes and sat forward, done remembering. I paced around Katie's living room until Ram passed on the message that the police were done at my house. Katie offered to let me stay at her place, but she and I had to work in the morning, and I didn't feel like crashing there just to get up extra early to return home. It wasn't as if I was going to sleep anyway. I'd rather toss and turn in my own bed.

Cooper's SUV was in my driveway when I pulled up. He stepped out of his vehicle the same time I did.

"Cooper, I am not in the mood tonight," I said, slamming my door shut.

"I know, I'm staying over tonight to make sure nothing else happens."

It would make me feel safer having him there, but I didn't want to have to tip toe around my own house trying not to wake him.

"Go home. I have a security system, I'll be fine."

He walked closer. "It's either me or Ram. He was the one who wanted to sleep over here tonight."

I leaned against my Jeep. "Why are you here then?"

He shrugged. "I figured, I'm fucking you, I'll protect you." I didn't even flinch at his crude answer as he held out his keys, threatening to leave. "You want me to call him?"

Not caring at this point, I made a sound of disgust. "Whatever." I turned and stormed back into the garage. "I'm getting up at five to workout. I'll probably keep you up all night with my tossing and turning. When you're tired tomorrow, don't say I didn't warn you."

Fuck, fuck, and fuck again. I felt horrible for my neighbor's murdered cat. My fault. The Creep was back. I was scared shitless, and supposed to go bowling in like, fifteen hours. How many people could say that? Just me.

I stared at the ceiling most of the night and came to a decision: The Creep's reappearance would not alter my life. I would not show fear or weakness. I would do everything I had planned on. Fuck The Creep and whatever sick game he was playing.

I hopped out of bed the next morning with my determination in overdrive. I bounced into work the next day and presented my lessons with over-the-top passion.

I showed up at the bowling alley and bowled better than I ever had. Even with Brenda as my partner, I still lost. Kyle, along with Shannon, finally bested me. I let him have his moment of glory and took all of his gloating in stride. I let him do his ass-smacking moves, his jumping all around, and pointing at me while taunting me with the phrase "Molly, Molly, big fat loser", and even his telling everyone in the bowling alley (all ten people) how he beat me at the bowling challenge because he ruled, and I sucked.

My smile was fake, and my laugh was fake, but I endured the day without anyone besides those involved knowing that my life was once again fucked up.

I also endured the next Wreckers Weekend almost as normally. Cooper and Ram stayed as close as they could to me, reminding me that I was still in danger. I played and sang as if my time on stage was the last performance of my life. With The Creep out there, it could be.

Kyle, Dave, and Mike showed up to tell me that they needed me for next weekend and that was it. Dave's cast was off and, after next week, they didn't have any gigs lined up for a few weeks. Fine with me.

It had snowed all weekend, so on Sunday I suggested to Katie that we go sledding. I still had this manic energy that I needed an outlet for. I was too hyper to sit and write music, or do anything mundane.

Once at our favorite hill, I went balls-to-the-wall sledding; standing up until I could make it to the bottom without wiping out. After that, I sledded down the really steep part of the hill that only stupid teenagers go down. I wanted to do something. . . dangerous. I wanted to be pushed to my absolute limit. When I got to the bottom of a hill, I would grab my sled and sprint all the way back up, and do it again and again and again.

After an hour and a half Katie, was done. She drove me home and came inside. I made us dinner and we relaxed, her more than me, while we ate on the couch.

She still hadn't broken things off with Brett. She said she was waiting for the right time. I knew she was scared of losing him if her plan didn't work. I also knew she didn't want to be alone on Valentine's Day. I would've bet a lot of money that she harbored a hope that Brett would propose to her that day.

Every day after work the following week I either threw on my shoe spikes and went for a nice exhausting run in the snow, went to the gym to lift, or spent hours in the lap pool. I hadn't swam for exercise in a while, and being in the water was the perfect activity to really wear me down.

I still felt like doing stupid, reckless stuff though. When I went running, I went without pepper spray and with my iPod blaring in my ears. Let The Creep see me. Let him come at me again. I didn't fucking care right then.

A couple weeks later I was still in overdrive. I really pushed myself in every single thing I did, but the exertion wasn't helping get rid of . . . whatever the hell this was. I was anxious all the time. Hyper and anxious. Almost as if I was in a constant state where everything was surreal.

One Sunday I got ready for bed knowing that I wasn't going to be able to sleep. Not that it mattered. The next day was President's Day, and there was no school, so I didn't have to get up early and go to work. I needed something to do that would help alleviate my manic state of mind. Nothing at my immediate disposal sounded remotely interesting.

I stood in the middle of my bedroom and tapped my foot to think for a minute. Cooper. Sex. It had been a while since we'd been together. Maybe what was wrong with me was that I needed to get laid.

I called Cooper and asked if he could come over. He explained he was waiting for a series of faxes at his house and couldn't leave. I told him I really needed him, that I would make it very worth his while, then asked if I could go over to his place. He gave me directions and ten minutes later, after I put on a black lace bra and matching panties, I was on my way.

Cooper lived in a loft in downtown Detroit. God, I hated driving in that fucking city. I supposed he wanted to live by his offices. Shortly after I got on the expressway, it started snowing, lightly at first, but by the time I got to Cooper's, flakes were coming down heavily. It had taken almost forty minutes in very little traffic for me to get to him.

Cooper let me in before I could knock. I took off my coat and gloves, and draped them on the arm of a chair and set my purse on the floor. Then I took a minute to look around. Not bad. High ceilings with everything except the bedroom and bathrooms being one large, open space. Lots of dark wood and clean lines made it look fairly modern. Fairly generic for a downtown loft. Nice furniture and things, but he'd obviously just bought what was comfortable and not much else. No way he did any entertaining there. Big surprise.

While I looked around, a fax came in. Cooper walked into his office area, a space most would've used for formal dining, to read it. I didn't come over to watch him read faxes, though. I waited patiently for a couple minutes. Soon he held two faxes in his hands and glanced between them.

Screw that. I stripped down to my bra and panties and leaned against the wall with my arms crossed over my chest. He stole a glance at me.

"Hold on a minute," he told me.

"I didn't come over to watch you work." I slowly walked toward him, took the faxes out of his hands, and set them on the table.

"You know, if anyone else did that, the consequences would not be good."

I hooked each of my index fingers into his side belt loops

and pulled him roughly against me so his hips were touching mine. "Maybe you should teach me a lesson."

Cooper opened his mouth to respond so I kissed him hard to silence him. I didn't let up until I was sure he forgot about the stupid faxes.

We had the actual sex in his bed, but the foreplay happened in various parts of his home on the way to his bed. It was extremely physical. It was rough and demanding. He didn't complain that I was being so aggressive; he went with it. Since all his floors were hardwood, we were both going to have bruising up and down our bodies.

I used all my strength on Cooper. He took everything I dished out and gave it right back. Our play became painful, not in the unpleasant way, and everything we did to each other was exactly what I needed right then. He let me be mad and crazy and take it out on him, and for that I was grateful. Especially since he didn't ask me to explain afterward what in the hell my energy was all about.

When we were finished and exhausted, I grabbed one of his T-shirts, put it on, then went to go retrieve my clothes from the floor in the living area. I took a peek out the window and noticed only white. It was snowing so hard I couldn't see the buildings across the street. Yikes, just the thought of driving in those weather conditions scared me.

"Shit," I said, walking back into Cooper's bedroom with my clothes. "I can't drive home in that, I don't think."

"You can stay here," he said.

Chapter 37

I awoke alone in Cooper's bed at seven the next morning. He had been there a few hours earlier because it woke me—for a minute—when he shoved me from the middle of the bed, back to one side of the bed.

Still in his shirt, and with the addition of my panties, I stumbled out to where I heard his voice in the kitchen.

He ended a phone call. "You're a bed hog," he declared. "Coffee?"

I plopped down in one of the kitchen chairs. "I've been sleeping alone for over thirty years and God yes." He poured me a cup then handed it to me.

I asked how the roads were, and he told me they were in the process of being plowed. His driveway and my car were still buried and would be until the guy he hired for snow removal showed up. The expressways and main roads should all be done within the next few hours. Then he said he'd be heading into the offices as soon as he could get his car out. He'd be working from home until then and told me to stay however long I needed to feel safe driving home.

I had drunk about half of my coffee when two things happened simultaneously. At the same time I spotted an item of mine on the floor and said, "Hey! There's my bra," Ram walked into the kitchen. I hadn't even heard him come in to the house.

My heart sank. I couldn't utter a sound. He took in what I said, looked at me in Cooper's T-shirt and my panties, and all the color drained from his face.

It took him a minute to recover. When he did he cleared his throat, looked at me and said, "I wondered whose car was here." Then he looked at Cooper. "Your guy is here. One side of the driveway is clear. I'm sure he's working on the other side, and Molly's car, by now."

I was beyond mortified. Getting caught in the act by Katie was one thing. But to be found out by Caleb Ramsey—the one man who I actually wanted to have a chance with—like that? Made me want to die right there in my chair.

That moment was the first time since I'd started having sex with Cooper that I felt ashamed of myself.

Screw that, I had no reason to be ashamed. I was a fucking adult and I could do whatever—and whoever—the hell I wanted. I put on a false brave face, grabbed my bra and stood up. "I really need to take a shower," I said, and walked out. I knew that statement pretty much threw the fact that Cooper and I had spent the night together in Ram's face, but what the hell? I wasn't going to deny it.

By the time I was showered and dressed Ram was gone. Thank freaking God, because the last thing I wanted to do was face him in Cooper's house the morning after having the most cathartic sex ever. I finally felt like I was back on earth. I don't know if the sex with Cooper, or being discovered by Ram cleared my mind, but I no longer felt like punishing myself.

Cooper told me he was going to head into the offices in a few minutes since his driveway and path to the offices were fairly clear. I guess it paid to have a big SUV with four wheel drive on days like that one. I rummaged around his cabinets for breakfast.

"You own a gun?" he asked me.

"No."

"Are you opposed to owning a gun?"

I found a box of Cheerios, a bowl, and spoon. "Not really, but I don't know how to shoot and have a small fear of shooting myself."

Cooper's smiles were rare. Seriously, the man was all business. Even in bed. He looked relaxed and happy after sex, but that look came without the smile.

He smiled and handed me the milk. "You're going to get a gun and learn how to shoot."

I rolled my eyes. "Super."

A few days later, Cooper dragged me out of my house and took me shooting. I felt stupid at the gun range because I'd never handled a gun before, and had no idea what I was doing. The place was grungy and smelled like metal, smoke, and other scents that puzzled me, but I tried really hard to ignore that.

Cooper handed me ear and eye protection. The girly part of me didn't want to wear them because I knew I'd look goofy, but I sucked it up and donned them anyway. I was trying to take this as serious as Cooper. He showed me the gun he'd brought for me to shoot with. I knew the difference between a revolver and non-revolver. That was as extensive as my gun knowledge went. This one was a revolver. Cooper told me that particular one was a snub nose .38 special plus P, Smith and Wesson. He gave basic instructions: this is how you load it, this is how you unload it, and don't ever point it at someone unless you mean it.

"Why a revolver and not an Uzi?" I really didn't know what an Uzi was, just that its reputation was bad ass. I could totally see myself with a bad ass gun.

"Because since you know nothing about guns or shooting we're going with simple. A revolver is idiot proof. It's simple and goes bang. It also has a second strike capability. If you pull the trigger and all that happens is click, then you pull the trigger again and it advances to the next round. Doesn't get any easier than that. For home defense, this is the best option for someone like you."

Idiot proof... someone like me... nice, asshole.

I meant to pay total attention, but I was thinking ahead to actually having to hold and shoot the thing. I was terrified of accidentally shooting myself or, God forbid, another human being. How embarrassing would it be to survive The Creep, only to die by accidentally shooting myself at a gun range while getting lessons? Ugh.

When he was done explaining, he made me hold the gun while he instructed me. I loaded and unloaded it. I always made sure the barrel was pointed at the ground or away from us. And if Cooper had a sense of humor, I would've struck a Charlie's Angel type pose.

He instructed me to explain what I was doing as I was doing it.

"Do it again," he told me.

"Why?"

"Because you need to practice until your hands stop shaking, and you can explain it with confidence."

So I loaded and unloaded the stupid revolver a couple more times. After the second time I stopped.

"Again," he demanded.

I set the gun down and put my hands on my hips. "I don't want to do it again. I got it."

"You're not good enough. Do it again," he said.

I took a deep breath because irritation was rearing its ugly head. I picked up the gun and loaded and unloaded again.

I glared at him when I finished.

"Most people get better the more they do something," he remarked.

"Cooper, this is new to me. Cut me a little slack."

"I was."

I stared down the alley-like space as we moved on to actually shooting. Without grumbling or bitching, I did everything he asked of me. Each part of the process was difficult. I didn't do anything up to his standards, or I did it just plain wrong, and he had no qualms about letting me know. My stance was no good. I didn't grasp the gun right. Even the way I pulled the trigger was crap. When he finally did let me fire a bullet I hit the edge of the paper, not the rings on the paper. I mentally cursed him out and became more and more frustrated with every passing minute.

"Relax your shoulders!" he barked.

I tried.

"Don't lock your elbows!"

I loosened them.

"Hips! Your hips aren't how I showed you!" He swatted my left hip.

I heated from anger. I slowly turned my head toward him and gave him the meanest glare I could.

"What?" he asked.

I set the gun down, then took off my glasses and ear muff things. "I'm done," I told him.

"You're not ready yet."

"Listen, Cooper. This is not working. You're a sucky teacher, and I'm a sucky student."

He looked offended. "I've taught lots of people how to shoot. You're the only one who's had trouble."

Figures. Part of the reason I grew so frustrated, though I hated to admit this, was that I was used to being pretty good at things when I really tried. I was really trying. Why wasn't I any good? Maybe I just needed to get my head together and give it another shot. Literally.

"Okay. I'll attempt this again," I told him.

He barked orders at me. He physically put my body in the proper position. When I pulled the trigger, I was lucky if it hit the paper. A couple of times I actually hit the target. We both knew that each hole in the paper was shit luck, though, and not skill.

I was done. Again. I set the gun down and took off the eye and ear protection. Again. "I'm done. Seriously. For real."

He gripped my upper arm. "Molly, you need to learn how to shoot, and you need a gun in your house to protect yourself."

I shrugged out of his grasp. "No. I need to get out of here before I shoot you. You're pissing me off."

He tensed, and his face reddened. "Do not ever joke about shooting someone in a gun range!"

Okay, I needed to put this in terms he understood. "Listen, Cooper. Here's the thing. I really want to hurt you right now. If you have any desire to keep getting in my pants, you will let me go home, and we will never repeat this experience again."

He took me home.

That night Cooper called to set up another gun range appointment, explaining that he would send another of his men to "get through my thick skull". Ass. My new tormentor would pick me up the next day after work. He didn't want me to meet his replacement at the gun range because he didn't trust me not to skip out. I would have, too.

Hopefully he'd send a woman to teach me how to shoot. Or at least a kind, understanding soul who understood I wasn't raised around guns, so I didn't have that natural comfort around them.

I shouldn't have been surprised when Ram showed up at my door.

Fuck. I was not ready to face him. I really hated when life forced me to put on my big girl underpants.

During the drive to the range, I expected him to bring up seeing me at Cooper's place. He didn't. He acted as if it had never happened. He was friendly, professional, and distant. Kind of like my mom, come to think of it.

We walked into the range, and the guy behind the counter

saw me and cringed. Fuck-knob. He and Ram shook hands, then they led me back to the torture chamber.

Ram had me show him everything Cooper taught me. I showed him how to load and unload, how to stand properly, and how to line up my sight.

"You're doing everything right," he said. "You were probably nervous. That affects your shooting."

I turned to face him. "I'm not comfortable with this. What if I accidentally shoot myself? Or someone else? I don't want to go to jail."

"That's not going to happen."

"How do you know?"

He put his hands on my shoulders and looked me in the eye. "Because I won't let it. Now you need to relax and clear your mind. I want you to watch me shoot."

He shot. All of his bullets landed near the middle of the target in a tight grouping. I sized him up to see exactly how his body was positioned. His stance was exactly how both he and Cooper told me it should be, and if I stood directly behind him I'd barely have to reach to lightly bite the side of his neck.

Damn it, focus.

After Ram emptied his gun and set it down, he turned me to face the target and stood behind me, keeping his hands on my shoulders. I put my body in position.

"Don't shoot yet," he told me. "Not until you feel yourself relax. Take your time."

I stood there with his hands on me. His touch gave me butterflies and relaxed me. He'd always had that effect on me.

After a minute of getting into the zone, I began shooting. One round missed completely, but the rest hit the paper, and several even hit the target. This turn was better than anything I'd done with Cooper teaching me. Who cared that my grouping wasn't tight.

I lowered the gun. "Huh. Look at that."

Ram told me "good job", then had me shoot more. And more, and more. Eventually, he was able to take his hands off me, and I still hit the target. My groupings were tighter. I wasn't good yet by any means, though I had the potential to be. I wasn't exactly comfortable, but I wasn't a ball of nerves anymore either. I was a work in progress.

He shot several more rounds, then I went one last time. When I finished, I turned around to look at him, and he was beaming at me. I beamed right back. Then we realized we were beaming at each other and let our faces fall.

He pushed his eye protection up onto his head since we were done shooting. "I'm supposed to convince you to get your permit to purchase, then convince you to buy the gun."

Ugh. It was one thing to go shooting and another to follow through and actually become a gun owner. "Tell Cooper what he wants to hear, please. I don't know about actually buying a gun, and I don't want him to bother me about it."

He agreed. We packed up, and as I left, I made sure to show the ass wipe behind the counter my target. With holes in it. From me.

We got in Ram's SUV and buckled our seat belts. Instead of starting the car, Ram stared at me. I turned my head to look at him.

"Molly, what—" he said, then stopped.

I knew exactly what was on his mind; what he needed to know. I spoke the rest of his question for him. "What the hell am I doing fucking Gabe Cooper?"

Chapter 38

Ram looked away from me and stared at his hands on the steering wheel. His knuckles were white from gripping it so tightly. "I wasn't going to be so crude about it, but yeah." He started the engine and pulled out of the parking lot.

"Who I decide to fuck is none of your business."

"The hell it isn't!" he yelled. He spent a minute calming down. After pulling onto the expressway, he told me, "You're right. It's not." After a pause, he added: "I still want to know."

"Ram, don't do this," I pleaded.

He gave an angry snort. "Do what? Wonder why you're sleeping with Cooper when I thought there was something between us?"

"Fine. Fucking. That's what I'm doing with him. Nothing more, nothing less."

"Stop using that word. You're making yourself sound cheap."

"It is cheap, Ram. Oh by the way, if there's something between us then why do you have a girlfriend?"

He took an exit that was not the one to my house. He pulled into a McDonald's parking lot right past the overpass, shut off the engine and turned to me. "*You* are not cheap, Molly." He raised his hands in the air and let them fall, then he resumed yelling. "I don't get it. I didn't peg you for this type of woman. He can't give you anything, Molly! He isn't capable of loving you or giving you what you need! He could never give you what I could have!"

"Exactly!" I yelled back. "He won't demand anything from me! And you're wrong. He can give me one thing you can't.

He can screw me and then leave me alone. Maybe that's all I wanted! Do you want to know how we hooked up?" I asked.

His head was shaking slightly from side to side, as if he didn't want to hear the story. I was going to tell him anyway. In an odd way, I owed him an explanation. But I couldn't look at him, so I stared out the window.

"My dad was getting remarried. He invited me to the wedding. I decided to go, since I made the decision to let him back in my life. I didn't want to go alone. Katie told me to invite you. She said that if I told you how I felt about you that you would leave your girlfriend for me."

"You knew I had a girlfriend?"

"It was fairly obvious you'd been dating someone. When she came to the softball game, I knew you'd been seeing her long enough to be a couple. Anyway, I couldn't do that to another woman. Believe it or not, I have some moral standards. So I asked Cooper. He agreed on the condition that I drop the idea of not letting 3D protect me anymore."

My hands quivered, but I took the opportunity to look at him. His eyes were closed, and his head was leaning against the back of the seat. His eyebrows were scrunched together as if he was working on a really hard math problem.

I turned back to the window and continued. "The wedding was far away, so we had to spend the night. We had separate hotel rooms. At the end of the night he walked me to my hotel room and kissed me. And you know what? I thought, *why the hell not?* I hadn't had sex in quite a while, and the man I really wanted . . . well, that didn't seem like it was ever going to work out. Why not let Cooper end a very long dry spell? I knew he wasn't the sick bastard who attacked me, so I trusted him in that respect. I knew he would screw me and leave afterward. I knew he wasn't going to expect anything from me, and I never expected anything from him." I turned and sat back in my seat facing forward.

"Is this like, payment for everything he's done for you?"

I snapped my head toward him and jabbed my finger in his face. "Fuck you. You did not just say that!"

He put his hands up in surrender. "That came out wrong."

"You're a jerk," I said, turning to face forward again. "Take me the hell home."

We were both silent for a few seconds. "Now!" I yelled. He started the engine, pulled out, and continued to my house. It took everything in me not to cry because it hit me hard—I had ruined everything. Everything I could have had with Caleb Ramsey.

When he pulled into my driveway, I reached to unclick my seatbelt when he covered my hand with his, stopping me. I looked up at him.

"I got a girlfriend because I wanted to see if any other woman could take my mind off of you. You kept pushing me away. It didn't work, and I broke it off. I'm sorry," he said.

"Don't, Ram. Don't be nice to me. We both know I don't deserve it." I pulled my hand out from under his, he unclicked my seatbelt for me, then watched me get out of the truck. "See ya," I said.

I shut the door and jogged into my home without looking back.

When your personal life is in the hole, you throw yourself into work. In my case, I threw myself into song writing and—shocker—working out. For the next couple of months, I forced myself into a routine. I went to work. I went swimming—my new favorite cardio activity—and lifted weights. I wrote like mad in my journals. I wrote music, both Wreckers and Gina stuff. There had only been hints that I would write for the next Gina album, because everything depended on how successful this first album was. I went running, still not being safe about my surroundings.

Although I loved and needed the peacefulness of the water, swimming gave me one hell of an ear infection. I woke up one morning with ear pain so bad it was painfully difficult to chew and swallow. The doctor prescribed me antibiotics and told me to say out of the water for at least four days. I felt better after two days, so I started back up. What do doctors know?

A few weeks later another, more painful case of swimmer's ear cropped up. This time the doctor actually yelled at me and put me on stronger antibiotics. I listened this time about staying out of the water. Doctors know a lot.

I saw both Cooper and Ram at the Wreckers shows. Ram acted completely professional. I wasn't his friend, I was his client. Period. I also noticed that he acted different toward Cooper. Either Cooper didn't notice or didn't care—probably the latter—because he acted the same as he always had.

I continued to have sex with Cooper. I figured, *why not*?

I told Katie what happened, about Ram discovering my and Cooper's affair. She was partially supportive. Mostly she expressed that I got what was coming to me. She told me that if I would've listened to her and told Ram about my feelings before the wedding that I wouldn't be in the boat I was in now. I knew she was right, but it still pissed me off to hear her say it.

One Sunday in March, we were hanging out at her house, trying to work on some new songs. Our creations weren't going very smoothly. Katie was in a bad mood, and mine wasn't all that great either.

Katie strummed her pick down her guitar, not even trying to make a pleasant sound. "This is going nowhere," she said.

"What? These songs or your life?" I meant it as a joke, kind of.

She huffed, louder than normal. "Oh, that's great coming from you."

"What the hell is that supposed to mean?"

She put her guitar down and looked at me. "Let's see . . . you make a crack about my life not going anywhere when yours is all messed up."

I knew my life was messed up, but I didn't feel like owning up to it out loud. "My life is fine. I have a job, I have money in the bank, I just have a bitch for a best friend."

Her eyes opened wide. "Oh, I'm a bitch? Why? Because I have the nerve to tell you when you're being stupid?"

I slammed my guitar down, then stood up. "Why am I stupid?"

"How many reasons do you want? One, because you started doing it with Cooper when you were totally into Ram."

"Can you please act like a grown up and call it sex?" I yelled.

She ignored me. "Two, because you continued to do it with Cooper when he doesn't even love you or want a relationship with you!"

"I don't love him or want a relationship with him either, you idiot!" I was defensive. She was my best friend so why wasn't she on my side?

Still ignoring me, "Three, at several times you could've spoken up and got the man you really wanted. Instead you let yourself be used. It's like you're trying to punish yourself! Don't think I didn't notice when you went all crazy for a while after the dead cat thing!"

She stood up too, and we screamed in each other's faces.

"Don't you feel even a little bit responsible for me sleeping with Cooper?"

Katie threw her arms up in the air and let them drop. "Why the hell would I feel responsible?"

I took a step even closer and pointed in her face. She hated that. "Because you were the one who set it up so I would ask Cooper to go with me in the first place!"

She swatted my hand away, but had no response to my accusation because it was true. Instead, she reverted to me being crazy. "You don't even try to lean on me when you're going through something! You try to push me away like you do everyone else! The only reason I know anything sometimes is because I don't take your bullshit excuses!"

"You know what, Katie Scarlett O'Suck-Ass? You have no fucking idea what it's like to be in my shoes!"

"That's because you keep everything inside, you stupid twit! I'm your best friend, and you don't even tell me everything! Best friends are supposed to tell each other everything! I tell you everything!"

I pointed in her face again. "Oh yeah?" I needed a comeback and now I wanted to hurt her. "Well, what happened to your brilliant fucking plan to dump Brett so he could see the light about how bad he wanted to be with you? Did you wake up and realize he could get a hundred other girls to replace you in the blink of an eye?"

Her jaw dropped. "That was mean! I'm gonna pull a Molly and say, I don't have to explain myself to you!"

"I don't have to explain myself to you either!" I grabbed my guitar and stormed out.

Katie and I had never fought so badly. It may be hard to believe in almost eighteen years of best-friendship that we'd never had it out like that, but we hadn't. If we were annoyed with each other, we took a break from one another for a few days or a few weeks. No big deal. Then we'd get together again and all was okay.

Playing with the Song Wreckers after our argument was tense. Katie and I talked to each other only when we had to. Mainly we ignored each other. Heather, Josh, and Courtney noticed but didn't say anything about it. Not to our faces anyway.

It was perfect timing when Kent called to tell me Gina's album was due to come out at the end of April. I needed *something* to be happy about. The first single being released was a song I had written called "Caught Misbehavin'".

Although a small part of me was happy, stress trumped my happiness. The Creep, Katie, Ram. And Gina's album. The weight of it really hit me after Kent's call. If the album failed, I failed. Gina was amazing. If it didn't sell it meant my songs weren't good enough. My stomach was in a constant state of twisted knots.

My dad had been consistently calling every week or two since the wedding. Usually I let the answering machine take his call. He wanted me to visit him, but I couldn't force myself to agree just yet. I wasn't trying to be a resentful bitch. I was trying to get to a state of mind where I wasn't a neurotic, stressed out mess. Was that ever going to happen, though?

The last time he called, he invited me to spend Easter with him and Joy, as well as her family. I figured I wasn't going to get emotionally better any time soon, so I accepted his invitation. Plus my mom was going to spend another holiday with Victor's family, and Katie and I weren't on good enough terms to spend the holiday together.

What was so pitiful was that everyone else had a set place they went for the holidays except for me. I floated around until someone grabbed me, or I spent them alone.

Pathetic, thy name is Molly Davis.

I blared Miranda Lambert as I drove to my dad's, singing my heart out about lost loves, crazy ex-girlfriends, and life's difficult choices. By the time Joy opened the door to let me in, I felt a teensy bit better.

Being around people who distracted me from my life for a while was refreshing. Since people in general liked to talk about themselves, I supplied lots and lots of questions. I steered all conversation away from me.

Then I told my dad about the Gina Swinger album and how her first single was about to come out, which made me the main focus. I kept the talk about the music part of my life. My work was the one part of my life that didn't suck.

I returned home from Easter to an email from Kent wanting a favor. Since he knew I was off work for the week due to Spring Break, he asked me to fly to Charleston, South Carolina to check out a couple of bands. I would fly to Charleston on Thursday, check out a band that night, another Friday, then fly home Saturday.

I scouted for Kent to keep myself occupied. Running away from my problems for a couple of days sounded really good, even if it wasn't exactly the grown-up thing to do. Katie was mad at me, so no hanging out with her. My mom was presumably out gallivanting with Victor. I had other friends, but running away sounded like the better option.

Before going to Nashville, I had never flown by myself. Now I was used to it. I wasn't used to going into bars by myself, however, so that was weird. I got a lot of looks. I didn't know if the constant peeks at me were because men were interested or because women usually didn't venture in bars solo. A couple of men offered to buy me drinks. I politely declined, telling them I was there to listen to the band, nothing more.

I made mental notes of everything about the two bands I was checking out: how they sounded, what the crowd's reaction to them was, if the quality of their playing declined as the night wore on, what they did when they were on break, how much they drank, the number of original songs versus cover songs—that sort of thing. I used my phone to record parts of their performances. I talked to the regulars at the bars and asked what they liked about the bands.

At the airport Saturday, I emailed Kent all the information I gathered about the bands, in addition to my opinion on them. My opinion was that the bands were good, and nothing more than that, so I worried that it had been a worthless trip. Sunday, he emailed back to thank me, telling me I'd done an outstanding job, and to say that most scouting trips didn't pan out anyway, so not to worry about it.

The next day was time to go back to work, and time to get back into a rhythm that would keep me from thinking too much. I threw myself into a routine of work, working out, and writing music.

When May rolled around I realized I had been overdoing it. I was tired of being pretty much alone all the time. I was tired of pushing myself to be non-stop busy. I was just plain tired. That routine of mine was getting ridiculous. I was making myself sick. My anxiety had been going on for so long I became nauseated. I pushed myself so hard physically that I skipped a period, and that hadn't happened since I was serious into dancing.

When the weather started getting nice outside, I could barely enjoy it. I sat on my couch, telling myself what an idiot I was for wearing myself down to such an extreme extent. I mean, there I was on a gorgeous day, dead tired, queasy, and my period still hadn't come.

Wait a minute.

Oh. Shit.

Chapter 39

Ohmygod. Shit. No way.

I sat up straight and squeezed the edge of the couch like a stress reliever ball. Squeeze, release. Squeeze, release. I couldn't be pregnant. I was on the Pill. I took it religiously. I had never not taken it or been more than a couple hours late taking it, and even that was rare. Oral contraceptives were like, almost one hundred percent effective. I may not have read all of the information that was given to me when I began taking the Pill, but remembered reading that perfect use pregnancy rate is .3%, making it 99.7% effective.

I was breathing so heavily my head spun. Where was a paper bag? On TV when someone hyperventilates, someone else sticks a paper bag up to their mouth. I didn't have any paper bags. Or a someone else.

Shit.

I closed my eyes and tapped my foot. *Calm down, Molly. You can't be pregnant.* I slowed my breathing, in through the nose and out through the mouth. Okay, better.

You can't prevent hurricanes, tornadoes, or earthquakes. You sure as hell could prevent pregnancy. Getting pregnant on the Pill is for people who forget to take it or always take it late. Irresponsible people. Not me.

I was tired because I'd worked myself too damn hard. I wanted to puke because I was stressed out over The Creep, Katie, and Gina's album. My period hadn't come because I killed myself at the gym.

Sitting around for days waiting to feel better or get my period wasn't an option, so I got my ass out of the house and drove all the way down to Monroe to a drugstore where I was positive I wouldn't run into anyone who might possibly know me. There was no way I was going to risk having a colleague—or worse, a student—witness me buying a pregnancy test.

I bought three tests and a bottle of water to start chugging on the drive home.

The first test came out positive.

The second test came out positive.

I didn't have enough pee for the third test.

Screw Katie being mad at me and the two us on bad terms with each other. I needed my best friend now more than ever. I called Katie to make sure she was home, and told her I was on my way. I wasn't sure if she understood what I was saying due to my super sobbing freak out.

She was waiting for me with the door open. I ran to her and threw my arms around her and cried. And cried. I eventually managed to get the words *I'm pregnant* out.

Finally I calmed down, and she led me to her couch. When I looked at her I saw her eyes were puffy, as if she had been crying too.

"What's wrong?" I asked her.

"Nothing. Don't worry about it. Are you sure, Molly?"

I nodded. "I took two tests. I have another one I want to take later, but I'm pretty sure I know what it will say."

"Cooper is the father?"

"Of course Cooper is the father! Katie, if you don't tell me what's wrong I'm going to strangle you!" The more I looked at her the more I saw she did not look good at all.

"I broke up with Brett."

I started blubbering all over again. "Oh my God! I'm pregnant, and you broke up with Brett."

We hugged each other for a while and cried our eyes out. When we were done she told me that she'd ended it with Brett the day before.

"Why didn't you tell me?"

She shrugged. "I didn't want to bother you with this."

"You're a liar. You always want to bother me with your problems." She handed me a tissue so I could blow my nose. "You know I didn't mean that like it sounded."

"I know. I *wanted* to bother you. Since we haven't been talking lately, I didn't." She grabbed a tissue for herself. "Molly, thank you for coming to me with this." She blew her nose. "I'm so sorry for everything! I love you, you know!"

I could barely see her through my tears. "I'm sor-sor-sorry, and I love you t-too. Katie, what am I gonna do?"

"I don't know!"

Here's what I did. I took the third test the next morning when I woke up, because the directions said that morning pee was the best.

Two pink lines. I dropped the test into the garbage with the other two.

Katie and I hung out for the next week, lounging around at one of our houses, letting ourselves be totally pathetic. I needed that week to let it sink in that I was really and truly pregnant. Like, with a baby.

I knew in this day and age a woman had options when it came to pregnancy. There was abortion and there was adoption. They weren't for me. I was going to have this baby.

I needed to tell Cooper, obviously. In general, people don't scare or intimidate me, but nothing scared me as much as having to tell Cooper that I was pregnant with his baby.

It took me two weeks to work up the nerve. First, I went to the doctor to give me yet another confirmation that, yes, I was pregnant. At the doctor's visit I found out I was six weeks along, due in early January. I also found out that antibiotics lessened the efficacy of the pill.

"How did you not know that?" Katie asked when I told her everything the doctor said. "Even I know that. Every woman knows that."

"Well I didn't!" God, I sure as hell did now.

"Didn't the doctor warn you when he prescribed them to you?"

"Obviously not."

"Weren't there little stickers on the side of the bottle that warned you?"

"The sticker told me to take with a meal and that antibiotics may interact with some medications."

"Yeah, well, birth control pills are one of those medications."

Fat lot of good that information was to me then.

I swore Katie to secrecy, and we discussed how I would tell Cooper. My plan was to tell him without any hesitation. Walk straight up to him and blurt it out. If I waited even a second, I had the potential to chicken out.

One thing I didn't tell Katie was that I was going to give Cooper an out. We didn't love each other. I'd bet every penny I had that he absolutely did not want to have this, or any, baby. I wanted an all or nothing situation regarding Cooper and fatherhood. I was giving give him two choices: be there one hundred percent, or walk away. If he chose to be a father, a *real* father, then great. My baby would have two parents. If he didn't want to be a part of our lives, then I'd lie and say I was artificially inseminated. As a child, it hurt too bad to know that you had a father out there who didn't love you enough to be in your life. I knew firsthand.

So I called Cooper and found out what time he was going to be home. I told him I had to run something by him and wanted to do it in person.

I was waiting for him in his driveway when he pulled in. As soon as he stepped out of his SUV, I walked toward him. He had been on the phone and let it drop to his side when he saw me approaching.

I saw he was done talking so I went right up to him, shaking, and gave my speech. "I'm pregnant with your baby.

I know this is unexpected and unwanted, but I'm having it anyway. Since this is probably the last thing in the world you want, I'm giving you the choice to walk away from me and this baby. I won't come after you for child support. I don't need the money. You need to decide to be there all the way or not at all. You know how to get a hold of me if you want to be involved. If I don't hear from you, I'll assume you're going to have nothing do with us." I stood there for a second then added, "I'm sorry."

I left him standing there stupefied in his spot with his hands down and his mouth partially open. Total surprise. I don't even think he watched me drive away because when I looked at him through my rear view mirror he was still looking at exactly the same spot, as if I was still there, talking to him.

Katie and I spent our spare time together. She was upset I gave Cooper the option I did, and refused to believe Cooper was choosing to opt out of fatherhood, even though I hadn't heard from him. She was convinced he just needed time to accept the baby. I knew better, and was really trying to be realistic about the situation. A small part of me got butterflies whenever the phone rang, thinking it might be Cooper. But I eventually stopped thinking he'd step up to the plate, though, and let go of the idea that he'd do the right thing.

As the days passed, I felt crappier and crappier. Nausea, fatigue, trouble focusing . . . was I pregnant or hung over? I had listened to several friends complain about how bad they felt during their first trimester, but you couldn't really understand until experiencing it firsthand. When I finally started puking, it would start around four in the morning and continue until about four in the afternoon. Since Katie was the only one who knew, outside of Cooper, I really had to be sneaky to hide it at work.

I loved when I was home and was able to veg out on the couch and do nothing. By five in the evening, I would feel well enough to eat, so I made make sure I had a nice big dinner to puke up the next morning. Since Katie wasn't with Brett anymore, she usually came over to join me.

It came as no surprise when we showed up on Friday for June's Wrecker Weekend and Cooper wasn't there. Only Ram, by himself, and he kept his distance.

I was super appreciative that I didn't feel too sick in the evenings. I just had to fight the God awful fatigue.

Katie kept worrying during the show, glancing at me often to gauge if I was all right. At least I helped keep her mind off Brett. They made eye contact occasionally. No talking.

Saturday morning, I was lounging on the couch feeling like shit, when the doorbell rang. Cooper?

I stood up to answer the door and got a major head rush. When the dizziness faded I looked to see who had come over. Ram.

I opened the door, and he stormed in with crazy, intense eyes, then slammed the door behind him.

"How the hell could you?" he screamed. He didn't wait for me to answer. "How the hell could you get pregnant by him and let him walk away?"

"He told you?" I gasped, shocked that Cooper would confide in Ram about this.

"No he didn't tell me!" he stepped into my personal space. "Here's a piece of advice: make sure when someone's on the phone, they press end before you start talking to them!"

So when Cooper dropped his arm down to the side he was still on the phone. With Caleb Ramsey.

Ram continued to yell. "Molly! How could you let this happen?"

I pushed on his chest and he backed up. "This is none of your business!" It wasn't any business of his that Cooper and

I had started off always using condoms. Then one night he didn't have any, and since I was on the pill . . .

He ran his hands through his hair. Instead of taking them out he got a good grip and held on. He was trying and failing to keep his anger in check, like the night of the attack.

"God damn it, Princess—"

"Stop calling me Princess!" I said, cutting him off. Then a huge wave of nausea hit me, and I ran to the bathroom to throw up.

When I came out of my master bathroom, Ram stood in the middle of my bedroom.

I pushed past him. "Hasn't anyone ever told you it's not polite to follow people when they're going to puke?"

He grabbed my arm to stop me. "Sorry. I was worried about you," he said. At least he'd stopped yelling.

"Well, don't be. It's only morning sickness. Back off." He let go and I marched around him.

Ram followed me to the living room and stayed standing while I collapsed on the couch. I noticed him look pretty intently at something and followed his gaze to the picture collage Alan and Garrett had given me for Christmas which I still hadn't hung. He flicked his eyes back to me. "I want to know what on earth you were thinking when you told him he could walk away. Do you know how stupid that is?"

I grabbed a throw pillow to snuggle. "This is *not* any of your concern. Why are you here anyway?"

"To see if you have even an ounce of sense! To see if it's really true! To have you look at me and tell me you're pregnant with Cooper's baby!"

I shot off the couch up to tell him off, but swayed when another head rush hit me. Ram hustled over to steady me.

As soon as I was sure I wasn't going to fall over, I shoved his hands off me. "Get away from me. I'm fine!" He backed up. "Yes, I have sense! Yes, it's really true! I. Am. Pregnant. With. Cooper's. Baby. Now go."

He stared at me several seconds in a way no other man had before—as if I'd tore his heart out and kicked it out of my way. He stormed out and tears welled in my eyes. I didn't let them fall. I went and dry heaved instead.

Chapter 40

So there I was, knocked up like a God damned teenager who didn't know any better. Unmarried. Pathetic. Pretty much alone.

Since all I really wanted to do was lie around, I had lots of time to think and make important decisions.

First, I had to move. I didn't want to raise a baby in a condo. I wanted a real house with a real yard. I wanted much more space that a baby and I wouldn't outgrow in a few years. Everyone I knew who had a baby said they couldn't believe how much space a baby took up. Between all the toys and baby gear, supposedly they needed their own mansions.

Second, I had to quit teaching. How could I go to work pregnant and unmarried and expect to have the respect of my students? As a high school teacher, I should be a role model. I should be an example to all the young women I saw every day. I barely even respected myself anymore. It wasn't as if I got pregnant by a serious boyfriend, so we could just go and get married. Nope. And honestly, I was embarrassed I was in this situation. Fortunately, I could afford to give up my day job because I had Gina money. If I kept writing and selling songs, I would be totally fine. In fact, even if I didn't earn any money for a while I would still be fine.

With a brave face I resigned from my teaching position at the end of the school year, citing wanting to concentrate solely on music as my reason. But God, I was beyond scared. I had to buy my own health insurance. Talk about adding even more stress—that shit's expensive. Now I *had* to make sure my new music career was successful. If not, I wouldn't be able to afford to live and have health insurance for me and the baby for more than a few years.

Everyone was surprised, and my department head and principal were upset at having to find a replacement for me over the summer. Luckily, I resigned so late in the year, the other teachers didn't have time to give me any sort of going away party. I couldn't have handled a party.

I hated giving up teaching, and on the last day of work, tears started falling as soon as I pulled out of the parking lot. Stupid hormones. Teaching was the one thing in my life that I hadn't fallen into. I was proud of that. My *mother* put me in dance class at the age of three, and I stuck with it and got good. *Katie* started me playing guitar and singing at the age of fourteen, and I stuck with it and got good. *I* chose teaching. Now I couldn't even stick with it.

I scoured the Internet looking for houses. Since the housing market in Michigan had started to tank, there were a lot of choices out there. Of course, that meant it would be more difficult to sell my condo.

I wanted to move farther away from where I taught—used to teach. That way, I'd have less chance of running into students—former students—while being pregnant. Katie thought it absurd that I went this route because I was pregnant and not married, but resigning and moving was the right thing to do in my mind.

When I called Kent to inform him I had resigned from teaching and was going to focus on song writing, he was thrilled. He reiterated that I should move to Nashville, something he'd been telling me since the summer. There was no way I could move away from Katie. She was my support system. Plus she'd kill me.

I still hadn't told anyone else I was pregnant. The only ones who knew were Katie, Cooper, and Ram. I knew in time I was going to have to go beyond accepting the pregnancy. I would have to stop hiding it. Embrace it. I just wasn't quite ready.

By the end of June, I felt so bad I wanted to die. Figuratively, of course. How was it possible to feel *that* bad without the use of an ungodly extreme amount of alcohol the night before?

I barely made it through July's Wreckers Weekend. I was completely caught up in my own drama—ohmygod I'm still pregnant, did everyone believe I had the flu or did they know I was lying—that I didn't see Ram until it was time to leave. As mad as he was at me, he still came to keep the band safe. He kept himself mostly hidden, but still, I didn't sense his presence at all. Weird, but I truly felt awful. In fact, we had to cut it short because I didn't have it in me to stand up on stage and exert the amount of energy needed for three entire sets.

I had been trying so hard to resume my normal activities, but couldn't. I was so tired and so crappy feeling I couldn't usually drag myself out for a run or swim. I was so sick of being inside the house all day that I dragged Katie out to dinner whenever I felt up to it. We usually went to Panera, where we ate dinner and lingered over coffee and dessert. (Fuck off, I was not giving up coffee!)

The outings with Katie kept me from going bat shit crazy. I needed out of my house. For a couple of hours, I felt like I was supposed to: excited with a side of nausea.

Preparing for a baby finally started getting fun. I had absolutely nothing, so had to start from scratch. Katie was thrilled, planning shit was her thing.

We were at Panera one evening, drinking fruit smoothies and eating bagels. It was too hot for coffee.

Katie leafed through a baby catalogue, deep in thought. "This is a tough one, Mol—gender neutral, or gender specific?"

"I kinda think—"

"Shh"—she waved me off—"I wasn't really asking you."

I rolled my eyes, not that she took the time to look at me. I don't really have a decorator's eye and gave her carte blanche to design my nursery, and she took her job seriously.

I sucked the last of my smoothie through the straw until the slurping noises stopped. "I saw a cute pattern online the other day," I said.

Only her eyes lifted. "You know I love you, Mol. But butt out. This is my—" her gaze went from me to over my shoulder. She raised her chin.

"What?" I asked, then followed her gaze to the person behind me. Ram. "Oh."

I looked at him for a few seconds, and gave him the smallest of smiles. I wasn't mad at him anymore for coming over to yell at me. Hell, I knew I deserved it. I waved to him.

He walked over to me and Katie. "Hi."

Katie said hello back, but Ram paid her no attention. His eyes stayed on me from the moment I had turned my head to see who Katie had been staring at.

"I see a gal from work over there, so I'm gonna go over and say hi," Katie lied. She was giving me and Ram time to clear the air with each other.

Once she left I motioned for him to sit down. "So what's up?" I asked.

He sat across from me. "You're being awfully civil to me considering how I acted toward you the last time we spoke."

"I'm not mad at you. Plus it's not like *I've* never yelled at *you* before."

"Well I wanted to apologize anyway for how I acted."

I smiled to let him know that really, I wasn't upset. "Don't. It's not a big deal, I had it coming, and I really don't care anymore, to be honest."

He leaned forward and put his arms on the table, took a breath, and looked me over while I shoved the last bite of bagel in my mouth. "How are you?" he asked.

"I'm okay. Promise." He didn't say anything. "So are you here to grab dinner?"

"No. I was in the area, and I saw your car here and wanted to see how you were and to tell you I'm sorry for acting like a jerk."

Ram's eyes held a concern I hadn't seen since the weeks after my attack. "You're worried about me?"

"Yes."

I put my hand on his arm. He covered it with his own, and I swear I saw his shoulders relax. "Well you don't have to be. I have everything under control. I had an offer accepted on a house over in New Boston, I have Katie planning what is probably going to be the most decked out nursery in the entire state, and I'm hoping soon that I'll be done with the morning sickness so I can feel relatively normal again."

He nodded, but looked unsure. Maybe there was something he wanted to tell me, or maybe he didn't want to be sitting there with me. Or maybe he didn't know what to say.

He pulled his hand off mine and sat up straight. After looking around he asked, "So do you think you'll take the rest of the school year off after the baby's born?"

"I quit."

He pulled his head back in surprise. "What?"

"I quit my job. I'm going to try writing music for a living. That way I can stay home with the baby and still earn a living."

Still surprised, he said, "Wow."

"Yup. I have it all worked out. I'm moving into a bigger house, I won't have to worry about daycare since I'll be working from home. I just have to hope I have more sellable music in me."

He had to leave, so we said our goodbyes. I wished when he walked away I didn't have to watch him until he was out of sight, but I did. He walked over to Katie and said goodbye to her for a couple minutes (why the hell did that take so long?), then left.

I was pretty sure I was able to ease his mind and get him to realize he didn't have to worry about me. If there's one thing I knew how to do, it was landing on my feet after taking a hit.

Truth be told, it made me sad to see Ram that day. I was reminded that he and I were never going to be anything more than friends. I'd also developed a pang of guilt for being excited over the baby, as if I had betrayed him in some way. How stupid was that? He and I were never really anything, we never got the chance to be. The contentment I felt when he sat with me, the butterflies I felt when I touched him . . . I had to ignore that from now on. Because my baby came first, and there was no use wondering what could have been. I would not look back. My focus was forward only from that point on.

When I began the second trimester, I started telling people about the baby. I told my mom, my dad and Joy, the band, Alan and Garrett, Kent, and every other friend I ran into.

Everyone was surprised, mainly because when they inquired as to who the father was I didn't tell them. I simply said that I was having a baby on my own.

Because the drama of an unexpected pregnancy and abandonment wasn't enough, I ended up being hospitalized for a couple of days when I was four and a half months along. I had lost weight and was dehydrated, and that, mixed with still throwing up daily, did not sit well with my doctor.

Of course Katie was there for me. She didn't dote on me too much in the hospital, but she kept me company. She kept me from going crazy once again. We were totally back to how we'd always been. The fight we had was forgotten. It was me and Katie against the world again. But now she was heartbroken, and I was pregnant, so we didn't have a whole lot of fight in us.

The doctor rolled an ultrasound machine into my hospital room. I lifted my gown and got cold-gelled up. She moved the wand thingy around my belly and pointed out images on the screen. I was glad she knew what was what, because I couldn't distinguish a single thing.

She moved the mouse around, clicked and made measurements. "See that?" the doctor asked. She had her index and middle fingers touching the screen. "I believe that's our main reason for how sick you've been."

I saw black and white fuzzy stuff and other little squirmy things. "Is that the Satan's child? Have I been impregnated by Satan and that's why I feel so bad?"

Katie shook her head. "No. I don't think that's the devil. I think it's maybe a space alien."

"Ladies, look." The doctor tapped the screen with her fingers. "There are two babies in there."

You know how you think you've finally accepted something? Then, *whammo*! You get more news that sets your head spinning all over again? Yeah. "Holy shit." I breathed. "Twins? Two babies? More than one? Twins? Are you sure?"

"Yup. Twins. Congratulations."

She finished the ultrasound, while I stayed in a state of mild shock, and Katie squealed.

When the doctor left Katie said, "I don't know why you're surprised. Of course you wouldn't have only one baby. You tend to be the exception and not the rule."

I didn't know whether to laugh or cry. I had two babies! Two babies, one me. Ugh.

I ended up laughing and crying at the same time.

Chapter 41

The next day I felt better. I accepted the idea of twins. I was rehydrated. The doctor didn't go so far as to diagnose me with hyper emesis, but said I had to be sure to get plenty of fluids in me, which would help with the nausea and make it easier to eat so I could gain the necessary weight. As long as I was doing okay, the doctor was going to release me the following morning. Twenty-four hours of time to fill while in a hospital room.

For entertainment, Katie had brought a big bag of rubber bands, and we were shooting them, using all of the things in the room as targets. Some of the nurses were amused and some of them were quite annoyed. To be fair, we did hit a couple of them.

There was a knock at the door. Katie answered it, then shot me a guilty smile, while Ram walked into the room with flowers.

"Well look at the time," Katie said. "I gotta run home for a while. See you later."

She left me alone with Ram. Again.

I stated the obvious. "I take it Katie called you?"

He set the vase of flowers on the windowsill and helped himself to the guest chair next to my bed. "Yeah. When I was leaving the restaurant a couple weeks ago I made her promise to call me if anything happened." He crossed his arms over his chest and smiled, so I knew he was being friendly. "So what'd you get yourself into now?"

"Ha ha. I was dehydrated. It's all under control now. I

get to go home tomorrow, thank God. I have so much to do it's not even funny."

"Like what, start writing baby songs?"

"No, smart ass. I close on my new house in a couple weeks, so I have to finish getting my house packed up to move. Then I have to move—or watch the movers move my stuff. Then I have to unpack and get my house settled. Then I have to start buying all the baby stuff. Get this, twins. I have to buy two of everything."

His eyes went wide. "Are you shitting me?"

"Nope."

He shook his head, as if to clear the shock. "Damn, Princess. As soon as I think you can't possibly surprise me anymore you . . . wow. Congratulations, I guess."

I smiled. "Thanks."

Although the movers had done almost everything up until that point, once they had delivered all of my household, the rest was up to me.

While my new house was more than I needed, 3,500 square feet, and would take more work than I was used to to maintain, I loved it from the first time I saw it. It was two stories plus a basement and sat on an acre lot. When you walked through the front door, you stood in a two story entryway. The living room was to the immediate left, which had a set of stairs leading to the second story. Straight ahead, beyond the entryway, was a large eat in kitchen with all the appliances and most of the cabinetry to the right side, along with the garage entrance. The left side of the kitchen was the eating area with additional cabinets, along with the stairs to the basement. Tucked into the back corner was a half bathroom. There was also a pocket door that led to a formal dining room. You could keep walking straight through the entryway and kitchen to enter the great room that was partially open to the kitchen. In the back left corner of the great room there was a second set of stairs that led to the second story.

The upstairs consisted of a long hallway with four bedrooms, three bathrooms, and a hall closet that could have been mistaken for a fifth bedroom if it had a window. The master bedroom had a large attached bathroom and a larger walk-in closet to die for. That was a powerful selling point for me. The three guest bedrooms were bigger than what I'd had growing up. Two of the bedrooms had a Jack and Jill bathroom, and the last bedroom had a hallway bathroom next to it.

The basement was finished, but bare. I'd have my new basement set up the same way my old one was set up, the difference being that nothing would have to compete for space.

I was glad to be officially in my new house, especially since it would make working from home easier after the babies were born. I'd be spending a lot of time indoors, and the extra breathing room assured I wouldn't feel trapped in a box.

I stood, hand on forehead, looking at everything in boxes. A bit overwhelming. I had to organize everything as to where it belonged, plus I had to paint and set up the nursery.

I walked around a bit. First, I should get my bed situated. How hard was it to set up a bed frame? Maybe I should call Katie to help me, or maybe I could just sleep on my mattress on the floor.

I heard a vehicle pull into the driveway. I looked out the front window and saw Ram. What the hell? He was obviously having Katie spy for him.

I opened the door before he had a chance to knock. "Well surprise, surprise. I guess a little birdie told you I moved today."

He smiled as a response, so I stepped back to let him in.

He took a quick look around. "Looks like we've got a lot of work to do," he said

"*We* don't. *I* do."

"So what's first?"

I gave a frustrated growl. "Ram!"

"Listen, Princess. I'm not going to let you move heavy stuff in your condition. I know how you operate. You'll feel bad asking people to help you, so you'll do everything yourself."

I didn't have a choice, really. He told me that unless I physically removed him, he was staying to help. I couldn't; he did.

He asked me where I wanted my furniture, and moved it into place. He set up my bed frame and mattress. He carried labeled boxes to the rooms they belonged in. He would've hung curtains had the previous owners not left some in place.

I knew I should have sat him down and told him to leave me alone. A couple of times I actually opened my mouth to do so, but what came out was . . . nothing. I was drawn to him, and I loved having him keep me company. Okay, so being around Ram wasn't healthy for me because when reality hit I would ride a slew of emotions I wasn't prepared for, but we got along great. I just couldn't push him away again.

It took a few days for the vibe to switch from unsure to easiness between us. We talked, we laughed, we gave each other a lot of shit. We were just two good friends hanging out. I would catch him looking at my baby bump. He would joke about me eating too much and getting fat.

He was so damn nice, and . . . genuine, sure of himself in that sexy, manly way. He was an all-around good guy. And all that made him even sexier than he already was to me. Fuck.

At August's Wreckers Weekend, I wanted to punch Ram. In the face. Hard. Okay, so maybe the hormones multiplied my emotions. God, he was on me like glue, as if any minute

The Creep was going to jump out and attack me again. I was surprised he didn't buy a giant wad of bubble wrap to put me in. He practically sat on the stage while we played and growled at anyone who stood too close.

Playing guitar with my bump was becoming difficult. I was obviously pregnant by that point and being on a stage singing about making men pay, going to hell, shaking my ass, or getting drunk while I had two little babies inside of me didn't sit right with me anymore.

Holy shit, should I quit the band? That's what passed through my head right smack dab in the middle of a song—one about shaking my ass. Molly Davis without the Song Wreckers. That was almost like Molly Davis without her arms. The Wreckers had been a part of me for so long, I'd never imagined life without them. But I was about to be a mother. Should I still be playing in bars? I panicked.

The color must've drained from my face—it sure felt like it—because Ram jumped up on stage to ask me if I was all right and felt my forehead as if he was checking for a fever. The band stopped playing and everyone stared at us. Katie announced a break, and he rushed me off into Brett's office and made me sit down. The whole band stood around me.

"What the hell did you do that for, you idiot?" I yelled at Ram. Multiplied hormones.

He sat down next to me. "You got this look on your face and went white. Are you okay?"

"I'm fine. I was just thinking about stuff."

They all stared at me. I addressed Courtney since she was the only other person in the room ever to be pregnant. "Courtney, you know how it is right? I was thinking about the babies, and it must've showed on my face."

Josh answered for her. "Yeah, that happened to Court a few times too. It was nothing."

I looked at everybody. "See? I'm totally fine. Go out

there, and I'll meet you in a few." I mouthed a *thank you* to Josh. I shooed everyone out.

Ram shut the door after the rest of the band left, then came back and touched my forehead again.

I pulled my head away. "What in the hell do you think that is accomplishing?"

"Are you sure you feel okay? This is not the time to pretend to be okay when you're not."

"Ram. Do you honestly believe that I would do anything to put these babies in danger?"

He hesitated, then admitted, "No."

Since he was still freaked out, I explained to him what I had been thinking that put the look on my face. My explanation calmed him, and he didn't argue with me when I joined the band back up on stage. I did make sure to threaten him if he ever did that without good reason again. Unfortunately, I don't think it scared him in the slightest.

I agreed not to paint or decorate the babies' room until I found out the sexes of them. Katie made up her mind that I wanted a gender specific décor.

"Oh that's cute that you think you're going to be painting." Ram said one night. He was hanging pictures, while I followed him around and watched, when I told him what Katie had decided.

"My doctor said as long as I open a window and take frequent breaks I'll be fine."

He pointed a hammer at me. "No. Absolutely not."

"You're not the boss of me, you know."

He turned and straightened the frame he'd hung. "I'll tell you what. You can do the tape work over the baseboards. That's it. No way am I going to let you do the painting or get up on any ladder. I don't know if the ladder could handle it."

Hilarious. There was no point in arguing with him. And anyway, I could always do it while he was at work.

"And if I think that you're going to do it anyway when I'm not around then I'll make sure that someone is here twenty-four seven to watch your every move and remove any paint brush from your pretty little hands."

God damn it. "I think you're going a wee bit overboard."

"And I think you don't know how far I'll go to make sure you're one hundred percent safe at all times."

"It's not possible for anyone to be one hundred percent safe at all times."

"Well I'm going to try." He set the hammer down. "You hungry?"

I was hungry, so he took me out to eat. Again, I knew I should be distancing myself from him, but I'd developed an addiction to him—his company, his friendship, the way he made me feel safe and grounded. I told myself every night when he left that I was being stupid, that he was not mine. He could never be mine because I was the world's hugest fuck up, pregnant with his boss's children. I was pathetic, and he felt sorry for me. End of story.

Chapter 42

Katie went to *the* ultrasound with me. The one that would hopefully let me know if I was having boys, girls, or one of each. She was hoping for one of each so she could decorate with both girl and boy stuff. I honestly didn't care what I had. I wanted to find out so I could be prepared.

When the ultrasound technician told me I was having boys, I started to laugh-cry. Not because I was upset, but because it became even more real. I couldn't wait to tell Ram. I debated with myself as to whether or not it would be appropriate to call him with the news.

Screw it, we plunked into her car after the appointment and I sent him a text with the news. He immediately texted back, *congratulations!*

"You've been spending a lot of time with Ram lately," Katie said when I shoved my phone back in my purse.

"He's been a good friend, and he's been helping me set up the house. You know that because you told him when I was moving and to come over and help me, remember?"

"You guys seem pretty close."

"We are, I guess." And that was the truth. He'd become someone I had come to totally depend on. Despite telling myself over and over that I should not let him do stuff for me, not let him take me out to eat and shop for baby stuff, not think he's smart and funny and everything that a man should be, I did it anyway. I was the Queen of Fucktards from the land of Fucktardia.

Ram and I talked about everything. I found out all the things that I'd ever wanted to know about him. He told me about his family. He even told me how he had been engaged to be married when he came out of the Army. His high school sweetheart waited for him all those years and dumped him when they found out he was unable to have children.

I felt devastated when I learned Ram would never be a father. Men like him—grounded, smart, trustworthy—*should* be the ones reproducing. As much as possible. He told me his story, but I became so angry at the woman who turned her back on him that I focused on her: Jenny Winters. The woman who said she loved him, then ran as soon as she knew her life wasn't going to be exactly like she'd planned out. What a bitch. She'd insisted they have complete physicals before the marriage because she worried about his health after spending time overseas. She'd seen a special news report on how these men were coming home from the military, and their wives claimed that having sex with their husbands made them burn "down there". They both wanted to start a family soon after getting married, so she wanted to make sure everything was physically okay with them.

It turned out Ram had damaged sperm ducts, which caused him to have very low sperm count. His doctor told him to count out having children that were biologically his. His fiancé then told him she changed her mind about wanting to get married.

I hated the idea of Ram almost marrying her, probably as much as he hated that I got knocked up by Cooper—who we briefly talked about. Ram told me that he'd confronted Cooper about the pregnancy and his lack of involvement. Cooper said what he did wasn't anybody's business. I didn't press Ram for any more details. As much as I wanted to know what the hell Cooper thought regarding this situation, I didn't want to find out that there was something about me so awful it caused the man who'd knocked me up to abandon his children. I'd never expected Cooper to step up to the plate, but it still stung.

I had some important questions for Cooper I hoped I'd get the answers to one day, but lately, the only questions I could concentrate on were for Ram. Why was he being so good to me, and what in the hell was I going to do when the babies were here and he wasn't?

As a band, The Song Wreckers agreed that we'd play September's Wreckers Weekend, then take maternity leave. For how long, I wasn't sure. Maybe I would continue after the babies were born, and maybe I would be done for good, although I really couldn't picture myself not playing with the band in the future.

Ram was the same overprotective oaf as last time. Fortunately, he didn't force me off the stage and try to check for a fever. The only incident was when he sat too close to a speaker and unplugged a cord by sitting on it.

We played our last song and I took off my guitar.

"Sorry about the cord," he said, hopping up on stage and handing me my towel.

I wiped my face and neck. "It's not a big deal, you plugged it back in right away."

Katie walked over. "Hey, Ram, don't leave without getting the nursery's paint colors. I have a diagram in my purse where everything should go."

He turned his attention to her, while she explained her plans. I shook my head and brought what I could to the back of the stage.

Katie had worked hard to finish designing my nursery. The furniture had been delivered, and the paint colors picked out. The room was still a blank slate, though, and it would take a lot of work to get it to Katie's standards.

Oh my God, I'm going to have a nursery. With babies in it.

Ram came over Sunday with the paint, trays, and a drop

cloth. I had the room as ready as I could make it—baseboards taped, light switch wall plate taken off.

We stood in the nursery, Ram ready to start. "You don't have to do all this, you know," I reminded him.

"I want to," he said. "And you're making me lunch for this, right?"

"Right."

So he spent the day painting. He stayed so late I made him dinner too, which helped lessen my guilt a bit.

He assembled furniture and hung curtains throughout the week when he wasn't working. I made sure he was well fed. Good God, the man eats a lot.

Katie stopped by a few times to make sure her plans were being followed. Why she's a choir director and not a professional decorator of some sort was beyond me.

When there were walls striped in three different shades of blue, sports themed wall hangings, two cribs, a big dresser, a rocking chair, and a changing table in the room, Ram called me in to see the finished product.

I stood in the middle of the room, one hand on my belly, the other over my heart. The room was perfect.

Ram put his hand on my shoulder. "Do you like it?"

Unable to speak without crying, I nodded. I walked around and trailed my hands over everything, just to make sure it was real.

"It's . . . wow. I love it." I couldn't stop the tears from falling. All the crying I did while pregnant was embarrassing, so I took a slow breath to help control my emotions.

Ram watched me from across the room. "You okay?"

I wiped my eyes and smiled. "Yeah. Hormones."

He closed the distance between us and hugged me. I couldn't help it, I threw my arms around him and let him hold me. "Ram, why are you doing all of this for me?" Asking him was easier with my face buried in his chest and not having to look him in the eyes.

He put his hands on either side of my face and pulled back to look at me. "Because I love you," he said. And then he kissed me.

And it was like everything in my life—all the fucked up decisions, the God-awful things that happened to me—made sense for the first time ever. Everything led to that moment.

I should have been thinking what a messed up situation kissing a man I had no business kissing was because I was five months pregnant, and not by him. I mean, this was wrong, wasn't it? Then why did it feel so damn right and so good and so natural? I tried to reason with myself to stop. It lasted one second.

He pulled away from the kiss, but I wasn't done. I put my arms around his neck and pulled him back to me and kissed him again. He gladly went along with it. I felt his smile against my mouth. I'm sure he felt mine, too.

When we were done kissing for the second time, I told him what I already knew. "I love you too."

He kissed me again. And again and again. Each kiss was deeper and more passionate than the one before it. He kept one hand on my lower back and one hand on the back of my head, as if he was determined to keep me right there with him.

My hands slid to his chest. There was a split second when I told myself to push him away. I couldn't do it. So I let my hands glide over his chest, stomach, shoulders, anywhere I could, and let me tell you, the man felt good under my hands.

Eventually I slid my hands down to join his. We reached the point where we had to decide—stop completely or let it continue and lead to where we both knew these kisses were headed. And God help me, but I didn't want this to stop. As fucked up as our desire for each other was, I wanted to finish what we were starting. I wanted Caleb Ramsey more than I'd wanted any other man in my entire life. I wanted him to have me too.

I looked into his eyes trying to find any indication that he wanted me to stop. All I saw was love and lust.

I pressed myself to him as best I could, but my bump prevented me from pressing into his groin. He got the point, and ran his hands over my body slowly, leaving goose bumps wherever his hands touched.

Ram took my hand and walked me out of the nursery and into my bedroom. He kissed me some more, then lightly stepped on my foot to stop the nervous tapping. He was about to see me naked for the first time and my body was way curvier than it ever had been, and I wasn't sure if that was a good thing.

He undressed me, and I became completely self-conscious once my clothes were finally off.

"Beautiful. You're beautiful," he whispered over and over.

And what do you know—I started to believe him.

It was my turn to undress Ram. I'd seen him without a shirt on before, so I already knew he was perfection. Muscles to showcase his strength, a light dusting of hair on his chest. Yum. There was still a tan leftover on his forearms, face, and neck, but his otherwise naturally light skin tone looked good enough to lick. There were no marks on his body. No tattoos, and if there were any imperfections at all, I couldn't find them.

He left me for a minute to arrange the pillows on my bed before laying me down so my top half was propped up. Then he lay next to me and continued to kiss me—my mouth, neck, chest, shoulders—while we used our hands to get extremely familiar with each other.

He took the time to touch and kiss each of my attack scars. Instead of feeling damaged, I felt treasured.

Here he was accepting me, flaws, and fuck-ups, and all.

Finally his hands made their way between my legs and I almost exploded as soon as he touched me. His every touch left a trail of electricity that made me crave him like nothing else.

He changed position. I was so ready.

He swept the hair from my forehead and kissed me, then whispered, "Let me know if this is uncomfortable, and I'll fix it."

I nodded. "Okay."

"Look at me," he said, still whispering.

I did. We were gazing into each other's eyes when he slid into me. I gasped, and he stopped. "I'm okay, I'm okay," I assured him. I wasn't prepared for how good it felt. Not because he was finally making love to me, but because this was Ram, the man I'd been waiting my whole entire life for.

It was about damn time.

He continued making love to me with lots of grunts, saying *oh shit* and *oh God*—his verbal tells apparently—and lots and lots of kissing. I didn't worry that he wasn't enjoying himself.

When those verbal tells reached a fevered pitch and I assumed he was going to come, he held off instead, and pulled out to concentrate solely on me. He licked a path, between my breasts, down my bump, then lower still. My knees were pushed further apart so he could work major tongue magic until I came. Then he slid back in me so he could do the same.

He didn't collapse on me for the obvious reason. Instead he rolled to the side and kissed down my arm.

"Are you okay?" he asked, between kisses.

I smiled. "Oh yeah. You?"

His buried his mouth in my neck. "Mm-hmm."

We lay in each other's arms for a while, not speaking, kissing and trailing our fingers over each other. After a bit, I looked over to see the time.

I didn't want my happy bubble to burst, but I had to ask. "It's late. Do you have to go soon?"

"Do you want me to go?"

Never. "No."

"Good, because I didn't plan to," he said.

I liked that. I didn't press for more details, because I was so freaking happy I wanted to enjoy the feeling for as long as possible.

Chapter 43

Not teaching anymore, I wasn't sure how my days would go, but I ended up getting on a pretty consistent schedule.

During the day Caleb—since he'd been inside of me I couldn't call him Ram anymore—would go to work, and I would mainly work on music. Sometimes I'd organize the little stuff that still had to be unpacked into its new spot, or go shopping for baby gear when I wanted to get out of the house. Caleb would come over after work and stay until morning. Even when work kept him late into the night, he would come over afterward.

On the days he didn't have to work, we hung out and did normal couple stuff, or normal for a couple having a baby. We continued making love and had a hard time keeping our hands off each other. If we were on the couch, his arms were around me. If we were at the table eating, he entwined his legs with mine.

We didn't talk about the future. Part of me was too afraid to ask and part of me was pretty sure he would always be there. Still, we probably should have talked about it.

By the time I was six months pregnant, I was as big as a house. By seven months, two houses. At the rate I was expanding, I didn't think I would have to give birth because I was pretty sure I was going to explode. Ka-boom, here's your babies.

I was physically uncomfortable, ready to get these babies out. That's what forced me to recognize that Ram and I weren't in a situation where we could let our relationship linger indefinitely. Yes, I was sure we loved each other.

But I had to keep telling myself that ours was not a normal situation to be in. If our relationship was going to end, it had to be soon. I was too close to a major, life-altering event to let the issue of "us" go unsettled, so in bed one night I started The Talk about The Future. Our future.

I heaved myself up to a sitting position to look at him.

"We have to talk," I told him.

"Okay," he said, not bothering to do more than glance at me from the papers he was holding.

Caleb often brought files home from work to read. In bed, which I never understood. I always had to grade papers in the kitchen or living room. Whatever.

Being a relationship retard my whole life, it took me a while to come up with the right words to start this conversation. "I love you."

"I love you too," he said, comparing one sheet of paper to another.

"We're a couple, right?"

He shoved the papers into their folder and set it on the night stand then sat up, realizing that this was going to be a serious conversation. "Of course."

"Are we still going to be a couple after the twins are born?"

"That depends."

Oh shit. Here I let myself fall madly in love with him, and *now* I find out our relationship is conditional? A jolt of dread shot through me. I closed my eyes. "On what?"

"On whether or not you marry me."

My eyes popped open and my jaw dropped. Instead of words coming out of my mouth, they ran through my head: ohmygod, ohmygod, ohmygod!

He adjusted us so that we sat across from one another, looking into each other's faces. "So will you marry me?" He smiled big enough to showcase his dimples.

Ohmygod. "You wanna marry me?"

"I want to marry you," he said without missing a beat.

"*You*," I pointed to him, "want to marry *me*?" I put my finger to my own chest.

"Yes."

Just to be clear, "You want to get married. To me." Not, *let's live together to see if it works out.* Not, *yes, I'll still be your boyfriend after you give birth.* Him man, me wife. Ohmygod.

"I, Caleb Ramsey, want to get married to you, Molly Davis." Most men propose on one knee. But I guess when the woman you asked to marry you was acted like a confused idiot you did things differently.

He took my head in his hands and brought our faces close together. "Molly Davis, will you marry me?"

I scooted my way to his lap to kiss him.

He pried my face off of his. "Is that a yes?"

"That's a hell yes." I hugged him tightly and buried myself in him. God, I loved doing that.

"Do you have any idea what you're getting yourself into? Babies, my weird life, and you'll have to put up with Katie."

He turned his head and kissed my temple. "I actually have your engagement ring back at my place. My plan was to make you a romantic, candle lit dinner and ask you over dessert. And by the way, I like Katie, I've grown accustomed to your life, and I want to be the father to the twins, if you'll let me."

Stupid hormones. I started crying. Not regular crying, but blubbering. Since I couldn't talk, I nodded while he held me. He laughed, the fucker, but the last laugh was on him because when I was done, we discovered that I had snotted all over him. And since he wasn't wearing a shirt the mess was kind of gross. I wiped off his chest with the blanket; the part that covered him and not me.

Three things woke me simultaneously in the middle of that night: the urge to pee, hunger, and complete, gut-wrenching panic. I wobbled up, used the bathroom then headed to the kitchen. Maybe a snack would help ease the panic.

Nope, not even close.

Caleb had asked me to marry him last night, and I said yes. I was completely and totally in love with him, so the idea of spending the rest of my life with him wasn't the cause of my panic. Just the opposite: the idea of having him by my side from here on out gave me the most peaceful, happy feeling. Could I do that to him, though? Being with me meant he couldn't have a normal relationship.

Did my loving him mean letting him go so he could be with someone who could give him everything he deserved?

"Hey. Oh, sorry," Caleb said, as he walked into the kitchen. I jumped when I heard his voice. I'd been so consumed in my worries, I hadn't heard him coming to find me. He wore boxers and rumpled hair, looking every ounce as sexy as he did during the daytime.

"Why don't you sit down?" he asked. I was standing at the counter eating a peanut butter and jelly sandwich. "Are you okay?"

I heard the worry in his voice, so I nodded. "I'm fine. I had to pee and eat. And I've been lying in bed for hours so it feels good to be on my feet for a few minutes."

"So what's wrong? Are you in pain?"

"I'm fine," I repeated.

"Princess, you're tapping your foot a million times a minute. You only do that when you're anxious, nervous, or worried." He plopped down in a chair and motioned for me to do the same. "Now please, talk to me."

I took my sandwich, set it on the table then sat down. I ran my hands through my hair and debated myself for a minute on whether or not to tell him what was really on my mind. I had to. He knew me too well and was too concerned for me to let this go since he knew I was worried. Plus I owed him the chance to get out of a proposal he might have rushed into. I lifted my head and looked directly in his blue eyes.

"Caleb listen. I love you. Completely and totally. But I don't know if you should be marrying me."

He pinched the bridge of his nose for a second. "Oh wow. Here we go. I've been waiting for this speech. I just didn't know I'd hear it in the middle of the night." He took a deep breath and leaned forward, arms on the table. "Let me guess the rest: Caleb, you need to be with someone who isn't already pregnant. You should be with a regular woman and have a regular relationship." He remained silent for a few seconds. "Did I get it right?"

"Well, you're downplaying it. I can't give you what other women can." The tears formed again which added annoyance to my fear, because I cried more during this pregnancy than I had my entire life. Times ten. Giving Caleb the chance to get out of our relationship was the hardest thing I'd ever have to do, and that included having to tell Cooper I was pregnant. The idea of not being with him was horrifying.

"You're right," he said. "You can give me so much more. Now let's go back to bed." He scooted his chair back to get up.

"Stop," I demanded. He stopped and remained seated. "You have to listen to me." My voice was starting to shake and the tears were now rolling down my face. "Caleb, we can't have a traditional—" I waved my hands around to think of the right word, "courtship. For God's sake, I'm pregnant with another man's children. We will have very little alone time before the babies are born. And it's not like we can spend the time until the babies are born frolicking around, because I can't even frolic anymore. You deserve more than this. You—"

"Enough," he said, cutting me off. He reached out and took my hands in his. "Come back to bed, and we'll talk about this in the morning."

"You're not taking me seriously!" I yelled.

He yelled back, "No, Molly, *you're* not taking *me* seriously. Why do you do this? Why do you insist on sacrificing your happiness because you want to make everyone else happy?"

I yanked my hands out of his. "I don't do that."

"The hell you don't! You got pregnant by Cooper and told him you didn't need anything from him and that he could have no part in his own child's life because you assumed that's what *he* wanted! A child needs both parents, Molly. You know that. I know that. But because you knew Cooper didn't want any children, you let him take the chicken shit way out leaving you to raise these kids by yourself."

"Is that why you want to marry me, Caleb? So these boys will have a father?" The idea that he wanted to be with me because I was pregnant had already occurred to me after he told me about him not being able to have children of his own. I'd pushed it to the back of my mind.

"No," he answered without hesitation.

I stared at him so he continued. "Do you think I didn't know what I was doing when I asked you to marry me? I'm not stupid."

"I don't th-think you a-a-are." Yup, I was crying again.

He reached back to grab some tissues from the counter, then handed it to me. I wiped my eyes and nose while he spoke softly. "Then be quiet and listen. I started falling in love with you a long time ago. Every day that goes by I love you even more. I don't care that we're not going to have a traditional courtship," he said, using air quotes. "I care that I get to be with you forever and raise these kids with you. After *a lot* of soul searching, I don't care that they're not mine. They're part of *you*. I'll love them and treat them like they *are* mine, though. I already do. I want to be a family with you. Do you understand? Do you believe me?" he asked.

I nodded, crying harder. Again, damn it. Those were the exact words I wanted to hear. He was the exact man I wanted and needed every single day for the rest of my life. I swear to God, I didn't deserve him.

"What if Cooper shows up and suddenly decides he wants to be a father?" I asked through the tears.

He seemed surprised by the question. "Is that what you want?"

"Answer my question first then I'll answer yours."

He put one of his hands over one of mine. He took a while to think before he answered. "I really don't see that happening. If it does, then we'll deal with it. Together."

He looked at me, waiting for the answer to his question.

"If he was going to be there permanently and not be an only-when-I-feel-like-it father, then yes." God I was a horrible person to say that, and it made more tears stream down my cheeks. "I'm sorry if that hurts you. I don't want to be with him, Caleb. No matter what, I want to be with you. If he comes into the picture, do you still want me?"

"Yes, but like I said before I really don't think that will happen. Princess, I can't explain why this is the way things should be for us. Maybe this is the universe's fucked-up way of letting us raise a family together since I can't have kids. Whatever. I just know that this is the way our lives were meant to be. *You* are the woman I was meant to spend the rest of my life with. I know I shouldn't be okay with the fact that you're going to have Cooper's kids." He raked his hands through his hair, let out a deep breath and looked up at the ceiling, avoiding my eyes. "I'm okay with it now. Don't get me wrong, the two of you together, creating a life—two lives—was a hard pill for me to swallow."

He trailed off and the only thing I could say was, "I'm sorry." It was true.

He looked at me again. "I tried not to love you. In fact I even tried hating you. I couldn't, so I told myself I would be your friend if you would let me, and for some reason you did."

"Because you're hot." Not the best time to make inappropriate jokes, but that's how I rolled.

I made him smile. "All I knew was that friendship wasn't cutting it for me because I loved you and I was going to do what it took to be together. Now, I get to have you *and* a family which I gave up on having. And if it ends up that I'm only their stepfather, then I'll deal with it. Of course I want these kids to have a father, but I wouldn't marry you for that reason."

He stood up, walked around the table and pulled me into his arms. He held me while I finished crying and let me get it all out. After a few minutes, he pulled back to look at me.

"You have to believe me that this is what I want. And to be honest I don't think it's possible to have a normal relationship with you. There is nothing normal about you, Molly Davis."

I smiled at that truth. "God I love you," I said and put my arms around his neck.

"And I love you, too, even after you tried to push me away for my own good. Now can we please go back to bed you giant cry baby?"

"In a minute. I have to finish my sandwich."

I let go of him so we could sit down while I finished eating. After my sandwich, I had a banana and a huge glass of chocolate milk. Then I grabbed a handful of pretzel crackers and shoved them in my mouth.

Caleb pretended to look disgusted at everything that I ate. "Do you think you should maybe save some food so we can eat tomorrow?"

"Shut up and take me back to bed."

"Well, now I'm all worked up so I need you to make me tired and relaxed. Suggestions?" He put his sexy smile on and raised his eyebrows a few times.

I laughed. "How do you know I'm even in the mood? Look at me, I'm gigantic."

He laid his arm across my shoulder and led me toward our bedroom. "I have three sisters, remember? All have been pregnant and shared too much information."

Yeah, right. He probably read that in *Cosmo*. Maybe they had a special pregnancy section. "I have several suggestions to tire yourself out. For example—"

"Just show me, Princess."

I did. And I wasn't bad for a big, fat, pregnant lady.

Afterward we lay together on our sides, face to face, our hands intertwined.

All I could think about was how lucky I was to have Caleb.

A man who loved me, who never made me feel dirty or damaged, who made sense of our unorthodox situation. "Thank you," I told him, though the words were inadequate.

"Mmmm." He was still in that post-climax haze.

"You gotta promise me that all of this. . . none of it's going to get between us. I don't want a huge elephant always in the room with us."

He chuckled. "I'm marrying a woman who's pregnant with another man's children who I'm going to claim as my own. Why would that be awkward?"

I swatted his arm. "Be serious, Caleb."

He kissed me very gently on the lips and said, "I promise, Princess. It is what it is, and I love what it is."

"I love you," I promised him.

"I love you too."

"Caleb?"

"Hmmm."

"Will you cancel your *Cosmo* subscription once we get married."

He snuggled me closer. "Sorry. I just renewed and put it in your name."

Ugh.

Chapter 44

I had never told anyone, besides Katie, who the father of my twins was. When Caleb and I announced we were getting married, everyone assumed that Caleb was the father. Like, people probably figured he got me pregnant, we had a falling out and split up, then reconciled. I didn't like that it made him look like the bad guy, but Caleb shrugged it off.

Within the week, he had moved into my house, we obtained our marriage license, waited our required three days, then went to the courthouse and became man and big, giant wife. No one else went with us except Katie, and that was only because she threatened me with death and then made me feel guilty for not giving her a wedding to plan. I wore a casual white tent—excuse me, dress—and Caleb wore khaki pants and a dress shirt.

We chose simple, white gold bands. I didn't want anything to detract from the absolutely gorgeous, princess cut—ah, the symbolism—diamond solitaire engagement he had gotten me.

Allow me to introduce myself. I am Molly Ramsey. Pregnant *and* married. Go me.

We used the weekend for a short honeymoon at a swanky hotel north of the city. We divided the time between lying in bed, going out to eat, and discussing names for the babies.

I slid under the covers. Caleb automatically pulled me toward him. Strong man, to be able to do that at my size.

"What about Harry and Ron?" I asked. I loved Harry Potter. What's not to love? Magic to get things to go your way—check. Strong friendships—check. Light romance and a happy-ever-after ending—check. Several big, nasty kick ass battles—check.

Caleb's hand, which had been stroking my arm, froze. "You're joking, right?"

"I don't joke about Harry Potter. Katie thinks Fred and George would be more appropriate since that's the names of the twins in the series. I say it's better to name them after the lead characters. What do you think?" I craned my head around to look at him.

Caleb looked horrified. "Uh. . ."

"I've pretty much ruled out the other characters' names, but if you like them we can talk about it. Besides Fred and George, there's Draco and Dean and Seamus and Neville. Cedric too, that's not too bad I guess. And then there are the professors' names, they're kind of stupid. Albus and Severus and Gilderoy and Remus and things like that. Why is that look on your face?"

"Is this up for debate at all?"

"Of course it is. You're my husband and their father. You don't want to name the boys after *Harry Potter* characters?"

"It . . . wasn't my first choice. Or my second. Or my hundredth, for that matter."

"Really?" Why would anyone *not* want to name their children after the best books in the history of books? "Okay. What do you like?"

"I was thinking of names more traditional, like. . . anything else."

We debated lots of names. At one point, we went to a bookstore, bought a baby name book and read over all of the bazillion names. We decided that we would split Caleb's middle name, Alexander, for the twins. Alex and Zander.

I hated for our brief honeymoon to be over. My uninterrupted naked time with Caleb was too short. It was time to meet each other's parents, and in his case, his siblings as well. He told me that his family was nice, so I had nothing to worry about. Yeah, let's see if I can not worry when he drops quite the bombshell: *Hi, Mom, here's my wife who's seven months pregnant with your grandchildren. That's right, I married to a woman you've never met, and you'll have two more babies to spoil in less than two months. So, what's for dinner?*

Then there was telling my mom, and my dad and Joy: *Hi! So remember when I told you I was pregnant but not who the father was? Well, here he is! Oh by the way we got married. So, what's for dinner?*

My mom was shocked, and thrilled I think, but mainly shocked. She had us over for dinner, and Caleb won her over whole heartedly. She acted pretty happy. She didn't ask much about us. But we learned all about a cruise to the Caribbean she and Victor were considering.

My dad and Joy gave us their surprised congratulations over the phone. We promised to get together when we all were able.

Once you knew Caleb, liking him was easy. I didn't have that same effect on people. Katie said I was more of an acquired taste, so maybe his family would like me eventually. I hated Katie sometimes.

The day I was going to meet his family arrived, and I was nervous as hell. The fact that it happened to be Thanksgiving didn't make it any easier. *Better to meet everyone all at once* is what I kept repeating in my head. Caleb called his entire family once we were married, so they all knew we legally belonged to each other, and that I was pregnant. His sisters, Catherine, Caroline, and Candice, were all married. His brother Carter was married as well.

The closer we got to his mom's house, the closer I came to hyperventilating, and there was no chance in hell I was able to put my head between my legs.

"Ow."

Oops. I guess I'd been squeezing Caleb's hand too hard. "Sorry."

We arrived, and once parked, he circled around the car to open my door for me. I slid out slowly and stood up to take a look around. Typical suburban house: two stories, attached garage, fenced in yard, pretty big. Caleb said his mom didn't want to downsize because of all the grandkids. The front porch was edged with empty flower boxes that probably brightened the whole yard come summer. A huge tree in the front yard looked as if it had been climbed many times over the years. The house had a relatively new paint job. It looked happy. It looked like only happy people came here. You might not enter happy, but you sure as hell would leave happy.

Late November was really cold. I took a moment to appreciate the chill—I was hot all the time now—when the front door flew open and about a hundred people, okay, more like twenty, squeezed out all at once. They all stared at us. I was stuck to my spot with glue called nerves. Finally his mom slapped her way through enough people to make her way to us first.

A woman in her sixties, as blond as Caleb thanks to her Swedish heritage, came up to us, smiling. She and Caleb hugged, and then she turned her attention to me.

"Mom, I'd like you to meet my wife, Molly. Molly, my mom."

"Hi, Mrs. Ramsey," I said.

"You're Mrs. Ramsey now too. Call me Char or Mom, whatever you're more comfortable with."

So I had to meet his entire gigantic freaking family, *and* make a split second decision as to what to call his mother? Shit!

As soon as I opened my mouth to respond to—Char? Mom?—she hugged me. "Come meet the family," she said and turned to the crowd of gawkers on the porch.

Since everyone was still staring at us she yelled, "Hey, everyone, meet Molly. Molly, this is everyone. They'll all introduce themselves once we get inside. Now get inside!"

Everyone took one last look and squeezed their way back inside. Caleb began walking, I was still frozen in place. He tugged me but I wouldn't budge. He put his hand on my lower back and gave a gentle push. I still didn't move.

"Molly," he said, and I turned my head to look at him. "Would you relax, please? Let's go in the house. It's cold out here."

"I don't really get cold anymore so I'm good out here. You go ahead."

"There's a lot of food in there. And I made sure there's a bag of bean sprouts for you."

Being pregnant made me love bean sprouts. Go figure.

"Okay. I can do this," I said, and finally put one foot in front of the other to move my ginormous self into the house.

If I was overwhelmed outside, inside I was damn near stunned where the excitement was a million times worse. I was the new factor into the family equation, and they all wanted to know everything.

How old was I? Thirty-two

What did I do for a living? Songwriter. (But, God not saying teacher was weird!)

How did Caleb and I meet? At a bar. (Technically that was true, and I didn't want to get into the whole Creep issue.)

Could they feel my belly? Sure. (I would even try not to cringe.)

How much weight had I gained? Forty pounds. (That I really tried not to stress about.)

Do we have names picked out? Yup. Alex and Zander. (Cue: awwwww. . .)

Was I having natural childbirth? Hell no! (Not if there was a God.)

And on and on and on and on. They were sweet. They were loud. They were everything I was so not used to when it came to family. Both my and Katie's families were tiny, so this was a total culture shock to me.

The women were horrified that, one, I did not attend child birth classes. I didn't need to since I had the Internet and Courtney's experience to rely on. And, two, I was not having a baby shower. Caleb and I had already purchased everything we needed (I hoped), so no shower was needed.

Dinner was served, and I was able to get lost in the sea of people, which helped me relax. Plus Caleb was by my side, and that always put me at ease.

His sisters would elbow one another whenever Caleb put his hands on my stomach. They thought it was cute that he liked feeling the babies move, and since I had been so nervous for most of the day, the boys were having a disco party.

After dinner came dessert, where the talk revolved around football (barf). For a minute, I waited for a fight to break out. There were hard core Lions fans in the house who did not appreciate speaking ill of their team. Then they calmed down, and I was disappointed. A fight would've really taken the focus off of me. And okay, I like a good fight. Sue me.

In the evening, the extended family began filtering out. His sisters and their families stayed, but the rest were gone by eight o'clock. I was tired, emotionally and physically. I couldn't bow out and go home because it would make me look chicken. I was *totally* chicken. I was also determined to let Caleb's mom say what she needed to.

I was sure his mom was disappointed she didn't get to attend her son's wedding or even meet her new daughter-in-law *before* she married into the family.

Caleb, his mom and I sat in the living room. The rest were in various parts of the house: watching the kids or cleaning up the dinner mess. The ten grandkids were all over the place. If I brought my babies there, they might get run over. Oh man, I was so not used to this sort of thing. Even with the extended family gone, the house was still full. My whole life it had been holidays for two: my mother and me. Now? I felt like I'd been adopted by the Duggar family. Twenty thousand kids and counting.

I wracked my brain for a topic to start a conversation. Global warming? Politics? The big, white elephant in the room?

I sat there like an idiot. A big pregnant idiot. A big pregnant idiot with the hottest man on the planet for a husband. That made me smile.

"Well finally," Char said to me.

There ya go, Char it is.

"I'm sorry, what?" Had I missed a question?

"Finally, a real smile. That's the first one I think I've seen all night."

Caleb sat beside me, one arm around me and the other resting on my stomach. I relaxed into him "Oh. Sorry. Nerves."

"We don't bite, dear."

I smiled again. "Dinner was great. Thank you." Oooohhh, look at me with the small talk.

"You're welcome." Char folded her hands and set them on her lap. "So, tell me everything."

I looked at Caleb for help, but all he did was pat my shoulder and keep quiet. Fucker. We had already agreed that nobody besides us, Cooper, and Katie was going to know the truth about Cooper being the biological father, so at least I didn't have to worry about explaining that one.

"How far exactly do you want me to go back?" I asked her.

"I want to know why it is I'm just now meeting you."

"Mom," Caleb said in warning.

"Honey, I'm not upset with her, I'm upset with you. How could you not introduce her to us before all of this?" She said, gesturing to my huge stomach and wedding ring.

Caleb took a deep breath and gave my shoulder a comfort squeeze. He explained how and why we met. He started out telling the truth. He told her about The Creep and the attack. He told her about me getting pregnant. Then he told his mom that we had a fight and broke up, then made up and eloped.

My story was a lot of information for his mom to take in. It was generally hard for people to be mean to big pregnant women, not to mention someone who'd been a victim of a violent attack like I had. And since I'm sure his siblings and their spouses were most likely eavesdropping on the entire conversation, I think she wanted to set a good example by welcoming me into the family.

We talked more about ourselves. Gradually, the rest of the family joined us and rehashed every embarrassing story they could remember about Caleb. As a kid, he was quite the little shit. I laughed so much I had to excuse myself to go to the bathroom a few times for fear of peeing my pants.

We left late, and in a much lighter mood. I had started out the visit extremely anxious and ended the visit completely relieved. I'd gone from being part of a tiny family to a large one, so that fact may take a while to wrap my head around. I used to barely celebrate the holidays. Now I would never spend one with less than a gazillion people around me.

We walked into our house, and Caleb turned to kiss me, but pulled back. "What are you smiling for?" he asked.

"Your big family. I'm okay with it."

"Well that's good, because you're stuck with them."

I laughed, mostly out of nerves, because that meant they were stuck with me too.

Chapter 45

"Where are all your Christmas decorations?" Caleb asked a couple weeks before Christmas. We still didn't have anything up.

"In the empty bedroom closet." Of the four bedrooms, one was the master, one was the nursery, one was a spare bedroom, and one was relatively empty, save for a few boxes of miscellaneous crap.

I walked to the empty bedroom with Caleb following me. I opened the closet, took out my Charlie Brown Christmas tree then handed it to him. "Here you go. All my Christmas decorations."

He looked as if I'd handed him a pile of dog poop. "This is it? A pathetic tree?"

"There's an ornament on it," I said, pointing it out. I never bothered decorating for the holidays. It annoyed Katie, so one year she bought me the Charlie Brown tree. The next year she bought me the ornament. Then she gave up. Usually I remembered to display them both by the time Christmas rolled around.

"Did you lose the rest in the move?"

"Nope. That's all of it."

He set the tree down on the floor. "Finish getting ready. We have shopping to do."

We came home with a tree, ornaments, lights, doodads, and whatnots. I followed him around the house while he Christmased the hell out of it. I wanted to help, but Caleb was clearly in his element. He enjoyed every second of it.

I followed him outside. He hauled out a huge ladder and began hanging lights. And whistling.

I yelled, "Oh my God you're one of *those* people," up to him.

"What people?" he yelled back.

"Your family decorates the house for every holiday, don't they?"

"Yeah. We used to win the city contest for best decorated Christmas house, and on Halloween we turned our garage into a really cool haunted house."

What the hell had I married myself into? "Okay then. Have fun."

By the time we went to bed, I had one of *those* houses. Like the Christmas spirit puked all over my house. Caleb put my Charlie Brown tree back in the closet. I set it back out on a side table when he wasn't looking. He grimaced when he noticed, but left it out.

Caleb and I woke up on Christmas morning and exchanged presents in bed. He got me a watch. One of those nice ones that are so simplistically beautiful that you knew it cost a fortune. I got him a watch. One that had so many different functions that it looked like it cost a fortune. It didn't; I found it on Groupon.

After eating breakfast and getting ready, we went to my mom's. Victor was there, and we had a pleasant, and short, visit. My mom acted like her newly happy self. And although she seemed genuinely pleased for me and Caleb, she hardly talked about the babies, which was weird since they would be her first grandchildren. Not to mention that they were due in a few weeks.

Char's house was a freaking crazy-ass zoo. Hyper kids, tipsy adults, an insane amount of food, football blaring on the TV (and again I say barf), and presents as far as the eye could see.

Shortly after arriving, I started feeling mild contractions. I didn't say anything at first because I wasn't sure, but after a few hours I knew I was in the beginning stages of labor.

I stood up to pee and silently motioned for Caleb to follow me. "I didn't want to say anything earlier," I whispered, then looked around to make sure we had privacy. "I'm in labor."

His eyes grew to twice their size. "What?"

"Sshhh. I wasn't sure if it was those fake contractions or not, but they're regularly twenty minutes apart."

"Holy shit."

"Yeah. We have a while, I think. We can leave in a few hours."

"Let's go now."

I didn't want to cut the celebration short. "Let me pee. We have time. Relax."

Of course my water broke while I was on the toilet.

I gave myself a moment to be thankful that my water didn't break while sitting on the couch or standing around other people, then screamed for Caleb.

He rushed me out while everyone shouted "good luck!" and "congratulations!" at us. On the way back home to get my bag and call the doctor, I made the necessary calls to my mom and Katie and Alan. My dad and Joy.

Alex and Zander Ramsey were born via C-section on the day after Christmas. My labor had stopped progressing after a certain point and the babies were in distress. I didn't read up on the C-section stuff, and Courtney had a vaginal delivery so I wasn't prepared at all.

My nurses were the best. I really wanted to breastfeed the twins, and they helped me tremendously. Caleb was totally hands-on. He changed the first several diapers since I was afraid to move too much. Katie provided tons of compliments: I was doing great, the boys were the cutest babies ever, that sort of thing. She took a bunch of pictures which I'm sure I'll appreciate later.

The first month was rough. Nursing twins while healing from surgery, not to mention trying to take care of myself, was extremely challenging. Caleb took a couple of weeks off work, and when he did go back, worked Monday through Friday, nine to five. Ish. He brought work home to do in the evenings occasionally. No big deal. The last couple of months, his work schedule was way more stable than it had ever been. He told me he and Cooper had agreed to this a while ago. Cooper apparently gave Caleb whatever he wanted at work now.

Katie came over a lot. She was so in love with Zander and Alex. I swore to God if they picked up her twang I was going to strangle her. She had deemed herself Auntie Katie Beans (God, she's a fucktard sometimes.). As in, "Who wuvs you? Auntie Katie Beans wuvs you. Yes she does. Yes Auntie Katie Beans does!"

I cringed every time she said it, reminding myself that she's been my best friend since high school, and I loved her like a sister.

The sister you sometimes had to force yourself not to toss her favorite jeans into the washer with bleach.

When the babies were about six weeks old, and I felt like a human being again, we headed over to Char's for lunch. She had been coming over our house fairly often, so I assumed she was simply reciprocating. As soon as her house was in view I saw a bunch of cars parked in the driveway and down the street.

I got out of Caleb's SUV and stopped to look at all the vehicles. I recognized most of them as either my new family's, or my friends. Katie's was there.

I looked at my husband, now standing there with a car seat in each arm. "Is there anything you want to tell me?"

He began walking into the house. "Nope."

He waited for me at the front door. When he opened it we walked inside and heard, "Surprise!"

I must've looked confused. Both our birthdays were long off.

"A surprise baby shower!" Katie explained to me, which would've been obvious had I taken the time to look around at all the light blue decorations.

I generally only liked surprises if I knew about them in advance, but I couldn't be upset at this. Katie had already been giving me shit about how she didn't get to throw me a bachelorette party, a wedding, or a baby shower, so I should've seen this coming.

Several people came up to me to hug me and look at the babies. The surprise of all surprises was when Alan came strutting out from the crowd of people.

He stood before me with a big smile and open arms.

"Oh my God! Alan!" He gave me a big, tight squeeze. "Ow, not so hard."

He released me and looked at Caleb.

"Alan, meet my husband Caleb, call him Ram. Caleb, meet Alan. My oldest friend." They shook hands and Alan took a minute to coo over the babies, which impressed me because I didn't think he'd ever been this close to one before.

All of the guys, except for Alan, retreated to the back of the house. The women and the kids who were interested stayed in the front of the house, and we had us a baby shower.

We received tons of stuff. Lots of clothes, toys, blankets, and keepsakes. Certain gifts I never wanted to use, but they were from women who already had kids and who swore by them. Was I really going to put my kids in a seat that bounced, vibrated, and stuck toys in their face? I'd seen one of those at the store and kept right on going.

After all the fun had been had, I was enjoying relaxing for a few minutes sitting on the couch, nursing one baby while the other was sleeping. Alan came and sat next to me. "You look really good, Mol."

He went for a hug. I stuck my hand out to stop him. "That has to wait, I'm nursing right now."

He leaned back and looked at me. "What exactly does that mean?"

"It means I'm feeding my baby."

The poor guy looked confused so I leaned over and explained in his ear exactly what nursing meant. I made sure to use the terms nipple, latching on, sucking, and breast milk.

His face turned bright red. "And you're doing that *now*?" He asked, part horrified, part fascinated.

"Yup."

His face lit up. "Can I see?"

"No way."

His face fell. "Oh. And you do that, like, in public and stuff?" He looked around the room to see if anyone was paying attention to what I was doing.

"If I have to. I try to find a private and quiet spot. I don't think most people know that I'm nursing. You didn't."

"I really want to see. Please?"

Everyone was mostly scattered all over the house and several people had left. Katie was twanging away in the kitchen, excited from getting to meet Caleb's family. I lifted the blanket that I was using as a cover and let Alan see what nursing a baby looked like. After his peek he had a million questions. I couldn't believe I was having this conversation with him, or that he was interested. After he got over his initial horror that is.

While Zander finished feeding, Alex wailed because he was hungry, too. Caleb heard and came into the room to see if I needed anything. I gave Zander to Caleb to burp and began the process again with Alex. Alan watched the whole process in awe.

"I let Alan see my boob," I told Caleb.

Alan's face had a flash of fear as he looked at Caleb for his reaction.

I shrugged. "He wanted to see what breast feeding was all about."

"Not the whole thing!" Alan quickly exclaimed. "I swear I saw the top and then the baby's head. Not the nipple or anything. I swear. Really."

Caleb smiled—the dopey kind men did whenever they thought of boobs. "They're big, right?"

"Caleb!" I whisper-yelled.

"I was wondering about that," Alan said. "I thought maybe she got implants."

"No, it's from her breasts filling with milk."

"Wow."

"Yeah."

Alan and Caleb were going to have a conversation about my boobs, and I couldn't punch either one because I was nursing!

Alan put one hand to his mouth, his thinking pose. "I would've been surprised if she did get implants," he said. "One time I was joking around and told her she should get some, and she punched me. Does it taste like regular milk you think?"

"Alan!" I swung my leg out to kick him. It didn't reach.

Caleb kept patting Zander's back. "I have no idea. She's not a cow, so I doubt it"

"Are you two done?" I asked.

Alan looked at me. "I don't know. I might have more questions later."

Chapter 46

I was glad Katie had been able to plan a party for me. It made her happy, and showing off the twins was fun. I know every parent thinks their kids are the cutest. Mine really were, at least to Caleb and I.

We stayed the whole day at Char's house. She loved doting over the babies, and being accepted unconditionally was awesome. I guess in large families that's what you did: spoiled the babies and accepted their parents, even if you didn't know about them until the last minute.

When we got home, we gave the twins a bath and put them to bed. Caleb had to jump into the shower as well because he got spit up on twice and stunk from it.

I sat on the bed, folding tiny little clothes when I looked up. My whole body flushed with heat, and I froze, mid-fold. Caleb had come out of the shower and into the bedroom while still drying himself. He was naked, the perfect amount of moist, and mumbling about how much soap it took to get the puke smell off of skin.

He wrapped the towel really low around his waist, and I squeezed my knees together, almost embarrassed at the *whoosh* I felt in my panties. How could he make me so wet, so fast?

Good God I needed to get me some of that.

He caught me staring at him. "What?" he asked.

"Uh . . ." I couldn't get myself to come out and tell him that seeing him like that made me hot. And it made me ready to resume our sex life.

I slowly looked him up and down. A big smile lit his face, telling me he understood what I wanted. "Does that mean what I think it means?"

I nodded. "Uh-huh."

See, here's where I think I actually *didn't* screw up in my and Caleb's totally untraditional way to the altar. Caleb and I didn't date for long before we got married. We were so new to each other we were still excited by each other sexually. And we hadn't even had sex while I wasn't pregnant, for crap's sake. That had to change. Immediately.

He walked over to the bed and I swiped all the clothes off. He climbed on, we lay down and started kissing. We had kissed and had a make out session or two since the twins were born, nothing rated R. It had been too soon. Not anymore.

"Are you sure?" he asked.

"I'm sure, just . . . go slow."

He did. He was slow and gentle. We did a lot of kissing and feeling for a long time. He smelled so good, he was lucky I didn't bite him. I could tell he was dying to get himself into me. I appreciated him not rushing right into it. This was new territory for us: making love while not pregnant, and for the first time after having the twins. He was hesitant, so I made a lot of pleasure sounds to let him know he was on the right track. And if his noises were any indication, then I was on the right track too.

Neither one of us lasted very long, and neither one of us cared. Even after the *woo-hoo-we're-back-to-having-sex-again!* giddiness wore off, he kept his body on me and in me.

"You're so flat."

You'd think after years of reading *Cosmo* he'd say anything other than that. "Thanks I think."

"I couldn't do this before. It's nice."

When I looked at my stomach I didn't see flat, but I knew what he meant. There was no huge mound o'babies in the way.

He eventually moved off me to lie next to me. He hummed softly. I imagined the lyrics to his made up song were, *Yay I get to have sex again. Yay I get to have sex again.*

I was in my happy place, determined not to move until I absolutely had to.

Which was when the phone rang. Without looking at caller I.D., I answered.

It was Alan Stupid Face. He had another question for me: Were my boobs going to look normal when I was done breast-feeding. I gave him an honest answer. I had no idea.

My life was back on a relatively normal schedule again, if chaotic and feeling overwhelmed was normal. Getting things done was hard during the day. I always got the basic necessities done—quick workout, quick shower, and everyone was fed and had clean clothes. I tried to work on song writing. But nursing two babies, changing diapers, and doing basic housework made it almost impossible. I just didn't have the time to be creative, and in the few moments I did, my mind was a blank. And lifetime of crappy sleeping or not, I was still tired from getting up a hundred times a night. How have women been doing this for thousands of years?

Evenings and weekends were easier because Caleb was home, but I didn't want our time home together spent apart by chores or me working. Plus, when the babies went to bed I was ready to crawl into bed too. Especially when Caleb was so excited to be having sex again he often couldn't be under the covers for more than two minutes before his hands started to wander. Then my hands would start to wander. Then before you know it we were both hoping we weren't waking the twins. Or in Caleb's case, the neighborhood.

Caleb and I had our first real fight as a married couple when I was venting one day about how accomplishing everything I needed to was damn near impossible, especially making time for music. We'd of course had disagreements by this point. Nothing that required yelling or apologies. I wasn't ungrateful for everything I had, I just needed to complain out loud to feel better. It worked for Katie anyway.

Caleb sat on the couch, leaning forward to click around on his laptop. In his defense, he was trying to be helpful when he said, "So why don't we hire a nanny to help out with the babies?"

But instead, he pissed me off. "What is it with you insisting I need professional help? I can raise my own children thank you very much."

"What is it with you insisting you never need help? There's nothing wrong with asking for help."

You see, Caleb's mom had been a shrink—excuse me psychiatrist—for thirty years. So he was raised believing the best course of action was to ask for help or talk about your problems. Well fuck that.

"Yes there is."

"Why?"

Honestly, I really didn't know so I stormed to the kitchen and took a drink of water to give me time to think of a reason. I stormed back to the family room. "Because I said so."

He stopped typing and pinched the bridge of his nose. "You're complaining how hard it is during the day to get things done, so fix it."

"I'm not complaining!"

"Yes, you are."

I totally was. "No, I'm not!" I yelled.

He must've been stressed out from work stuff because he was usually the calming factor in our disagreements that kept me from raising my voice. He yelled right back at me, "Molly, there is nothing wrong with admitting you need help!"

"I don't need help!" I pointed in his face. "Maybe you need help!"

He gently pushed my arm down. "Oh yeah? What do I need help with?"

"You need help with . . ." *Think, think of something.* "With your fucked up notion that I always need professional help! I don't need help! And you're stupid!" Oh my God, I couldn't stop being an idiot!

"Oh, I'm stupid. That's nice. Well you're immature."

"I know you are but what am I?" Hormones. I still have hormones raging through my body, right?

He slammed his papers down. "That . . ." He shook his head unable to finish the thought. "When did I say I think you always need help?"

I crossed my arms over my chest. "At the batting cages you told me to get help, and now you told me to get help."

"If you're struggling, you should find someone to help you!"

"What? You want another woman in here raising your children? I can raise my own children!"

He shot up from the couch. "Then hire a housekeeper to do all the house stuff so you have more time for your other stuff!"

That was actually a really good idea. "Huh," I said. *That* type of help I could accept. Caleb did help out around the house, but when he came home from work, he wanted to relax and help with the babies, not clean and do laundry. "Fine."

He stared at me for a minute, waiting for me to yell at him more. When I didn't he said, "Fine. Are we done arguing now?"

"I guess." I scrunched my face, embarrassed that I acted a wee bit adolescent-like. "Are you mad at me?"

He clenched his jaw. "Maybe."

"I'm sorry for calling you stupid." And I was, but I was also half-waiting for him to walk out.

We stood face-to-face. My foot started tapping. I thought he was about to turn and walk away from me, but he took a step and covered my foot with his own to stop my tapping. I put my hand on his chest and felt him relax.

One corner of his mouth pulled up, showing off one dimple. Playful Caleb. "You really hurt my feelings, you know. Deep down I'm a very sensitive soul."

I breathed a small sigh of relief, but oh please. *Cosmo* probably said that women liked sensitive men. I rolled my eyes to match his playfulness. "Whatever."

He crossed his arms over his chest and went straight faced, but I'm pretty sure he had to work to hide his smile. "I'm serious. You should really try harder at a better apology."

I crossed my arms to match his pose. Hmmm, I needed a better apology. One that said, *I'm sorry for being an idiot and thank you for not making it into a big issue.* Because, let's face it, I was bound to act like a five year old again someday.

It didn't take long to come up with an apology that would definitely get his mind off our fight. I sauntered (yes, sauntered) over to him and pushed him back down to sitting on the couch. I dropped to my knees, undid his pants, and spent the next five minutes apologizing without saying a single word.

When I was done and re-zipped and buttoned his pants, he lounged smiling from ear to ear. "That, Princess, was the best apology of all time. And to think I was going to ask you to make a batch of cookies or brownies."

I didn't keep much junk food in the house, and I knew he missed it. "Okay, so next time we fight, and I call you stupid, I'll preheat the oven when we're done and start baking." I walked out of the room to get the twins, who were now awake and crying, but I didn't miss the disappointed look on Caleb's face.

Hiring a housekeeper was one of the best things I ever did, besides getting knocked up by one man then marrying a much better man. Ugh, that sounded bad. My house was always clean, the clothes were laundered, and I was a more relaxed wife and mother. I still struggled, but I was able to spend a lot more time writing music.

Katie would come over and help. She was a good sounding board and missed playing as the Song Wreckers.

"Think Brett will let us resume our Wreckers Weekends?" I asked Katie one day while sitting in the basement, tinkering on our guitars.

"Of course. We were the best thing to ever happen to his bar." She continued to play softly. "You really ready for that?"

Caleb and I had talked about it. I really needed to play with the band again. I wanted to get out of the house for non-baby related stuff every once in a while. (Did that make me a bad mother?) Also, I missed it, and performing helped my song writing. "I am. I called Heather, Josh and Courtney, and they're on board with the idea." I put my guitar down. "You wanna call Brett or do you want me to?"

She stared for a few seconds. "I'll do it."

"You sure?"

"Yeah. We need to talk to clear the air anyway. It's been too long."

A couple mornings later I answered the phone to this: "Good Lord, Mol! He did it!"

"Uh-huh." Coffee hadn't entered my bloodstream yet.

"I called him about Wreckers Weekends, and we started talking, then he came over then we . . . you know. Then he said living without me sucked and would I marry him! Can you believe it?"

"Wait, what?" I was without caffeine and proper sleep, I was changing a diaper and trying not to get peed on, so my comprehension and attention span was low.

"Molly, listen. I called Brett about playing at the bar again, and we got to talking. Then he came over, and we ended up doing it. You with me so far?"

I fastened the diaper and set Zander down. "Did what? Changed the oil in your car? Climbed Mount Everest?"

"Molly, shut up! We spent the last couple of days together and talked. Really talked. A lot. About everything. He said being without me this past year sucked! Then we talked some more about a lot of other things. Then he asked me to marry him last night! Can you believe it?"

I damn near dropped Alex in shock. "Oh my God!! What did you say?"

"I said yes, you twit!"

"Congratulations! When is the big day? What does your engagement ring look like? If he wanted to marry you, why didn't he call you?" I cringed at what I shouldn't have said out loud. "Not trying to spoil the moment, though. Congratulations!"

"Haven't set the date, don't have a ring yet, he said he wanted to call me but wasn't sure I'd even talk to him. Listen, I gotta go to work. I'll come over after, and I'll tell you everything."

I shouldn't have stopped for a second to send a quick prayer for her to leave some of the details out, because that's when I got peed on.

Chapter 47

Everyone, especially Brett, was more than ready to have The Song Wreckers resume their first weekend of the month shows. We held one practice and declared we were ready to start rocking it out yet again.

Caleb pulled into the alley behind Brett's. Talk about different. For one, I was married with children, and Caleb was next to me. Second, I was nervous as hell. Char was watching the twins. I knew she was the perfect sitter for us, but what if the boys thought I was abandoning them? What if the house blew up, or she couldn't handle caring for two tiny babies?

Caleb shut off the engine and looked at me. I looked at him and started the kind of crying that made it difficult to talk. He knew exactly why I was crying, so he leaned over and hugged me.

"I think I changed my mind," I said into his neck. "Do you think everyone will hate me if I cancel?"

"You want this. Just call my mom so you'll feel better."

I called Char and didn't hear any crying. She reassured me everything was fine. Was I pathetic for not being able to leave my kids for several hours twice a month without breaking down? Maybe being at a bar while my children were at home without either parent made me feel kind of trashy. But there was no way in hell Caleb would've let me come without him for protection. And honestly, I wanted him here with me.

I dragged myself out of the car to start unloading the equipment when Josh and Courtney's van pulled up. Josh saw me and smiled. "Court had a hard time at first, too. Go talk to her."

Courtney told me that I would feel like this the first few times. Eventually I would stop once I saw there was no harm done. I hoped she was right.

I faked happiness when the crowd saw us setting up and began their hoots and hollers. I was too busy trying to convince myself that my babies weren't home plotting against me for leaving them.

Years ago, I found out playing with a sore hand sucked (you know, from punching bitches in the face). Playing while trying not to cry sucked even worse. I tried to focus on the silver lining—the twins would get lots of quality time with their grandma, and apparently I was lucky that the twins would take a bottle from anyone except me. If I was feeding them they had to have a boob. Caleb, Katie, and Char (okay, and once the housekeeper because both boys were screaming bloody murder, and I didn't know what else to do) could feed them from a bottle and they didn't care.

What really got me through the night was Katie. She was so freaking happy she glowed. Brett had presented her with a beautiful two carat solitaire engagement ring, and they set a date for the summer so she would be married before the school started. She wanted to start the year off as Mrs. Jensen, not start Ms. Culver and then have to change to Mrs. Jensen. Her enthusiasm made up for my lack.

Caleb showed pictures of the twins to anyone who looked in his direction, the goober. My goober. He had spent enough time at Brett's over the past couple of years that he knew all of the regulars. He divided his time between analyzing everyone in the bar that he didn't know and whipping out his wallet and showing pictures to anyone who told him *congratulations*.

I found out when I arrived at Saturday's show another reason why Katie was in such great mood. Mama had come to town. She and Katie both wanted to surprise me, which they did. Mama jumped out of the car with Katie, waited until I registered that she was there, then she ran over and gave me a big hug.

She didn't hug me for long, though. She let go and walked over to Caleb. Nice and slow, and with her feet crunching on the gravelly alley it made for a dramatic show. "So you're the one who got my baby pregnant and married her at the last minute."

I didn't say anything. Mama wasn't being mean, she was being protective, and I owed it to her to let her get this off her chest.

Caleb played his part of the humbled husband. "Yes, ma'am," he obediently replied.

Mama said, "hmph," so he took out his wallet and showed her the pictures (even though I emailed her pictures every week) and all was forgiven. That did it. She hugged him and gave me a smile and a thumbs up.

Mama and Katie came over Sunday to spoil the boys rotten. I had no babies to take care of since they wouldn't let me, and of course Zander and Alex took a bottle from Mama too, so I made everyone a huge lunch and we talked while gathered in the kitchen. Caleb went down in the basement to workout and give us privacy.

Mama was really disappointed in my mom for not showing more of an interest in the twins. She'd come over a couple of times because I'd invited her, but preferred to talk more about what she and Victor had been doing and the travel plans they had, and any talk of Alex and Zander came up because *I* mentioned them.

I was starting to be less happy about my mom moving on, and more bitter about her not showing more attention to my—her—new family.

Yet I still stuck up for her. "What do you expect? She lost a baby at ten months old. It's probably hard for her."

Mama traded babies with Katie. "Why do you defend her like that? It was over thirty years ago."

I didn't know why I still defended my mother's emotional distance. I loved her. I felt bad she had experienced losing a baby. I was hurt by her, I also didn't want to hurt her back by making her feel bad about not being the mother I needed. Water under the bridge. I wanted to start fresh with her, like my dad was attempting to do with me, only she wouldn't take her head out of her ass. She should jump in and start being a grandma. I still wanted to talk to her about my sister and my dad, but I was too afraid of hurting her feelings. And now that she was so happy with Victor, I didn't want to ruin it.

"Molly," Mama twanged, just like Katie. "You need to talk to her. She should be over here today fawning all over these sweet babies." She held Zander up by the armpits so he was right in her face. "Yes you are the sweetest little bitty babies. Yes you are. Yes you are. Give Meemaw some kisses."

Oh God, my babies had a Meemaw. Shoot me.

I changed the subject to the wedding and that was that. Katie updated us on everything. She had been planning our weddings since we were teenagers, so she knew what she was doing. If she made me wear an ugly, poufy bridesmaid dress I was going to wring her fucking neck. She might do it for revenge of not being able to plan my wedding for me. Just what a new mom wants to wear: a big bow on her ass and nineteen eighties-style sleeves.

Mama went back to Mississippi. I had played my first Wreckers Weekend since the twins were born, and everyone survived. I was happy, Caleb was happy, the twins were happy, Katie was happy, life was great. I mean, what was there to come and kick me in the teeth?

Just The Creep who'd almost killed me and was still out there, the biological father to my kids who could possibly pop up and decide he wanted in our lives, a mother who was moving on in life without me, and my absentee father who didn't want to be absent anymore and whom I was trying to include in my life, but struggling to do so.

For now I'm good. Great, even. I love Caleb more than I thought I could love a man. We'll deal with life as it comes at us, because there was no way in hell I believed I didn't have some sort of fight out there waiting for me.

But I'm Molly fucking Ramsey. I've kicked ass before, and I'll do it again. Then I'll get that damn *Cosmo* subscription out of my name once and for all. (Right, and monkeys will fly out my ass.)

CPSIA information can be obtained at www.ICGtesting.com
Printed in the USA
LVOW12s0245120515

438144LV00027B/450/P